CAPTIVE LOVE

Trembling at the thought of lying beside Rhiannon, Moira tore her gaze from the bed to the fire. She was lost, helpless, among enemies. Her greatest enemy, the wolf himself, held her captive. "W-where shall I sleep?" Her voice shook with nervousness. Although she knew the answer, she could not suppress the question.

Rhiannon raised an eyebrow quizzically, his wolfish grin twisting the corner of his mouth. His fingers touched her hand, staying it from carrying more wine to her lips, his eyes searched hers. "If I gave you the choice of a warm bed beside me or an icy dungeon alone, which would you choose?" he asked.

Her flesh quailed. Trembling, white to the lips, she set the tankard down abruptly. Her hands clenched.

Watching her narrowly, Rhiannon waited a moment. When he spoke, his voice was warm with sympathy. "No. Do not answer. The choice is not yours." He kissed her forehead, released her hair, and placed the tips of his fingers on the fillet still bound around her throat. "You are mine," he said softly. "No one else shall touch you. . . ."

EXCITING BESTSELLERS FROM ZEBRA

PASSION'S REIGN by Karen Harper   (1177, $3.95)

Golden-haired Mary Bullen was wealthy, lovely and refined—
and lusty King Henry VIII's prize gem! But her passion for the
handsome Lord William Stafford put her at odds with the
Royal Court. Mary and Stafford lived by a lovers' vow: one day
they would be ruled by only the crown of PASSION'S REIGN.

HEIRLOOM by Eleanora Brownleigh   (1200, $3.95)

The surge of desire Thea felt for Charles was powerful enough
to convince her that, even though they were strangers and
their marriage was a fake, fate was playing a most subtle trick
on them both: Were they on a mission for President Teddy
Roosevelt—or on a crusade to realize their own passionate
desire?

LOVESTONE by Deanna James   (1202, $3.50)

After just one night of torrid passion and tender need, the dark-
haired, rugged lord could not deny that Moira, with her
precious beauty, was born to be a princess. But how could he
grant her freedom when he himself was a prisoner of her love?

DEBORAH'S LEGACY by Stephen Marlowe   (1153, $3.75)

Deborah was young and innocent. Benton was worldly and
experienced. And while the world rumbled with the thunder of
battle, together they rose on a whirlwind of passion—daring
fate, fear and fury to keep them apart!

LOVESTONE

BY DEANA JAMES

ZEBRA BOOKS
KENSINGTON PUBLISHING CORP.

ZEBRA BOOKS

are published by

KENSINGTON PUBLISHING CORP.
475 Park Avenue South
New York, N.Y. 10016

Printed in the United States of America

To Rachel Andrea
Dearest Daughter, Dearest Friend

One

Moira of Lorne stopped her horse on the rise and strained to get a view of the returning horsemen. The wind whipped her long brown hair across her face, and she brushed it back impatiently with her slender fingers. Her left hand held the reins firmly as the black gelding tugged at the bit and half rose, pawing the bracken. She patted his lathered neck, speaking soothingly to him. As he pranced and tugged again at the restraining hand, she raised her head to stare hard at the approaching riders. They were traveling more slowly than they might have been under ordinary circumstances. Deliberately, she pressed her lips together, pulling them in between her teeth. Her hand tightened on the reins. Many wounded, exhausted men meant unhappy women at Lorne's Rock.

They were moving past the rock outcroppings, now entering the far side of the plain spread out before her. She pulled her horse's head about to turn him down the side of the slope. Where the rough field flattened out, her progress was slowed as she wove back and forth avoiding gray rock upthrustings and small bushes. She rode astride like a man with knees and heels gripping the horse's barrel, but with a full skirt of tawny wool billowing behind her.

Her father, Lord Peter of Lorne, rode in the lead, his brown-gray hair and beard blowing back from his hawk's face. As she approached at a lope, he raised his hand in salute. She saw his white teeth gleam in a smile of welcome. Pulling her horse up, she answered with a smile, a bright flash in a day otherwise cold and grim. When his horse sided against hers, she grasped his arm in greeting, as a son would do.

"Did it go well, Father?" She turned her horse to ride beside his gray stallion. The horses increased to a hard gallop again.

She looked back over her shoulder at the men riding behind. Captives were tied on short ropes behind several horses. Forced to run and stumble through the coarse bracken, they were pulled painfully by their wrists, bound and stretched taut before them.

One man was tied to her father's saddle. Lord Lorne chuckled grimly. Deliberately, he spurred his horse to take a short jump over a low bush, dragging his prisoner ruthlessly behind him. The prickly scrub caught and ripped the man's *chausses* tearing the flesh beneath, leaving bloody scratches. Blood trickled down his muscular thighs exposed now to the chill wind. His face was gray with fatigue and cold; his mouth gaped with the effort to draw breath into his laboring lungs. His eyes glazed with the strain. His leather tunic showed a dark stain at his left shoulder and his chest, bared by the vee of the tunic, showed several nicks. Muscles and tendons, now strained to the limit, stood out as cords on his arms. The clenched hands were empurpled from lack of circulation. Only will, dominant when all else failed, kept him moving upright.

Moira's face registered recognition. The man's long

8

black hair, plastered with sweat against a tanned forehead, was bound by a gold and leather braided fillet. In the center of the headpiece, a golden bird spread its wings. The beak was parted; the head and talons thrust forward viciously from the foreshortened body. The wings swept back to the temples of the man's head. The screaming eagle, symbol of Rhiannon ap Breannon. She gasped, her eyes flying to her father's face. He stared straight ahead, a satisfied smile on his lips.

One mile. Two. The pace continued unabated. The party moved up from the bed of the plain past the rise where Moira had stopped her horse. A cleft in the rocks formed the natural base of the stronghold of the Lornes. Rhiannon stumbled. Falling heavily on his side, he was dragged mercilessly along through the brush and rocks. He could not hope to rise, but buried his face in his updrawn arms to protect his eyes from the cruel thorns. In another thirty feet the horses reached the cut.

When Lord Lorne drew his mount aside, Moira followed suit, holding her horse in tight behind her father's as the men slowed behind them. One by one they began to pick their ways through the passage up the narrow winding trail beyond.

Rhiannon's semiconscious body lay beside Moira's horse. He groaned faintly. Then rolling onto his right side, he struggled to get a knee under him. One man's horse brushed against him as he sought to balance himself without the use of his bound hands. He fell, sprawling almost under the feet of Moira's mount that snorted nervously and reared again. The ironshod hooves hung over the black head beneath her. Then she pulled her horse sharply back, its feet coming down to straddle the prone body. So protected, the prisoner was able to hunch himself forward to the rock face and pull himself upright. His left shoulder left a scarlet smear on the rough gray boulder. His head fell back; sweat mixed with dirt to make his face a gargoyle mask. His mouth gaped again as he painfully sought to draw air into his aching lungs. Moira moved her horse in tighter behind her father's to allow the men to move more easily through the passage. Rhiannon's face, gray as the granite, lolled back close to her left thigh which was encased in buckskin *chausses* and soft boots laced and drawn above her knee to give maximum protection for rough riding. Dispassionately, she gazed down into the face only a few feet below her.

He was the enemy. This man and his family had robbed and raided, kidnapped and killed members of her own clan for the last fifty years, since the Lornes had come from across the sea to take this land for their own. Within the borders of her father's lands the man was a curse, the most dreaded of his fellows. Now his fate lay in her father's hands, hands that would undoubtedly be cruel. No ransom for this one, she thought. Peter of Lorne had placed a price on his head—no, a bounty. He had been declared a wolf's head. Like a vicious killer animal, he could be killed on sight and fifty gold pieces would be paid to whoever brought his dead body to the stronghold.

Her father's brothers were dead because of this man and his father. Patrick, Claighmore, and Lawrence, all were dead. Her brother Matthew was also dead although not in battle—five years now. Only she and her father were left amongst widows and small children. Hatred mixed with grief shook her frame for an instant. She caught her breath sharply, gritting her teeth in an effort to maintain control.

The prisoner's dazed eyes opened, unfocused at first, but then clear. Coolly, she met their hot blue gaze under straight black brows. They widened, acknowledging her sex, then slitted in a grimace of pain. He half-raised his bound arms toward her, the stiff fingers swollen and discolored. Her lip curled in disgust as she interpreted the gesture to be one of supplication. Her expression hardened as the fingers sought to close on her knee and drag her from the saddle. The will was there, but the muscles refused to respond. In surprise, the man looked at his useless fingers dabbling feebly with the effort of closing about the boot.

Moira laughed, a bitter metallic sound. Raising her whip, she brought it down lightly but sharply on the defenseless forearms. The hands fell away instantly. Their eyes met for a long moment as hatred leaped across the space between them, making a bond which each was unwilling to break.

The last man rode through the gap beside Moira. She spurred her horse into the passage. Her father followed last with the prisoner now on his feet stumbling behind.

Two

Men and horses milled in noisy confusion in the muddy courtyard before the door of the hall. The captives who had been dragged through the passage, a rocky incline strewn with loose rubble, were to a man fallen unconscious in the yard.

One was dead; his head had struck a rock as he was dragged upwards. The man who had the corpse roped to his horse cursed and slashed at the rope, allowing the body to roll free. He yelled at two guards, standing at ease curiously watching the proceeding. They sauntered over to the body, rolled it over, searched it for any valuables that might have escaped the notice of the rider. Finding nothing, they grasped it, one by the bound arms and one by the feet, to haul it away.

Moira guided her horse to the steps of the hall and swung down, handing her reins to the ostler standing there to receive them. Mounting the steps, she stood waiting at the hall door as her father dismounted. The unmoving body of Rhiannon ap Breannon lay in the mud at the foot of the steps. The slight expansion and contraction of the ribs was the only sign of life. Glancing back over his shoulder, Lord Peter of Lorne smiled coldly at the sight of the fallen man. With a quick slash of his knife, he parted the rope from the saddle. While the boy led the two horses away, Lord Lorne stepped down to catch the toe of his boot under the right side of his captive's chest. The upper part, arms, head, and chest moved, but the lower half remained flaccid, threatening to pull the upper half face down again. Lorne quickly rammed a boot into the abdomen just below the hip bone. The limp body flopped over on its back in the muddy filth. Lorne grinned at his daughter, then bent to stare intently into the face of his foe. His grin disappeared.

"God's nails! Almost dead!" he cursed. "No! No, my lad! No, not you! Not yet! If you had a thousand lives, they would not be nearly enough for me. You will scream for death. 'Twill come slow to you, but not yet. Not yet. Thomas!" he thundered for a man-at-arms standing to the side. "Bring buckets of water to douse him down. Take those ropes off. Put chains on him instead. Heavy chains. The heaviest we have."

Turning, Peter of Lorne mounted the steps to the hall to stand beside his daughter. They were of a height, both almost six feet tall. She, slender and supple, he, heavier and much broader. Too much ale had coarsened his figure and reddened his face. His thumbs hooked in his scabbard, pushing it down farther as he sought to ease some of the strain after the long ride. Moira stood just behind his left shoulder. Together they watched the scene in the courtyard.

Riders turned their mounts into two narrow archways that led to the right and left of the hall. The courtyard emptied quickly as darkness gathered. Some dragged a captive; some greeted a woman, lifting a bag of loot from the raid for approval. A pair of torches smoked, then flared into life. The guard, Thomas Tech Duinn, with two others brought buckets of icy water. Drawing back, one

13

guard tossed the contents of his bucket full in the face of the unconscious man. Rhiannon gasped and choked. His body flexed in a small spasm as the icy water flooded his nostrils and half-open mouth. He turned half on his side, but the other guard doused him again. The water's force slapped him back into the mud where he lay coughing weakly. He raised his head and shoulders, attempting to sit up despite his bound hands. Laughing now, entertained by their sport, the men threw another bucket of water into his face and chest. This time he tried to roll away, pulling his knees up against himself.

The guard called Thomas reached forward with the trailing rope and wrapped it around and around his wrist. Rhiannon was pulled close up against the man. Thomas threw a loop around his captive's neck. The action hauled Rhiannon's clenched hands up under the chin at the same time Thomas dragged him to his knees. Lifting strongly as Rhiannon grimaced in pain, Thomas hauled him to his feet, then stepped back. Rhiannon swayed, his head bowed, his body shuddering, while icy rivulets of muddy water streamed down and pooled about his feet. Three more buckets of icy water doused his shivering form. Finally, when Thomas slashed the bonds about Rhiannon's wrists, the arms fell free to his sides. After being tied so long, Rhiannon could not move his arms or feel his hands. With the captive helpless before him, Thomas leisurely fastened heavy manacles to the lacerated wrists. A six-inch chain ran between them and a three foot lead chain dangled almost to the ground. Enjoying himself, the grinning guard dragged the shivering, reeling captive up the six wide steps to present him to Lord Peter.

"My lord, he's ready for your pleasure," he bowed.

"Daughter, will you enter?" Lord Peter bowed in turn in high good humor.

"Indeed, Father. I had almost given up hope of our

getting any supper tonight."

"Come, wolf," Lord Peter jerked up the chain, wringing a groan from his captive's white lips. "You have a reckoning awaiting you inside." He laughed, mockery thick in his tone, as the doors swung open.

The hall with its line of benches and boards was hazy with blue smoke. Torches lighted the way. The fire in the fireplace at the left was roaring, sending warmth into the chill damp atmosphere. At the end of the hall opposite the door, some thirty feet from the archway, was a dais reached by climbing three short steps. On this platform, the family had once eaten in their numbers. Tonight all who survived had eaten and retired for the night except Moira and her father, for only two widows and three small children remained beside themselves of the once large family. Moira ascended the steps, nodding to the servant to bring the chalices of mulled wine to warm them both. Her father strode after her, laughing as he pulled his staggering prisoner behind him. Rhiannon was almost fainting now from the pain, as his numbed hands began to feel the agonies of returning life.

"Thomas!" barked the lord to the man-at-arms following close in his wake. "Place a stool for our guest."

Grinning, Thomas pulled a stool from the end of one of the tables to the center of the hall before the dais. He made a comic show of dusting its surface, cocking his eye toward his master to judge the effect. When Lorne jerked the chain, the captive lurched forward on trembling, quaking legs. Gratefully, he slumped down on the stool. His hands clenched and then convulsively opened. Even in the torchlight's flicker, his shuddering was visible to Moira seated ten feet away and above him. No sound, however, escaped his compressed lips.

"Head up, lad! Let me see the face." Lord Lorne grasped the wet black hair to jerk the man's face up to the light. "See, Moira, my darling. The face of the enemy.

15

The face of the wolf. We kill wolves. We kill enemies, but first we run them awhile for sport. Snarl, Wolf, and show your fangs for my daughter."

The sapphire blue eyes opened. First, they focused on his captor's grinning face looming triumphant above them. Then they slid sideways to the woman standing at the side of the table holding the two chalices. They followed her as she descended the steps of the dais to bring a hot drink to her father. His lips moved slightly as his eyes followed the passage of restoring drink from one hand to another.

As she thrust the refreshment into her father's hand, Moira stared at the figure before her. Lord Lorne chuckled as he lifted the chalice to his mouth and drank deep. The ruby wine trickled into his beard. Against his will, the prisoner licked his lips. Lorne caught the motion and laughed out loud.

"Good wine," he bellowed, one hand still clutching, tightening, worrying the head of his captive. "Warmth on a chill day. Puts heart in a man."

The blue eyes glazed as the chattering teeth clenched together, not quite able to suppress a groan. The man's eyes closed as his body relaxed and slid off the stool, dragging down the hand which tormented him.

"Bah! He's fainted again. Thomas, bring him to."

As Thomas lumbered forward, Moira spoke, "Please, Father, let us eat and drink. He will be here for you as long as you wish him. Let us eat now. You can tell me the whole story."

"Good. Good, Moira, my girl." The Lord of Lorne turned away from his sport without a backward glance. He mounted the steps of the dais, drinking from the chalice and emptying it at the top of the steps. A servant approached as the lord rounded the end of the table, but the burly man waved the lout away. He seated himself in the high-backed chair. Broken meats, bread, some small rounds of cheese, and wine in a tall pitcher were set before the lord and his daughter.

Thomas shook the still form huddled on the hall floor. He gave the body a stiff kick at the back above the hipbone, but no sound came from it. Instead, it slumped over from side to front to lie like a broken ragged thing, its face hidden from view. A dark stain from the shoulder began to seep into the filthy rushes strewn carelessly upon the hall's dirt floor.

Lord Peter studied the body with avid interest. "Get a poker from the fire, Thomas, and close that wound in his shoulder before he bleeds to death. I gave him that, Daughter." He smiled at her as he signaled the servant for more wine. "Yes, I gave him that." He looked at Moira, keenly measuring her face for signs of revulsion, pity, or horror, for signs of any womanish weakness. Her face remained impassive. Well-satisfied with what he saw, Lorne patted her hand resting on the table beside him. With his other hand, he raised the chalice and tilted it back again.

A shriek of pain slashed through the air. Moira shuddered, but forced herself to let her hand lie still relaxed under her father's. The scene before her was not unlike the torments of hell. Carefully, she sought to detach her mind from the reality of the torture, to replace it with a coolness which she felt she must maintain. Rhiannon's face, turned toward the pair on the dais, was a study in suffering. The closed eyes were sunken in the head. The mouth gaped open as the broad chest heaved to encompass the labored breathing. The wildly beating heart responded to the excruciating pain which had penetrated even the depths of unconsciousness. A smell of singed flesh and hair filled the room.

"Father!" Moira exclaimed. "Is this really necessary while we are eating?"

Her father laughed again. "Leave him, Thomas. He

will go nowhere for a long time now." As he laughed, he drank again from the chalice.

Glumly, Moira regarded her father. Where was the kind and gentle man who had loved her and her brother so? Was he gone forever, consumed in a merciless obsession for revenge? Was she prepared to commit herself to this course of cruelty which he had set for them? She swirled the wine in the chalice, staring at its contents as if she sought to read the answer in its red depths.

Three

The hall was silent, deserted except for three people. Lord Peter of Lorne slumped drunkenly in his chair. His eyes gazed steadily straight ahead. He stared for long minutes at nothing, then swung his head to the side to stare at his daughter who leaned back quietly against the chair beside him. Her eyes were closed, their lashes resting on the darkened circles beneath. He drew one more deep swallow from the chalice, swiped at the purple stream that trickled from his mouth into his beard, hiccupped, and allowed his head to sink gently onto his arm.

Opening her eyes, Moira stared at her father. Her hand reached out to gently smooth the rumpled hair. Rising from her chair, she stretched her tall body. Her arms straightened above her head, the fingers arching in the air. She yawned widely, then relaxed, dropping her arms. Quietly, descending the dais, she started across the hall. Her garments were perfectly suited to her status and her activities. She still wore the boots and leather *chausses* while the tawny gold gown, slit both back and front to act as a skirt, partially concealed the length of her legs. The gown itself was worn over a rare silk blouse of palest cream. She strode lithely across the hall, passing close to the huddled form of the captive who had not moved since Thomas' crude cautery. As she passed, she heard a moan followed by a dry whisper.

"Mercy, lady," came the sibilant breath as if the supplicant were too weak to do more than expel the air. To form the speech and articulate the sound was beyond his powers. She hesitated, staring cautiously at the form. Warily, she circled back until the face was turned toward her. The blue eyes were open, the cheeks flushed.

"Please, my lady, water." The voice seemed slightly stronger, a croaking sound.

Moira moved back slightly, remembering his attempt to grab her boot in the pass. Surely the man was too weak to be a threat now. No water was in evidence in the room. Some wine perhaps remained in the pitcher on the table. She reached up, hefted it, picked up her own chalice from the table, and drained the dregs into it. Cautiously she approached, studying the figure for the slightest sign of movement. She set the chalice down amid the rushes on the stone floor, within arm's length of the limp form. Against her will, Moira's eyes flickered again to the white face, drawn by the expression in the blue eyes. They seemed to strike sparks from shadows. Blue fire glowed from out of the darkened hollows of pain. Shivering, she drew back a step farther. He was indeed a wolf, cruel and altogether implacable.

Rhiannon's hands flexed, his arms strained to move forward to reach the chalice. Curiously she watched the muscles tremble in his arms. Some damage or serious dislocation must have been done to his shoulders during the drag up the trail to the hall. Rhiannon's face contorted. His body tensed as he attempted to sit up. He managed to raise his head and shoulders only a few inches. A groan slipped out from between his clenched teeth as he fell back down again. His eyes closed as his breath escaped, deep and shuddery. Moira watched as his eyes opened again and focused on her. Again he tried to reach for the chalice. Again with a sigh, he dropped back full length on the rushes. His head rolled weakly; sweat bedewed his brow.

Sharp pains pierced Moira's vitals at the sight of his pain. Rhiannon was the enemy, true enough. Her father's careful training forbade her to pity or comfort him. Yet . . . She shook her head, then cautiously approached again. Lifting the chalice nervously, she knelt on one knee beside him. Her eyes never left his face as she held the wine to his lips. Lying on his side, he could not drink. The wine dribbled from the corner of his mouth. Warily, Moira bent farther, placing one hand hesitantly under his head. With his cooperation, she raised and turned him slightly. Scanning his face for the first sign of deception, she supported him as he greedily swallowed the contents of the chalice.

For an instant, she became aware of him as a man. His cool damp black hair curled about her hand while the back of his neck felt burning hot to her touch. His cheekbones were flushed a bright red. His sapphire eyes seemed to pierce through her.

A sixth sense warned her of her danger! Quick as her reflexes were, his were quicker. She sprang to the side. The cup flew from her hand to clatter against a bench. Rhiannon's hand like a wolf's jaw caught her heavy divided skirt, tripping her on its folds. She sprawled headlong. Quick as thought, she pulled away, but he was on her, straddling her hips before she could get her knees under her. His chained hands flashed down across her face. Before she could cry out, the six inches of chain separating the manacled wrists clamped about her throat cutting off her air and bruising her tender skin. Her senses began to swim. She bucked under him once, trying

21

to get her fingers under the chain around her throat. Her nails clawed at his hands.

"Be still!" he hissed in her ear. His eyes darted round the near-empty room, penetrating its darkest corners. Her hands clawed feebly at the rushes; one leg kicked futilely. "Be still!" he repeated, never loosening his hold. His eyes flew to the dais where Lorne lay sleeping. The drunken snores continued rhythmically; the clattering cup and the sounds of the struggle had not disturbed him.

Moira could not move by this time. Pressed down into the rushes on the dirt floor, her hipbones were painfully abraded. Rhiannon's buttocks and thighs rested his full weight on her lower back. Her spine arched; her head pulled back impossibly; she was almost paralyzed by the increasing pressure around her throat. Her eyes closed; her resistance faded.

Slowly Rhiannon eased the chain. Immediately, Moira sucked in a deep breath. His lips spoke at her ear. "Scream and 'tis the last thing you ever do. I can break your neck *and* your back with one motion."

She knew he was right. Her eyes filled with tears of anger, frustration, and pain, but she did not let them fall. She lay still beneath him, her body hard and tense. Suspended in time, the two antagonists marshaled their forces. With her body enclosed by his thighs, he judged it, surprised to find strength where he expected softness. For her part, Moira became aware of his labored breathing. The unnatural heat of his lower body, undoubtedly the result of fever, burned through her clothing.

Taking a deep breath, he slid his feet under him and pulled her up as he heaved himself back. She dangled, strangling from the chain around his wrists, until she too could get her feet under her. Upright at last, he held her against him, where she leaned, dizzy and only half-conscious from lack of air. They were almost of a height although he was perhaps two inches taller. In her ear he whispered, "Where is your chamber?"

He released her throat enough for her to reply in a pained whisper, "Behind the hanging at the right of the dais and up the stairs."

"Lead the way, my lady."

Together they stumbled across the room where he shouldered her roughly behind the hanging. Once on the stairs he again relaxed the pressure fractionally, but by that time Moira's throat was too badly bruised to emit any sounds.

"Do you have a serving maid waiting for you to retire?"

She hesitated.

"If you do, we go out into the cold and we are without cloaks. We shall probably not survive."

Moira shook her head.

"If you are lying and she screams, I swear I will kill you and her before I let them take me. Also consider that no one would pay much attention to the feeble cries that you two might utter in this pile before I dispatched you both."

"There is no one awaiting me," she croaked. They were at the door.

"Open it," he ordered.

Moira did so and he pushed them both sharply into the room. His eyes searched out every corner, satisfying himself that they were alone. Releasing his breath in a long sigh, Rhiannon pushed his captive face down on her bed lifting his hands from about her throat. At the same time, he planted a hard knee in her back.

"You can make this very uncomfortable for yourself if you wish to struggle uselessly and cry out," he said in a husky voice.

Moira lay limply on her bed. Her hands massaged her throat as she tried to speak. No sound came except a dry whisper. She swallowed convulsively.

Cautiously Rhiannon eased the knee off her back. A profound sigh escaped him as he stretched his long form beside her and closed his eyes momentarily. Acute trembling brought on by weariness attacked him. So intense were his sensations that he feared for a moment he would lose consciousness. His head pounded. Brilliant flashes of light streaked across the insides of his eyelids. The longing to sink further onto the bed, to ease his wounds, to sleep, to let the delirium of fever overcome him was almost overpowering. He squeezed his eyes tighter, trying to drive out the agonizing pains in his head.

His eyes flew open as he became aware of movement on the bed beside him. Moira had turned to look at him. Her eyes met his with a coldly calculating look. Inches separated them. He returned her gaze, judging her in his turn. Who was weaker? Who would be the victor in this war? His eyes measured her. No weeping woman here. She did not beg him for her life or her freedom. No bargains, no pleas for mercy. Her body tensed as he passed a hand over his eyes. He could see her gathering herself to meet whatever move he made.

Rhiannon pushed himself upright on the bed. Fighting the dizziness the slightest movement caused him, he glanced around him until he found what he sought. A large chest stood to one side of the small bed.

"Your clothes, my lady?" he asked with mock politeness.

She followed his look. "Yes," she whispered. Again she gagged. "Yes," she repeated in a stronger voice.

"Open the chest."

As she rose from the bed, he did too, following her to stand beside the chest with his shoulder propped against the wall, his manacled hands held in readiness. Opening the lid, she began to pull out her clothing. First on top

24

was a full length fur-lined cloak of heavy, dark brown wool.

"Put it here," he ordered, kicking a small three-legged stool closer to the chest.

Next was a gown of woad-blue wool. "Go past the gowns and women's garments," he said impatiently. "What other clothing have you to keep the body warm?"

Bending over the chest, she silently rummaged through the soft materials until she pulled out a vest of sheepskin, the wool clipped and brushed. It laced up the front to close and retain a maximum of body heat. He indicated that she was to drop it on the stool also. Again she bent to the trunk; her hands feeling among the soft goods. She straightened at last with a long woolen scarf held in her hand extended slightly in front of her toward him. As he nodded toward the stool again, she lunged, quick as a cat. The knife concealed in the scarf grazed his ribs as he sidestepped her. With a curse, he chopped his manacled wrists down on her back and shoulder. She fell hard against the wall.

He leaped on her, even as her body slipped down stunned by the blows to her head where she had hit the wall. Knowing she would have but one chance, she had risked all on the one lunge. Angrily, he grabbed her shoulder with his manacled hands and hauled her up to her knees. With his left hand fastened in the neck of her gown, he slapped her, a stinging blow with his right hand, first forward, then backward. The blows lacked force because of his shortened chain, but were sufficient to snap her into consciousness.

"Bitch!" he snarled. He slapped her back and forth again, then flung her to one side, overturning the stool. Callously, he stepped over her body. With a dry laugh, he bent to retrieve the knife. Turning to the chest, he flung her clothing right and left until he found what he sought. Straightening, he slipped the knife into the scabbard and the scabbard into the belt around his lean middle. Then he swung back to her.

"Up!" he ordered, giving her a kick on her hip. She grunted from the pain and scrambled to all fours, dizzily swinging her head. "Get up!" he repeated as he picked up the clothing. She managed to stand, swaying groggily.

"Turn around," he commanded. "Put this cloak around my shoulders and fasten it."

As he bade her, she swung the cloak around his broad shoulders, settling it upon them. With unsteady fingers, she fastened it at the throat. As she did, he searched her face. In the flickering candle beside her bed, he could see the bruises already staining her cheeks and throat. Her lower lip was swelling. A trickle of blood slipped down her left temple where she had struck the wall. Still no tears.

"Slip on the sheepskin," he commanded when she had finished. She did as she was bidden, then remained standing beside the stool.

He pushed her to the bed again. "Tear a strip from the sheet," he commanded. She did so thinking he meant to bind her arms. "Tear another," he ordered. She silently handed them to him, turning her back to him.

He came toward her and looped the wool scarf through his belt. A quick turn brought it through hers also, so that they were bound together with only a few inches separating them. He knotted the scarf securely. Then with the two strips of sheet in his hand, he reached up to her face. He stuffed one strip into her mouth bringing a groan from her as he pressed roughly against the wounded lower lip. The other he clumsily wrapped around her head, thereby holding the other strip firmly in place. She choked, making a strangling sound as the rough linen filled her mouth, but he ignored her discomfort.

"Now, my lady, we are ready to go." He knotted the strip tightly at the back of her neck. Together they moved in lock step across the room to the door.

26

The hall outside the chamber was dark and empty as he hurried her down its length and down the stair. "The stables?" he whispered in her ear. She shook her head. Grasping her left arm next to his body, he twisted it up behind her back. "Will you lose your arm here in this dark hallway without even a scream to sound the alarm?" Her body arched frantically, dancing on tiptoe.

When he released the pressure, she stumbled to the right through a small side door. They came out into the dark yard, lighted only by pale stars. Almost immediately he spied the building, small, dark, deserted. As they entered the interior, he smelled the familiar odors of the animals. He smiled grimly to know she had not led him wrong.

"Where is your horse?" he questioned.

For a moment she stopped, turning her head from right to left as if trying to get her directions. Then she led him to the second stall. In the faint light he made out the shape of a horse standing with two ropes attached to each side of the stall. A leather tack jingled as the animal tossed its head and snuffled.

"Untie him," her captor whispered.

She did so, joining the two ropes and offering them to Rhiannon.

He did not take them. Instead his husky voice asked, "Now where is your father's?"

She shook her head and pulled away, but he grasped her left wrist again, twisting hard, stilling her. Reluctantly she led him to the first stall where Lord Lorne's horse stood. When she paused, he pushed her wrist higher without comment. Stolidly now with little hope for her life, she released the two ropes on the gray offering them all to Rhiannon.

With these wrapped around his wrists, he pushed her before him to the door of the stables. There he untied the wool scarf from around their belts and boosted her onto her horse's back. Quickly he looped and tied the wool scarf around her left ankle. Slipping under the horse's neck, he pulled the thick material underneath its belly and secured her other ankle.

"Now, my lady," he muttered hoarsely. "Don't fall."

In another moment he had gathered the ropes. With a swift graceful movement he vaulted onto the gray stallion that was her father's pride. Together they trotted forward cautiously into the darkness, through the archway, and out into the bailey.

Pulling the gag from her mouth, Moira looked around frantically for guards to intercept their progress. She sought to give the alarm, but her throat was so bruised and her mouth so dry, that speech was impossible. Silently, helplessly, she cursed swinish churls who drank themselves into insensibility at the least excuse.

Once on the pathway, Rhiannon's booted heels jabbed viciously into the gray's ribs. The breakneck pace downhill in the freezing dark terrified Moira. Tied as she was to her horse, she stood no chance if it should fall. She gripped with all her strength, winding her hands in the horse's mane to keep from sliding from its back and being dragged and trampled.

Four

When the trail leveled out across the flat, Moira realized that the horses were slowing their breakneck pace. Whether from the dictates of her captor or their own exhaustion, she could not guess. Her own mount was relatively fresh, but her father's had been ridden hard that day.

Able to relax the terrible physical strain, she allowed her thoughts to dwell despairingly on her future. Where was he taking her? How long would he keep her alive? She had tried for a while to concentrate on the trail, but it soon became hopelessly confused as her captor turned, twisted, and doubled back, emulating the wolf her father had dubbed him. With only a few pale stars to follow, she lost all sense of direction.

Hours passed in a confusion of dizzying movement and darkness. Finally the horses slowed to a trot, then to a walk, then stopped, lathered sides heaving, heads hanging. Beside her, she heard Rhiannon dismount in a soft clank of chains. Looking into the gloom which she recognized for the first streaks of dawn, she could see his dim form resting his head and manacled arms against the shoulder of the mount. Finally, he turned away in a dazed manner. Intently she watched him. He swayed, shook his head, and then staggered toward her, stumbling over uneven ground as he did so. At her side, he fumbled at her ankle and unbound the wool scarf. Reaching upward to grasp her arm, chains clinking softly, he pulled her down beside him. Pins and needles shot through her feet and up her legs, but she managed to retain her balance while they both swayed precariously together at the horse's side. His arm settled heavily about her shoulders. His body was burning hot, but his teeth were chattering. He must be very sick, Moira thought. Hope shot through her as she wondered how long he could keep going. She must wait and watch. He would not last long.

Together they staggered blindly away from the horses to the trunk of a small twisted tree. Realizing that he was panting and shivering beside her, Moira suddenly turned in his arms. With all her strength she gave him a vicious push full in the chest. He cursed vividly as he reeled away, for her hand had thrust hard against the wound in his shoulder. The sharpness of the pain momentarily revived his flagging senses. As she darted for the horses, he flung himself on the trailing wool scarf still bound about one ankle.

Moira's breath was jolted from her body by the stunning fall. She lay limply as he again thrust his knee in her back. Grasping her right arm and then her left, he brought them together behind her. With the trailing end of the scarf, he bound her wrists together, leaving her leg doubled back painfully. As he jerked the knot tight, he uttered a hoarse chuckle. Then, as if his body had exhausted itself completely by that final spurt of energy, he collapsed away from her body. As she felt his weight leave her, she turned her head in time to see him slump down beside her. Gasping for breath, he felt for his shoulder. A deep groan escaped him. He pushed the edge of the cloak back to reveal the ragged tunic and raw wound. Moira swallowed when she saw it in the misty light of the dawning day.

The pain he endured was excruciating. Rhiannon raised his head from staring aghast at the wound to catch her looking at him. In the contact that passed between them, his suffering as well as his hopelessness was clearly revealed. Alive with sympathy and understanding, answering his *cri de coeur*, her own blue eyes met his.

Only for a moment, then each remembered who and what the other was. Her eyes became hard with triumph; his slid off her contemptuously and back to the wound.

Glancing around her, she realized they were halted in a small copse which effectively shielded them from long-range peering eyes. A stream of water trickled over some rocks a few yards below them. The horses had already moved down the bank to drink.

As she watched, Rhiannon swung his head in the direction of the water. He rested his chained hands on the ground, then drawing a deep breath, he sought to push himself up to a standing position. His strength was too far gone. The events of the past twenty-four hours rolled over him. Emitting a faint sigh, he slid forward in a faint.

Wasting no more time on him, Moira contemplated her own predicament. Her hands were tightly bound. Her leg already ached from the unaccustomed stretching of the thigh muscle.

When she tried to roll over and sit up, the movement almost dislocated her left shoulder. She had no choice but to lie as he had left her. Her face dropped to the moss-covered rock beneath her cheek. She shivered with cold, praying that the sun's rays would soon shine into the copse to warm her body. From the damp earth beneath her, a clammy chill rose to quickly penetrate the layers of her garments until she felt she was lying on rough wet rock. She was thirsty too, but for the moment exhaustion

31

claimed her. She closed her eyes and slept.

The sound of murmuring and moaning awakened her. She opened her eyes to see Rhiannon still asleep or unconscious, talking and moving restlessly. She calculated that they must have slept several hours because the sun was overhead, a pale blue ball, appearing and disappearing behind shifting swathes of mist and clouds. The copse was sheltered from the wind, but the chill of the damp earth had not abated.

In his fevered sleep, Rhiannon had thrown off the cloak. Now he shivered, plucking aimlessly with his chained hands, trying to find some covering. She swallowed, licking her dry, chapped lips. "Rhiannon," she croaked. "Rhiannon ap Breannon!" she tried again. This time her voice was stronger and clearer. "Wake!" The movement and murmuring ceased. The eyes half-opened, then closed again as if exhausted at the effort. "Wake! The ground is cold and damp. We need food and water."

His eyes opened, focusing on her face. At first, he appeared puzzled, then recognition dawned. His eyelids flickered. Wearily, he rolled his head away from her in the direction of the stream. His dry, cracked lips moved as he swallowed. His tongue slipped from between them to moisten and relieve them.

"We need water, my lord. You especially need to bathe your wound. Will you allow me to assist you? Release my foot and you can lean on me. We can walk together to the water." Moira made her voice as gently coaxing as she could manage with the pain in her throat.

He glanced back at her, allowing his eyes to slide contemptuously over her body. Painfully, he pushed himself to his knees and bound hands, but when he tried to push up, he almost fell on his face.

"Please, my lord," she begged anxiously. "Allow me to help you."

He swore then, calling her a foul name as he staggered to his feet. Tottering to the stream to fall full length beside it, he drank, sucking noisily at the clear cold water. Finally, when he could hold no more, he sat up, tearing a strip from his ragged tunic to wet in the stream. Carefully he dabbed at the cuts on his chest and thighs. The water was icy to his feverish skin. Gasping and shuddering, he persevered, sliding the cloth along his belly, dabbing away at several nicks and scratches, all the while dreading attending to the serious wound.

Finally, he bent over again and splashed water into his face. Unable to delay any longer, he clumsily folded the icy cloth and pressed it against the shoulder wound. The shock coupled with pain tore a cry from his lips. Grimly he sat, head bowed, as the pain receded, leaving him drained and trembling. As his hands fell limply away from his wound, he bent again to drink from the stream. To his parched throat it was like nectar. Refreshed somewhat, he rose unsteadily and approached the horses.

Fortunately, they had not wandered far. He was able to catch them with little difficulty and untie one rope from the black's halter. With the rope and the three-foot length of chain swinging from his hands, he came toward Moira.

Thinking he meant to kill her now, Moira closed her eyes and breathed a silent prayer. When the chain clinked softly above her head, she cautiously opened her eyes, craning her neck to get a glimpse of her captor's face. He looked down at her from his great height, grinning sardonically. The chain links touched her shoulder. She winced.

"Praying for mercy, my lady?" He coughed, dropping to his haunches beside her. His eyes were points of sapphire ice, blazing his hatred for her and triumph at his escape. Lightheaded from pain and fever, all the trappings of civilization stripped from him, he roughly

33

pushed her over onto her side, eliciting a muffled groan from between her clenched teeth.

"How quickly the battle shifts," he snarled. "I had not thought to gain so useful a slave when I set out yesterday. My lads and I were only out for a few cattle, mayhap some small coin." He chuckled as his eyes rudely appraised the length of her body.

"Thief!" she rasped. "Murdering villain . . ."

Angrily, he smote the ground before her face with the three-foot chain. Bits of pale gray lichen struck from the stone spattered onto her cheek. "A slave does not use that tone of voice to her master." His voice changed to deceptive gentleness. "What a great deal of pleasure a man will have in taming you. I do not think you will calm easily. Lorne has raised you too wild. You will suffer a great deal of pain before you learn submission." He smiled at the thought.

With eyes steadily gauging her reaction, he ran his hand across her shoulder and down her breast, enjoying her outraged exclamation. Roughly, his hand dove beneath the wool of her gown to rasp across her nipple covered only by the raw silk of her blouse. As his hand closed over the soft mound, his teeth bared in a vulpine grin.

High color rose from her throat into her cheeks as she squirmed impotently. Shamed and alarmed at his fondling, she could only set her lips tightly and endure.

Gradually, to her surprise, his touch lightened, the fingers kneaded gently, as his hand warmed itself against her flesh. To her horror, she felt less outrage as the gentle caress shifted to the other breast.

Abandoning the fierce pride that had made her blaze defiance from her eyes when her very flesh had quailed beneath the cold iron, she shut her lids tightly, hiding from his gaze the effect his touch engendered.

Abruptly his hand fell away. The angry sardonism

34

faded. Her eyes flew open to study him narrowly. Suddenly, he looked old and pale with dark circles beneath his eyes. A deep hacking cough bowed him over his knees. When he could recover his breath, his voice seemed much weaker.

"So, my lady, are you ready to ride again?"

She closed her eyes for a moment, releasing her breath in a silent sigh of relief.

"Not ready to assist me?" He laughed again at the memory.

His hands were dry and hot as they fumbled at her wrists. When her arms fell free, she struggled to rise, but to her consternation, she was so stiff that she could hardly move her leg. Biting her lip to keep from groaning, she took her thigh in both hands and pulled it forward against her chest.

Pain and cramp accompanied her efforts to move toward the water. Finally, she managed to limp to the stream's edge, slump down on her stomach, and drink her fill.

She became aware of him standing beside her as she finished.

"Stand up!" he commanded.

Lightheaded, with a hollow feeling in her stomach, she struggled to her feet, her back to him. He bound her wrists firmly behind her, using the wool scarf again. Touching her shoulder, he motioned her to her horse, boosting her onto its back. He tied one end of the rope to her ankle, then walked around to the other side of the horse and tied the other end to the other ankle. The rope was not as tight as the scarf had been the night before. He looked up grinning mirthlessly, his bloodless lips peeling back from his white teeth. "No problem for you, my lady, unless you think of jumping off the horse and running."

"I shall not do so, cur," Moira replied coldly. "I shall

35

see you dead, preferably by my own hand, before we part."

Ignoring her threat as if she had not spoken, he caught up the gray and hauled himself laboriously onto its back. Carefully, he gathered the ropes attached to the halter as well as the lead rope on her mount into his right hand. Painfully, he tucked his left hand into his belt for support. The ordeal painted his face gray with strain except for the high color on his cheekbones. He set his teeth to endure the ride. Settling himself on the horse's back, he glanced over at her.

"I shall surely not send you back to your father when I reach Hawk's Keep. I do intend to make a slave of you," he jeered. With pleasure, he noted her stiffening body. "Yes, perhaps I shall give you to our men for their sport and then make you a scullery wench."

Her eyes flashed fire. "My father will come for me long before we reach your stronghold."

"He is probably just now waking from his drunken slumbers and wondering where we are. He does not yet know that you are missing."

Moira clamped her lips together and looked stonily ahead.

Laughing, Rhiannon twitched the ropes. "You will make fair sport for my men," he repeated. "The more you struggle, the more they will enjoy it." He dug his heels into the horse's ribs. It bolted up the slope of the copse, pulling Moira's black along behind.

Five

For two hours Moira and Rhiannon rode obliquely across a valley whose walls were outcroppings of stones. Riding her horse behind and to the right of her captor, Moira observed how he drooped. After an hour he began to moan and mutter to himself. When his horse stumbled, Rhiannon tumbled forward on the gray's neck, almost dropping the reins. For a couple of miles he seemed to straighten and regain consciousness, but soon he slumped helplessly again, oblivious to his direction. The pale blue sun disappeared completely; the dampness turned at first to fine mist and finally to drizzling rain. Rhiannon's horse stopped, no longer feeling the movement of the manacled hands laced through the tangle of mane and ropes. Rhiannon hunched, moaning with every breath, too sick to respond.

Moira kicked her horse close. "Rhiannon," she spoke sharply. "Wake, sir. Wake. You must find shelter for us or we shall die. Wake." Leaning over, she nudged him with her shoulder.

At first he did not stir, then wearily he turned his head to stare at her. His eyes brightened; he smiled.

"Why, my lady, what is it? How may I serve you? You are cold and wet. I must get you to shelter." He coughed a deep cough, bowing his head in pain. When he could straighten, he stared helplessly around him. Clearly, he had no conception of where he was or who his companion might be.

With a thrill of excitement, Moira realized that he was delirious. "Indeed, Sir Knight, you have rendered me great service, already bringing me away safely from the castle. I beg you to release me from the bondage others have imposed and let me direct you to shelter." Twisting in the saddle, she presented her bound hands to him. Trembling in fear that he might refuse her, she waited anxiously. Finally, she felt him fumble with the scarf. Then her hands came free. Agonizing pains shot through her shoulders as she pulled her arms around in front of her body and rubbed her chafed wrists. He sat beside her, docile, shivering. A feeling akin to panic swept over her as she faced their terrible predicament. Neither could go much farther. For several hours hunger had gnawed relentlessly at her stomach. Now she felt faint as she trenched her fingers distractedly through her sopping hair. The cold rain soaked her garments, water dripped off her nose and lashes.

Staring wildly around her, she could not think where to go or what to do. She saw no sign of shelter except for some small trees a few yards ahead. Plucking her horse's rope from Rhiannon's unresisting hands, she moved off. His horse followed hers. As they approached the grove of trees, she realized with a pang of disappointment that it was too small to offer much relief. They must find some place where they could dismount to build a fire to warm their bodies and dry their clothing. Not the faintest trace of human habitation could be seen anywhere. The landscape stretched monotonously in all directions—dead gray, dark green, muddy brown.

She continued along the side of outcroppings. The way rose upward toward a small opening at the end of the valley. She headed the horses in that direction, kicking hers into a trot. Poor beasts! They too were tired, wet and hungry. At the top of the rise, she surveyed the countryside before and behind, breathing a small prayer. Luck was with her for she spied a small rooftop of thatch perhaps a mile down in the next valley. She kicked the tired black's sides with her heels and headed it toward the building. Behind her she heard the plodding hooves of the gray horse and Rhiannon's cough and moan. Glancing back, she saw that he could no longer hold his body off the horse's neck. Unaccountably, she felt a wave of pity for him. So much pain, such agonizing suffering.

As they moved closer, she saw to her chagrin that the building was deserted. It had been some crofter's hut, but now the side of one wall was fallen in. The roof still remained, but water was undoubtedly leaking in. Pulling up the black, she waited for Rhiannon's mount to come alongside.

"Rhiannon," she leaned over to speak in his ear. He moaned, mumbled something, but did not raise his head. "Rhiannon!" she spoke again. "Stir yourself, sir. Get down from the horse." Still he did not move.

Reaching over, she grasped his shoulder and tugged him upright. His head lolled back; his mouth hung open to the rain. As the icy water hit his face, he opened his eyes, shaking his head and muttering in protest. At length, he looked at her questioningly. "Dismount!" she ordered, "and unbind my ankles." He allowed his body to slide from the horse, but his numbed legs refused to hold him. He slid forward into the mud at the horse's feet.

"Rhiannon!" she screamed. "For your life, man, do not lie there. Unbind my feet." He stirred, trying to rise, but slumped back cradling his face in his arms. Frantically, she struggled to reach her ankle with her hands, but drew back in fear as she almost slid from the horse's wet back. "Rhiannon!" she cried. "Rhiannon! Help me!" This time he heard her, or perhaps the cold muddy water against his face had restored him somewhat. He rolled over, blinking against the pelting rain, looking up into her agonized face.

She was a long way off. His hands were heavy and painful. As he raised them toward the rope knotted around her boot, he felt a tearing agony in his left shoulder. He contorted his face in pain. A dull whimpering issued from his mouth.

"Stop that!" she commanded fiercely. "Stop that immediately! Release me and we shall go into the house. Soon we shall be warm and dry."

He tried again. This time he succeeded in grasping her boot and pulling himself half up. His weight almost dislodged her, but she grabbed for the mane and saved herself. The knots, swollen by the rain, were impossible to budge. He looked up at her helplessly, his eyes hopeless.

"Your knife, fool!" she hissed.

He looked at his belt in surprise. With great concentration, he placed his hands on his belt and drew the knife from the scabbard. He was very nearly unconscious. Pitifully, he sawed at the offending rope. His weakness coupled with the terrible pain of his shoulder overcame him before he could get through it. His hands dropped back to his sides. Again he looked up at her helplessly, shaking his head, so exhausted he was beyond speech.

"One more try," she coaxed. "Then we can go inside. Maybe we'll find something to eat. Please. I know you can do it. Lift your arms just one more time and cut through the rope. Good. Good. It is parting. Just one more effort. Thank God." She muttered this last as she felt the rope part. She was free. Immediately, she swung down hanging for a minute to her horse's mane as her legs found the ground, adjusting to the stiffness and cramp. Then she stumbled to the broken wall and looked in.

The hut was disappointing: a bare enclosure of rocks and thatch with three sides standing creating a barrier. The roof seemed to be in fair condition. The floor, of course, was dirt. A hole in the middle of the roof had been left to allow the smoke to escape. Still, Moira breathed a prayer of thankfulness and climbed over the rubble and into the room. Charcoal remained in the firepit and, wonder of wonders, pieces of flint. She had never built a fire that way before, but she could certainly try.

The sound of a horse stamping made her remember her responsibility. Climbing back over the ruined wall, she slogged through the mud to the two horses. Gathering the reins of the miserable beasts, she led them into the lee of the hut where an overhang from the roof offered them partial shelter. A large stone outcropping afforded her a place to groundstake their ropes for the night.

She returned to the side where she had left Rhiannon. When the rope broke, he had slumped back into the mire, his last strength exhausted. His mouth hung open like a dead man's. She stood staring down at the face of the enemy, the gray wolf's face. Her sneer of triumph faded before the sight of the pale sunken features. He was another human being; she could not leave him drowning in the mud.

If he could move enough to get in out of the rain, she could help him to get dry. She could always leave him tomorrow and return with her father to claim him. He was too ill to be a threat. Almost against her will, she bent over him and called, "Rhiannon! Wake! Help yourself. You are too heavy for me to lift." She shook him roughly. His only response was a groan and a cough. Again she shook him, slapping his face sharply. He rolled over on

41

his side, drawing his knees up toward his chest as the cough cut through him like a knife.

"Get up!" She straightened her weary body and nudged him with her boot. Again he mumbled, but could not seem to move farther. One hand flexed feebly. "Come, get up. Rhiannon. You must. Get up for me." Again she bent over him. "Come, Sir Knight. I must have some protection. You cannot leave me alone. They will come and take me away."

Her words reached him, dragging him out of the darkness. "My lady," he whispered. After several tries, he rolled himself up on his elbows and knees. His breathing was a painful rasp. He started to slip down again. "My lady, I cannot . . ."

"No!" she cried. She grasped his shoulder and tugged. A smaller girl would have been unable to bring him up, but she put her tall frame to the test to haul him up straight from his knees. He swayed. "Come, sir. Get your feet under you. 'Tis but a few steps."

He tottered forward to reel against her. She supported him with her arms. He succeeded in mounting the crumbling wall. At the top, a loose stone rolled under his boot and he fell heavily, sliding down the inside of the mound. She could not rouse him from where he lay in the shelter of the roof and out of the pelting rain. Her cloak was soaked with water and mud, but she drew it around him covering him as best she could. He could afford to lose no more body heat.

She began to shiver uncontrollably as she stumbled in the fast dying light to the charcoal hole in the floor. She fell on her knees beside it, found the flints, and laid them at hand. A few sticks and some bits of wood had been left in the hole by the crofter. Looking around the hut, she spied dry grasses growing out of the rubble of the wall. Crawling on her hands and knees, she pulled them up by the roots for tinder. Returning to the hole, she gathered

42

everything together. Drawing a deep shuddering breath, she leaned back on her heels and rubbed her numbed hands together to restore the circulation. Then offering a silent prayer, she leaned forward and struck with the flints. Sparks jumped, but to her consternation did not fly in the right direction. Again she tried. Again. And yet again. Finally, when she was almost weeping with frustration and painful cold, the little bit of dried grass caught. Quickly, she added little sticks, carefully waiting as they caught. Then bigger sticks and bits of bark. Finally, she added the bits of charcoal and blew on the whole as she had seen the servants do at home. She was rewarded with a puff of smoke from which she fell back coughing with her eyes and nose streaming.

Nevertheless, she persisted and soon had enough flame to cast a meager warmth around a small circle in the hut. Working as swiftly as her bone-weary body would respond, she gathered more dried grass from the floor of the hut and from the rubble by the wall. Several good-sized sticks had been left by the crofter to be used as kindling when he returned. In another few minutes, she had a beautiful blaze going, reddening her hands from the increasing heat. Blissfully, she basked in its life-giving warmth. At last, somewhat restored, she shrugged from her sheepskin, spreading it on the dirt floor next to the fire to dry. Her gown and shirt were equally wet, but she wrung the water from the two halves of the skirt and ignored the rest.

Her companion moaned softly. Hunching herself over to kneel beside him, she regarded him critically. His wrists were rubbed raw; blood trickled from beneath the manacles. Curiously, she lifted the edge of the cloak to reveal the burned and bruised wound.

Suddenly, his eyes flew open. At first he stared unseeing, then recognition lighted the blue eyes. She saw him tense his body where he lay on the ground. Like a wild creature, his eyes swept round the hut investigating the surroundings. He drew in a deep breath at the sight of the fire and immediately coughed. His body spasmed in pain as he raised his legs up toward his chest, then let them slump back weakly.

"Can you drag yourself closer to the fire?" she asked as she moved back out of his way. Painfully, he hunched himself over on his right elbow. Dragging his body like a dead weight, he finally got there. Less than a yard away he sat, crossing his legs, placing his elbows on his knees. In this position he bowed his head, trying to breathe with control to stave off a fit of coughing.

Neither spoke. As the firelight grew brighter, Moira was able to survey the surroundings. Above the fire to the right and left along the beams of the roof were several hooks for smoking or dressing meat. She lifted her sheepskin from the ground and draped it on one of the hooks to dry more swiftly in the rising heat. At first she hesitated, then with a shrug she bent to remove the sopping cloak from around his shoulders. The water dripped from it, so she hung it on the farthest hook from the fire. The scarf with which her hands had been bound, she twisted and wrung. Heating it over the fire, she moved around to where he was sitting. With the hot damp cloth, she wiped his face and swept the heavy wet hair off his neck. There she spread the cloth, pressing firmly with her fingers for a full minute. The convulsive shivering stopped. Rhiannon's head fell forward beneath her hand.

"Take off what is left of your tunic," she suggested. "We will try to dry that over the fire."

Her arms reached around his body and unbuckled the heavy studded belt from his lean waist. Wordlessly, he pulled at the neck of the tunic slipping it over his head and along his arms. At the same time, they remembered the manacles. He stared at them, at first surprised, then

44

bitter. Moving around to his side, she pulled the shirt out to the end of his wrists and spread it over his hands.

"Let it dry there for a while," she said. She removed the wool scarf from the back of his neck and hung it over the fire again to reheat.

Almost immediately he began to shiver again. A frenzy of coughing bent him over, convulsions ripping over his body. He drew his knees up, groaning, tears starting in his eyes despite his efforts to restrain himself. She turned back and spread the heated scarf over his back, rubbing it. Pressing her hands against the shoulder blades and ribs through the scarf, she again massaged his back. The coughing died away as she felt the shivering cease.

"Can you turn sideways, so I will not have to crouch in the fire?" she asked, half laughing. He did so. She approached him with the scarf outstretched and pressed it against his broad chest. He gasped at the heat, for the scarf was almost dry now.

With her left hand pressing it against the center of his chest, she slowly dried his belly with the end. He was badly cut. Three nicks, not deep but long and bruised, crossed his lower ribs. They all seemed to be healing cleanly. The black hair curled over the edges of the scarf to tickle her fingers as she gently stroked him. A faint tremor disturbed her body, causing her to shut her eyes to conceal her puzzling reaction. Nevertheless, she continued to rub while he sat hypnotized by the warmth and gentleness. Finally, she turned away and again draped the wool scarf over the fire.

"I wish we had something to eat," she said a little nervously. The contact with his body, the feel of his firm flesh had caused a peculiar feeling to course through her own body. "Unfortunately, nothing in here appears edible." She turned back to him and rubbed his uninjured shoulder, then draped the scarf over his back.

"Now turn back to face the fire," she suggested.

He did so, resting his good arm on his knee and cradling the left in his lap against his bowed body. She leaned around and respread his shirt. No more wood lay within reach. Trembling with weariness, she hoisted herself to her feet and tottered to the back wall. Fetching a stick, she added it to the fire, then glanced narrowly at her companion. With his head bowed, his eyes shut, he sat, breathing shallowly, not noticing her. Reassured, she stripped off her filthy gown. The silk blouse underneath was plastered to her skin, but she plucked it away shivering. Hanging the gown on the hook with her sheepskin jacket, she sat down across the fire from Rhiannon.

For several minutes they sat in silence. She sneezed. He coughed. The rain continued to drum on the thatch and to splatter the crumbled wall. Her head began to nod as she let the exhaustion of the grueling day overcome her. The ground was hard, but close to the fire it was dry. She roused and spoke, "We must take turns watching the fire. If it goes out, it will be difficult to start again and we need its heat to dry our clothes."

"Put some more fuel on it," he said, "and bank it."

"What does that mean?"

Surprised, he looked across the fire at her. "Bring me sticks from against the wall and I will show you."

She hesitated, unwilling to stand up before him in only her blouse and *chausses*. Still they needed the fire and she doubted she could stay awake more than a few minutes longer. Blushing furiously, she fetched the remainder of the fuel and knelt beside him.

"Break up the sticks and lay them on top of the fire. Then scrape up the ashes from around it and make a mound over the whole thing."

Again she did as she was bid.

"Now it will burn slowly and when we wake we will still have fire in the coals to start a new blaze." His voice was a

46

croak, painful to hear. He could scarcely keep his eyes open.

She started to rise, but he held out his hands, covered with his shirt. "Be so good as to cover my back," he requested. She turned the garment back over his head and shoulders, extracted the wool scarf, and drew the shirt down over his back and hips. He caught her arm, as she braced herself to leave his side. "Lie here with me. We can keep each other warm."

Horrified at the suggestion, she started to struggle. "No," she cried. "No!"

"I will not hurt you, my lady. I could not hurt you. If you want to pull away, you can. I am much too weak to stop you. But we can give each other warmth this evening. Truce?" His eyes, devoid of hatred and contempt, met hers. His hand relaxed its grip on her arm.

Suddenly, she could fight no longer. She was so tired, so wet, so hungry. No one would know or care. Nodding, her eyes closed and she collapsed against him. Stretching out on his right side, he pulled her down beside him, facing the fire within the circle of his manacled hands. The feverish heat of his body settled over her like a blanket. Briefly she moved, finding a more comfortable position, then lay stiffly against him, not allowing her back to rest against his chest and abdomen.

"Relax and sleep," his deep voice rumbled above her head, his chin on her hair. "You keep me warm."

Surprisingly, she was asleep almost before he had finished speaking. Her body melted into his. He shifted, trying to find a comfortable place for his head; then his senses too drifted away in a haze of pain, hunger, and exhaustion.

Six

Rhiannon dreamed that his body was in flames, chained to a stake. The manacles cut deeply into his already lacerated skin. Blood flowed from his wrists. Blood flowed from his wounded shoulder. The lord of Lorne beat him with a great whip of fire and as he writhed, flames sheathed his body again and again. He screamed at the pain. Again the grinning man-at-arms thrust the hot iron against his shoulder, holding it there. Then suddenly he was cold. Rain and icy water slapped his face. He tasted mud in his mouth mixed with the blood from his own wounds. He choked, struggled, finally screamed again for help. He was drowning, burning, freezing.

"Hush," a soft voice whispered. Soft hands caressed his face, his hair. His forehead was relieved of the pressure of the fillet. Cool hands rubbed his temples. "Hush," admonished the voice again. "'Tis all a nightmare. All will be well."

Rhiannon's blue eyes opened, blinked in the half light, focused on the white face above his own. He could not remember who she might be. Her cool hands continued to caress his cheeks and forehead. Her soft voice came soothing him from out of the horrifying darkness. Gratefully, he pressed his body against hers. He raised his manacled hands to clasp the back of her head. She stiffened, her spine pressing backward away from him, but before she could utter a protest, he raised his head to kiss her full on her soft mouth. Tenderly, he touched his tongue to her lips, insinuating it between them as she gasped in anger and disbelief. His passion stirring, he thrust deeper to explore the interior, caressing her tongue with his own.

Terrified at his treatment, Moira wrenched her head out of his hands, freeing her mouth. Simultaneously, she thrust her arms straight on each side of his head, pushing herself away. Ducking her head out of the circle of his arms, she scrambled away to the other side of the fire. "Cur!" she hissed. "Dog!"

Startled, Rhiannon stared at her angry face now feebly illuminated across the glowing space. Then with a sigh of recognition, he closed his eyes. He remembered now. Everything. He had not intended to violate her trust, but she would not believe him. What did he care what she thought! She was the enemy, his captive. Eventually, he would have her if he wanted her. But not now. More pressing needs occupied his attention now.

Stiffly he sat up. The hunger in his belly made him dizzy. Today he must find food, he thought, or he would be unable to continue. The day had dawned gray and ugly, but blessedly free of rain. A cold wind whistled around the walls. Rhiannon readjusted the gold and leather fillet about his brow, gained his feet with an effort, and straightened painfully. For a moment his legs trembled with weakness, but then his will took command. Ignoring Moira, who scrambled away as he rounded the fire, he moved to the edge of the hut to pick up the last two sticks of firewood. Returning to the hole, weaving

49

slightly as he walked, he poked aside the ashes. He thrust the two sticks in amongst the coals which immediately glowed cherry red in the fresh air. When the flames began to lick around the edges of the wood, he straightened again. Walking stiffly to the mound of rubble, he mounted it and stepped down outside into the mud.

The cold wind struck him full force. Gritting his teeth, he struggled to orient himself in the light of day. Lorne Rock lay somewhere to the north, perhaps less than a day's journey. Moreover, since his own lands lay at least ten days' journey farther north and east, the men of Lorne stood between him and safety. His only hope lay in traveling south and slightly east for at least another day. Only then, perhaps by swinging wide and north again, could he hope to avoid pursuit.

His thoughts turned to his fair captive. He must keep her with him for at least three more days as a hostage in case her father's patrols intercepted them. Then . . . He did not know. She had been kind to him last night. When he was at his most vulnerable, she had given him aid. He stamped from one foot to the other uneasily. He could not keep his threat to make her a scullery slave. Yet she was the daughter of the enemy. Her captivity might give them a means to hold off Lord Lorne, if he valued his daughter at all.

The sun threw no shadow to tell where the east lay, but the icy wind blew down against his back from the north. He would trust to riding before that wind for at least another day. The crofter's hut was a good sign. People had lived here. Perhaps farther down the valley would be an inhabited hut. Undoubtedly, they would be serfs of Lorne, but they might be persuaded by the presence of the girl to part with food.

He rattled his manacles and snarled in frustration.

Perhaps someone would have the means to free his hands.

When he turned, she stood poised on top of the mound of rubble. She had put on her gown and sheepskin vest and seemed about to spring upon him. When he spied her, she hesitated, then relaxed.

"May I go now?" she inquired politely.

"Get back into the hut," he commanded. As he unsteadily mounted to the top of the pile, he grabbed for her arm.

"No!" she snarled suddenly. With all her strength, she pushed him down into the hut. At the same time, she jumped outside. Her foot slipped from under her on the icy surface sending her sprawling, but she struggled up, heading for the horses.

Roaring a curse, Rhiannon threw himself at the rubble, mounting it in one bound and springing down on the outside. He reached her as she flung herself belly down onto the horse's back. Both hard hands closed around her ankle.

She kicked him in the chest with her free boot. Though the kick lacked force, he grunted as the heel caught his injuries. Angry at her violent resistance, he jerked backward. She fell on her arms, chest and face in the mud, her jaw cracking against a rock. Without a whimper, she slumped lifelessly.

Dropping down beside her in the mud, he sucked in deep, agonized breaths. A coughing fit seized him. In agony, he bent over and rested his manacled fists on her back. Finally, the fit ceased. Unceremoniously, he rolled her over. Another time he would have laughed at the comical picture she presented, her face caked with gray mud and sprigs of dried grass, but her chin was swelling fast. A trickle of blood slid down from the point of her jaw to her throat. She groaned.

51

Sure she would not try to move for a while, he left her side to catch the horses. They had bolted at the struggle, but were too tired to move more than a few yards. Catching the trailing ropes, he led them back to her side. Again he dropped down beside her. This time he slapped her face sharply. Moaning, she opened her eyes. A fierce light of hatred flamed in them.

She struggled wildly to sit up, then fell back on her elbows. The throbbing pain in her jaw made black specks dance before her eyes. Raising a shaking hand to her chin, she drew away bloodstained fingers. "Well, I am truly punished," she muttered.

"As you deserve," he snarled, prodding her to her feet. When she swayed unsteadily, he grasped her arm and led her to the side of the hut. They leaned against it, panting, bravely able to suppress their anguish. Bending over against the pain in his chest, Rhiannon found the knife where it had fallen the night before. With a grunt of approbation, he swept it up, feeling somehow whole again. Wiping the mud from the hilt and blade onto his *chausses,* he grasped her arm again and guided her around the corner and up over the rubble. The fire still burned feebly. He bent over and picked up his studded leather belt. "Fasten this round me," he commanded.

Slowly she obeyed, taking it in both hands, passing it around his waist, shuddering when her fingers touched his body. He brushed her aside when she fumbled at the heavy bronze buckle and girded himself, tightening the belt in the first notch.

With her legs too weak to hold her any longer, Moira dropped crosslegged on the ground, her muddy face hidden in equally muddy hands. No sound escaped her, but her whole body shivered. Kneeling, his own toilet completed, he tore a piece of cloth from his ragged tunic and gently pushed her hands down to wipe her face. She kept her eyes closed during his ministrations, but could not still her quivering lips. Deliberately, she pressed them together and pulled them in between her teeth.

When her face was clean, Rhiannon waited for her to open her eyes. Her temple was bruised from the night in the castle when she had slammed into the wall. Now her chin had a rising bump on it. Both wounds had broken the skin. Her hair was a bedraggled tangle. Beneath her eyes were dark circles. Her cheeks were hollowed with fatigue and deprivation.

"Kill me," she whispered.

Her calm words startled him. He shook his head.

"No, my lady, you are too valuable to me alive. Although a great deal of trouble," he added ruefully.

Bowing her head in acceptance of his statement, she nevertheless clenched her fists in anguish. A torrent of bitter self-reproach poured from her lips. "Last night I saved your life. I could have left you lying in the mud, shivering with fever, delirious, coughing. You would have been dead when I came out this morning. I could have mounted the horse and ridden back to my father in triumph. Instead I showed mercy to an enemy . . . a thing my father told me never to do. He told me I would pay the price if I ever showed weakness. Now that I am tested, I have failed."

For a minute there was silence. The fire crackled. Puzzled at first by her speech, Rhiannon finally smiled sardonically. "My lady, I thank you for your mercy. You are after all a woman in your heart. I am free because of you, not suffering the tortures Lorne had planned. If I could, I would release you. This I swear. But if I do, you will return to your father to tell him my route. I apologize beforehand for the inconvenience you may suffer, but you will accompany me for the next several days. You may do so at ease if you promise not to attempt another escape. . . ." He waited.

She did not speak, but looked steadily into the fire.

He shrugged, leaving the sentence unfinished. The fur-lined cloak was still very damp and smelly. Clumsily, he swung it about his shoulders, the chain striking his body. As he settled it about himself, its dampness set him shivering. The fever still burned in his body. Regretfully, he held his swollen hands over the dying fire, savoring the last of the warmth. Moira had not moved from where she sat.

At last, he could prolong the departure no longer. The chain connected to his wrist chain, brushed her shoulder. She looked up into his face. Her expression stung like a blow, so hate-filled was it. Without assistance, she got to her feet and climbed the rubble, stepping into the biting wind. In the muddy yard, she approached her black gelding, but he stopped her.

"Mount the gray, my lady, in front of me," he commanded. He boosted her up, then swung up behind her. "Reach back and pull the cloak around us both," he instructed.

As he turned the horse away from the hut, she bowed her head in the icy wind. Her teeth began to chatter as the cold wind struck her wet hair. He pulled the woolen scarf from inside his shirt and thrust it into her hands.

"Wrap this around your head and ears," he bade, "to protect yourself."

He set heels to the gray and they moved slowly away toward the south.

Seven

Midway down the valley they encountered a faint trail slanting away southeast toward the pass at the head of the rocky crest. The gray horse stumbled from their combined weight. Dismounting, they walked along the narrow trail where rough, gray rock rose on either side of them. Two more faint paths converged below the ridge. The trail grew steeper. Ahead the clear gray sky appeared lighter than the rocks. Rhiannon panted from weakness, coughing deep painful coughs which tore out of his chest. Moira plodded on, weaving sometimes as her foot turned on a rock.

At the top of the grass, a steep rocky cliff trail led down into a valley. At the end of the valley, a wisp of smoke rose from a small misty clump of trees.

Rhiannon breathed a sigh of relief. "Look, my lady," he said. "Look! There is help. We will find something to eat and some way to get dry." A spasm of coughing racked him back against the gray's shoulder.

She watched him carefully. His coughing was much worse, deep and scraping. Tears sprang from his eyes only to freeze on his sunken cheeks. He wiped them away with the back of his hand before he assisted her to mount her black. A stone turned under his clumsy feet causing him to stagger against the rock, but he finally managed to haul himself atop his mount. The horses started down carefully along the rough trail.

They rode silently, side by side for several hours, both too miserable and weak to do more than cling to the manes of the horses. He did not lead her mount now, but it followed of its own accord, head down and shambling.

As they neared the hut, Rhiannon pulled up. As she drew abreast, his manacled hands snatched her rein from her grasp and halted her horse. "My lady," he said, "I cannot have you betraying me. I shall ride in. You must wait here. Dismount."

Obediently, she slid down from her horse. He came around and grasped her hands. Their iciness touched him. She was blue with cold; her lips pinched; her fingers stiff. How could he bind those pitiful fingers? Pulling the wool scarf from her head, he wrapped it carefully around her hands. Then he pulled the gold and leather fillet from his own brow, wrapping it tightly around her wrists. Clumsily unfastening the cloak from around his own throat, he swung it over her slender body. After fastening it, he escorted her to the shelter of a rock where he bade her sit.

"Do not be afraid. I will return in a few minutes." He touched her cheek with the back of his fingers as he smiled down into her cold hostile eyes. At his touch, she jerked her head aside. With a thin smile, he pulled the ropes of the two mounts together and flung himself up on her black.

Moira sat shivering for several minutes. The cold was so terrible that she thought her bones would crack. Her body was stiff and all her garments damp. The cloak he had put around her was like a cold heavy rug which did nothing but cut the wind. Her mind refused to function.

Numbly, despairingly, she contemplated the shame of her position. She had had a chance to escape, but had not done so. She had aided the man who was her father's mortal enemy. She could have ridden home in triumph today. They would have drunk her health at her father's table in hot wine. Her enemy would cower before her in chains. Instead she sat frozen and hungry, huddled in the middle of nowhere, her hands bound with a fillet from his head.

She stared down at the bindings. The golden bird stared back at her, its screaming beak and thrusting talons reaching for her. She twisted and tugged at her wrists in frustration. Tears formed in her eyes, but she winked them back. Tears would do her no good. She must plan. She must wait for her chance with him and seize it when it came. Or if he did not return in a few more minutes, she might suppose that he was in trouble, perhaps dead or captured by the people in the hut. They were assuredly her father's people.

She started up at the sound of returning hooves. Rhiannon rode toward her. At first, he swayed over the horse's neck, but as he saw her, he straightened, smiling wanly. As he came to her side, he reached down his right arm, still chained, offering it to her. She grasped it and swung up before him. He heeled his mount into a stumbling lope.

"An old woman is alone in the hut. Crazed, I think. She appears to know nothing. And the hut is warm and dry. We can have a fire and food. You can have some privacy in a small inner room." He barely got the words out before a violent spasm of coughing wracked him. He reeled in the saddle, finally, clutching her body at the waist and burying his face against her cloaked shoulder. His breath blew hot as fire on her neck. When his fit ceased, he slumped against her body.

She stiffened when she thought he had lost consciousness, but he rallied as the horses pulled up at the door. Wearily allowing his body to slide down, he nevertheless held up his right arm for her. When she haughtily ignored it and slipped off, he caught her upper arm and spun her roughly to face him. His eyes, hard as sapphires, bore directly into hers as he untied her wrists and unwrapped her hands. In a voice that brooked no argument, he delivered his ultimatum.

"Listen to me, my lady. I can kill the old woman with this dagger. If you try to enlist her aid or try to get away, I will do so. Do you understand?" He shook her by her shoulders. "I have told her that we are man and wife. She does not understand that I have chains on; she did not even notice them. She is fixing us a warm meal even now. I will care for the horses. Do not try to escape and we will be safe for the night."

Moira nodded. To lie down. To be dry. To have food in her belly after forty-eight hours of hunger. She must gain a little strength before she could plan again. She opened the door of the hut and stepped in.

The rude interior was dirty and disorderly, but a cheerful fire burned in a crude fireplace along one wall. A table that listed slightly to one side bore a jug, a plate, and a loaf of hard black bread. A long, sharp knife stuck out of the bread. Moira's eyes glittered when she saw it.

She started toward the table, intending to pull out the knife to conceal in her clothing. Two strides into the room, her way was blocked by a crouching figure clad in drooping, filthy rags. The creature's yellow-white hair was twisted into a greasy knot on the top of her head. Her mouth was entirely toothless and her generous nose hooked over almost to touch her chin. Moira could not repress a shudder when the old woman laid crippled, bony fingers on her arm. Ignoring Moira's shaking and hanging back, the beldam tugged the girl away from the bread and knife.

"Here, here, pretty pet," she quavered. "Be taking off that cloak and warming yourself beside the fire."

Before Moira could move, the crone's calloused fingers were scrabbling at the neck of the cloak. Drawing it from Moira's shoulders, she shuffled across the room to hang it on a peg on the wall. Gratefully, Moira extended her hands to the fire, unable for a moment to move as the delicious warmth seeped into her extremities. An iron pot hung over the fire, its contents bubbling and hissing. Moira swallowed painfully as the odor of mutton and leeks filled her nostrils. As she braced herself against her weakness, the crone came up behind her to help Moira remove the sheepskin tunic.

When the old woman turned away the second time, Moira darted toward the table. Her hand closed over the knife. At the same moment, the door of the hut swung open to admit a swell of icy, wet wind and Rhiannon. Moira jumped guiltily. His eyebrows lifted, he glanced meaningfully at the hostess and tensed. In that electric moment, their roles of captor and captive were clearly defined. Moira's frame slumped. Head down, she grasped the loaf in her left hand, cut an end of bread from it and handed it to him. He grinned wolfishly as he bowed over her hand and accepted the bread.

"Wait, my lord, wait," the old woman hurried forward. "Sit yourself down whilst I bring hot food to warm you as well as bread." She darted around to the fireplace where she lifted the iron pot from the hook. She set it on the table and began to hollow the bread to make a trencher. Deftly, she ladled some of the contents of the pot into the hole in the bread, divided the piece hollowed from the loaf and handed them each a half. "Sit yourself down, my lady, beside your lord and I'll bring you a cup."

Loath as Moira was to sit down beside Rhiannon, to share the same fare with him, she saw no choice. Her acute hunger caused her hands to tremble. Her head swam dizzily. She actually staggered as she sought to lower herself to the bench beside him. She did not feel his hand grasp her arm to guide her down. Thankful, she rested her elbows on the table and leaned her head in her hands. Black spots and crashing suns distorted her vision.

She tried to come alert when she felt Rhiannon's hand against her upper arm. His fingers, dry and hard, intruded between her arm and the curve of her breast. She could feel his hot fevered breath against her cheek at the same time she realized he held a piece of bread sopped in the brown stew less than an inch from her trembling lips.

"Eat," he said softly. "Eat and you will feel better in a minute."

Too exhausted to resist, Moira obediently opened her lips. He slipped the bread into her mouth. When she sought to chew, she almost choked. His hand left her arm, but returned immediately with a cup. A rather foul ale burned her mouth and throat, but the alcohol gave her strength as well as warming her stomach. She straightened to look directly into his concerned blue eyes. The thought flashed through her mind that he had not eaten perhaps for a day or two before she had, yet he was suppressing his own need to fulfill hers.

She stared at the face so close to hers. He had replaced the fillet around his brow. Under the golden eagle, his forehead creased in a hard line of pain. His blue eyes looked out from deep hollows with dark smudges beneath them. His nostrils and cheeks were pinched white and drawn except where a hectic flush stained the area over the high carved bones. His mouth was dry with compressed cracked lips, which showed evidence of having been gnawed and bitten in agony. A bruise showed dark blue along his right cheekbone. A black stubble of beard covered all.

"Drink yourself, my lord." She pushed the clay cup from her lips and held it to his.

Gratefully, he turned up the cup. Closing his eyes as he did so, she saw his hands shake as he drained it. Reaching across the table, she lifted the pitcher to pour another draught. "Drink more, my lord wolf. It will put heart into you."

He smiled thinly at her. She drew back, aware that she was sitting side by side with her enemy, their shoulders, hips, and thighs touching while she drank from the same cup and ate from the same loaf. Hunger, however, asserted itself with cruel pangs stronger than her hatred. She tore off a piece of her bread and dipped it into the trencher. He joined her. Rapidly the stew disappeared along with the bread that had held it.

Moira realized that she could have eaten much more, but she also realized that the old woman might have nothing else for herself.

Rhiannon pushed back from the table first. Carefully, he studied the room, looking for some tool with which to rid himself of the chains or at least to part them. An ax was buried in the corner in a small pile of logs and faggots. His chains would part easily enough if Moira would swing the ax, but he could not trust her so far. She would undoubtedly kill him given such an opportunity. Perhaps the old crone had a grinding stone or file with which to sharpen the ax.

He rose, approaching the old woman where she sat staring into the fire crooning a soft muttering tune. "Mother, I and my lady thank you most heartily for your food and drink. I would do you a favor if you would allow."

The old woman turned in surprise, seeming to start from a daze to regard him as if she were seeing him for the first time.

"I see you have an ax in the woodpile," he nodded in

61

its direction. Her eyes moved vaguely over to the corner and focused on the tool. "If you have ought to put an edge on it, I will gladly do so and chop some firewood for you."

"Not needful, not needful," the old one insisted. "Get you and your lady to bed." She hoisted herself up and shuffled across the room to hurriedly draw aside a curtain concealing a small alcove. There, a few inches above the floor, was a frame supporting a rope bed thinly covered with a ticking of grasses and a few grubby wolf pelts. The whole sagged wearily to one side and the distinct odor of musty dampness wafted into his nostrils as the cold air was released into the room.

Rhiannon hesitated in disappointment, turned back to Moira expecting to see her look of triumph, but beheld her drooping figure, her hand supporting her head, her eyes closed. Glancing back at the bed, he shrugged wearily. Wayfarers could only take what was available. He turned back to pull her to her feet. She was as limp and as easily guided as a child when he led her into the alcove. The old woman dropped the curtain behind them.

Moira, her garments still wet, began to shiver helplessly in the chilly compartment once the dividing curtain was in place. Shaking in every muscle, she dropped down on the bed and attempted to pull off her boots. Rhiannon watched her futile struggles as he swayed forward and backward in the dimness. He dropped down on his knees before her to grasp the boot at the toe and heel. It came off suddenly and he fell back on his haunches. Her hose underneath was wet. He stripped it off, too. The long, thin toes were wrinkled and blue. He grasped the foot in his hand and began to rub it briskly.

"I beg you, stop," she gasped through clenched teeth.

"Does it pain too much?" He paused, grasped the other boot, and pulled it off and the hose with it. Instantly she pulled her foot away from him, tucking

62

both feet back under the bed. His task completed, he stumbled to his feet and lifted the curtain.

As she allowed herself to slip sideways onto the musty furs, she heard him confer with the old woman. When he returned to her side, he saw that Moira was shivering again.

"Sorry, my lady, but she has nothing to warm your feet with." Moira did not respond. She had pulled her feet up and clutched her toes in her hands in an effort to warm them.

He gazed down at her, marveling that no tears trickled down her cheeks. No woman in his experience would have endured such as she had without weeping, moaning, possibly fainting dead away. As he watched, her shivering became convulsive. Helpless moans escaped from between her clenched teeth. She could not control herself. He reached down, lifted her by the shoulders, and stripped the gown from her body. Then, before she could protest or because she was too weak to do so, he pulled her blouse off. Her hands grasped futilely at her clothing, but his movements caught her by surprise. He pushed her back gently onto the bed. His fingers fumbled at the tie of her *chausses* and he pulled them off over her legs. Struggling feebly, she sought to move away from him, but he piled the pelts on top of her. Turning, he sat down on the bed beside her. He pulled off his boots, one by one, and the *chausses* under them. He straightened and unbelted the heavy leather belt and laid it and the knife carefully on the floor beside the bed. He padded to the curtain, lifted it, and saw the old woman curled into a ball beside the fire. Swiftly, he gathered up the girl's clothing and his boots and *chausses*, carried them into the main room, and spread them before the fire. Then drawing off his breeks, he spread them, too, and turned back to approach the bed. She saw him coming naked toward her and moaned in fear.

63

He lifted the pelts and crawled into the bed beside her and gathered her against his body. She struggled weakly but frantically.

"Hush, my lady, rest easy. I will not hurt you. Believe me, my lady," he said sarcastically, "I have neither the strength nor the inclination to do anything to a willing woman tonight, much less an unwilling one. Especially one who is almost as tall as I am with the strength and courage of a lion."

She stopped struggling. Her face was turned toward him in the dark. He could see its expression in the glow of the fire while his was shadowed from her. Her face reflected exhaustion, bewilderment, fear, distrust, and finally resignation. When she relaxed against him, he gathered her into his arms as he had done the night before. The feverish warmth of his body lulled her to sleep almost immediately. Waiting until he felt her relax, he gathered her more closely against him. Her pliant body fitted each curve of his.

Speculatively, he ran his fingers along the smooth arm under the covers. What could he do with her? What should he do with her? His thoughts whirled away into oblivion.

Eight

Moira could not remember being so painfully sore. Her entire body was one huge ache. From her toes to her face, her skin was cracked and burned from exposure to the elements. Her muscles were strained and stiff. Her throat was a raw wound; her nose, stuffy and dry.

Aware of hot breath against her neck, she turned her face to the side. Warily, she gazed into the flushed sleeping face of the beast who held her captive. Through his parted lips, his breath sighed as he exhaled. Somehow with his eyes closed, with the snarl faded from his lips, he did not look like the wolf her father had named him. Instead he looked very young. Almost a boy. He could not be more than a couple of years older than she.

As she watched, he coughed painfully and grimaced. His eyes opened dully, then focused on her. For a full minute she stared into his blue eyes before a blush began to rise on her face. She was pressed against his body from shoulder to hip. One of his legs was slung across her thighs pressing her down. One of his arms rested casually on her upper body, the forearm crossing between her breasts. Even as she watched, the cruel grin curled his lips, exposing the straight white teeth. The pressure of his leg increased as he shifted his leg back and forth along her thighs.

"You are soft, my lady," he whispered, his breath fanning her ear. "So soft." He hunched forward, letting his upper body slide across her arm and shoulder, further pinning her to the bed.

The warmth of his body soothed her, comforted her, making her senses turn traitor to her mind.

His breath brushed her earlobe, an instant before his lips gently took her soft flesh, tugging at it lightly. Involuntarily, she shifted her shoulder as her response sent shivers through her muscles. His teeth inflicted a tiny nip on its soft skin before they returned to her ear, catching the lobe between their sharp edges. A muted growl seemed to rumble from his throat.

Held immobile by his body, she could not stir. The inside of his thigh moved higher, bearing down on the sensitive mound at the joining of her legs. The roughness of his hair tickled her, adding to the multitude of sensations she was already experiencing. Helplessly, she moaned.

Heat surrounded her as blood fired by his heat and touch raced through her veins. Not fully awake, she could feel her body melting in that fire.

His lips abandoned her ear to slide along her cheek to the corner of her mouth. There his little nibbling kisses made her squirm again.

She raised her free arm to grasp his, but her strength melted. She ended merely clasping the hard muscles of his forearm where it lay between her breasts.

His mouth closed over hers, devouring hers, his tongue pushing into her satiny interior.

What is happening to me? I cannot seem to think. I want . . . No man had ever kissed her on the mouth. How could such a feeling be possible? Rather than unpleasant, the sensation was exciting. She had not known that anyone kissed anyone else with such intimacy. He was actually thrusting his tongue into her mouth, caressing her own tongue, tasting her. As her mouth opened to receive him, a fire began to grow. As if his fever were burning her body as well, she sighed. The taste of him was not unpleasant, she decided. Evidently, he liked the way she tasted, too. His tongue flicked in and out of her mouth, rippling over her lips, along the edges of her teeth, touching the tip of her own tongue with quick little caresses.

Almost against her will, her tongue moved to touch his and follow to the edge of his lips.

Suddenly, he coughed and once begun, he could not stop. His body spasmed as if he were flailed by whips. Jerking his head away from her mouth, he buried his face against her shoulder.

Quickly she turned her face away. Next to her left ear lay his manacled hands. The hands themselves were square and strong and brown, the long tapering fingers clenched with his efforts to gain control of his body. The wrists stirred her to pity.

With a sigh, she turned back to face him. His spasm had passed, leaving him shaken, his eyes blurred with involuntary tears.

"If you will go for our clothing, I will bathe and bandage your wrists for you." Her hand resting on his upper arm patted him soothingly.

With an effort, he lifted his arms from around her upper body and tried to hoist himself up. Another fit of coughing racked him and he fell back limply. His lips were dry and cracked; his head rolled helplessly on the mattress. "I believe I cannot get up just yet," he whispered. "Let me lie here a minute longer."

Moira turned to face him and raised up on one elbow. With her left hand, she tested his forehead. "You are burning with fever, my lord."

"Do not think to escape, my lady," he cautioned her. "Remember the old woman."

She curled her lip at him. Gathering one of the pelts from atop them, she crawled to the foot and across his legs. As she swung her feet over the side of the rude bed to stand, she groaned and staggered. She caught her lip between her teeth and straightened. Pulling the pelt tight about her shoulders, she tottered to the opening.

The fire had died down on the hearth, but the old woman slept on, curled in a tight ball. Bending stiffly, Moira picked up her blouse. Grateful to find it completely dry, she dropped the pelt and pulled her garment over her head, groaning again as her stiff shoulders protested from the effort of lifting her arms over her head. Her *chausses* were another matter, as was her gown. The usually supple leather was damp and stiff. The heavy thick wool of the gown was still quite wet. Fortunately, her hose were dry enough to don, however. Her boots, carefully oiled and cared for, felt flexible and dry. She decided against putting them on. She knotted the pelt around her waist to act as a makeshift skirt.

Wearily, she turned all the garments to expose the other side to the heat. Then she returned to the bedside and slumped down as he moved over to accommodate her. For a long time, she stared at the beams and the thatch above her head. Gradually, however, her body relaxed to allow her senses to begin to drift away.

She was awakened by a hard palm pressed over her mouth. Glittering eyes glared down at her malevolently from out of a face covered with grizzled, greasy hair. A purplish, veined nose and broken teeth lowered themselves closer to peer intently at her.

A cold draft chilled her skin as the covers were pulled off and then the protecting pelt she had wrapped around herself. The palm shifted to fasten in her hair. She felt a hard greasy hand on her inner thigh, pinching her.

Her mouth freed, she hissed, "Leave me alone, animal!"

Still, the rough palm pushed hard against her crotch as the calloused fingers probed and pinched. The face spread in a grin of evil malice as he twisted her hair, seeming to delight in the pain he caused.

She gasped and writhed. He let go of her hair to strike her sharply across the cheek. The blow angered her. Grasping the hand that had struck her in both her own, she fastened her teeth on it. The man yelled and cursed, trying to shake her off. She tasted blood before a blow sent her floating away. She could feel her fingers and her jaw relaxing against her will.

When Moira opened her eyes, she felt that she was suffocating. Her arms were wrenched behind her back and rough cords bound her wrists tightly. Raising her head out of the pelts, she found herself practically cheek to cheek with Rhiannon. His teeth were bared in a snarl.

"What—?" she began.

A blow in the middle of her back accompanied by a guttural command silenced her. Then ungentle hands pulled them both to their feet. Rhiannon was naked and still chained while she wore only her silk shirt reaching just below her hips.

Their captors pushed them into the main room of the hut where some half dozen men in motley dress argued. Two pawed her wool cape. One had donned her sheepskin vest. Another attempted to gird Rhiannon's wide belt around his waist. As Rhiannon stumbled out behind her, a man younger than the others sprang forward with a cry. Roughly, he jerked the gold and leather fillet from Rhiannon's forehead. Immediately a cry went up from the others as they began to argue and gesture frantically. The younger one stoutly defended his prize. The others were determined to take it, but uncertain who among them would possess it.

In the corner of the hut as far away as possible crouched the old woman. She crooned to herself oblivious to all that was occurring around her. Moira and Rhiannon were herded over beside her. Rhiannon's captor gave a cruel shove that sent the chained man crashing against the side of the hut on his wounded shoulder. A cry of pain tore from his lips, but then he was silent.

Defiantly, Moira turned to face the men. "My father is Lord Peter of Lorne Rock. Release me and bring me to him and I will personally reward you, as will he."

The men appeared not to hear her.

"My father is Lord Lorne," she tried again desperately. "Lorne!" she commanded imperiously.

The men continued to ransack the hut for food, clothing, weapons, anything they might steal.

Moira felt the old woman tug gently at her sleeve. Turning slightly Moira saw the old one trembling and shaking her head. In dawning hopelessness, Moira stepped back out of the circle of light left by the fire and slid down the wall to wait for what would come.

Beside her, Rhiannon struggled to rise, then slumped down on his face. After a few minutes he moved, moaning softly. At last, with an agonized grunt, he twisted his body, then hunched and raised his back against the wall. They sat together; the crooning old woman lost in her own thoughts, Rhiannon ap Breannon, his cheeks flushed with fever beneath eyes burning like coals, and Moira of Lorne, her lips pulled in and pressed hard between her teeth.

The six men had found some food which they ate greedily as they drank from a skin they had brought with them. The odor of sour ale permeated the hut. That along with the smell of unwashed bodies, made more pungent by the heat of the fire, made the air close and stuffy. Two men slumped down over the table. Another dragged his body off the bench and flopped down on the wool cloak before the fire. A fourth kept watch after a fashion, nursing his skin and sipping occasionally. The younger man who had claimed the fillet and the one who apparently was the leader were muttering together in harsh, angry tones.

"My lady," Rhiannon's voice was raspy in her ear, "turn slowly to let me untie your hands."

Carefully she shifted her body until she felt his fingers fumble at the hard knots at her wrists. When he released her, she remained as she was with her arms behind her.

Again she felt Rhiannon's breath at her neck. "I shall attack them. This chain will make a strong weapon. When I do, run for the door. The horses must be outside. While I hold them off, you get away."

Moira nodded her head, but her eyes darted around the hut to rest on a heavy rake leaning against the wall in the corner some six feet away.

Behind her, Rhiannon rose from the darkness. The three feet of chain hanging from his wrists swung back. With a low growl, he lunged at the pair who argued. His first swing wrapped the chain around the younger man's face. Screaming in agony, he staggered into his leader.

The guard started up too late. Moira was also on her feet and slammed the rake handle into his head just below his left ear. The leader blundered forward, but Rhiannon's chain lashed at him, bringing him up short. Again as the man dodged, Rhiannon feinted with the swinging chain. His eyes glittering in his hairy face, the man lunged under the chain straight for Rhiannon's body. He connected with a thud, his arms closing around Rhiannon's ribs to crush the breath from him. Before the grip could tighten, the manacled wrists slammed down on the back at the base of the skull. With a grunt, the leader fell away.

Whirling, Rhiannon faced the two·men who sat stupe-

71

fied at the small table. Across the room, Moira raised her heavy rake handle. Together they moved toward them. Terrified, one rose backing toward the door, his hand held out to ward off the terrible weapons of the two. The other sidled over to the fire to rouse his companion who had fallen asleep in Moira's cloak.

The sleeper roused and scrambled up. As he started for the door, Moira darted forward to pull the cloak from his nerveless grasp. The young man with the crushed face was still moaning on the floor when Rhiannon bent over and extracted the gold fillet from his pocket. Grasping his injured opponent by the shoulder and neck, he half-dragged, half-flung him out the door after the others.

As he stood at the door, Moira came up behind him and flung the cloak around his shoulders.

"The horses," she warned. "See that they leave the horses."

Nodding, he swiftly followed the four men outside. Two were already sprinting over the hill. The third was helping his wounded companion, but all were fast disappearing on foot.

With a grunt of satisfaction, Rhiannon re-entered the hut.

Nine

Her body tall and slender, outlined with firelight, Moira faced him across the table. As he entered, he grinned at her. For an instant an answering smile flickered on her lips before she stiffened and backed a step away. Her fingers tightened on the rake.

"Peace, my lady." The firm lips widened into a smile of delight. "A truce between us until we can at least put on clothing. Your body is delightful in firelight, but I am sure you must be—as I am—chilled in the limbs."

Embarrassed, she lowered the rake. Together they sorted through the bundles before the hearth. Turning her back to Rhiannon, she began to dress. As she bent to pull on her *chausses*, her lovely form was again outlined against the fire.

Still grinning, Rhiannon picked up his own leggings from the floor and pulled them on. She constantly amazed him. She could have run, probably escaped. Instead she had caught up a weapon and protected his back. Different from any woman he had ever known, her courage and endurance equaled those of most men. He shook his head wonderingly.

Dressed at last, she started toward the man whose head she had crushed to retrieve her sheepskin vest. Rhiannon watched curiously as she knelt beside the body and started to turn it over. Suddenly she gagged, letting the bloody mess slump back on its face. Her face went sickly pale, her hands trembled.

Rhiannon started forward, bracing her with his hands against her back. "Let me get the vest for you, my lady. Even you need help now and again."

She shuddered. Together they took a few steps to the rude bench where they had sat the night before to eat.

He held her hands in his as she shivered with reaction and weakness. With her head bowed, he could not see her expression, but the icy chill of her hands told him much. From somewhere within himself he felt a wave of tender feeling.

"My lady, again I must thank you for being at my side. You could have escaped, but you stayed and fought. Perhaps you saved my life." His hands tightened on her own, lifting them as he lifted his own to bring them up under her chin. "Why did you so?" he asked, looking into her eyes.

"Why did you untie me and tell me to run?" she countered. "You could have left me tied to await the outcome of the fight."

"I could not leave you at their mercy," he replied arrogantly. "I had brought you here, but only as a hostage for me. Not for other men. Certainly not for such as those. You are *my* captive."

She drew herself up coldly. "And I could not run out into the cold and rain clad only in my shift and blouse. I would not have lived to reach my father. Be certain though, that I shall survive and see you destroyed."

With those words, she snatched her hands away from his. Angrily, she strode to the bundles and began extracting the food the thieves had packed to take with

74

them. The old woman moved forward and crouched beside the fire, quietly watching as Moira began to prepare a simple meal to break their fast. With water, oats, and salt she began to mix a porridge in the black kettle that hung from the fireplace.

Shrugging, Rhiannon searched the two dead men, removing their coats as well as Moira's sheepskin. With a strange feeling of detachment, he noted that his hands were trembling badly. After a few minutes, dizziness overwhelmed him so that he was forced to leave the task. He slumped in weak helplessness beside the fire, his eyes staring dully into its flames.

Dimly, he was aware when Moira came toward him with a clay cup containing some of the ale they had drunk the night before. Downing the ale in a long gulp, he coughed painfully. Heartened, nevertheless, in a few minutes he pulled himself up to sit cross-legged before the fire.

Among the leader's variety of weapons was a slender dagger. By the light of the fire, Rhiannon began to pick at the lock on his manacles. The work was awkward and he gave it up in despair as Moira returned with a bowl of the porridge. At first, he ate gratefully. However, after only a few spoonfuls, weariness swept over him. He set the bowl down to lean his head in his hands.

His face felt on fire, his throat was an open wound. His shoulder ached devastatingly. Curiously, he drew aside the shreds of shirt to look at the seared surface. A hard brown crust had formed over the whole, but the entire area was circled with angry red flesh. The minor wounds on his chest also looked swollen and discolored. Touching the wound tentatively with his fingers, he gasped at the pain even the slightest pressure gave him.

Helplessly he glanced around him. Moira's eyes met his from across the room where she was finishing her bowl of porridge.

"Let me heat some water, my lord," she offered, "to make a poultice to draw some of that infection out." As good as her word, she rose to draw water from a crock in the corner beside the hearth. Pouring several dipperfuls into a smaller kettle, she swung it over the fire to heat. Next, she began to tear strips from the shirt of one of the dead men.

When the water had begun to simmer, she sat again beside him. Gingerly she dipped a strip of rough cloth into the hot water. Grimacing, she pulled it out and squeezed some of the liquid out of it.

"This will be hot, my lord, but it should soften the crust and let the wound drain and ease somewhat." Draping the strip across his shoulder, she reached for another while he set his teeth against the searing pain. Steadily, she worked until several thicknesses of hot steamy cloth were lying across the wound. Finally, taking a dry strip, she bound the whole rather loosely around his armpit and across his chest.

Taking another strip of cloth, she wet it and carefully began to clean the area around the cuffs on his wrists. Despite himself, he flinched as she dabbed at the blisters. When she had washed the areas thoroughly, she carefully drew strips of cloth between the manacles and his wrists to pad the awful cuffs and give him some measure of relief.

Without looking at his face, she withdrew to the other side of the fire where she took some more porridge. The old woman helped herself also and they ate together in companionable silence.

Left alone, Rhiannon shivered at his own weakness. Carefully he reached into his pocket to draw out the fillet. In his hands, it seemed to glow and writhe in the firelight. With eyes burning from the effects of the fever, his hands trembling with weakness, he lifted the fillet to his forehead and bound it in place. Finally, it was accomplished and the feel of it around his brow gave him a moral comfort that he had not hoped for. I must get home to my father's hall, he thought. I must leave now.

With great difficulty he got to his feet. "Come, my lady, we must move on. Morning is far gone. I would be miles farther from your father by nightfall."

Moira looked up swiftly to see him sway in the light of the fire. "Are you sure you are capable of moving on, my lord?" she jeered.

"Capable or not, we shall." He held out the sheepskin vest toward her.

She flinched at the sight of the blood stain, but Rhiannon insisted. "'Twill keep you warm, my lady. He will not need it, nor anything."

Collecting her wool cape from the floor, he handed it to her also. Methodically, he drew on the leader's wool cloak and weapons and bent to drag the body outside the hut. Using one of the leading ropes from the gray, he secured the dead man's foot and swung himself up onto the animal's back. The big stallion pranced nervously as the body dragged along behind it. A hundred yards behind the hut lay a small ravine. Dismounting, Rhiannon untied the body and rolled it into the wash.

When he returned to the cabin, Moira had packed a small parcel in a roll made by the cloak of the other man. At his wary look, she laughed bitterly. "Some food, my lord, which our kind hostess insisted that we take."

Nodding, Rhiannon dragged the other man's body from the hut. At last, he re-entered and approached the old woman who huddled by the fire.

"Thank you, mother, for your many kindnesses. My lady and I must continue on our journey." He smiled. "We will remember you with great fondness for your charity."

The old woman bobbed her head at him. "You are welcome, my lord," she quavered.

Placing his hand over Moira's arm, Rhiannon drew her out the door with him into the dim half light of the cold morning. When they mounted, she on the black, he on the gray, he led the way to the wash where he disposed of the body.

When he had returned to the saddle, she spoke, "Which way now?"

He raised his head to calculate the sun to his left. "South."

Surreptitiously, she tested the handle of the knife hidden in the sleeve of her gown and kicked her horse out after his.

Evening found them alone with no shelter in sight. She had long since given up trying to sit the black with any purpose and merely slumped dejectedly as the horse plodded along. Rhiannon was sometimes alert, sometimes dazed and delirious, but always they continued to the south.

The sun had moved across over their heads and descended on the right. A harsh wind had sprung up in the midafternoon, but had also died with the sun. Now a frosty mist surrounded their horses' legs as they rode through the early evening.

At last, Rhiannon steered toward a copse of trees which appeared out of the mist to their left. Within their protection, he stiffly dismounted. Moira followed suit. As her feet touched the ground, she moaned, her legs buckled under her, and she sat down beside the horse.

Walking stiffly to her side, Rhiannon took the reins of the tired animal from her hand and led both of the horses away. Staggering back to her, he discovered Moira on her hands and knees, trying to feel around in the waning light for some small sticks with which to build a fire. Together they lighted it with a flint she had brought from the old woman's hut.

When the fire began to burn falteringly, she spread out

the food that they had between them—a small loaf of hard black bread and a smaller piece of cheese. He broke the loaf in half and handed her one. With his knife he divided the cheese. Together they chewed the rough dry rations.

Beside the feeble flame they huddled cross-legged, Moira's right knee brushing Rhiannon's left. As they leaned forward as close as they dared to catch the warmth, the flickering glow lit their faces starkly, accentuating the suffering they had endured.

The fire would scarcely last half an hour, Moira realized dismally as she stared into its center, allowing it to draw her eyes hypnotically and in some small way desensitize her aching body. The wind sighed mournfully in the tops of the trees as its damp chill brushed a long strand of hair across her cheek.

The thought of escape flitted through her tired mind, but she could not seem to organize her thoughts. Hunger and fatigue deadened her mind until the whole world receded into the tiny pale flames that curled above the pitifully small collection of sticks and dead grasses.

The breeze carried a wisp of smoke into Rhiannon's face. He coughed, bowing his head in his misery and dragging the cloak more tightly around him.

One of the horses whickered faintly. Moira roused, turning her head in their direction. Poor beasts. Used to warm stalls at night and grain in plenty, they must be puzzled by the lack of care. Aching in every bone, she uncrossed her legs and wearily attempted to push herself up on her knees.

"Where do you go?" Rhiannon's hoarse question was barely intelligible.

"To loosen the girths and stake them in grass, if I can find some," Moira replied, getting one foot under her and placing both hands on her knee.

"Stay still," he commanded. "I will see to the horses."

His weary sneer reminded her of their antipathy.

A slow flush rose to her cheeks as she realized that in her misery and exhaustion, she had not been thinking of herself, but of the misery of the animals. It galled her to think that she might have risen and tended both mounts without flinging herself into the saddle of one and leading the other one away at a gallop. Her failure to seize even the most obvious opportunity shamed her. She subsided, hugging herself even tighter, into a ball of pain, her head cradled in her crossed arms.

When he returned, Rhiannon gazed down at her curiously. At last she is crying, he thought. I knew it would be just a matter of time before she would break. She is like every other woman. He knelt beside her, hand on her shoulder, thinking to turn her and gather her into his arms. At his touch, she raised her face. To his astonishment, her cheeks were dry. But her eyes . . . They were dark pits of sorrow. Like a man, she faced him and he recognized in her eyes what he would have felt if he had been in her position. The shame, the self-condemnation.

His eyes drooped. Gathering his cloak around him without a word, Rhiannon stretched out beside her, turning on his side with his back toward her body.

The fire died while she sat staring at it. Long she looked into its coals, watching as they each became coated with gray ash. Fool! She chastised herself. Coward! Staring into the dying fire like some lady in a *romans courteois*. Do you expect your life to go out like the flames. Ridiculous. Rest tonight. Plan tomorrow.

Encouraged by her resolution, she stretched out at his back. The fire ceased to give off even a faint warmth. She shivered as the wind whispered through the copse.

Body heat, he had said. She would not deny herself this one small comfort. Determinedly, she turned her body to face his back and pressed herself against him. Her arm pushed through the slit of his cloak and passed around his waist. Her palm rested against his lean middle, gaining warmth from the delicious heat emanating from him. Involuntarily, her fingers caressed the smooth texture of his skin here and there encountering the curly hairs. He moaned softly, but did not seem to waken. Turning her cheek into the wide space between his shoulder blades, she pulled herself tight against him and relaxed.

Ten

Rhiannon swung down from the horse and for a full twenty seconds rested on his knees, trying to find the strength to pull himself up on his numbed and weakened legs. Moira was no better than he as she felt helplessly for the strength to slide from the saddle. Her thighs and back ached appallingly. She could feel nothing from her knees down.

Above their heads, the church tower loomed with the evening star just appearing in the square of one arm of the cross. The buildings of a small monastery huddled in the gloom.

Finally, Rhiannon pulled himself to his feet and staggered to her side. "My lady, can you dismount? Here is shelter and food."

Moira looked down at him in the darkness. His face was a white spot, unfocused and hazy. She swayed and then straightened abruptly. "I cannot dismount, my lord," she whispered, "unless you can catch me. Perhaps you should summon help from the house before I try."

Nodding, he staggered away to the door and pounded on it. No sound came. No answering call. He shouted. He pounded again. He rattled the doorlatch. No reply.

In defeat and despair, he staggered back to her side where she drooped on the horse. Her face was lowered over the neck of the horse as she slumped helplessly. "There is no answer," he groaned.

"Perhaps there is a stable at the back," she whispered.

Gathering their horses' reins, he led them behind the small outbuilding. Sure enough, a dark opening yawned in the side of a hill. Staggering with weariness, he led the animals in. Darker than a pit, the cavern smelled unmistakably of mouldy hay and horses. Returning to her side, he placed his hand on her thigh. "My lady, can you reach the flints?"

Obediently, Moira fumbled them from the pocket in her cloak and into his hand. Kneeling down, he scraped with his hands to form a little pile of hay and clear a circle around it. A few strokes with the flints, and magically the little fire sprang up, driving the darkness back into the corners of the stable.

A quick glance around revealed a lantern on a hook at the stable door. A small stub of a candle remained in it. Lifting it from its hook, Rhiannon lighted it with a piece of straw from the small fire.

Behind him, Moira slipped from her horse's back to fall on her side in the hay as her benumbed legs refused to bear her weight.

"How is it with you, lady?" he asked, coming to her side.

"I am but weary from the long ride," she responded. "Help me to rise and I can tend our fire while you see if you can rouse anyone in that building. Perhaps they are at prayer and would not answer the call."

Grasping her arms, Rhiannon pulled her to her feet. She staggered against him and would have fallen, but he shifted his grasp and supported her. Leaning her against his good shoulder, together they took a half dozen painful steps to and fro before the fire.

Moira staggered slightly as the feeling came back into her feet, needles of fire shot from her soles to her knees. At last, taking a deep breath, she straightened. Almost on a level with him, her eyes looked into his with answering blue fire. "I am all right now," she said. "I will stay here with the horses, tend the fire, and try to rub them down. The poor beasts need attention."

Rhiannon carried the lantern out into the night. Immediately, Moira began to gather handfuls of hay to add to the flame. A couple of rough boards lay beside the entrance. She dragged them to the fire and carefully stuck their ends into the hay. As they began to smoulder, she added more hay, holding out her hands thankfully to the heat.

The stable was very small. With a back wall and one side of sod, the small hovel contained only one partition. Despite her weariness, she tied the black in the far stall, rubbed him down with handfuls of hay, and piled a goodly amount of the hay in front of him.

After caring for the gray in the same manner, she turned to the fire again. Beside its welcoming blaze, she sat down and extended her feet and hands to it, luxuriating in the warmth. Gradually the pains and aches subsided. Her head drooped, her eyes closed.

Abruptly she jerked awake. Rhiannon had not returned. Stirring restively, she glanced around her. She dared not leave the fire untended, yet she thought he might need her.

Suddenly, she angrily shook her head. What was the matter with her? If he did not return, she would escape and ride out in the morning directly west until she encountered her father's lands. She should be glad that he had not returned.

At that moment he entered, his face white and his mouth set in a grim line. "The place is deserted."

"What can have happened?"

"Probably plague," he replied. "I brought as much food as I could carry, but I feared to spend the night in the place. 'Tis dangerous to eat the food, but I think we can go no farther without it."

He swung a bag down from his back and allowed the sides to fold down. In it were several loaves of hard black bread, some dried meats, and two small jugs.

When he passed her the vessel, she uncorked it gratefully and took a tentative sip. The fiery liquid burned her throat, causing her to choke and sputter.

"Good stuff," he smiled. "For that reason alone, I was sure that they did not move away or leave voluntarily. Too many jugs, along with casks of ale and beer in the larder."

"Did you investigate the rest of the house or did you remain with the drink?" she inquired sarcastically, reaching for a strip of meat.

He looked at her questioningly. "What mean you by that?"

"I meant that a robber and coward such as you and your kind would be uninterested in offering help to anyone who might be in need, perhaps in another room in the house."

Before he answered, Rhiannon opened the second jug and took a long pull. The brandy seared his raw throat, warming him as it coursed down through his body. It warmed his belly and imparted strength to its weakened limbs. He broke a loaf of bread, giving half to her as he dropped down beside her. She moved away slightly, but accepted the bread, biting into it gratefully with her strong white teeth.

Rhiannon took a bite of bread and then another pull at the brandy. "My lady," he began, "I searched through all the rooms of that small house. There was no one there, but things were in disarray, as if the brothers had left in

85

a great hurry. As you see, there were baked bread and meats still in the larder. More important, among the implements in the kitchen I found this.''

He sneered triumphantly at her. Moira gasped as he held up a file. It was a heavy, cumbersome tool, but its very weight gave it great effectiveness. Rhiannon began to saw at the ring on the manacle where the chain joined the cuff. The file screeched as metal scraped metal. The cuff bit cruelly into his wrist. Fresh blood stained the pad she had made to protect him.

Unable to bear the sight of his set, white face clammy with perspiration, she hitched herself closer to him, placing her hands on the cuff where he braced it on his knee. ''Let me help you to steady the thing, my lord,'' she said softly. He glanced quickly at her face, his eyes alight with speculative fire. She would not look at his eyes, but kept her head down, her gaze concentrated on the manacle.

At length, he paused gasping, to drink deeply from the jug. Moira looked at him from beneath her lashes. His face was gray and pinched, except for bright red spots which blazed above his cheekbones. ''Eat a bite of meat and bread, my lord,'' she advised. ''You will make yourself ill with the strong brandy and lose what little strength you may have gained.''

Panting, he laid the file aside and bowed his head. Offering him the bread, she watched as he took a bite. While he chewed, she added more hay to the fire and pushed the boards farther into the blaze as they had begun to burn down. ''Now a bit of meat,'' she urged him. Again he complied, tearing the bite off with his strong white teeth and chewing slowly as if in weariness. ''Stretch out, my lord, and I will look at your wound and rebandage it.''

He sat up deliberately. ''No!'' Taking another drink from the jug, he picked up the file and again began with renewed vigor to rasp away at the link.

She placed her hands tightly around the manacle and held fast. The iron began to heat. She looked out from under her lashes at the face of the man bent perforce with his head close to hers. His forehead gleamed with perspiration. His lips curled back from teeth clenched with determination. The rasping went on and on. Moira's nerves were being rubbed raw along with the terrible screeching sound of the file.

Again Rhiannon fell back, dropping the implement. Desperately, he reached for the jug, but she stayed his hand. "No, my lord, do not," she begged. "Bread and meat first."

Throwing her a look of exhausted annoyance, he nevertheless reached for the bread. This time, he lay back at length, his wrists lying limply across his loins, while he stared at the roof of the stable. When he had finished chewing the bread, Moira handed him a piece of meat which he stuffed into his mouth without comment. Again he chewed slowly.

Finished, he sat up, glanced sardonically at her, and reached for the jug. "With your permission, lady."

She smiled.

For the first time, he saw her face light up with a brief flicker of warmth. In that moment, he caught a glimpse of a rare beauty. Her eyes, surrounded by long dark curling lashes, were an unusual shade of pale blue. They seemed to glow with a luminous light. He looked into the eyes for an extra moment as he lifted the jug to let the fiery liquid trickle down his throat. Embarrassed under his gaze, she took a large bite off the bread. Immediately, she choked on the dry stuff, reaching hastily for her own jug. Tears stood in her eyes from the choking and the fiery brandy. She coughed, cleared her throat, and finally glanced up at him with a watery smile. Her eyes lit up her whole face.

He caught his breath in wonderment. Hastily, he

picked up the file and began again to rasp away at the link. She took another bite of meat, then set her hands against the manacle to hold it steady.

The file screeched through the link. With a sigh of relief, Rhiannon grasped the six inches of chain in his right fist. He nodded as she placed her hands around the manacle. Drawing a deep breath, he pulled with all the strength of his back and shoulder. The chain spanged through the break in the link.

He was free!

Chuckling exultantly, Rhiannon spread his arms wide, stretching his long-cramped muscles. As his arms extended out a full six feet, she fell back. He was like some huge, frightening creature unfolding himself before her eyes. The three feet of chain that had been attached to the six-inch piece fell away. He chuckled again as he felt the freedom.

Only for a minute. Then he winced, lowering his left arm to his side. He probed gently with his right hand, then looked at her inquiringly. "You were saying something about rebandaging my wound?"

Wordlessly, she nodded, watching him as he unfastened the cloak and began to gather the edges of his ragged tunic. Again the wound hindered him. His left arm hung limp. Witnessing his evident distress, she rose on her knees to help him slip it off.

Clinically, she regarded his torso. The black hair curled crisply against the white skin. The muscles rippled along the rib cage. The two sword cuts on his body were scabbed over and no longer red or inflamed looking. The whip mark across the chest still showed a blue-green bruise. Unwrapping his shoulder, she carefully withdrew the pad she had made hours ago to soften and draw the wound. To her relief, the angry red had faded somewhat and the swelling had decreased. Throwing the old pads into the fire, she bound the wound loosely with the outer bandage. Then she sat back on her heels.

"My lord, I believe that you will be quite all right. The wound is clean. Everything else is beginning to heal nicely. Apart from a scar, you should have no memory in a month."

"My thanks, my lady," he replied. "You have saved me and cared for me. Believe me, I am most grateful." He grinned. "I also remember that you were very helpful in freeing me from your father."

Immediately, she stiffened, starting to draw away, but he caught her arm and pulled her back against him. "My lady, you fought me well. I would not despise to have you among my men-at-arms," his breath brushed her forehead, "except that you are too beautiful. . . ."

Angrily she twisted, vainly seeking to pull away from him. "Gently, gently." He talked to her as he would to a small child or an animal.

"No!" she protested. "No! No! You shall not do this thing to me now that you are free."

"What thing, my lady?"

Shivering, she ducked her head away from him and his piercing blue eyes. "I am yet a maid," she said so low that he could barely hear her words.

At that, he laughed softly. With a mocking sigh, he pushed her away from him. In the same movement, he reached for the jug of brandy and turned it up, letting a hearty swallow warm him and bring a pleasant light-headedness to his tired frame. Saluting her companionably, he broke off another bite of bread and chewed it slowly as he slumped back into the hay.

Moira scrambled halfway around the fire from where she stared fearfully at him from under her lashes. When he closed his eyes with an exhausted sigh, she reached for the food. Tearing off another bite of meat, she chewed morosely. Her many aches and her exhaustion became apparent to her. Taking a firm grip on the jug, she swung it up to her mouth as she had seen him do to let a large swallow sear her throat. She gasped, coughed, and almost gagged. A smothered laugh reached her from across the fire. Hastily, she set the jug down. Refusing to look at him, she instead reached her grimy hands up to her face and hair.

To her disgust, Moira realized that she was as filthy as she had ever been in her life. Her hair was a witch's nest of snarls and tangles. In all the time of her captivity, she had not touched it. With difficulty, she found the leather strings that bound the end of her braid. After much fumbling and tugging, she untied them. However, when she sought to pull them free, she could not do so. Her hair was so matted that she could not extricate them without her mirror. Her hands dropped to her lap as she sighed disconsolately. Her body slumped back dejectedly.

Rhiannon had been watching her with some amusement from across the fire. "Come back here and let me help you. You can trust me," he chuckled. "I think that the least I could do for you would be to help you with your problem since you have been so gracious as to help me with mine."

Moira hesitated. She stared hard at Rhiannon. He raised his jug, saluted her, and drank off another swallow. He smiled pleasantly at her and gestured lazily.

One hand went self-consciously to her hair. She lifted her jug, took another swallow, and stood up. Carrying her drink and food, she moved determinedly around the fire to his side. Carefully, intent on preserving her dignity, she lowered herself onto the hay. As she did so, she staggered slightly and sat down a little harder than she had expected. Murmuring irritably, she carefully righted herself and presented him with her back.

Rhiannon deliberately began to tug at the leather strips that bound her heavy braid. The hair, mixed with bits of dried grasses, was knotted crazily around the leather. As he worked, he paused from time to time to take a bite of bread and to wash it down with liquid. As one of the strings came out, a long wisp of hair came away with it.

Moira whimpered in protest. The other strip came away and her coil of hair rippled down her back. Long and brown, with red and golden lights, it glinted in the fire.

"There." Rhiannon dropped his hands. Moira swung her hair around between her breasts and turned halfway around to sit beside him. With a smile of gratitude, she began to comb her fingers through the mass, starting at the end and working up. Before she had gone very far, she paused, aware that he was watching her intently beneath half-closed lids. Quizzically, she looked at him. Her head tilted to one side, her fingers busily tried to untangle the snarls.

Rhiannon smiled again as he proffered her the jug. She accepted it, drinking with hardly a gasp or grimace. Her hands fell to her lap while she waited for the liquid fire to warm her stomach.

His smile widening, Rhiannon lifted the braid and began to comb his own long fingers through it. Something like a purr escaped her as she sat perfectly still, mesmerized by her exhaustion, the drink she had consumed, the warmth of the fire and the feel of his hands in her hair. When he was done, she raised her head to stare into his eyes. Hers were luminous in the reflected light. "Thank you," she murmured. "Now, can I go to sleep? I am so tired."

Rhiannon raised his hands to her shoulders. His thumbs came up to rest under her ears and tilt her head back. The vulpine look faded from his mouth as he searched the dirty, tired face surrounded by the cloud of red-brown hair. Her body was relaxed and pliant from the liquor. She was dazed beyond thought.

"What is your name?" he asked softly.

"Moira," she replied.

"Then, Moira, I am going to kiss you, after which you may go to sleep. Raise your lips to me. Come. That's a very good girl."

Gently his lips brushed hers, his tongue licked the brandy from her lips and tasted her mouth tentatively. Her eyes closed as he gathered her into his arms.

Eleven

Moira awoke as the light of morning dimly filtered through the stable. Her body felt warm and rested, but her head pounded fiercely. When she opened her eyes, the light stabbed them so painfully that she moaned and turned her face away. As she did so, she encountered the bearded neck of her captor.

Her moan of pain changed to one of horror. What had occurred? She could not remember past beginning to take her hair down. Her next conscious thought concerned flight. She must get away from him. Perhaps tonight when he slept—if she could get enough food. She had always been able to stay awake. Perhaps tonight.

Rhiannon stirred beside her. His eyes flicked open. Breast to breast, they faced each other. She regarded him warily, searching his face for some sign of his intent. Gradually, she became aware of the rise and fall of his chest against her bosom.

Drawing her lithe body into the circle of his arms, Rhiannon pressed her spine with his hands. As she stiffened and sought to push away, his touch hardened. One hand moved upward through her hair to cup the back of her head. Again she moaned in protest as he pressed her toward him.

Shuddering, she twisted her head, trying to writhe out of his caress, but he was everywhere. His lips, his tongue, his hot breath and where his lips and tongue led, his teeth followed.

Every muscle, every nerve strung tighter and tighter as the strange touch forced responses from her, driving her body farther beyond her control. A light dew of perspiration formed on her skin. His tongue tasted the salt in the soft curve at the corner of her mouth. He chuckled faintly. At his laughter, she stared hard into the sapphire blue eyes glowing in the dimness. His eyelashes, long and black, drooped slightly, hiding his expression from her. As she tried to find the reason for his humor, his mouth met hers. She felt acutely the soft tangle of his beard.

Like fire, his kiss melted the strength from her muscles at the same time that it strung her nerves even tauter. She was sensation, quivering, tormented, responsive sensation, sensually played upon by the master lover. How long the fiery pleasure might have continued, she feared to think. Dimly in the recesses of her mind, her rebellion began. Arching her weak body as strongly as she could, she dug her heels into the dirt of the stable floor.

"No!" Her voice was somewhere between a plea and a command. "No! You have no right to do this thing to me." She struck out at him at the same time she wrenched and twisted her body from beneath his. Her right hand slapped his cheek a resounding whack before he seized her wrist. Twisting it behind her back, he rolled after her, pressing her body more firmly into the hay. Reared up over her now, his body terrified her—he was *so* hard, *so* strong. His weight pressed her down, holding her almost immobile. His chest flattened her soft breasts. His thighs gripped on each side of hers. His belly ground down against hers, so she could feel the hardness of his sex.

Fear tore at her vitals. She had seen the pitiful shuddering wrecks her father's men brought home and enslaved after a raid. Once a group had become more drunken than usual and had taken their turns with a slight, dark-haired gypsy creature before the dais in the hall. The pleas, the screams, the sobs trailing away to pitiful whimperings had rung in her ear for weeks. Now his chuckle and his hard hands working their implacable will on her body brought back the drunken scene in startling clarity.

He was but one! And wounded! She must marshal all her strength, goading it with fury and outrage, to force him to stop. If she could not, then he must at least pay dearly for the pleasure he sought. Her father's face rose before her, stern, grizzled, a fierce scowl on his brow. She had made the mistake of aiding the enemy, not once but twice. She had disobeyed Lord Lorne's sternest command. Her spine stiffened. A charge of fury burst in her brain and burned fiercely as hot blood coursed through her body, revitalizing her muscles.

"Beast!" Her voice was a desperate hiss of rage. "Cur! Take your hands off me. If you do not, I shall kill you. Indeed I shall never rest until you lie dead at my feet."

His hands tightened momentarily on her wrist and in her hair. "Go on," he muttered against her ear. "Fight me! You will give me greater pleasure. Your rage delights me. All the good lads your father's men have killed will watch your struggles."

She writhed uselessly under him, groaning with the physical effort, her legs thrashing ineffectually as she tried to bring up a knee between his thighs. Wrenching her hair from his grasp and ducking, she sank her teeth into his left shoulder. The warm salty taste of his blood was sickening on her tongue.

Howling, he tore himself away and slapped her. "Vixen!" he snarled. "No more biting. Understand." The blow dazed her, although he had used his open palm rather than his doubled fist.

Taking advantage of her momentary immobility, he sprang upright rubbing his shoulder. The bloodstains on his fingers brought a fierce growl from his lips. Bite him, would she?

As if she were a rag doll, he grasped her boots one at a time and dragged them off her feet, allowing each leg to flop weakly back. Dropping to his knees astride her thighs, he fumbled at the tie at her waist. Her eyelids fluttered as he pulled the *chausses* down around her hips. Her feeble hands were struck aside as he rose lithely, jerking her hips upward and ripping the garment down off her legs.

Her mouth opened in a soundless scream, but she did not utter it. No one would hear her. No one would care. She was alone. He was so quick and so very, very strong. Something of her despair must have shown in her eyes, for he grinned his feral grin as, in one violent sweep, he flung the material across the stable into the shadows.

Free of his weight, she struggled violently to push her body away from him. With a frantic scramble, she succeeded in turning herself over in the hay and getting one knee under her. Her scalp prickled as she felt rather than heard the swooping movement with which he straddled her. Dropping to his knees, he pressed his weight down on her pelvis, trapping her between his legs. As she writhed futilely, panting and gasping, he sat upright on her.

"Steady, girl." His voice was strangely soft in her ears. "Steady."

She felt his hands in her hair, gathering its snarled strands and smoothing them into a skein.

"Steady," he repeated. As he bent over her, he lifted

the hair aside and touched her ear with his lips. His hands slipped under her and grasped her breasts.

Shocked at his touch, she redoubled her efforts, digging her toes into the dirt and bucking to try to throw him off. For a moment, her strength was almost equal to the task. As she got one knee under her, her hips lifted his full weight.

Laughing grimly, he sat upright and slapped her rump hard.

Her breath groaned from between clenched teeth, as inexorably his weight bore down upon her until she collapsed helplessly. Her head sank into the dusty hay where she coughed weakly.

Again she felt his hand in her hair, stroking her gently. "Ready to submit, my lady?" His voice was cold, in marked contrast to his touch.

She coughed again. Her whole frame shuddered as she turned her face to the side to draw a deep breath. "Never!"

His weight lifted momentarily to allow the hand on her breast to tighten roughly. It was joined by the other at her hip as he rolled her over onto her back. Immediately, his weight settled on her again, this time astride her pelvis.

"Now, Moira of Lorne. Now." His voice was tight. "You shall feel what it is to be a woman. For me."

Her blue eyes flashed sparks of hatred as she lay panting from her useless exertions. His fingers trailed a path down her cheek, touching a pale streak where sweat had plowed a trail down her dusty face. Too weak for the moment to resist, she lay quiescent under his touch. Taking his time, he opened the lacings of her vest and then of her gown. Finally, the silk blouse was beneath his fingers. Watching her eyes, he closed his hands over her breasts, squeezing them gently.

As if she had run hard, she panted, flinging her head

from side to side. The nipples sprang up as he massaged them. Feebly her hands closed around his wrists, but her pressure only made him pinch her harder. As the raw silk rasped sensuously under his fingers, she closed her eyes. Desperately her mind commanded her body to fight, but his touch coupled with her exhaustion from her violent struggles had weakened her. As his fingers continued their relentless movement, he could imagine what she was feeling as she shuddered beneath him. The muscles of her belly tightened and shivered with her violent struggles. As she bucked upward, he pressed his body down to meet her violent thrusts.

"Oh, my lady," he moaned at last, "you stir me so."

Her face whitened. Ice blue eyes flashed open, dilated with fear and horror. In his eyes and his voice, she read the fate of all captive women.

Beneath his fingers, the wide leather belt at his waist fell away. Grasping the bottom edge of his tunic, he pulled the ragged garment over his head, exposing his hard naked flesh with its black curling hairs and fearsome scars to her horrified gaze. The wound on his left shoulder where she had bitten him was a swollen red mound crested by a tiny smear of blood. Blue veins traced across the muscles of his shoulders and upper arms. Mesmerized by the sight and scent and heat of a naked masculine body so close to her own, she drew in a shallow awestruck breath. Thinking her beaten, his hand reached almost casually for the fastenings of his breeches. As he did so, she made an extraordinarily violent movement. Her anger strengthened by terror gave her the unnatural force to overbalance him and send him sprawling on his side in the hay.

She had but one chance left. Her right hand flashed to the sleeve of her blouse, withdrawing the dagger. On her back, she could only strike upward and across. Quick as she was, his warrior's reflexes detected her action and lunged to grasp her wrist. "A knife," he snarled as he twisted her wrist cruelly. "Not gentle, my vixen! Not gentle at all. I warned you—no more fighting." Wrenching the knife from her hand, he flung it after her *chausses* into the depths of the stable.

Rearing up on his knees, his muscles flexed, his eyes wary, he paused. "Any more clever tricks, my lady?" he invited politely. "Any more daggers hidden about your person?" His eyes swept over her half-naked body, searching for tell-tale bulges.

Unable to conceal her despair, she flung her hand to her head, pressing hard against her temple. Her eyes flickered round the stable, searching vainly for some means of escape, some source of help.

"Relax," he chuckled, edging forward. "You will find . . ."

"Noo-o-o-o!"

Her breath sobbing in her throat, she struggled to her feet. Two steps she took before his hand closed like a vise round her ankle. She fell hard. Her air rushed out of her lungs as a murky blackness threatened to overcome her vision.

The next impression she had was of chilled air striking her ribs. Her gown and blouse were tugged away. Hay pricked the skin of her back and shoulders. Suddenly, she was naked!

Again she sought to struggle feebly, but the fight had gone out of her. Shocked, breathless, exhausted, she opened her eyes to see him straddling her with his legs outspread as he bared his swollen manhood. Huge and terrifying, it leaped out at her from beneath the arch of his scarred chest and lean belly. With a moan, Moira recognized the extent of what he would force into her body. She felt no comfort in the fleeting realization that all of her sex had been fashioned to accept such a thing. Instead the limp form of the ravaged gypsy, bruised, bleeding, her eyes staring in dull, unfocused despair, haunted her vision.

Rhiannon dropped down beside her in the hay, pressing himself along her naked body. His hands began at once to warm her flesh, suddenly gone so cold that it startled him. The perspiration had chilled. Even her nipples looked shrunken somehow. Where only a few minutes before she had writhed sensuously beneath his hands, now he felt her tremble.

The shrinking of her flesh slowed him. Suddenly he drew off. Relieved of his weight, she opened wary eyes, but closed them as he laid his body alongside hers.

Propping himself on one elbow, he began a new agony for her as he stroked her breasts. His long, hard fingers closed around her quivering white mound and slid firmly toward the nipple. Gently, he rolled it between this thumb and finger.

"Beautiful," he crooned. "Beautiful. So fine. So silky." His hand strayed down from the rosy peak to the dimple of her navel, and even to the crest of pale brown hair at the top of her thighs.

"No, pl—" Stubbornly, she bit down on the word, refusing to beg mercy from the enemy. He would do what he would do. She could not stop him. To beg would only increase his pleasure. She would gain an honorable defeat, if defeat it must be.

His fingers caressed the insides of her thighs, pushing them gently apart, insinuating his fingers in against the warm flesh. With a shock, she felt his fingers begin to tease the silken skin. New sensations began immediately in the depths of her body. Nervously, she writhed under his hand.

"What softness," he commented. "What a beauty you are! I cannot believe your skin is so fine when you have used your body as you have, riding astride and such as that . . ."

100

His hand stroked up across the skin of her hipbones, tickling her ribs and cupping her breast from beneath. As he caught her nipple again, she twisted sideways nervously. His hand clasped her ribcage, drawing her back close to his side.

"No, my lady," he crooned in her ear. "Relax. You will only hurt yourself if you struggle. Relax and let me give you pleasure. I know you are a virgin. For a virgin, the first time can be painful and frightening or there can be little pain and much pleasure." He bent his head. Despite the shaking of her head and the tiny murmur of protest, his lips closed over one nipple circling it lightly with his tongue as his fingers and thumb continued to caress the other one.

Under his ministrations, Moira's flesh began to burn and throb. Her body suffused with her blushes; from chest to hairline her skin glowed a deep pink. Moaning in her shame and helplessness, she grasped his hair in her two fists and pulled with all her might. The leather fillet came loose as he cursed at the pain.

"Witch!" He gripped her wrists. "Still you fight me! Enough, I say!" Viciously he squeezed the slender bones together, forcing her to release her grip. His expression murderous as his patience dissolved, he transferred both of her wrists to his left hand and with his right pulled the leather fillet from her nerveless fingers. Ruthlessly, he bound her wrists tightly together as he had done once before.

Her mind rebelled against the binding, but her body was too weak to resist. Mindlessly, she clenched and unclenched her fingers, vainly struggling against the leather. To be bound, helpless. Only bindings around her ankles were lacking to have her stretched on a rack.

Pulling her hands over her head and holding them there with his left hand, he reached down and pressed his palm hard against her soft mount at the top of her thighs.

When his fingers slipped lower, gently but firmly fingering her soft, tender places, she cried out in shock and twisted violently against his strictures. Rotating his palm slightly, ignoring her cry, he teased and tantalized the never-before-touched spots. Inexorably, he forced his knee between her thighs, spreading them.

One last try, her mind screamed. One last attempt! Surely, you have strength enough for one more. Wearily, she gathered her muscles for the herculean task she was setting them. Fierce blue eyes, filled with violent hatred, swept open to lock with his.

Her tension communicated itself to him. "Strive no more, my lady," he advised. "Only a very stupid person cannot see when the odds are overwhelming. You are overmatched. Yield yourself." His smile was almost gentle.

Her eyes slid down his body to stare at his rampant organ, at the black hairs curling over his belly and chest, at the wide shoulders and the thin film of perspiration covering all.

He was right. Oh dear God, but he was right. Her glittering blue eyes swept upward to his face, her mouth twisting in self-contempt.

"I cannot fight you off," she admitted tonelessly. "Do what you will. I shall not beg. Nor shall I attempt to resist you any further. But get it over with." The last words hissed between her clenched teeth. Her body went rigid as she resolved to face the ordeal.

A shuddering breath escaped him as he took in her rigid form now still before him. He nodded his head shortly as he released her hands from his grasp. As if he still held them above her head, she lay unmoving except for the tremors which racked her body from toes to head. Her eyes stared steadily at him. Not for her the executioner's hood. The blue eyes glowed in the white oval of her face.

The stable's early morning dimness had given way to stronger light that allowed each to see the other's face clearly and judge the emotions that played upon it.

Gentle now that he was assured of her passivity, he stretched out upon her, placing himself at her soft entrance. Her warm flesh raised a throbbing in his loins. Her sheath waited for his sword. Her quiescent body soothed his hatred for her and her family. She became female in his arms. Nothing more sinister nor dangerous. Thoughts of vengeance dissolved in a flood of anticipation.

Gathering her into his arms against his chest, he clasped one hand around the point of her shoulder to aid him in holding her body firm. Then he moved slowly but steadily forward. As he entered her, she tensed and threw her head to the side, biting her lips together between her teeth. Her body shuddered beneath him; tiny whimpering sounds escaped her throat.

"Relax," he whispered softly in her hear. "Relax. 'Twill be easier for you." His hand tightened on her shoulder catching her body as if it were in a vise. Drawing a deep breath, he lunged forward.

She screamed!

Like a dagger through silk, he tore through her virginal tissue, burying himself deep within her body. His belly ground against hers. Her world went suddenly dim. Nor could she move. Her whole body seemed numb from the impalement. Well-sheathed within her, he waited, his only movement the throbbing of his weapon filling her. Savoring his excitement, delightfully tormenting himself, he waited to give her a chance to stretch to accommodate him. Finally, when he felt a slight tremor in the exquisite clasp of her body, he began to move slowly, pulling himself almost out of her, then thrusting back in again.

Moisture glistened in her eyes as the searing pain

103

of his withdrawal was only surpassed by the agony of his thrust. She was being torn in two. Only pride forbade her to cry out. In truth, he stretched her upon the rack. Even the whip on her back could not be so bad as this deliberate abrasion of her inner body. And yet again he pushed into her, but the pain was not so intense. From within a moisture began to gather, easing his way. A shudder ran through her body as she speculated as to the nature of the lubricant.

The pain was definitely receding. Could such a thing be? Her body began to loosen; her limbs, to relax.

As if he felt the change in her, he whispered something unintelligible in her ear. His mouth pressed warmly. His breath came gasping as words fell from his lips. "Yes . . . ah, yes . . . Relax . . . ah . . ." His hand shifted from her shoulder to her breast. Not surprisingly, he found the nipple a diamond point, the entire mound hardened with excitement. "Ah, my lady," he whispered. "Your body . . . so soft, yet so firm . . . so warm . . ."

With these words, he seemed to lose control of his actions, to push harder and move faster. Each successive thrust roused traitorous feelings which she could not name, but that nibbled subtly at the nerve endings of her body. Suddenly at the peak of one deep, cruel thrust, he gasped for breath, cried out, and collapsed upon her. Numbly, she lay in the wake of his plunging motion, wondering what would be next, her senses reeling, her eyes closed.

At last, with a profound sigh he withdrew from her. At the same time, a trickle of warm fluid bedewed her thighs and the lower curve of her buttocks. Pulling himself off her body, he glanced down at himself now limp and relaxed. The proof of her virginity was unquestionably on him and on her smeared thighs.

His eyes flew to her face, pale as death, her lips bitten,

a tiny ruby of blood on the lower one. Pity stirred within him at the sight of the blood. Anyone who bore pain well roused his admiration. He was familiar with the screaming and wailing of women, whom he regarded as rather hopeless, cowardly creatures, useless for almost everything except the one thing they were created for. Her stoic façade pleased him. The thought struck him that she was different from most women. She would undoubtedly make a good slave when she was trained to serve. A warrior all his life, he knew that blood could not be shed without pain. Although he did not understand the precise nature of virginal pain, he imagined it to be intense. After her first cry, she had been silent. Now she lay still, not moaning nor writhing about, not weeping like an hysterical fool over something that was over and done. Her mouth was still. Her eyes were closed.

Her hands remained doubled into fists above her head, the leather cutting deeply into her crossed wrists. Without speaking, he reached up to grasp her wrists and pull them down across her belly. Untying the knot, he unwound the fillet, noting where the leather had cruelly bruised her. Thoughtfully staring at her face for some flicker of emotion, some hint of woman's tears, he massaged the weals with his thumbs and third fingers. Gradually, she relaxed and finally drew a shuddering sigh. Her eyes remained closed, but she caught her already bitten lip between her teeth to still its quivering.

The sight made him wince, although he could not have told why. Surely, he did not pity the plight of his enemy. Hastily, he rose and sought the supplies he had brought from the monastery the night before. Among them were several lengths of cloth undoubtedly intended for bandages. He tore off a length, moistening it slightly in the brandy from one of the jugs.

Returning to her side, he knelt and spread her legs again. The bleeding had stopped and gently he began to clean the area. The brandy stung her thighs and the torn edges of her strained, abused flesh.

She moaned again in surprise and half sat up, reaching for his hand in protest. Now, her face reflected the emotions of shame, pain, and fear as he fended off her hand.

"Softly, my lady, softly. I will do you no harm. Let me just clean you a bit here and there. Then we will dress and be on our way."

She fell back on her elbows, regarding him with a mixture of fear and wonder. How could he be so gentle now, when he had hurt her so desperately only minutes before. Of course, in the end, the pain had receded and with it some of her fear. Through half-veiled eyes, she regarded his serious face. Now that the tension waned, she felt drained. Color had left his face also. Dark bluish smudges stood out under his eyes. Lines around his nose deepened. More a lean, gaunt wolf than ever, he drew a deep breath as he finished. Tossing the rag aside, he sat back on his haunches regarding her steadily, a lupine grin curving his lips. "Moira of Lorne," he addressed her formally, "you are beautiful and you are a woman now. My woman."

His words took her by surprise. She could only stare at first. Then angrily, she scrambled away from him. "Never!" she exploded. "You may have raped me and perhaps rendered me worthless for any other man, but I shall never be yours nor submit to what you call your possession. You do not own me, my lord. You have merely bound me to your will for the present. I shall never cease to fight you and resist to the utmost limits of my strength."

"So be it," he nodded sardonically, "except you have too much sense to fight uselessly when the battle is hopelessly lost. You did not resist today," he reminded her.

Shamed, she bowed her head over her clenched fists. "No, but I shall not contribute to your pleasure in any way. Even though you possess my body, you cannot take my mind and heart and soul. Some day I will find the means to be avenged." She stared up at him. Blue eyes met in a fierce clash of wills.

Laughing softly at her defiance, he allowed his gaze to deliberately drop from her eyes to her body. "Think you so, my lady," he grinned. "Your beautiful body already knows I am your master. Next time will be easier. And the next easier."

"You lie!" Her hands clenched and then curved like talons as if she would fly at his face.

For answer, he insolently inspected her body with great deliberation. Beneath his gaze her breasts heaved, their nipples pink and turgid; her taut muscles pulled her belly firmly flat between her narrow hipbones. At the joining of her thighs was the triangle of curling hair which he remembered was soft to the touch. Her thighs were smooth and her legs tapered down to long, slim feet.

Lazily his eyes returned to her breasts, studying them as a rosy blush suffused her throat, spreading upward to her cheeks and downward to the white mounds. As he stared, she gasped and hastily grabbed for her clothes. With hands that shook with rage and fear, she began to draw on her *chausses*. Her blouse, gown, and vest followed in quick order.

When she turned back to face him, her vest tightly laced about her body, he had drawn the tunic down over his head. They faced each other much as they had before—yet something more lay between them. She did not want to recognize her newfound knowledge of her body. Later she would do so, she thought, when she was more prepared to analyze what had happened and what it meant to her. Moving hastily to avoid his self-satisfied expression, she reached for her boots. The world receded to a pinpoint of light as she slumped to her hands and knees and then limply sprawled over on her side, her eyes closed.

"Moira!"

She did not hear the real alarm with which he spoke her name as he reached for her. Dropping down beside her, his fingertips sought the pulse in the side of her throat as one arm slipped under her shoulders. Soft and relaxed in his arms, her head fallen limply against his shoulder, she seemed more vulnerable than he had ever seen her. With a feeling of relief, he found the pulse strong but slightly irregular. Shock, intensified by exhaustion and fasting, had undoubtedly overwhelmed her.

Even as he brushed her hair back from her forehead, her eyes fluttered open and she stirred. "Softly," he crooned. "Softly. Lie still and let me care for you. I will take care of the horses while you rest. Then we will have some food and you will feel better."

"What happened?"

"You fainted."

"Not I," she denied softly. "I did not! I have never fainted. You hit me. I must have tripped over something and fallen."

Her mouth set in a stubborn line, she dizzily rolled her head against his shoulder. From somewhere, she must find the strength to pull herself up and show him that he was wrong. But she was so weak. His shoulder under her head pillowed her so comfortably. One palm trailing limply in the hay pressed downward weakly as she sought to push herself to a sitting position. To her surprise, her arms felt like rubber. Her eyes flew accusingly to his smiling face.

"Why did you hurt me again?" she questioned wearily. "I can be of no use to you as a hostage if I am too weak to ride with you. You have surely punished me

108

enough, using my body to satisfy your lust for vengeance."

He quirked a black-winged eyebrow. "Moira, I did not punish you. Although the experience was not pleasant for you—this first time—you must surely know enough about human nature to realize that the presence of a woman, any woman . . ." he declared insultingly, ". . . beside a man at night for some enforced time gives rise not necessarily to a lust for vengeance, but simply to a lust for her body. And a very beautiful body you have, I might add." His hand slipped inside the lacings of her clothing to find her heart.

When she gasped in protest, he smiled. "Just checking to see if your faint has left you too weak to be left alone."

"I did not faint," she insisted.

"You pitched over headfirst when you reached for your boots."

"I have never done so before." The left hand pressed against his chest as she flexed one knee.

Smiling, he shook his head. "Moira, why are you so certain that you did not faint? Why do you care so much? You are human. More—you are a woman and sorely driven. In just such circumstances, I fainted in your father's hall. I begged you for water and you gathered me into your arms even as I do now. If you will lie still, I will leave you for a moment to bring you a reviving drink."

But her struggles increased.

"Lie still! By God, you are a wild one." Carefully, he lowered her to the hay. "Now stay there," he commanded sternly when she would have pushed herself up. Efficiently, he brought her cloak and covered her, tucking its ends under her chin while she stared at him mutinously.

Turning away with a weary smile, he gathered their belongings into two bags which he tied across the withers of the gray horse. Their meager supplies packed, he

109

approached her, holding out a piece of bread and one of the jugs. "Sit up now if you can," he commanded. "Eat and drink. We both need strength."

She took a bite of the bread, so hard she had to gnaw it through with several small cutting movements of her teeth. As she chewed the tasteless shingle, she forced her tired arms to knot a leather thong around her wildly disordered hair.

He broke off a piece of bread and choked it down with a small sip of brandy. Clearing his throat, he glanced in her direction, taking in her pale face and trembling hands. Pity stirred him, but he sternly put it down. "Mount and we will ride on. At this rate, we will take all day to eat and we might as well be moving."

As she sought to lift her leg to catch her toe in the stirrup, Moira's courage flagged. The muscles of her thigh twisted in agonized knots, while the other leg trembled so violently that she had to grasp the saddle and hang on to remain standing upright.

Observing her trouble, Rhiannon moved to her side. "Now together," he whispered. "One. Two. Up!" His hands around her waist and under her buttock boosted her across the saddle. There she hung while his hands supported her and she struggled to haul her leg over the back of her mount. Her faint groan changed to a gasping cry as her nether parts came in contact with the hard leather of the saddle. Each inch of movement by which she straightened herself in the saddle added to her torment, until her face was white as chalk.

Beside her on the ground, Rhiannon held her wrist, expecting to catch her fainting body any minute. Worriedly, he took in her pain. If she could not ride, he would have greatly compounded his problem. Of course, he could leave her afoot. It would take her days to get home, if indeed she did not die on the way. Something in his very soul rebelled at the idea of leaving her to the

110

vagaries of chance. Better to tie her on the horse, stopping at intervals to take her down for a rest. "Can you bear to ride?" he inquired at last.

The sight of his concerned frown stiffened her. "I can always ride," she announced between set teeth. "You need not doubt my strength. I promised vengeance. I shall have it." Her blue eyes stared straight ahead; her face carefully composed itself into calm lines.

"So be it," he nodded harshly, offended that she had rejected his sympathy. Haughtily, he swung himself up on the gray horse's back, setting himself and gathering her reins together with his own. With a stab of his heels, he guided the horses out into the morning of a cold but blessedly bright day. A yellow winter's sun was moving the mist off the moors. Rested and fed, the horses moved out at a good pace. After the first few steps, Moira knew the dull ache between her thighs would be bearable. I can endure that, she thought.

But she could not take another bite of the dry bread. She choked on the piece in her mouth and spat it out onto the road. Tiredly she gave her body up to the pain of the ride and the hunger which caused strange fancies to flit through her mind and before her tired eyes.

Twelve

Rhiannon felt good. His body was more easy than it had been since his capture. The bread and brandy were giving him heart as he rode, nibbling at the loaf and sipping at the brandy alternately. His pleasure in the morning's conquest of the body of his enemy was keen, although somewhat uneasy because of her obvious terror and shame. Her virginity was a triumph, he thought to himself. What pleasure she had given him! What sport he would have relaying the message to his father and to her father!

His wounds were healing rapidly. Even the one in his shoulder only ached slightly. The sun warmed his bones as the brandy warmed his insides.

He glanced over his shoulder at her drooping form. Her hands crossed over the horse's withers where she seemed to be bearing some of her weight on her arms. He flushed uncomfortably as he realized how painful the ride astride must be for her lower parts.

He pulled up his horse and let her black come up beside him. "Is it bad, lady?" he inquired.

Her head snapped up, her eyes flashing. "Cur! When I

ask for sympathy, then you may give it. Leave me." Haughtily she turned her horse aside.

Chuckling softly, he shook his head in wonderment and in something very like admiration. She never cried, he thought. Never asked for quarter. Never begged. Absolutely refused to acknowledge that she was hurt.

"My lady, you are as brave as any man I have ever known. My sympathies and my respect are with you. I do wish we could rest for the day, but you know that I must be riding to my father. He will be wild with grief and the desire for revenge if I cannot reach him soon."

"I care nothing for your father," she snarled. "May he rot in hell and you along with him."

"As you will. May your father experience the same and worse." He kicked his horse into a fast lope that snapped her head back and caused her to draw her breath and bite her lower lip to still a cry of pain.

They rode for almost two hours without stopping. Finally, beside a small stream which crossed the road, he called a halt, pulling her horse and his to the side into a grassy spot.

Moira dismounted stiffly. Grabbing the horse's mane, she let herself to the ground. Oh, dear God, she thought, I cannot stand. As her feet touched the ground, sharp pains shot to her knees. For a minute, all her weight was on her arms. Then she began to feel her feet and get them under her. She tottered the two or three steps to the bole of a tree where she braced herself while she tentatively bent and arched first one foot and then the other.

Rhiannon in the meantime was producing a jug of brandy, some dried flat pieces which in many ways resembled leather but were in fact salted meat, and a small cloth bag containing some dried fruits of uncertain type, but which he presumed were apples.

"Come, my lady," he said. "Sit and eat. We will both feel better and the rest from riding will ease us. You

113

particularly should be glad of the relief." He chuckled, handing her the jug as she slowly and carefully made her way to his side.

Flushing, she would have refused to share his food, but she reasoned that to do so would only weaken her further. Surely, she would have some chance to escape before they reached Hawk's Keep, his father's castle. Sinking down beside him with a sigh she could not conceal, she accepted the proffered jug. Despite her aversion to sharing food with him, she tilted her head back to let the fiery liquid burn down her throat and into her stomach. Closing her eyes against the tears in them, she set the jug down, bent her head, and stretched her neck forward slightly to ease the strained muscles around her shoulders.

When she opened her eyes, her gaze fell on a bit of dried fruit resting on his outstretched palm. When she looked at him, a question in her blue eyes, he smiled back companionably and sympathetically. What a foul creature, she thought, to hurt her so, to laugh at her and kidnap her and abuse her, to rape her and then to offer her a bit of dried fruit as if it were a friendship token.

Sullenly, she took the fruit from his hand and bit into it. It was almost flavorless and so tough that she had to worry it back and forth in order to separate the piece she had between her teeth from the piece she retained in her hand. After a few half-hearted motions with her jaws, she realized that the effort to chew was wasted. Turning her head away from her captor, she spat the offensive bite out on the ground.

"May I try a bit of the meat?" she asked.

He grinned at her in a friendly way and cut a bite from the end of one of the leather-looking strips. "Take it into your mouth and chew slowly. Do not try to swallow or to chew fast. You will choke for sure."

She did as he instructed and the saliva did indeed begin

to soften the meat and make it at least chewable. Tentatively, she felt the first dawnings of hunger as her stomach accepted the first food it had had since the night before.

"You will make a good companion when you are tamed," Rhiannon interrupted her thoughts. She stiffened at his implication. "Yes, I have been thinking about what I shall do with you when I get you back to Hawk's Keep. You shall be my lackey. My personal servant and companion. My squire. I can have you with me. You are strong and tall. You could be most useful. Tamed to my hand, what an advantage to me!" He grinned in satisfaction at the thought. "I could take you with me on raids. After a while, when you got to accept your situation, you would be the best man I have ever seen. You are strong and brave. You bear discomfort well. Better than most. We could share the furs at night and keep each other warm. After a few more times, you will begin to love what I can do for you. You will be as eager for it as I am." As he talked, his face lit up with boyish enthusiasm at the plans he was making.

She stared at him in unbelieving silence, carefully making her face impassive. The idea that she would be his servant was utterly repugnant to her. Furthermore, the idea that she would go on raids with him against her own people was absurd. What had she done to make him think that she would be amenable to such an idea? "My father will offer a rich ransom for me. Surely you would prefer to accept, my lord, and . . ."

He interrupted, "No! I will not take any gold for you. You are mine by right of conquest and besides I could never find anyone like you. No woman I have ever known is like you and no man either. Call me 'Rhys' instead of 'my lord.' My friends do, and perhaps you will be my friend after a while."

Moira's eyes dropped to her lap as she reached for the

115

jug of brandy and took a strong swallow. "What if I should conceive?"

For a minute he was silent. "Ah, well. That would be a problem, but nothing serious. There are dozens of brats running around the keep. One or two more will make no difference. My nurse is still living with us. I can have her take the babe off our hands and raise it for us. We can dedicate it—or them—to the church." Here he looked at her quizzically, gauging the effect of his words. "And I can promise you that I will pay for their admission to an order as soon as they are old enough to leave home. Of course, if you were so minded . . ."

Moira's scream of rage completely stunned him as she rose from her place to launch herself at him. He had no time to throw up his hand before the brandy jug came crashing down on the side of his head and seemed to explode in his brain. Falling sidewise off the knoll, he rolled over onto his face, the brandy splattering his head and clothing.

Moira stood above him for several seconds, trembling and panting. Cautiously, she nudged him with her foot, but he seemed deeply unconscious. Hurriedly, she gathered up her belongings, her warm cape, a small bit of food, and his knife, and swung onto her horse. Her thoughts were triumphant as she gathered the reins to the gray horse as well. When Rhiannon recovered, she would be miles from him on the way home. She would ride west until she encountered familiar territory. By changing horses from time to time, she could make good headway.

Horrid creature, she thought as she turned her back on him. The vanity of men. How had he ever gotten the idea that she would be pleased to serve him! Worse! How had he conceived the idea that she would gladly and graciously give up her child to be cared for by someone

116

else and to be given to the church when it was tiny. Monster!

Swiftly, she kicked the horses into a gallop, heading north along the road. As she rode, her pain eased, but she alternated between sharp clarity and a sort of fuzzy vision wherein her attention seemed to wander. At these times, the tired horses slowed to a walk, while she wavered in the saddle unaware of her plight. After perhaps two miles, she came to a faint trail crossing the road and leading westward. Home, she thought; I cannot rest. She had ridden for only a short time, but her body was beginning to warn her with a weak trembling of her hands on the reins and a gnawing ache in her belly that she was in trouble.

A stream cut across her path. She stopped to rest and water the horses. Digging into the sack, she pulled out the remaining jug of brandy. As she did so, she smiled at the thought of Rhiannon smugly announcing his intentions for her. Tamed, was she? She almost laughed out loud.

In celebration of her victory, she uncorked the brandy and took a strong pull at the jug. Immediately, a false warmth spread through her. This was really good. Why had she never been offered this before? She replaced the cork, returned the jug to the sack, and dragged out a piece of meat. Resolutely, she began to gnaw and chew at one end.

Pulling the horses' heads up, she headed them across the stream and up the side of the small declivity. She rode steadily for several minutes, but then her attention began to flag again. The horses were harder to guide; the brandy was a nauseating fume in her head as she began to struggle to see. Helplessly, she felt her body struggling to disgorge the contents of her stomach. Oh no, she thought. Sliding from the black, she staggered to the side

117

where she retched. After the first passage, she had nothing to give up, but she continued to heave until finally she thought she would lose consciousness. I will feel better now, she thought.

She turned to see the black horse and the gray still standing dejectedly where she had dropped the reins. Slowly, carefully placing one foot in front of the other, she walked to the side of the black and gathered up the reins. Now a new problem faced her. She was unable to put together the necessary spring to mount. Her unsteady legs felt as if there were no bones in them. I must move on until I find a fallen log or something I can use for a mounting block, she thought. The horses dragged her back, but she persevered some two hundred yards down the trail. There she spotted a stone that would give her the necessary height to raise her body onto the horse's back. Unfortunately, when she reached it, she could only sink down on it for a minute, holding her head in abject misery. Again, she resorted to the brandy, sipping cautiously at the stuff which she realized now was making her sick. Again the false warmth spread through her, enabling her to mount the gray horse.

She kicked the animal into a trot which for a few minutes carried her along at a fair pace. Soon, however, her weakness forced her to allow the animals to slow to a fast walk. Encumbered as she was with bag of food, reins and lead rein from the black, she had no hands with which to ease her body off the horse's back. Her bruised inner thighs were too sore to stand the bumping while her weakened legs would not hold fast and give her the support she needed.

She would have to abandon one horse. Regretfully, she transferred her belongings and herself to her black which she trusted. Then she dropped the gray's lead rein, allowing him to fall back. She draped the sack on one side and brandy jug on the other. This arrangement enabled her to rest her hand on her mount's withers and give herself some support. Nevertheless, she drew her lips tight in between her teeth. Once or twice when the black stumbled on the rough trail, she moaned.

How long she continued in this daze of pain and fatigue, or how many miles she had covered, she did not know. Once she regained consciousness as from a dream to find the black stopped stock still and cropping grass beside the trail. The sun seemed to be sinking, the shadows, lengthening, but her will drove her on when she could feel nothing from the waist down except the terrible burning of her abused thighs.

Her horse climbed a rise slanting upward some twenty feet along the trail. She paused to allow him to blow and to search in her pack for something to chew on to try to gain a little nourishment. As she looked back over her trail, she was pleased for a minute to see how far she had come. The vantage point gave her a feeling of freedom. She was going home. She smiled to herself as she kicked her horse down the opposite side of the mound.

As evening approached, she realized she had to find shelter for the night. Tonight she would rest and eat as much as she could force down her throat. None of this fainting and retching again. Tomorrow would be better.

Another hour and she would stop, she told herself. Deliberately, she made for the copse of trees that lay at the end of the trail that looped around the basin. Again she required all her concentration to keep her mind from wandering. The horse kept slowing and stopping. She kept swaying as she drifted in and out of consciousness. The trees tossed and shimmered. Just as she entered the copse, she straightened her body, shaking her head in an effort to clear her vision. The effort of shaking her head caused her to reel drunkenly.

Suddenly, painfully, she was swept from the saddle. A body slammed into her side and bore her crashing to the ground. Her breath was jolted from her body. Blinded, she lay limp, paralyzed from the shock of landing on the hard ground. Her body was roughly turned face down. A piece of cord tightened painfully around her wrists. Still her eyes remained closed. Incapable of thought, she could only muster a faint groan of protest as hard hands jerked her shoulders about and raised her body half off the ground. One hand held the front of her vest tightly. Then her head reeled as a flat hand slapped her cheeks, first right, then left. The sharp punishing blows served to clear her head. She opened her eyes to stare into the hard angry eyes of her captor.

"Rhiannon," she gasped. "Oh, no!"

Thirteen

Rhiannon ap Breannon had regained consciousness within minutes after Moira of Lorne had galloped away from him. His anger exploded when he realized she was gone. How dare she! How dare she rise up and strike him down! He ignored his pain at the blow on the head as if it did not exist. Pausing only long enough to gather the remaining victuals into the sack, he slung it over his shoulder. When he felt for the knife and realized that she had taken it, his curses were uttered in low, furious growls. Lunging out onto the trail, he followed the tracks of the horses at a ground-eating lope.

In those first minutes, he was as deadly and dangerous as a wounded wolf. If Moira had risen before him in that moment, he would have struck her down with a howl of vengeance. His anger carried him swiftly north for two miles before he found the point where she had left the trail. At this junction he stopped, his chest heaving, his breath coming in hard, painful grunts.

She had obviously turned toward home. Indecision halted him. Should he continue as quickly as possible on foot to reach his father's territory? In all likelihood, he would meet a patrol or a friend from whom he could get a horse and follow her. Why follow her at all? Let her make good her escape and get home. He would get her again, he vowed.

And yet. He wanted her now! He wanted her beside him when he returned in triumph to Hawk's Keep. He wanted to present her as a fitting substitute for the men he had lost. His father would be proud beyond all measure. He would be acknowledged the second in command, the heir to all his father's power. Moreover, he wanted her beneath him to yield her flesh to him again.

"You are mine!" he growled, facing the westward trail. She had struck him unconscious. She would pay. Yes, she would pay. He pulled a strip of meat from the sack. As he turned down the trail, he chewed on the meat.

Clearly he could see the tracks of her horses as he jogged along at a steady pace. Constantly he chewed the meat and regularly stopped for rest. Shortly, he came to the stream where Moira had drunk and watered the horses. He found the spot where she had knelt to drink and noted that she had moved to a tuft of grass and sat. The foliage was still crushed down from the weight of her body. His smile was grim as he realized he was gaining on her. She thought herself safe. Let her take her time. Chuckling, he followed the tracks up the bank.

Minutes later, he came to the spot where she had stumbled from the horse. She was sick. Clearly he read the signs as he followed her stumbling track. No pity stirred within him for her plight. Instead, increasing eagerness hastened his steps as he realized that she was traveling more and more slowly. I will catch her easily, he exulted.

With interest, he noted her struggles with the horses; she was forced to stop frequently. Undoubtedly, the horses were too tired to go on. She was losing time leading one. His excitement over the chase was exhilarating. His aches and pains were forgotten; his stride was steady.

A horse whickered in the brush beside the trail. For an instant, he froze and then could have shouted for joy. The gray horse raised its head from its diligent cropping of grass and moved off a couple of steps. Rhiannon approached it cautiously, talking soothingly. The horse recognized him and stood quietly while he mounted.

Rhiannon laughed aloud as he wheeled the horse down the trail. Shadows began to lengthen. He would recapture her soon for she would stop for the night. He was almost out of the grove of trees when he glimpsed her. She was urging her horse over the top of a rise perhaps a mile ahead.

Galloping the rested gray along the trail, he tethered it halfway up the rise and crept up the last ten feet. From the rise, he watched her circling the edge of the valley. She rode slowly now, her body swaying in the saddle. His first impulse was to ride after her at full gallop and run her down. Instead, he grinned. The trees would make an excellent place to spend the night. He would make his way along the ridge just below the crest, out of her sight, and capture her as she reached the trees. Let her enjoy her freedom for a few minutes longer. He chuckled as he withdrew down the ridge. Mounting, he spurred the gray across the slanted surface, careless of rocks and brambles. He felt an impulse to throw back his head and howl with delight.

The rough going was little problem to the big animal. Rhiannon reached the copse well ahead of Moira. Riding down into the trees through the precipitous ravine, however, required some skill on his part and some cautious footing from the horse. At one point, he was forced to cross a tiny open area from which he glimpsed Moira riding unsteadily across the valley. Again he chuckled. She was almost done. Fool that she was. She

123

would be glad that he caught her. Indeed he was glad himself that he had. Without him to aid her, she would never survive. She was too weak from hunger; he was saving her life. He swelled with pride.

But first he would punish her a little. Just a bit to show her who was master and who must be obeyed from now on. Her proud spirit must learn its lesson and know that she must exert herself to do his will, not to try stupid things like fighting him and seeking to escape. Lorne Rock was behind her now, he thought. The only time she would ever return, he vowed, would be with the men of Breannon when they captured the place and made the men of Lorne swear fealty to his father and himself.

Tonight she would sleep beside him again. He would hold her warm in his arms. After he had given her a strong lesson, he would build a fire and feed her and hold her body against his. In all his twenty-four winters, he could think of no thought that had pleased him more.

He tethered the gray back in the ravine and loped swiftly through the trees and large rocks that tumbled out of the declivity. A rather large boulder caused the trail to circle it and here he waited, thinking as he did so that it would give him a springboard to drag her from the horse as she came along the way. Sinking silently into the grasses some six or eight feet behind the boulder, he waited. His heart beat fast; his muscles tensed expectantly as he heard the stumbling hooves of Moira's mount.

As Moira of Lorne entered the copse, she straightened her tired body and shook her head. The trees had darkened her vision which had been accustomed to the last rays of the setting sun. Cautiously, she slowed her horse as it approached the huge boulder that blocked the trail.

As Moira pulled the reins to the side, Rhiannon rose from his hiding place. Silent and powerful as a wolf, he

124

covered the intervening space in two steps, vaulting the rock at full force. His lunge propelled him crashing into his prey, sweeping her from the saddle, and slamming her to the ground with all the force of his lean, strong body.

"Rhiannon," she gasped. "Oh, no!"

"Oh, yes, my lady!" he snarled. "You are going to learn right now who is master and who is to be obeyed. You left me unconscious, afoot, unarmed . . ."

"I could have killed you as you lay," she whispered.

He paused. His anger subsided. Slowly, he allowed her to sink down upon the ground. Freed of his punishing grip, she rolled on her side, curling her body into a tight ball. He regarded her steadily as she tightly shut her eyes. As he watched, she shuddered visibly, her body twitched, and her hands opened and closed convulsively.

Satisfied that she was helpless, he turned away to catch up the black horse and stake it near the gray. Immediately it began to eat from the sparse grass. Farther away from the trail, Rhiannon cleared a small space and gathered dry sticks and grasses to make a fire. Lighting it with a flint from the pack, he set out the food and drink. At full dark, he strolled back to Moira.

She lay where he had left her, her eyes closed, her body still. In the dim light from the stars and moon, he bent over to shake her shoulder.

She stirred slightly and moaned. Had she been asleep? Hoisting her, he sought to set her on her feet, but she collapsed immediately onto her knees.

"Stand!" he hissed sharply, jerking her upright again.

Again she tottered, slipping out of his hands.

With a muffled curse, he jerked her upright, slipped his hands behind her knees, and let her fall forward over his shoulder. Too late he remembered his wound as her weight descended on him. Handling her like a rag doll, he pushed her off his left shoulder and transferred her to his right.

"'Twould be easier if I made you crawl to the fire," he grumbled.

She made a muffled reply which he could not understand as he carried her roughly over the ground, her head hanging down behind his back. He knelt down beside the fire and allowed her feet to touch. This time she straightened and swayed. Her strength seemed to have returned, enabling her to stand before him.

"Now what?" she asked. "Will you keep me standing here all night? Or perhaps you would like to tie me to a tree and beat me?"

"Tempting, indeed," he agreed evenly. "Do you think you deserve better?"

Wearily, she sank to her knees before him and then slipped to her hip. Because of her bound hands she rocked precariously before she could gain her balance and keep from falling on her face. Her clumsy movements brought her face directly in front of his. "You were a prisoner and you escaped," she reminded him bitterly. "Do you deny me the same chance?"

Silently, he regarded her. Then he moved around behind her and unbound her hands. "No," he said softly. "No," he said more strongly. He laughed. "By God, my lady, you are a wonder. I will never let you go. You will be my companion. Together we can face and best anything. No other could have done so well against me," he boasted happily, "and you would have gotten away from any other man. I am your master, for no one else could ever hope to tame you." He laughed with delight while she stared at him in incredulous anger. He reached his arms around her body and pulled her back against him, laughing, kissing her ear, and holding her tightly.

Then just as suddenly, he released her and sprang up. "You must be hungry," he said. "True?"

She nodded wearily, licking her lips. He was truly a strange man. One minute he was threatening to beat her;

the next he was hugging and kissing her and offering her food. Gingerly, she pulled her stiff arms around to the front of her body.

He returned with dried meat, fruit, and a last bit of brandy. "You wasted some of the drink," he chided, "but I will share with you. Drink up."

She reached for the jug, then drew back. "I was sick today. This is too strong for me."

Looking at her solicitously, he offered her a piece of the fruit. "Eat this then and have some meat."

She did as he bade and they chewed in silence. His appetite was so good that he ate several pieces of the dried fruit. He failed to notice that she ate only the one. Then he cut off a bite of meat with his knife, handing it to her.

At last he rose. "Lie down and make yourself comfortable. Wrap your cape around you and face your body to the fire as close as you can without being too hot." He disappeared into the woods for a minute and returned, adjusting his clothing. He sank down behind her, gathering her into his arms. For several minutes she lay stiffly, but her body was too exhausted and her mind too confused to manifest her fear for long. Her breathing became even.

Possessively, he rubbed his hand along her shoulder and arm, then up and down across her belly and breasts. He pressed his hand firmly against her rib cage beneath her breasts, forcing her body closer against his until they lay with her body touching his at all points, from her hair pressed against his chin to the soles of her feet in her soft boots resting against the instep of his. She felt so good to him as he kneaded her belly gently.

She moaned slightly in her sleep, then placed her hand over his. He was surprised until he realized that she was asleep. He kissed the top of her head very gently.

Fourteen

Rhiannon woke as the first faint streaks of dawn filtered through the trees. His body was stiff and he was ravenously hungry. In his sleep, he had moved so that his head pressed against Moira's neck and cheek. She had turned on her back sometime during the night. He had moved his leg up across her thighs and his arm across her breasts. Never had he felt such warm softness beside and beneath him.

Her breasts brushed softly against his arm. In the pale light of dawn, her face was composed. Her lashes lay long and brown and thick against her fine cheekbones. Only the hollows beneath the eyes and the pinched look around her mouth bespoke the exhaustion and deprivation which had begun to take their toll in this journey of almost a week.

Rhiannon lay recounting the past days and the reserves of endurance that she had been forced to call up to ride with him. He was forced to acknowledge a profound admiration for her. When he got her home, he would feed her well and dress her in clean garments.

His gaze drifted down her body swathed in the cocoon-like cloak. Gently, he drew it back until her breasts in her tightly laced sheepskin vest were exposed. For a moment, he toyed with the lacings as he imagined what pleasure he would find. He could bare those soft breasts, kiss them, and rouse her to wakefulness with his passion.

With a sigh, he drew the cloak back across her body. He had sorely used her yesterday. Still she would undoubtedly fight him. He could not but feel that she would be unable to ride today if she expended much more of her energy.

Bending his head, he kissed her gently on the lips. She did not stir. He kissed her again, then allowed his mouth to slide across her cheek and down to her ear. He blew softly into it before he took the lobe between his teeth and tugged gently. She stirred, groaned, and half opened her eyes. Immediately, she blinked them shut and turned on her side away from him. He kissed her ear again and whispered, "Moira, my lady, rise," ending with a sibilant hiss that blew his soft breath into her ear again.

She turned her body half back again, gazing at him through eyes still drugged with sleep. For just an instant, he saw the corners of her mouth twist as if in the beginnings of a smile. Then the eyes closed as her mouth set firmly into a hard line.

Abruptly she made as if to sit up. "If you will move your arm . . ." she said hoarsely.

Without hesitation he did so and she sat up throwing back her cloak. He heaved himself to his feet, stretching his arms wide. The manacles still encircled his wrists, and the six inch chain dangled from his right arm. Then he slipped his arm under her shoulder to help her to her feet. Indicating the thick bushes where he had disappeared the night before, he suggested that she might like to relieve herself while he extinguished the fire.

Blushing, she hastily strode into the bushes. Behind her, he chuckled as he recognized her embarrassment.

She would get over that when they traveled together. He would keep her from being embarrassed by other men and she would learn to be at ease with him. When she returned, he ruefully handed her another strip of the meat and a handful of dried fruit.

"The fare grows more and more monotonous," he apologized. "Perhaps we can find something more appetizing as we ride along today. There is a small stream over this way." He grasped her wrist in his right hand and drew her with him in its direction.

A small trickle of water pulsed down the side of a large gray boulder at the foot of the ravine. He tasted it and smiled, "Drink your fill, my lady. 'Tis sweet and so cold your teeth will tingle. 'Twill be better for you than the brandy that makes you sick."

Kneeling, she pressed her mouth to the stone to allow water to trickle into her mouth. "I believe nothing has ever tasted so good to me in my life," she said when she raised her head. "I was so parched that I could not have swallowed any of that food to save my life. We are in luck that you found it. Now, my lord, drink you."

He knelt on the other side to follow her example, pressing his lips to the same spot she had drunk. Twice more each drank, kneeling and facing each other, like children. At length, he sat back on his heels. "We must be going."

She threw her head back proudly on her slender neck. "My father will be coming for me. Let me go and I can ride to meet him. We can prevent war between our two families."

"There will always be war between us," he sneered. "Do you think you could stop the blood feud? My family has been killing your family for more years than either you or I have lived."

"Then kill me," Moira demanded. "Perhaps you will be forced to when you get me home, if you get me there.

Your father will not let you keep me in the way you have described. He will take me from you and perhaps torture me. Give me a clean death."

"Be quiet!" Rhiannon lunged forward to cover her mouth with his hand. Roughly, he pulled her down in the bracken and wild grasses beside the little spring. Cautiously, he raised his head, then sprang up with delight.

"Owen!" he shouted. "Owen Llewellyn!" He strode forward into the clearing in an instant.

"My lord!" shouted the man. "Praise be to God! You are safe. We were scouting widely, for your father has massed his men to rescue you. We thought you captured."

"Dafydd! Huw!" They slid from their saddles and gathered round him, laughing and clapping him on the back. He embraced each one in turn and clasped each hand.

"Are you wounded, Lord Rhys?" the one called Dafydd asked, anxiously noting the bandage through the rents in the tunic.

"Nothing. Nothing at all. A flea bite. Besides I've had the best nurse a man could have." Rhiannon bounded back into the bracken and around the boulders to the spring.

Moira sat huddled in silence where he had left her. Her attitude was one of great weariness and defeat, but when she heard him coming, she straightened her back and faced him sullenly. There would be no hope for her now. They would guard her. She could not escape.

Chattering to her in his enthusiasm about the friends he had met and how they were safe, he pulled her to her feet. They would have good food and an escort to the keep. His spirits soared high while hers sank to such depths that she had to clasp her hands together tightly to still their trembling. Never since she had been a small

131

child had she felt so close to weeping. But now was not the time. Now would be the worst time. She would not break before him, she vowed.

He felt her hesitancy and stopped. He had gripped her wrist with his right hand. He turned to face her. "You need not be afraid. No one will treat you as your father would have treated me," he said sardonically. "I shall make clear to everyone that you are my property, my prize. I know how you despise the word, but you must accept it. You are my slave. Remember that. School yourself to submit and you will be safe and well-cared for."

Her eyes flashed in anger as she snarled her hatred and defiance. "Never turn your back on me, my lord. You will find just what a slave I am."

He grinned wolfishly as he tugged her into the clearing before the three men. They regarded her narrowly. The two called Dafydd and Huw were young. Dafydd appeared to be no more than sixteen. His long blond hair was caught back from his face by a leather thong. His cheeks had soft blond down in front of his ears, and his eyes were friendly and exceedingly cheerful. "My lord," he exclaimed happily as he studied Moira's tall graceful body and flashing blue eyes, "you have brought home a prize in your escape."

The other young man, Huw, hung back. Older than Dafydd, he carefully studied her face until a look of puzzled half-recognition began to dawn. One eyebrow quirked as he glanced inquiringly at Rhiannon.

The man called Owen Llewellyn started visibly when she appeared. His face twisted into a sneer and then to a smirk. His heavy grizzled beard bristling, he spat contemptuously on the ground in her direction. "God's precious wounds!" he exclaimed. "'Tis the Lorne bitch. I always said that you, my lord, were your father's own true son. Ah! But 'tis true. How true!" He grasped

132

Moira's shoulder in his heavy hand. Brutally squeezing with his thick thumb into the hollow of her left shoulder, he forced Moira to her knees before Rhiannon, who held her firmly by the right wrist, was truly aware of what he was about. "Who gets first turn with her?" He cocked his head, leering at Rhiannon as he continued to grind his thumb and fingers into the vulnerable spots above and below her collarbone.

Moira's face twisted in pain. She tried to pull away from the excruciating agony of his grinding grip. Her mouth opened and clamped down hard to suppress a scream.

Angrily, Rhiannon stepped forward and laid his hand on the arm which tormented Moira so. "I have claimed her," he declared. "She belongs to me for the time. Since no one aided me to capture her, no one shall be allowed to share her with me."

The three men stared in amazement. Owen Llewellyn snarled and spat again. "She deserves no favored treatment. She is Lorne's daughter. Her father killed your brother, your uncle, and who knows how many other members of the clan. Her body should be given to all to wreak whatever vengeance we might do." He turned angrily. "We will see what the Lord Gethin says. He will back me in this. See if he does not. Captives are for the common until they can be divided among those who deserve them."

Rhiannon regarded the three closely. "Those laws apply to raids," he reminded them. "Do you dispute that I captured her by myself and not in a raid?"

Owen whirled. "You were on a raid when you were captured yourself. What about the brave lads who died or were captured?"

Rhiannon spoke in a voice that brooked no further argument. "They failed to bring back anything. I am the only one to return. So the spoils belong to me."

For a minute, the air was charged with tension. Then Dafydd spoke softly. "No one denies your right to your spoils. You have plainly captured her and she . . ." Here he placed an arm placatingly about the older man's shoulder. ". . . she is only a woman after all. Come, Owen, this is not like you. What care you for one wench more or less?"

"Aye," rumbled Huw. "See here. We are lucky to find Lord Rhys alive and well. Let us get him on horse and guide him to his father." He looked inquiringly at Rhiannon. "There will be a reward for us in the way of favors and honor."

Rhiannon smiled and dropped Moira's wrist. Stepping forward, he placed an arm around Dafydd's shoulders and held out his arm to Huw. "For friends such as you who have brought such help and comfort, my father and I shall be always grateful and shall show gratitude in material ways. Come, Owen, here is my hand."

Llewellyn turned and frowned wickedly. "Keep your hand until your father has spoken to you. Mayhap you will have another reason to shake hands."

Rhiannon drew back rebuffed and not a little angry.

Again Huw stepped into the breach. "Let us be off then! Your father is beside himself with fury and fear."

"Where is he?" asked Rhiannon.

"He has left the keep and ridden to attack Lorne Rock," came the reply.

"Then he must be stopped. There is no need to attack now, for I am safe and we have not enough men to take the place. I have been there and I know," said Rhiannon in alarm.

"Aye," growled Llewellyn, "and we do not need to attack with a hostage like her to force tribute from them."

Rhiannon grinned at Moira as she knelt on the ground. Her head snapped up and her eyes flashed. "My father will pay for me in blood," she said, "your blood."

Ignoring her threat, Rhiannon continued, "We should split up here. Two can take her back to the keep while two ride to intercept my father. That way the news will reach him no matter where he is."

Dafydd spoke up eagerly. "I will gladly ride with you to reach Lord Gethin. My horse is fast and strong. Together we can go like the wind. I could ride out ahead of you while you followed at a slower pace and rested your animal." He indicated the gray with a toss of his tawny locks.

Owen Llewellyn nodded agreement. "Aye," he said, "Dafydd is the one to ride with you, my lord. His horse is freshest from carrying the lightest load these many days we have been out."

Rhiannon hesitated, glancing at Moira still kneeling on the ground where she had been forced by Owen's hand. He wanted to keep her with him, toying with the idea of leading her horse with her bound upon it, looking properly downcast as he rode up to the camp of his father. Perhaps the camp would be in sight of the lookouts from Lorne Rock. What a triumph!

On the other hand, he thought of returning to Hawk's Keep with her beside him to see his sister's eyes shining, his mother smiling proudly. Either place, his father would witness this great turnabout which he had accomplished.

Another glance at her drooping figure changed his mind. She was tired. She had eaten practically nothing and had slept hardly at all under harsh conditions for days. Her strength was sorely tried, he knew. He could not take her with him riding at such a fast pace to head off his father.

The others were watching him closely to see what his next orders would be. Owen was smirking scornfully, Huw looked puzzled, Dafydd stared with open mouth from one to the other, sensing some problem in the air that he could not fathom.

Rhiannon took a deep breath. "Up, slave!" he addressed Moira peremptorily. When she did not move, but only glared her hatred at him, he gripped her left arm above the elbow and hauled her to her feet. "She is proud and haughty yet," he boasted, "but she will soon know her master. Huw, take her in tow and conduct her to the keep . . ." He looked at Owen, who sneered unpleasantly. ". . . and bestow her safely there to await my return."

"Is she to be given any special treatment? Mayhap your mother's apartments, your sister's clothes?" Owen growled.

"No! Treat her no different from the way you would treat any other captive." Rhiannon watched uneasily as Owen smiled in anticipation. "But, look you, she is not to be harmed. She is too valuable for that." His next words included the company. "We can expect rich tribute from her father and a time of peace so long as she is in our keep."

"Oh, aye," said Owen sarcastically, "we will not be harming her. She is a very valuable captive. But she is a captive and as such is dangerous. She is Lorne's bitch, after all."

Dafydd and Huw stirred apprehensively as they stared at Moira. Although she swayed from exhaustion and hunger, she stood almost six feet tall. Dafydd came only to her shoulder and Huw measured his thatch at her eye level. Owen was the same height as Huw, but his bulk made him seem larger and more dangerous.

Rhiannon turned Moira to face him and stripped the fillet of gold and leather from his brow. One hand raked his fingers through his black tousled hair while the other dangled the fillet across her wrists. "I shall not bind you, my lady," he said softly, "if you will give me your word to accept this binding around your brow until I return for you. It will protect you from those who would use you harshly and kill you. You are my property. When you and I are reunited, then 'twill be time to renew our battle. Will you cry truce and accept me?"

"No!" Moira spat furiously. "I would rather be dead than bound to you and branded with your symbol. I shall escape or I shall die trying. And look you and hear you," her voice rose to include the other men, "I shall not die easily."

Rhiannon's face flushed with anger at her defiance. Spinning her around, he jerked her wrists up behind her into the small of her back forcing her to bend over as she stifled a cry of pain into a muffled moan. He looped the leather and gold tightly twice around her wrists. The talons of the eagle were upper most on the outside, but the sharpness of the wings bit into the tender flesh.

Then grasping her by the shoulder, he hauled her back and thrust her stumbling into Huw's surprised arms. "She is a haughty bitch and must be taught the duties and the behavior of a slave. You may use your discretion about releasing that tie before you get her home."

"'Tis three days hard riding back to Hawk's Keep," said Owen with satisfaction. "Three days with her hands bound behind her will teach her whatever you want her to learn. She will not soon forget her place."

"True," Rhiannon agreed. "For me it was a day of being bound at the end of a tether to a horse. I ran all the way with a wound in my left shoulder. Let us mount now and ride," he commanded. "Huw, give me your horse. You take the gray. He's a good animal. Lord Lorne's own mount." He chuckled. "Keep the woman mounted on the black. He is her animal and about done in. She should not be able to make any time on him if she managed to get away.

"Up, Dafydd, lad. You and I will ride and eat in the saddle. Is there ration in the pouch?" He bent to look for himself as he swung up into the saddle of Huw's sturdy gelding. Without a backward glance, Rhiannon wheeled his horse and heeled it out of the clearing. One hand held the reins, the other held a piece of beef jerky from the pouch.

Moira concentrated through a haze of pain. Her hands tingled with approaching numbness, but the muscles of her arms and shoulders ached with blazing fury from being stretched and strained into this unnatural position. She had had no food since the night before and only a sip of water. When Rhiannon rode away without a backward glance, she felt a thrill of fear as the other two men stared at her. The heavier one with a leering grin caught her shoulder and then her hair in his hamlike fist, twisted her head around, and forced her back down to her knees.

"Get the horses, Huw!" he commanded. "I take no chances that she might try to run while you fetch them." He put his knee in the small of Moira's back between her arms and pushed hard while at the same time he pulled back on her thick switch of brown hair.

"Best leave her alone," Huw advised. "She is valuable as he said and I would not want to cross the boy. He is a fierce fighter."

"I will have her in the end," sneered Llewellyn. "Lord Gethin owes me this one for deaths of my family. When we have drained the Lorne of everything we can, then this one will be mine to destroy. Like a mad bitch!" He kicked her side and snarled in frenzy.

Huw pulled the frantic man back from Moira's inert form and sought to soothe him. "Easy, Owen. You will kill her and then both Lord Gethin and Lord Rhys will have your head. I know. I know. You are hard used."

Owen's breath slid out in a sob between his clenched teeth. "My wife. My sons. All gone. If she were three times what she is, she could not draw my vengeance from me. Just looking at her makes my blood boil and my stomach sicken." He clenched his fists and turned away, blundering into a tree. In his rage, he grasped a limb as thick as his wrist, thrust out at a right angle from the trunk. With a shout, he wrested it from its place, and strode away, flailing the underbrush as he went.

Huw was pale as he lifted Moira's limp form across the back of his horse and swung up behind her body. Steadying it with his right hand, he guided the horse back along the trail from whence they had come.

"Bring the horses, Owen," he called.

Within half an hour, Moira began to stir and moan, trying to ease her position.

Owen rode up beside Huw leading Moira's horse alongside.

Huw reached down to lift Moira's left leg at the knee and guide it across the back of her horse. Catching her by the right shoulder, he straightened her while Owen grasped her left leg and hauled her over upright. She was erect on the horse's back without wasted motion and without stopping. Both men retained their hold on her arms until she seemed to be gripping with her legs. Huw released her first and spurred his horse away. Owen Llewellyn gripped her left arm between elbow and armpit and squeezed cruelly hard.

"Feel that, woman," he snarled. "That hand can throttle the life from you in a quick twist. Just like twisting the head off a pigeon. Ride quietly and you will get to the keep in one piece. Give trouble and you will arrive without fingers. Understand."

Moira nodded dumbly. Her despair was as black as her pain was intense. She was at the mercy of these animals. She could not feel her hands while her shoulders, arms, and breasts ached as if they were in flames. She moaned softly when he released her and automatically gripped her knees around the black's barrel as she was jerked forward by the pull of the leading rein.

139

Fifteen

Rhiannon was furious as he rode out of the trees with
Dafydd trailing after him. How dare she speak to him so!
He took a vicious bite at the jerky. She would need a stiff
dose of taming when he returned home with his father.
Only when she was broken to his hand could he trust her
to ride with him and be the companion that he wanted.
She was the ideal partner for his adventures. He could
imagine her beside him in his long rides, beside him in his
furs at night, warming him with her soft body as she had
done this morning. She would be brave, and what a
fighter!

Suddenly he grinned. She had spat defiance at them all
just as he had when Lorne had captured him. He admired
her courage and was amazed that she was only a girl. A
woman, he corrected himself with some satisfaction. She
was only a woman, but she could ride as hard as any man.
He remembered the way she had killed the churl in the
old woman's hut.

Yes, she would be worth the taming, he thought. Just
as any good beast, horse, falcon or hound, was worth the
taming, she would be without equal when he had finished

140

with her.

So chewing, thinking of her and making his plans, he rode toward the west. One day's hard riding should see signs of his father's force. His shoulder pained him only now and then; his torso stretched in exhilaration as he shifted in the saddle to catch the position of Dafydd, flanking him back two lengths. Rhiannon drew his lips back in a wolfish grin and Dafydd answered with the same look. Together they kicked their horses and urged them forward at an even, ground-eating lope.

Riding and resting, they traveled through the day. The sun disappeared and the twilight brought a cold mist up from the fields. Down into a valley thick with gorse and rubble of gray granite outcroppings the two rode. In a small declivity where a large strata of rock arched over and provided a shallow cave, they halted their horses as the twilight deepened. The black, cloudy night blotted everything but their shadowy forms. Together they dragged furs from rolls on the flanks of the horses and made a swift dry camp. Rhiannon was too tired to do anything but roll himself into his covering and into a dreamless sleep. Dafydd staked the horses, rubbed them dry with a bit of cloth, and pulled dry broom from the rocks to give them some fodder. Then he too rolled into wolfskins and gave himself up to sleep.

Two more days of hard riding brought them to within the first signs of his father's progress. Lord Gethin had circled and redoubled his tracks, traveling slowly and sending scouts in all directions in an effort to find where his son's party had been attacked and captured.

Rhiannon sobered as he came upon the valley where his men had been seized upon and made prisoners. He noted the cairns of stones erected by his father's order above the bodies of his men who had died that day.

"We must hurry," he remarked to Dafydd. "We were only one day away from the stronghold."

"Lord Gethin will be there before us," agreed Dafydd as they spurred their horses along the broad trail.

Through the night they rode. Dafydd valiantly fought to stay awake in the saddle. Rhiannon was dizzy with fatigue and numb with pain as his shoulder ached where half-healed muscle and tendon were called upon to do the work of solid, perfectly conditioned flesh. Finally, just before dawn, they sighted the lights of small fires among the rocks.

Rhiannon's horse reared in terror as shadowy figures rose from beside the trail to grasp its bridle and pull the rider from the saddle. Dafydd, riding some yards behind, was dragged from the saddle, also. The sharpness of a knifepoint pricked Rhiannon's throat.

"Who rides in the dark?" came a rough whisper close to his ear.

"Rhiannon ap Breannon," said the exasperated rider. "Let me up, Henry Fletcher. Where is my father?"

"Good God and blessed Jesus!" exclaimed the Englishman. "He is sitting in his tent worrying himself to death. The lying bastard Lorne sent a message today. He would cut off a piece of you every hour that your father remains after sunrise tomorrow and send it to him."

"He will cut off a piece of some poor lad, be sure," growled Rhiannon, "but 'twill not be me. Quick! We must get to my father and rouse the camp to withdraw. Several good lads are his prisoners up there."

"By the dear Lord, we thought you were a dead one and us along with you, if your father had any say in it. He has been all for taking the charge up Lorne Rock to the keep, with us knowing full well that we could not make it." Henry trotted, panting, drawing breaths between his words as he led Rhiannon and Dafydd over the rough terrain up the slope toward the fires. Another man followed more slowly with the horses while others had resumed their watches in the bush along the trail.

142

They broke into the circle of light before a small tent; a guard sitting just outside the light rose with a murmur of protest, but Henry waved him back. "Lord Gethin! Come out. Praise to all the blessed saints and to all the angels. Here's Lord Rhys!"

From within the tent came a roar of deep laughter, a booming shout that echoed off the cliffs, and through the tent flap burst a copy of Rhiannon. Gethin ap Breannon was as tall as his son and his weight was the result of hard muscle developed by twenty more years of active living. His hair was as intensely black as his son's and his eyes struck blue lightning in his pleasure at the sight of Rhiannon returned.

"Oh, God!" he howled, throwing back his head on his shoulders. "Thine be the praise!" He swept his son into his long corded arms, hugging him against his powerful chest. Indeed, Rhiannon felt he might be crushed, so overpowering was his father's hug. His ribs creaked as his father almost lifted him off the ground.

"Gently! Father! Please! You will kill me with your joy."

"I must be sure I am not embracing a ghost. I looked to be a ghost tomorrow or find a ghost when I got to the top of yon rock. How came you here and how did Henry find you? I swear he was to guard the back trail. Did you take a party out on your own, Henry?"

As the man shook his head, Rhiannon interrupted, "Father, I have been free of Lorne Rock for almost ten days now."

"No!" ejaculated Gethin. "That damned bastard! He said you were still his captive and that he would torture you if I did not leave. He promised terms of ransom within a month. How came you to get free of him? Have you eaten, my son? Henry, stir up something in the way of hot food. Are you injured? I see rents in your clothing and bandages on your shoulder. Sit! Sit! Tell me all." He grabbed Rhiannon again and hugged him.

Henry turned and vanished from the lighted circle. Rhiannon dropped down beside the fire, suddenly drained of all strength. His goal achieved, his body screamed for relief. He had thought to sit cross-legged, but his legs had slipped nervelessly from beneath him so that he sprawled, half reclining. His father snapped an order. A guard brought a pallet from the tent and spread it in front of the saddle to prop under his son's shoulder and head. Fondly, Gethin then slipped both hands under his boy's shoulders and helped him hoist himself onto the pallet.

Rhiannon's head sank wearily back on to the saddle and he closed his eyes for a moment. Never had he felt such relief. A wave of weakness rode over him, and he clamped his teeth together to keep from moaning at the pain. For a full minute he lay still, feeling his father's eyes on him but unable to respond.

Footsteps penetrated his fading consciousness, dragging him back into the circle of light. Henry Fletcher had returned with a round loaf of hard black bread, a bowl containing a hot stew, and a cup containing hot mulled wine. Greedily, Rhiannon took a long drink of the wine. The liquid burned his tongue and seared his throat, but its heat spread throughout his body from the warmth in his belly to the ends of his fingers and toes. Rapidly he ate the stew, sopping the pieces of bread into the liquid and scooping the pieces of meat into his mouth. Finished, he lay back against the saddle totally at ease, clutching the cup to his belly with both hands. He sipped it from time to time as he began to tell his father the story of his adventure.

When he came to the wound and the treatment that Lorne's man had inflicted, Lord Gethin growled and moved forward to check the shoulder himself.

"'Tis no matter, Father. 'Tis almost healed," protested

144

Rhiannon, but Lord Gethin would not be satisfied until the wound was bared and he had satisfied himself that there was no infection. Fortunately, the slash was closed. The burn had scabbed over and the flesh around it was pink and healthy.

"'Twas a lady who really saved me, Father," said Rhiannon with a grin.

"What's that?"

"Lorne's daughter."

"No! Never say so. That cruel creature. That's his only living whelp. We have heard stories about her. They must be exaggerated."

"Not really," Rhiannon insisted. "She is as big as you have heard them say. Almost six feet tall. Strong. Brave. Fierce. I saw her kill a man." Here Rhiannon shuddered and drained the cup with the thought of how close his death had been on at least three separate occasions. "Father, we must get away before light. The story can be told later. For there are many of our lads up there in the Rock and someone will be tortured in my place while Lorne seeks to deceive you."

"I have already told Henry to order the men to strike the camp. We will be away before sunup. But you must rest in the next two or three hours. You will not be able to sit a horse. I shall order them to rig a litter for you."

"I rode in. I can ride out. But truly now, I do not believe that I can talk anymore." Rhiannon's eyes closed and his breath evened as he spoke the last word. He was asleep.

Gethin regarded his son. He pressed his thumb and index finger against the inner corners of his eyes and bowed his head. After his prayer, he turned. From his tent, he brought a heavy soft fur robe of carefully sewn wolf skins, the finest gray and beautifully matched. Spreading this over his sleeping son, he tucked the edges in around the body. Then he motioned the guards forward to strike the tent and prepare to pack his weapons and armor.

In two hours, as the men of the Hawk moved out at dawn, they carried the still, sleeping form on a litter strung between two horses. Rhiannon had not moved nor felt them when he was carefully lifted, pallet, saddle, furs and all, onto the litter and borne along. The strain of the past days, the physical agony and the mental fear, the crushing weight of responsibility and defeat, all had combined to drain his body. When the relief came, he could not be roused.

Sixteen

Late in the afternoon of the first day of the ride with
Owen Llewellyn and his companion, Huw Llengaron,
Moira of Lorne had slipped unconscious to the ground.
The pain in her shoulders and breasts, the thirst and
hunger, had combined to overcome her fighting body.
The three had ridden without pause at a loose lope,
slowing periodically to a walk to blow the horses. Owen
Llewellyn and Huw had shared jerky and bread in the
middle of the morning, but Moira's hands were bound.
When Huw had held a bite beneath her nose, she had
turned her head away. He had shrugged and they had
moved on.

In truth, her body was so numb to all sensation except
pain and fatigue that nothing of hunger and thirst could
penetrate the agony her shoulders and arms were
relaying to her brain. She could concentrate only on
attempting to ease the suffering somewhat. Finally, she
could no longer will her muscles to do anything. She
accepted the pain and the strange hallucinations of light,
sound, and motion as the afternoon wore on.

They were traveling north. The clouds had obscured

the sun and the wind was cold. She could not feel her hands. From somewhere, she felt a knife was cutting into the back of her wrist. The talons of the screaming eagle were pressed against her left wrist and had finally clawed through the skin. A trickle of blood wound its way down her hand and dripped off one swollen, bluish fingertip.

With the freshening wind, Owen sniffed and decreed that a sharp rain would drench them before long. "Find shelter or be miserable all the night." They had whipped the horses into a gallop. As the black was jerked forward sharply, Moira's head snapped back on her spine. Colored lights flashed before her eyes as the horizon reeled dizzily around her. When she closed her eyes to steady herself, her legs relaxed their precarious hold. She slipped to the road and lay with her face pressed into the mire.

Owen cursed roundly as he and Huw turned their horses back to a halt beside her. Dismounting, Huw shook her shoulder, then regarded her disgustedly. "She's done."

"Throw her up there in front of you and ride for yonder grove." Owen wheeled his horse, thudding off without a backward glance.

Huw bent over Moira, scooped her up in his arms, and slung her face down over the mount's back. As he swung up behind her, he adjusted her body by grasping her swollen, bloodstained hands. He was not naturally a cruel man and to continue to torture someone so obviously beyond pain went against the grain of his conscience. He unbound the fillet and allowed the girl's arms to dangle over her head at the side of the horse. Thrusting the fillet into his tunic, he spurred his horse after Owen.

Once in the grove, darkness seemed to fall upon them like a door closing them from the light. Huw found Owen crouched under a tree, his furs pulled up around his shoulders, moodily chewing on a bit of jerky. The heavier man greeted him with a grunt as Huw swung down. Turning, he grasped Moira about the waist and lowered her feet to the ground.

Her body fell back against his chest, her head against his shoulder. Her hands slid over the horse's withers to drop lifelessly down against her thighs. Her eyes flew open and she uttered a muffled shriek of pain. Huw steadied her and whispered in her ear, "Easy, easy, girl. 'Tis the blood returning to your hands. 'Tis lucky you are, for they could be dead at the end of your wrists and then where would you be? I have seen a man's hands turn black and rot and him still alive and screaming in pain."

At his words, Moira became aware of her surroundings. The icy rain dripping through the overhanging boughs, the gray chill twilight, her captors, and foremost the incredible pain in her hands. With each pulse beat, throbbing red-hot twinges shot up from the nerve endings in her fingertips to pierce her brain. She could not as yet clench her hands, but had to endure helplessly the throes of returning life. His arm around her waist, Huw guided her to sit against the trunk of a small oak whose large leaves gave her a considerable degree of protection from the rain. There she made a lap of her knees and skirt and regarded her hands lying helplessly, throbbing painfully. In the gray afternoon, she could see that they were gradually turning from bluish purple to bright crimson. She sucked her lips in between her teeth and bit down hard to still her desire to shriek and weep from the pain.

Huw regarded her suffering in silence before he brought a fur from his horse and tossed over her. Her face was white as chalk in the thickening evening. Her eyes gazed up at him like black holes with specks of light in their depths. Surrounded by her mass of tangled, matted hair, her face looked like something from a nightmare. Surreptitiously, Huw crossed himself as he

149

turned away. Getting his other fur from the back of the gray horse, he crouched down under the tree with Owen who proffered him a strip of dried meat.

"Give me a piece for the girl," said Huw.

Owen's brows rose and he looked as if he would refuse.

"She will be unable to ride tomorrow if she gets naught tonight," insisted Huw reasonably, glancing in her direction. "We do not want to carry her. She is a big one," he chuckled.

Grumbling and cursing under his breath, Owen dug in the pouch and produced a smaller strip which he tossed onto the ground at Huw's feet. "Feed the creature, if you have a mind to. But leave me be."

Huw rose with the meat in hand and gathered the fur more securely around his shoulders. His hair was dripping from the rain and he was already uncomfortable. It would be a wet, cold camp that night for certain. He was already regretting that he had given the girl his ground cover. To build a fire was impossible. As he approached her, she raised her face to him again. He thought she spoke to him. Her voice was so low that he could not catch the words. Kneeling at her side, he bent his ear close to her face.

"Thank you," came the dry whisper in his ear.

He cocked his head, gazing into her eyes only inches from his own. Her mouth was set in a thin line and he could see her shivering.

"Can you move your hands yet?" he inquired.

"Yes." The answer was stronger.

"Then give me your hand."

She pulled it from under the fur. He placed the piece of meat in it and closed the weak fingers over it. She moaned in pain, but seemed able to retain a grip on the food. He patted her hand clumsily and started to rise.

"Is there some water?" her voice came again huskily.

"Surely you can lick your lips and get all of that you

150

need," he chuckled, "but I think I have some of the sourest ale in the north parts in a skin on Owen's saddle. Would that brace you?"

Nodding, she raised the leathery meat to her mouth. When he returned, she was trying vainly to grasp the strip tightly enough to break off a piece to chew.

He pushed her hand aside and grasped the meat. "Bite," he commanded. While she chewed, he took the piece of meat and tore it into small pieces and laid them on a stone beside her. Then he handed her a small skin. She allowed some of the ale to gurgle into her mouth. Abruptly she coughed and gagged.

"See!" he chuckled. "I told you it was foul stuff. The only reason to drink it is that there is naught else. Come now! Another pull and I must get myself a place and feed myself. Night is coming down hard upon us."

She did as he bid her and handed him the ale.

He started to rise, then changed his mind. "Girl, bend your head forward," he commanded.

Too exhausted to disobey, she did as he ordered. He pulled the fillet from inside his tunic. With rough hands, he swept her hair back from her forehead and away from her face. Deliberately, he wrapped the leather and gold around her head. In the dark, it was some seconds before he had positioned it correctly, but nevertheless the eagle's tiny golden wings swept back from her forehead to her temples and the claws and beak stretched forward from above her eyes. "Do not remove it," he commanded. "It will protect you when nothing else can."

Forestalling any protest, Huw returned to Owen's side and selected a tree nearby.

"Did you bind her?" Owen growled.

"Aye," replied Huw. Turning on his side, he sought a bit of peace and comfort with his meat and his sour ale.

Left alone, Moira picked up another piece of meat with fingers that she had to watch in order to direct them to

151

the spot where the meat lay. They could not feel anything very well, but she managed to pick up a bite and transfer it to her mouth. Her head fell back against the trunk as she chewed. She raised her hand to touch the sign of her captivity and of Rhiannon's ownership.

She wanted to drag it from her head and fling it away, for in her imagination it burned like a brand of Cain on her forehead. She felt the raindrops on her face and wished for a moment that she could allow herself the luxury of tears. Sternly, she forbade herself this shameful act and instead concentrated on analyzing her own predicament. If she removed the fillet, on the morrow they would bind her tightly again. She would suffer greatly and perhaps not survive. She clenched her right hand weakly, pleased to feel that though the fingers were very swollen and tender, nevertheless, they all moved. She thrust her hand under the fur and grasped her left hand. Although still partially wooden in her grasp, the flaming pain assured her that it would be normal soon. If I can bear to wait, she thought.

She clasped her hands under the fur and bowed her proud head. She was a captive. A slave. The men with whom she traveled would kill her if she made any effort to escape. They hated her. Rhiannon . . . Suddenly she longed for him. For his enthusiasm. For his warmth. She recalled the last nights when she had lain beside him. He had warmed her with his body and held her fast against the cold and wet. No one else had held her that she could remember. Her mother was long dead. Her nurse, too. Her father was not demonstrative. Her brother had hated her. He had been too jealous of her size and strength to approve of his sister.

With her right hand, she selected another bite of food, chewing it reflectively. Her only course lay in getting to Rhiannon. He would make arrangements to get her back to her father. He would keep her safe until such time as the exchange could be made. She would accept the binding; she would only wound herself by fighting against these underlings.

The thought was hardly framed in her mind when her head fell sideways on the fur and she lost consciousness, her mouth still containing the bite of food she had been chewing on.

From time to time during the night, she stirred. Her miserable stiff, aching body, cold and damp, awakened her even through the drugged sleep of exhaustion. As she dreamed of some terrible torment or some awful pursuit, she jarred herself awake to find her body chilled and shaking, her hands aching, water dripping down her face and neck. Fortunately, periods of awareness were short, for kind nature mercifully blotted out the horror and she drifted again into restless slumber.

In the half dawn, she jerked awake with a grunt of pain. Her eyes flew open. Through the mist and the glare of the icy morning, Owen Llewellyn's shaggy head rose, a black blot against the filtered light. He stood above her, snarling his hatred. His booted toe rammed into the small of her back below her ribs. Fearfully, she raised her arms to protect her face as he drew back his boot and aimed another kick at her.

Huw stepped forward to protect her. "Leave her alone, Owen. See! She wears the binding of Breannon now. She has accepted her slavery. She belongs to him."

Owen cursed. "You did that last night. You bound her, Huw Llengaron. Are you soft in the head? You saved her for that whelp when there are good men lying dead out there because of him and his wild ideas and because of her and that hound of a father." He spat on the ground between the two of them and stalked off to gather the reins to the horses.

Huw stared after him as Moira struggled to rise. A look of pained surprise crossed her face when she tried to get her feet under her. She was so cold and stiff from lying on the ground that she could hardly move. She lurched forward onto her hands and knees. By grabbing the bole of the tree and pulling herself up hand over hand, she managed to gain her feet. Her arms and hands ached and her head felt dizzy. Huw caught her under the arm to steady her and she gasped in pain at the touch of his hard grasp. She was sure every inch of skin on her body was bruised and flayed.

As Huw rolled up the fur at their feet, Owen rode up, leading the other two horses. Her mount still had no saddle and she had not the strength to pull herself onto his back with her weakened arms. Huw made a step for her with his hands and boosted her into her place.

Out of the grove, they rode into the lightening dawn. Today was much easier for Moira, for she could use her hands on the horse's withers to relieve her feet and her legs. She could grasp the black mane as they climbed up the steep road into the northern Cambrian Mountains of Wales.

At good strong light, they stopped and dismounted to blow the horses. Owen Llewellyn, with a contemptuous snort, opened his *chausses* and made water in the road in front of her. Moira gasped and ducked around the side of her horse. Without waiting for permission, she moved off around a boulder to the side of the narrow trail and relieved herself. Behind her, she heard Owen's howl of laughter and Huw's mumble of protest.

When she returned, they had mounted again and were waiting for her. Leading her black to the boulder, she climbed up on his back without help. Huw handed her a small round loaf of hard black bread from his kit and they were off again.

For the rest of the day and through the night they rode. Moira was uncertain as to the way for they were climbing and doubling back. She only knew that sometimes they

154

rode single file and sometimes Huw and Owen rode abreast while she was led behind. At first light, Owen pulled up.

"Look girl!" exclaimed Huw. "There's our destination. Hawk's Keep."

Following his pointed finger, Moira of Lorne saw with sinking heart the prison to which she was being taken. Rising out of the rock ahead of them was a massive fortification. Much of the keep had been hewn out of the rock itself, taking advantage of natural walls at its back and one side and adding hewn stone to form its front. So natural was it that it seemed to grow from the earth. The only way out for her, she sensed, was death or ransom. Her father and his men could never hope to take such a steep and impregnable fortress.

"The sea is at our back," said Huw. "There's the village beneath the keep on the sea. Colwyn Bay runs into the land below and to the west. We can hold off an army and they can neither starve us nor storm us."

Owen Llewellyn grinned evilly. "Aye, take a last look around you as you ride in. Freedom for you is over. When you ride into yon stone keep, you never ride out again. I promise you that on the grave of my kin."

Moira shuddered, but straightened and met his eyes. "Which man can say who will be captive and who will be free for any period of time? I vow to walk a free woman from that place. I can swear on the graves of my kin also and I do not doubt that I have just as many kin lying dead because of you and your cruel masters."

Owen snarled and drew back his whip to strike, but Huw shouldered his horse between the two, grabbed Moira's leading rein and led her forward.

Seventeen

With open disgust, Lady Branwen ni Rhiannon regarded the stinking, filthy, ragged captive. Proudly, Moira flung her head back to face her judge, but Owen Llewellyn's hard hand on her shoulder forced her to her knees before the chatelaine of Hawk's Keep.

"Who is this creature?"

"My Lady Branwen," declared Huw Llengaron, "this is Moira of Lorne, captive slave of your son Lord Rhiannon."

"My son is alive?" the woman's voice faltered. "Oh, dear God, where . . ."

"Yes, my lady, and even now he is with Lord Gethin if he has had any luck in his travel at all."

"Was he well? Had he any serious hurts?"

"No, my lady. He was very well and insisted that he ride to join the lord, to avoid battle with the men of Lorne."

Here Owen Llewellyn interrupted. "He had been held captive within the enemy's keep, my Lady Branwen, and believed that Lord Gethin would not take it without much bloodshed and great loss of life."

"'Tis very possible, indeed true," Lady Branwen replied. For several seconds, she sat silent with head bowed. Her lips moved; her hands twisted in her lap. Then she raised her head and stared at Moira's kneeling figure. "And this is my son's slave." Her lip curled and her nostrils quivered. "I see the fillet binding her brow. What orders did he give to accompany her removal here?"

As Huw hesitated, Owen replied, "That she be brought here and treated as any other captive. The chains and dungeon would be good for her. She threatens to escape. Lord Rhiannon himself said she was a haughty bitch who needed to be taught."

Huw clamped his lips together as he listened to Owen. Lady Branwen seemed well satisfied with the answer.

"So be it," she declared. "See to it, sirs. Say you he was well?"

"Aye, my lady."

". . . and that he rides to join my lord?"

"Aye, my lady."

Lady Branwen rose from her chair without another word and paced from the hall.

Owen Llewellyn hauled Moira to her feet and shoved her across the floor. "I said that you would never leave here. We have a dungeon that has not seen a light since the stones closed round it. It will be my joy to dispose of you there."

Moira was silent, but her lip trembled. Owen caught her under her left arm and dragged her from the hall down into the depths of the keep. The temperature dropped as they descended along a way lighted by small sconces which smoked dismally in the chill air.

Huw followed behind, but when once Moira cast a glance over her shoulder, he dropped his eyes.

At a heavy oak door, Owen knocked and was admitted by a stooped, brutish fellow heavily clad in smoke-darkened, musty-smelling skins. The room into which she was ushered was small. The smoke from torches and a brazier of coals in the center had blackened the walls and ceiling. A small table, two rude benches, and a chest were the only other furnishings in the room. The man clanked as he turned. Moira saw a ring bearing several large keys dangling from a wide studded belt beside a weighted leather thong. Grabbing his forelock, the brute waited as Owen Llewellyn surveyed the room with some satisfaction.

"This woman," he said grandly, "is the only whelp of Lorne, the bastard who killed your brother, Ian. Lady Branwen has ordered that she be chained with heavy chains in the lowest dungeon."

A low grumbling noise issued from the guard's throat as he opened the chest and dragged out heavy iron fetters and manacles with a connecting chain.

"Not fetters, too," whispered Huw. "'Tis not necessary."

"I say it is," growled Owen.

"No! What if Lord Rhiannon remembers her and finds her sorely crippled? Think, man! Would you destroy yourself for her discomfort?"

"He will not remember."

"But suppose he does."

"Oh, very well." Growling angrily, Owen turned to the guard. "Manacles only, but see you chain her to the wall."

Moira stood quietly, white to the lips, her eyes blue chips of ice as the cold iron clamped round her sore and blistered wrists. The manacles were rusty and smears of red dust ground into the wounds. She winced, but restrained herself from drawing away. The guard locked a connecting chain around the six inch chain between.

Owen reached forward speculatively and weighed the chains in his hand. His wild cruel eyes rolled at Moira.

Raucously, he laughed as he gave the chains a quick twist. She was caught off guard and staggered helplessly.

The guard chuckled, received the chain as Owen handed it to him with a nod of satisfaction, and tugged her across the three or four feet that separated her from the inner door. He paused, selected a key from the ring on his belt, and opened the heavy portal. A wave of icy, fetid air swept into the room.

Owen Llewellyn laughed again.

The guard pulled a lantern from its hook on the wall and led her into a narrow tunnel. The surface beneath her feet was uneven and slippery. One of the walls against which she brushed was also rough and uneven like the wall of a cave.

Moira's knees were trembling. Was she truly being buried alive? Was there no help? She slipped and the guard gave the chain a jerk and muttered something incomprehensible. Suddenly he stopped and Moira collided with him in the dim light. Cursing, he dropped the chain, swung the leather thong, and struck her full force along the left arm and shoulder. Thrown back against the wall, Moira allowed herself to slide down the damp stone and huddled against it to protect her body from further blows.

Fearfully, she waited for the shock which did not come. The guard instead had lost interest in her as he unlocked the small door only four feet high in the end of the tunnel. As it swung open, he turned and fumbled for her chain.

"Up with you and in you go." He goaded her with the stiff leather thong. She scrambled through the short door, coming up inside a tiny cell which in the flickering light from the guard's lantern appeared to be hollowed from the rock. Dampness glistened on the walls and dripped into a pool in a corner beside the door. At the back of the cell was the only other sign of human intercession, a rusty iron staple set three feet off the floor. Crossing the space in two steps, the guard dragged Moira to the wall and locked the chain in place. Then he stepped back to the door.

"'Twould do me better to see your sire in your place," he remarked.

Moira swallowed convulsively.

"Silent, huh? There are quiet ones and cursing ones, but they all ends up the same way here—mad and dead." He laughed. "Mad and dead."

Moira shivered helplessly. Her teeth chattered so loudly that the guard could hear her and see her shaking in the dim light.

"It does get chill here. But no rats. Rats like their comforts. This place is too cold and wet for them."

He studied her for some sign of weakness, but she did not respond, only stared at him from deep hollow eyes in a pale face. He stooped and took the lantern out of the cell, the door swung to, and the key grated in the lock.

A thin ray of light filtered through a slit in the door where the boards had been improperly fitted together. Moira concentrated on that for the tiny space of time that the guard remained in the tunnel. She could hear nothing through the door for all sound seemed muffled by the rock. Then the light disappeared. She was buried in total darkness!

"Father," she whispered into the icy blackness, "you were right. I am indeed punished. And, oh, this punishment is hard to bear."

Her thoughts became frenzied as a great wave of claustrophobia rolled over her. She sought to tug her arms apart, but the manacles restrained her. She set her knuckles against her teeth and bit down hard. The pain calmed her somewhat and she became aware of the chill. Her body began to tremble and her lack of food and sleep overcame her. She slid down the side of the cell wall, gathered her ragged cloak around her, and slipped miserably into oblivion.

Much later, she awoke to the sound of the key grating in the lock. The door creaked open. The guard's harsh voice echoed in the cell.

"Back against the wall!"

Moira giggled hysterically. The chain which held her to the wall was only three feet in length. She could sit or lie nowhere but back against the wall and the cell was too short for her to stand erect.

The guard entered and set his lantern down at the door. Over his arm he carried a ragged, greasy fur which he flung at her. "Huw Llengaron said you were to have this. He is a strange one, he is. Soft." He regarded her as she gathered the odorous pelts around her. "Not many females come down here. Generally, they be house slaves or more like bed slaves to the ones upstairs."

He waited, but Moira made no move. "Could be you might not stay in this cold cell, but could come up and share my room with me. I've a charcoal fire and a bench to lie on."

He waited again. He shuffled forward, warily reaching his hand toward the front of her cloak. He was a black bulk in front of her, his face in darkness from the lantern light behind him. Moving slightly to the left, so he could see the expression on her face, he sought to gauge her reaction to his suggestion. Her expression warned him even as she bit at him. Instead of sinking her teeth into his wrist, she missed. He jerked back swiftly.

"Bitch!" he cursed. "Need to be taught a lesson, huh! No food for you today." He drew from his belt his leather thong. He turned slightly to the left so that she could see its dull surface in the light. His teeth gleamed in his hairy face as he grinned at her.

"No biting," he ordered as he raised his arm. She ducked her head and flung up her manacled hands.

161

Someone was screaming. The sound was piercing and thin, despairing and weak. She suddenly realized she was the source.

At last, his blows stopped. She heard his harsh breathing behind her. "I like my females willing. No food for a couple of days. Then you'll come out and eat and be friendly with me. You'll be gentle, too. I like weak, helpless ones with no thought but pleasing a man." He backed out closing the door.

Moira lay shuddering and moaning. Gradually the pain in her hands and in her body began to fade. Grasping her chain between her hands, she raised herself painfully to a sitting position in the total darkness. Thankful for the slightest favor, she struggled to arrange Huw Llengaron's furs around her. They gave blessed protection to her buttocks and thighs from the stone floor.

She was thirsty and her throat was raw from screaming. Turning her face to the wall beside her head, she ran her fingertips along the stone. They encountered only damp and slimy surfaces until she was almost ready to give up and turn back to the other side. At last, however, her finger encountered a smooth spot where a tiny stream of water pulsed down the side of the rock. She withdrew her finger and tasted. The water was cold with a faintly metallic taste, but she could not be concerned.

Carefully she felt again until she found the spot, then placed her lips to the smooth stream and sucked greedily. She remembered the morning when she and Rhiannon had drunk together from the rock.

"God damn him!" she exclaimed aloud. "I was such a fool." Her voice resounded against the stone, hollow and thin. The blackness was impenetrable. Moira buried her face in her hands. Her skin was chilled and layered with a film of grime and grit. Her hands were slimy from contact with the walls and floor of the cell.

162

As her shivering increased, she pulled herself into a tight ball and closed her eyes. In her imagination she sought to conjure images of warmth and pleasure from her childhood. Meager though they were, her mind dwelt upon them until her body drifted away so she was temporarily oblivious to discomfort. She dozed, but then her head slipped onto the wet surface and she awoke.

A soft whisper penetrated her consciousness and she realized that she was perilously close to tears. "Stop that!" she told herself sternly. "That only expends energy and does not help a bit." Shall I go mad? I am talking to myself out loud. Her thoughts raced and turned and twisted on themselves. No help. No aid will come. Perhaps I should go with the guard. At least I could warm myself and have a bite of food.

She pressed her hands against her face and her fingertips encountered the fillet still binding her forehead. The talons were outstretched and sharp to her touch. I can kill myself if I cannot endure anymore, she thought. I carry the means to save myself with me. Huw Llengaron was right. This will protect me when nothing else will. Her right hand rubbed over the golden bird with the wideswept wings. Perhaps the guard might come into the cell when she was asleep or unconscious and see the piece and steal it. Carefully she removed the fillet and retied it around her throat, hiding it beneath her blouse and gown. She pressed her hand against the bird and felt oddly comforted as the gold warmed to her touch.

"I have not gone beyond the point where I can decide my own fate," she said aloud. "I am still in control. I still have a choice. But, oh, I am so cold and hungry."

Hush, she thought to herself sternly. You are talking to yourself again. I must think of something to occupy my mind. Her thoughts returned to the source of her trouble—Rhiannon ap Breannon. "How shall I kill

163

him?" she asked herself aloud. She adjusted a corner of the fur and pillowed her cheek against it as she lay huddled against the wall of the cell beneath the staple. One hand curled beneath her chin and held tightly to the fillet. The other clasped her chain to ease the strain from the manacle on her left wrist. So thinking and plotting, she drifted off to sleep again.

Eighteen

Lord Gethin ap Breannon made camp early in the day,
after precipitously leaving the siege camp beneath the
walls of Lorne Rock. His only son lay unconscious in the
litter slung between two horses. When his father had
tried to rouse him at noon, he had merely muttered and
fallen again into a deep sleep. His days without rest,
tortured, hungry, in pain, had accumulated to strike him
now with full force. Rhiannon could not rouse himself,
although he heard his father's voice.

Lord Gethin ordered soldiers to fetch water from the
stream beside which they camped. They heated the water
in cooking pots and, inside the small tent Gethin carried
for his own use, they stripped Rhiannon of his ragged,
bloodstained garments. Henry bathed the young man's
body carefully with warm water. Under Lord Gethin's
direction, he applied ointment to the many cuts and
inspected the half-healed wound in the shoulder.

"This has had good care," Henry observed, "or else
you might not be lying here so lazy and contented right
now."

Rhiannon stretched his arm and shoulder apprecia-

165

tively. "The lady put a poultice on it and drew the poison from it. When the wound was drawn, the fever went down."

Grunting, Gethin lifted his son's wrist. "We can get these off you only when we reach home. The locks are rusted by the look of them and the armorer will have to saw them off."

"With the pads that the lady put on me I have suffered naught since we got the chains cut through. They can wait."

"Tell me about the lady that you speak of," Gethin ordered.

"She is Moira of Lorne, the daughter and only child of the lord, I believe," replied Rhiannon, looking to Gethin's confirming nod. "I tricked her into helping me escape and came away with her as my captive. Now she will be my slave when I return home."

"By God!" exclaimed Gethin, "you are a cool one. My son, indeed! What a wonder you are! To be captured and turn such shame into a victory."

Rhiannon grinned a wolfish grin at his father's words.

Gethin continued, "What a ransom we can get for her! Lorne will squirm and twist, but he can do naught. She is his only girl and built like a man I have heard."

Rhiannon nodded, but his grin faded somewhat. He did not want to think of giving Moira back to her father. In his mind, he still dreamed of her as he had the night when they had lain together in the stable. She would go with him. She would be his slave and his companion. He had not brought her so far and put his stamp so firmly on her flesh to be giving her back for a bit of gold.

"I would keep her, Father," he declared. "She will ensure peace between us and a quiet time. They cannot take her back. We can get back all our lads who survived the raid and keep all safe."

Gethin raised his hand. "She will be worth the lives of

166

all those men and much gold as well. I doubt that Lorne would consider her worth peace and an end to raiding when he has made his living that way for so long. He would get another heir and forget her. But no! When we get back, we will arrange for exchange and gold."

Rhiannon opened his mouth to protest, but his father rose irritably and strode from the tent. Gethin ap Breannon hated to be crossed. Only his son could do so without a great shouting and beating about. Even his son could not cross him without Gethin revealing his anger.

Later, at supper, both men were silent, each too stubborn to relent. At the end of the meal, the father left without a word to see to the deployment of the camp. Rolled in the furs, within the tent, Rhiannon lay staring moodily at the ceiling. She was his. He had captured her, ridden with her, eaten with her, slept with her. He thought of the warmth of her soft body, the courage in her ice blue eyes, the gentleness in her long steady fingers when she bathed his wounds. His hands stretched as he remembered reaching out to touch her belly and breasts with their smooth, firm white skin. He closed his eyes. She would never be anyone's again but his. He wanted her with him. As she grew tamer, she would be easier to be with. They would ride together. She would learn to laugh with him and smile for him. He had seen her smile once or twice and he longed to see her do so again. He concentrated on her smile as he drifted off to sleep.

He was awakened at first light by Henry. Differentially, the man requested that Rhiannon rise so they could be off. With him, Henry brought fresh clothing, sweeping up the rags Rhiannon had worn for almost a fortnight.

Rhiannon dressed himself with some pleasure. Even though he had to wrap his father's tunic and lap his own belt around his lean middle, he welcomed the clean feel against his skin. By the time he had eaten, squatting beside the campfire, he felt almost his old self. When Henry led forward a fresh horse, a shaggy brown gelding with a wicked white eye, Rhiannon eagerly swung into the saddle. Proudly, he moved to his place beside his father at the head of the band.

For three more days, they rode through the mountains and valleys of central Wales. Their progress was slower now, for a festive air communicated itself to the whole group. About mid-morning of the first day, Gethin's irritation disappeared. From then the company saw him smile, then chuckle, then throw back his head and sound his hearty laugh. By the time of the midday rest, father and son were again friends. By tacit agreement, they did not speak of the slave that awaited them when they returned to Hawk's Keep.

On the third day, riders had gone out at dawn to bear the news that the party would arrive home before dark. Just at sunset, Gethin and Rhiannon rode together across the bridge that separated the outlying area from the winding mountain trail that led up to the bailey of Hawk's Keep.

Lady Branwen and her daughter Edain greeted them on the steps of the hall. With tears in her eyes, Branwen embraced first her son and then her husband. Edain shyly bowed to her brother and then laughed as he embraced her with a great hug that lifted her off her feet and set her braids swinging. Unable to contain their happiness, the four embraced again, joining their arms about their bodies in affection and thanksgiving.

"All is prepared," gasped Lady Branwen when she could free herself from the laughing embraces. Tears stood on her cheeks as she clasped her son's face in her hands and kissed him on the mouth. "Come into the hall. Everyone waits to do you honor and welcome you home. We had thought you perhaps dead. We had heard that you had been sorely wounded . . . your wounds!" she exclaimed. "Have they been seen to?"

"Truly, Mother, I am fine. The sores are practically healed and I am hungry as a bear. I have eaten nothing but rations since I left. And I have not tasted ale such as we make here."

As they entered the hall, the musicians in the gallery struck up a piece. All was light and warmth. A great fire blazed in the hearth, the boards were laid with the fine family plate, and candles gleamed from every candelabrum. Rhiannon was seated on the dais between his father and his mother with his sister on his mother's left. Edain beamed over this honor and the prospect of being allowed to stay to dine with the family at her young age.

When they all were seated, wine was poured into the chalices and the kinsmen and ladies were seated in order of their rank in the family. The feast began.

Rhiannon's body craved nourishment. At his mother's signal, course after course of soup, fowl, pork, beef, fish, and vegetables was served. Fine breads and pies and pastries of all kinds as well as good cheese accompanied each course. Finally, he could eat no more. After plates were cleared away, fine brandy was brought. As Rhiannon sank back in his chair with a sigh of pleasure, a bard strode forth to sing of Rhiannon, goddess of the white horse, who was the mother of all and the ancestress of the family. She who was bravest in battle and strongest in magic had given her name to the family and, he concluded, the young man who bore her name was the most glorious of her descendants.

The old legend was made new by the addition of the deeds of Rhiannon ap Breannon, son of Gethin ap Breannon and of Branwen ni Rhiannon. When the bard began to sing then of the capture of the daughter of Lorne and her subsequent humiliation, Rhiannon remembered Moira. Hastily, he glanced around.

His eye caught Owen Llewellyn sitting halfway down the table, but Owen avoided Rhiannon's look. Rhiannon turned to his mother. "Where is the slave, Moira of Lorne, whom I sent here with Owen Llewellyn and Huw Llengaron?"

Lady Branwen sat puzzled for a minute. "Truly, I do not remember." She wrinkled her brow. "Oh, now I do. She was barely human, as I recall. Filthy and ragged and she stank. When Owen informed me that you were safe, I was so overcome with joy that I could not think of anything else. He said he would dispose of her as you had ordered, so I left the hall to go to my prayers. I knew that I should thank God so many times for your safe escape and your return."

"Mother," Rhiannon sought to put an end to her ramblings which were common when his mother had had a bit too much of the stout ale and sweet wine, "where was she disposed?"

Branwen passed a hand over her eyes. "I cannot think. Perhaps the dungeon . . ."

"No!" exclaimed Rhiannon. "How many days ago?"

"Why, 'tis at least three or four since I heard of your safety! My son, worry not. She will be safely kept until the feasting is over. She cannot escape. Owen saw to it that she was chained. I remember his saying that you ordered her taming and that the chains and the dungeon were at your command."

Rhiannon thrust back his chair with a muffled curse. He was making a fool of himself, he knew, but he could not bear to think of Moira lying in chains in a foul dungeon. She was his. If she needed taming, he would tame her. None other. Hurrying from the hall, he grasped a torch from its sconce as he strode along the corridor and down the stone steps into the depths of the keep.

Behind him in the hall, few noted his departure. The guests were generally sprawled at their ease on the

170

benches in the alcoves or had begun to move off toward their rooms. The fire had gone down in the hearth, the musicians had retired for the night. Gethin and Branwen exchanged looks as she sought to explain.

"Let be!" he commanded gruffly. "See to your daughter, madam. And we will to bed. The boy may be a fool on his own. All explanations can wait until the morning."

Rhiannon pounded on the oak door of the guard room. From within came no sound. He pounded again and again, using all his strength and the iron of the manacles still attached to his wrists.

Finally, the door opened and the bleary-eyed guard stood before him, half-drunk and scratching himself. "Wha's the matter? Can't a man have a bit of sleep?" His manner changed abruptly when he saw the young lord of the keep standing before him. Abruptly, he straightened his back and saluted.

Rhiannon brushed past him into the room. "Where have you lodged the lady who was brought here some three or four days ago?"

The guard laughed nastily. "Oh, I put her down in the lowest cell as you ordered, sir. 'Tis might cold, but Owen Llewellyn said you wanted her tamed proper. She be still a bit haughty. Tried to fight me a few days ago and her still chained. But she be different now, I vow. No bread, I said. The ones what bites gets no bread. I whipped her good and proper, too. She be ready to do whatever you want now."

Rhiannon's face paled. "Have you fed her nothing? Is she still alive?"

"Oh, aye," responded the guard proudly. "I checked on her each day. She stares at me with those big white eyes of hers and dares me still, but yesterday I offered her a piece of bread and she took it, so she be taming down right nicely."

171

"Take me to her," choked Rhiannon.

The guard led him across the room, chuckling at this success with the lord's slave and pleased with himself for his efforts.

"Be not often I get female prisoners down here, you know, my lord," he said as he fumbled for the key to the inner door. "Mayhap you might find my way useful for later. Of course, Huw Llengaron sent her some furs. I figure they was a mistake. She would be broken and ready for your bed if she had been cold all this time. Every day I stuck my head in and said she be mad and dead if she did not give herself to you willingly when you come for her. Tried to bite me once she did."

When he opened the door, an icy, fetid stench assaulted Rhiannon's nostrils. "Dear God!" he gasped. His lady, his companion, his enemy to be sure, but she had offered him wine when she thought he was too weak to lift a cup as he lay in his own blood on her father's floor.

The guard ambled along the dark tunnel swinging his lantern. He was well pleased with himself that he was able to demonstrate his methods to the lord's son. Now if the girl would just cooperate and present a properly servile demeanor, he might get more opportunities with women. True enough, he had not really had any success with this one. She was still as angry as ever, still refusing to come with him, but he felt sure that she would have broken the next time he visited her cell.

He stopped at the door at the end of the tunnel and fumbled with the key. Finally, the door rasped open.

Shouldering him aside, Rhiannon called in a voice filled with concern. "Moira, my lady! Come out!"

"She cannot, my lord. She be chained to the back wall of the cell with a three-foot chain. She cannot stir much more than stand up. I keep the prisoners well. Nobody gets out of here unless I allow it."

172

Seizing the lantern from the guard's grasp, Rhiannon shoved it into the cell ahead of him. When he bobbed through the door, he banged his head against the top of the cell. Violently, he cursed, his voice a growl. How had she survived? She who was so tall and free.

The flickering lantern revealed a huddled form, hardly more than a heap of grimy clothing, lying on cold stone, damp and fetid.

"Moira, my lady. Dear God!" He thrust the lantern into the guard's face and dropped down beside her.

She stirred slowly. A chain rattled as she struggled to raise her body.

Another growl rumbled from him. At his touch on her shoulders, she shrank away with a faint whimper. He could feel her damp clothing, the convulsive shivering of her body. Rage fought with pity as he sought to pull her upright before he realized that neither of them could stand erect. She whimpered again as the chain brought her up short. His strong arms pulling against it twisted her body. He could see her wrists were chained with manacles such as he had worn and a connecting chain attached to a staple in the wall.

"The key, fool!" he barked to the guard. "Unchain her immediately."

The man fumbled to obey.

Numbly, Moira half crouched, her matted hair brushing against the clammy stone above her. Her pale face was expressionless except for her lips which were set in a grim line. Dark green slime begrimed her hair and face on the right side where she had lain against the wet dripping stones.

Raising his hand, Rhiannon caressed her cheek—his touch was supremely tender. The manacles fell to the floor with a sharp clatter. Rhiannon slid his arm around Moira's shoulders to lead her forward. At the first step she stumbled, then as they bent to leave through the lower cell door, she collapsed.

Rhiannon dropped to his knees beside her. "My dear, just a little farther. I will take you out of this. Come! Brace up!"

Saving her breath for the effort, she got her feet under her. By steadying herself with her hand on the stones in front of her, she managed to move through the low door. Once outside, she straightened, swaying, blinded by the light, dizzy with the effort. Following behind her, he immediately caught her and supported her in his arms. Through the fabric of her gown, he could feel her ribs. Poor girl, he thought. How many days had passed since she had had a fair meal? They had all but starved after his escape.

His arm around her waist propelled her through the maze of passages that brought them behind the great banquet hall of Hawk's Keep. At his command, a wench scurried away to bring wine, a thick soup, and a custard to the lord's rooms immediately.

"Come!" he said again as he returned to her side.

"Where?" she croaked, pushing her body away from the wall where she had weakly supported herself.

"To my rooms," he replied.

"No, my lord. Return me to the dungeon. I will not share a bed with you. My father will rescue me soon enough or I will die, but I will not sleep and eat with you again."

She jerked her arm out of his grasp and spun around. Two steps she took toward the tapestry separating the passage from the hall before she felt everything begin to go black from her sudden movement. Oh, no! she thought, I must not faint in front of him. Please let me be strong. But her admonition was for naught as the light faded from her vision and her knees buckled.

He caught her before she fell, lifting her high into his arms against his chest. Her head hung limply over his arm, her defiant blue eyes closed. Her weight stirred him to sharp pity. So light was she that he knew he could have carried her for miles. There was almost no flesh on her body from the deprivation she had endured.

Swiftly he mounted the stairs to his room. Already she was stirring in his arms as he laid her down on the bench before the fireplace. Leaving her, he strode to the door to shout for the boys who brought the bath. Peremptorily, he instructed them to bring the copper tub and extra amounts of hot water, towels, napkins, and soap.

Hurrying back to her side, he laid a gentle hand on her shoulder. "Lie back, Moira. Do not try to move around now. The wench will be here with food in a moment. You need not stir yourself. Then I will feed you and give you a good warm bath and then to bed."

She sank back on the bench, her eyes moving restlessly around the room seeking escape, help, some means of release from his hateful presence.

The knock at the door brought the wench with the food he had ordered.

"Shall I serve, my lord?" She curtseyed and set the tray on the table.

"No. I will do it. You may go," he replied.

She dipped again and left, closing the door quietly behind her.

Rhiannon walked to the table and ladled soup from the brown earthenware crock into a bowl. Picking up a spoon, he returned to her side. She stiffened at first and closed her eyes, determined to refuse to eat.

"Moira," he called softly. "Moira. Moi-i-ira. Smell this. Doesn't this smell good?" He held the bowl beside her head and watched the steam curl upward. Teasing her like a devil, he blew across it to cool it. The vapor wafted across her face. She swallowed convulsively. Their eyes met, his blue and smiling at her, hers smoky and agonized.

175

"Can you raise yourself?" he inquired.

Slowly she swung her legs off the other side of the bench. Like a rheumatic old woman, she hunched miserably, her feet toward the fire. Dipping the spoon into the bowl, he held the broth to her lips.

"I can do it myself," she said, reaching shaking hands for the bowl.

"No," he said, moving it out of her reach. "You will spill it or eat too much too fast and be sick." Gently he continued to feed her the soup.

In too short a time, Moira turned her head away. "Had enough?" he asked. She nodded her head, shivering slightly.

Setting the bowl on the table, he poured wine into a pewter tankard. Handing it to her, he came round the bench, knelt with his back to the fire, to grasp her foot and remove her boot.

Glaring defiantly, Moira drew her feet back under the bench.

Rhiannon desisted with a chuckle. "Drink your wine, my lady. It will relax you." He was relieved to see her fighting spirit had not left her.

A knock interrupted what he might have said. At his command, the door swung open to admit three lackeys, grinning sleepy towheaded boys. Obviously, they were brothers very close together in age. The largest boy bore a yoke with two large buckets of steaming water. The second carried an oval copper tub decorated with brass braiding around the lip. It was perhaps two feet deep and about four feet at its widest point. The smallest boy rather ostentatiously carried a pile of neatly folded linen towels and napkins topped by a small cake of perfumed soap.

Rhiannon indicated the spot to the left of the bench, then turned back to Moira and gestured. "Drink up, my lady."

As Moira did, she felt a slow warmth stealing over her. She took another generous sip. Her exhausted mind began to blur. Although she tried to watch the boys preparing the bath with alarm and suspicion, she found focusing somewhat difficult.

At last, the boys scuffled out, noisily closing the door behind them. Rhiannon moved to the table where he cut off a slice of dark brown bread. From a small pot, he drizzled a thin stream of golden honey over the bread. Taking the tankard from her hand, he replaced it with the food. Obediently, Moira took a bite. The honey spread to the corners of her mouth and suddenly Rhiannon was beside her, wiping it carefully away with a napkin. Gently, his mouth followed his hand down to kiss her lips. His tongue flicked quickly over them, then darted into her mouth, licking the honey and at the same time tasting her.

"Sweet," said Rhiannon. Moira stiffened in protest, but he caught her hands in both of his. "Now," he said, looking deep into her eyes, "stand up and I will undress you."

"No!" she gasped.

Inexorably, he pulled her to her feet. When she swayed weakly, he turned her shoulder against his body and began to unfasten her vest. Feebly her hands caught at his, but he tugged determinedly at the strings. As the lacings came loose, he drew it gently from her body. Forestalling any protest she might make, he pulled her gown off over her head in a deft movement. Her silk blouse followed.

"Oh, no, please . . ." Her voice trembled, but too late. She was nude from the waist up. Like a barbarian princess she stood with a golden bird at her throat, her proud breasts outthrust.

His awed expression changed to an angry frown as his eyes inspected her. Livid bruises stood out on the white

177

skin of her arms and shoulders and here and there along her ribs. Angrily he touched one, surprised at the slight trembling of his fingers. So sensitive was her skin, so deep were the bruises, that the light pressure of his hand caused her to wince. Her involuntary reaction drew a soft growl from Rhiannon's throat as he drew his hands away. His eyes rested on the golden bird around her neck, glinting warmly from the contact with her skin. Gently placing his fingers on her collar bones, he rested his thumbs on the wings of the eagle. "You wear my symbol," he said quietly. "When did you put this on?"

For a minute she would not answer him. Her eyes dropped as a shamed blush crept into her cheeks. But he shook her slightly, letting his eyes rove over her gaunt body and beautiful white breasts. "Tell me," he insisted softly.

"Huw Llengaron put it on me the night after you left. My hands were blue where you had bound them. He was afraid that I would lose them if I remained bound as you and your bestial henchman Owen intended."

"Did he put it around your throat under your clothing?"

"No, I did that in the cell. I knew I could kill myself with it if need be and I was afraid the guard might snatch it away from me."

Nodding silently, he frowned at the use she would have put it to. She bowed her head and did not see his expression. Helpless and a little drunk, Moira crossed her arms over her breasts. Almost tenderly, Rhiannon guided her down on the bench and tugged off her boots and *chausses* despite her soft moan of protest.

Slipping his arms around her shoulders and under her knees, he carried her to the tub where he lowered her to her feet beside it. "Test it," he suggested.

She shuddered and shook her head, too embarrassed to raise her eyes. The enmity of the morning in the stable

178

had been exchanged for this peculiar gentleness. She could not fathom it, nor could she fight it. Her exhaustion merely added to her confusion.

He bent and tested the water with his left hand, keeping his right arm around her upright body. "Feels right to me," he said, ignoring her ineffectual squirming. He lifted her again and deposited her in the tub.

She squealed, a most amazing sound for her, and tried to rise, but his arm on her shoulder prevented her. Thoroughly enjoying himself now, he picked up the ladle from beside the tub to pour water over her shoulders and back. "Relax," he chuckled. "The worst is over. I told you once before, my lady, you should allow me to keep you warm and comfortable."

Slowly she relaxed as he poured water again and again over her upper body. He dipped the napkin into the water to wash her face and neck. She could not conceal a small sigh of pleasure as the grime of the cell was sponged away from her cheeks and chin. Then he picked up the soap and began to lather her back and shoulders. Closing her eyes, she leaned her head forward, sunk her chin on her chest, inhaling the warm steam from the tub. It warmed her body from within where it had been too long exposed to the chill air of the cell.

When he had finished, he poured water over her back and rinsed her before he tipped her head back. Her eyes flew open as he lathered her breasts and belly. Tensing, she half-raised herself to spring away from him, but he placed his hand firmly on her shoulder. His eyes like deep blue mountain lakes reassured her somehow. She wanted to trust him. His hands were doing such vaguely soothing and at the same time sensuous things to her body. Round and round her soft breasts in gentle circling motions, his palms and fingertips lathered her. Like a cat stretching with pleasure, she could not stop her chest from arching slightly as she drew in a deeper breath than she might normally have done.

"I think you do not hate my touch so much," he teased, feeling her involuntary movement. A soft flush crept into her cheeks in answer and he chuckled softly. Again and again, he ladled that part of her, admiring the way the water coursed down over her breasts and beaded on her pretty pink nipples. She was truly lovely, he thought, even with her ribs showing stark and shadowed.

"If you kneel in the tub, I will wash your hair," he whispered.

Doing as he bade without demur, she knelt in the tub leaning on her hands with her head bent forward. As he ladled water over her hair, he admired the fine, clean line of her back. Silvery water glistened on her breasts. Her buttocks were exciting curves of glowing pink from the heat of the water. As he washed her hair, they gradually faded to paler pink and then to soft cream, the shade of the rest of her body. He felt his own excitement begin to stir again. Finally, he rinsed her hair for the last time and wrapped it in a towel.

"Stand up, my lady." He placed a hand under her arm to assist her to rise.

His breath caught in his throat as she obediently stood, slender and tall, perfectly formed, her skin white as alabaster. Sparkling silver streams sluiced down her legs, outlining their graceful curves. From his position, his face was alongside her hip close enough to feel the heat of the bath radiating from her skin, to smell the perfume of the soap.

Desire rose strong in him to clasp her against him and ease himself in her depths where his first experience had created more pressure than it had released. His eyes slid up her body to the thin hands, one clasped tightly within the other before her breasts, to the chin whose quivering seemed stilled only by the grip of the white teeth on the lower lip, to the deathly pale cheeks and closed eyes. She

180

swayed slightly.

She was too weak to stand for very long. She has endured much, he thought. The idea of having her against her will, for she would surely resist to the limit of her considerably diminished strength, seemed shabby somehow. His act would be the act of a bully taking from the weak and helpless. The thought did much to cool his ardor.

With a sigh, he dipped the soap into the tub and lathered and rinsed her long legs as she stood still, her feet in the warm water. Finally, he patted her dry.

When he had finished, he slipped her into a warm wool robe of his own and escorted her to the bench. Feeling dizzy from the nearness of her body, he poured two tankards of wine. Seating himself beside her, he handed her one. Together they drank, he grinning, she impassive.

"What now?" she asked him.

"Why now, Moira, my lady, we go to bed. Finish your wine while I call the lackeys back."

Immediately they came scrambling in. Grinning widely, two cleared away the paraphernalia of the bath while the third, the youngest, scuttled coals from the hearth into a long-handled warming pan which he carried to the bed, a high, draped structure in the dark corner of the room.

Trembling at the thought of lying beside him, Moira tore her gaze from the bed to the fire. She was lost, helpless, among enemies. Her greatest enemy, the wolf himself, held her captive. "W-where shall I sleep?" Her voice shook with nervousness. Although she knew the answer, she could not suppress the question.

He raised an eyebrow quizzically, his wolfish grin twisting the corner of his mouth. His fingers touched her hand, staying it from carrying more wine to her lips, his eyes searched hers. "If I gave you the choice of a warm

181

bed beside me or an icy dungeon alone, which would you choose?" he asked.

Her flesh quailed. Trembling, white to the lips, she set the tankard down abruptly. Her hands clenched.

Watching her narrowly, Rhiannon waited a moment. When he spoke, his voice was warm with sympathy. "No. Do not answer. The choice is not yours." He thrust the tankard back into her hand again. "Drink up."

Suddenly, nothing mattered. Rhiannon had taken her virginity; he could not hurt her anymore. At least she was not lying on the cold wet stones in the dungeon. With this comforting thought, she clutched the tankard more tightly, lifted it to her lips, and drank deeply. Soothed by the wine, she was becoming more and more sleepy. She was hardly aware when Rhiannon began to dry her hair. From somewhere, he produced a brush and began to brush with long, steady strokes down through the heavy brown mass.

Mesmerized by his attentions, Moira allowed her head to fall back as her eyes closed. Almost bereft of consciousness, she felt as if she were floating suspended in space somewhere above the bench. She tilted her head forward with great effort and took another drink from the tankard. "'Tis all gone," she said softly in the hurt voice of a child.

"You need no more tonight, my lady," her captor chuckled, relieving her of the vessel. "Come, let us to bed."

In a dream she moved across the floor with him. Almost casually, he unbelted her robe, sliding it off over her shoulders. When he turned back the covers, she obediently sat down, then swung her legs into the bed which was blissfully warm from the pan of coals placed in between the sheets. Rhiannon covered her to her chin before placing a kiss on her forehead. Quietly he returned to the hearth, snuffed the candles, banked the fire, and removed his clothes beside the chest in the other corner of the chamber. Turned on her side, Moira watched him with eyes that struggled to stay open. Her body relaxed quiescent in the delightful luxury of the clean, warm, soft bed.

When he crossed the room to climb in beside her, she did not, could not object. Instead, she merely snuggled down against him, closing her eyes as his arms went around her.

He stroked her hair, pressed his lips again to her forehead, and smiled in the darkness. For just a few hours she would allow herself to relax and enjoy the truce. She was a brave girl who had suffered much. Again he thought as he had done so many nights ago about what he would do with her. The feel of her warm, pliant body against him made him more determined than ever to pursue the plan to make her his companion as well as his slave. To have her with him in field and in keep would gain him much.

She stirred vaguely against him, settling herself more comfortably into the warmth of his embrace. Her movement made him want her, but he was content to wait until morning to avail himself of her.

So thinking, his arm around her waist, his hand shaping the curve of her breast, he fell asleep.

Nineteen

Moira dreamed she was being buried alive in a tiny coffin. Only icy, smothering, enveloping blackness filled her eyes. She fought, striking upward and outward, trying to kick out before the coffin was buried in the ground. Arms caught hers, a voice whispered in her ear. Someone was with her, she was not alone. Frantically, she clutched at the body beside her. "Help me. Help me," she pleaded frantically.

"Hush! You are all right. Everything is well. I will help you. You will not be alone. Go to sleep." The voice whispered in her ear. Lips touched her cheek, her forehead, her mouth.

Clinging tightly to the arms that encircled her, she pressed her face against the face hidden from her by the smothering darkness. She breathed in the scent of the person beside her, curling her body against his.

A warm, strong hand stroked her back and hip, stroked gently again and again until gradually she relaxed. Her fear subsided as the comfort evoked by the caressing hand and voice blended into a dream of other places and other times.

184

When next she opened her eyes, a soft gray light filtered in through the shutters of a window recessed in the wall. The tapestry had been drawn aside to allow the light to enter. A fire burned in the hearth. The room was quite warm, the bed soft. She raised herself to stare around the room. Empty. She looked down at her body; her clean hair streamed over her shoulders and breasts. He had washed her, she remembered, and afterward he had brushed her hair. She lifted her hands and inspected them. Those rough scars would probably be there forever. Great patches of skin were scoured raw on both sides and chilblains encircled the wrists like grim red bracelets. Her hands and forearms were bruised from the guard's beating. She felt her face and decided that it must be all right except for a tender spot on her cheekbone below her left eye.

Hunger gnawed at her insides until her hands began to tremble. She had not been able to eat much last night. She clenched her hands tight and started to push herself off the bed. As she did so, the door opened and Rhiannon strode into the room. Behind him came a wench and two lackeys carrying a tray, a kettle of hot water, and an armload of clothing.

Rhiannon grinned as she hastily jumped back under the covers, pulling them tightly under her chin. "Good morrow, Lady Moira," he said making her a sweeping bow. "I have brought food to break your fast. Will you please to rise and wash?"

Moira glared at him and remained under the covers.

"Ah, but I forget. You are as yet unclad." He spun and dismissed the servants with a wave of his hand. The lackeys left impassively, but the wench stared hard at Moira and then sneered as she went out and closed the door behind them.

Rhiannon turned back to her and walked toward the bed. She braced herself, not daring to think what might

185

come. He was dressed in a long, elegant robe of soft dark blue material belted at the middle with a gold cord. Embroidery decorated the neck and edges of the long full sleeves. His feet were encased in sleek black leather boots. His black hair was brushed back from his forehead and his eyes seemed bluer than ever in his dark, tanned face. To her eyes, he looked alien and altogether frightening. She was at his mercy.

At the side of the bed, he paused to stare down into her upturned face. "Do not be afraid," he soothed. His hand reached out to the covers under her chin and she sucked in her breath. He touched the covers and pulled them down and placed the tips of his fingers on the fillet still bound around her throat. "You are mine," he said softly. "No one else shall touch you and I swear that I will not hurt you." He spoke as if in token of a pledge.

She looked up at him with frightened eyes. Never had she felt so vulnerable. She lay in his bed, naked, his family and cohorts all around. His hand moved from her throat to her shoulder and caressed her gently. As Moira shuddered at his touch, a tiny whisper of sound escaped her lips. She was unable to totally repress her shame and fear.

"'Tis morning," he murmured half to himself, "a time for pleasant things." He made to draw the covers slowly down.

"Oh, no," she whispered, clutching them tightly to her throat.

"Oh, yes," he replied softly. "I want to see you in all your beauty and touch you from your head to your toe. Then I want you to see me and touch me. Then I shall have you, and we will be very, very happy."

Despite the mesmerizing quality of his voice, she gasped, flattening herself tightly against the bed. Her eyes, wide with terror, darted toward the door.

His hands unclenched her fingers one by one. "Moira,

186

you cannot escape. I have had you once. You suffered great pain when you lost your virginity. But you need not again. If you will submit, your feelings will be pleasurable. If not, they may be very painful, but they will still occur."

As he spoke, he peeled the covers down to her waist. The sight of her body stirred him almost unbearably. He trembled as if about to experience his first woman.

Her breasts rose and fell with the urgency of her breathing. "Do not touch me," she commanded futilely.

He stripped the blue robe from his body. "I must, my lady."

"I hate and despise you. Only undying enmity can ever exist between us. How can you say there will be pleasure?"

Her hair fanned out across the pillows. He gathered a lock of it into his hand. "Ah, but there can be." Slowly he wound the hair around his palm as he drew closer to her, bending to her, covering her over. "Do not fight me. Surrender yourself. You have no choice. Even the strongest citadel will surrender if there is no chance. The submission brings with it always the hope of future victory."

His palm rested on her cheek, pale now as snow. Her body trembled. Too little food, too much deprivation, too much emotion. She was unable to struggle against his superior strength and will.

Numbly she turned her head away to the wall.

"You will do as I command," he stated simply.

"Yes," she whispered.

He kissed her forehead, released her hair, and climbed beneath the covers, finding his spot casually as she shuddered with each movement of the bed.

Supporting himself on his elbow, he studied her at leisure, feeding his own desire. Her body was creamy white with soft shadows beneath her breasts, in the hollows of her ribs, in the arch of her abdomen, in the cup of her navel.

"Open your eyes," came his soft voice.

Her ice blue eyes were pools of despair when he looked into them.

"You are very beautiful," he soothed. Moira knew she had touched the depths of humiliation as she lay quiet, submissive, in his bed.

One hard hand with strong, lean fingers reached out and caressed her shoulder, her arm, her soft breast, her narrow waist. With his thumb he pressed against her nipple, circling gently until the small nub of flesh hardened.

Her breath hissed through her teeth as she stared into his eyes in surprise at what his hands had accomplished.

Chuckling softly, he continued his soft circling until she moaned and twisted slightly. "Steady," he commanded. "Lie still. I know this is new to you, but you must learn to submit and obey." Sitting up straight in the bed, he moved his hands down over her belly, concave from the enforced fasting. Gently he stroked her, tickling her soft hair and flesh at the joining of her thighs. Again she trembled beneath his fingers, moaning softly as she slipped farther and farther beyond control.

Abruptly, he bent to her, kissing her fiercely before he drew back.

"Now you shall look at me and touch me!"

He tossed the covers to the foot of the bed, exposing them both. "Now, my lady, see what you have to become accustomed to. Indeed, I do not think either of us will have any trouble becoming used to the other."

White-faced, she studied his lean, hard shoulders and torso, already so familiar to her, scarred and bruised as he had been. The black hair curled crisply across his chest. Rearing up on his knees, he placed his fists on his hips.

The muscles stood out corded and firm in his upper arms. Black hair shadowed his armpits as well. His ribs were covered with a swath of rippling muscle and the cage arched over his flat belly. At that point she could look no lower. Instead, she closed her eyes.

His voice was merciless. "Look, Moira."

And she did. Below his waist line, his hip bones jutted forward and from a nest of black hair his manhood lanced upward. Below that his thighs were like columns, firm, long, and lean.

"Do you like what you see?" he invited. "Perhaps you would like to touch."

"No!" she exclaimed. "I cannot. I will not." Her voice failed her. Embarrassment overcame her. She squeezed her eyes tightly shut.

Instantly, she was lifted into his arms, swept up, and held high on his chest. "Enough. I did not mean to cause you pain. Enough, sweet Moira." His hands stroked her hair and her cheeks.

She could not protest. Her head rolled limply on his shoulder. The strength of his arms, the hardness of his chest tormented her with her own weakness. When he lowered her again to the pillows, her eyes closed. She was almost unconscious.

He was gone for a moment, then knelt again at her side and raised her shoulders. "A sip of this, Moira. Drink, dear girl."

Helplessly she obeyed him and brandy warmed her lips. Sipping slowly, she felt it burn her throat and revive her failing senses. "False strength," she muttered, remembering the nausea she had experienced when she had sought to escape him.

"'Twill serve," he replied sardonically.

His weight came down beside her in the bed and he gathered her against him. "Now," he said, "we begin.

You have much to learn about pleasure. Your life has been the spartan life of a man. Your father spared you nothing in your upbringing. I think there is very little in your past life of pleasure. Is that true?"

"My father was good to me," she whispered, leaping to deny Rhiannon's accusation. "He made me hard. The very strength of which you boast was created in a stern setting."

"My father was good to me, too," he argued. "He made me brave, but he did not deny me pleasure." As he spoke, he began to caress her breasts.

When she would have answered him, his mouth closed over hers in a deep, lingering kiss. Gently his tongue caressed the inside of her mouth, tasting the brandy. She pressed her hands up against his shoulders, but his weight was too much for her. Her hands slid upward to lie limply across his back.

With one hand, he supported her head and caressed her breast while with the other he played his fingers up and back over her belly, teasingly touching the soft joining of her thighs and then withdrawing.

She felt awake only in the sense that her body was being tormented. Her sense of self was dimmed. She felt only that she was a body submitting to these pleasant manipulations over which she had no control. Her nipple hardened under his fingers. He bent his head to kiss it, then took it into his mouth and pressed his teeth around it in a soft bite which made her squirm.

Suddenly she was aware that her thighs had relaxed and lay open to his questing fingers. Immediately she tensed, brought them together, but he raised his head and whispered against the side of her mouth.

"Do not, sweetheart. Do not close to me. You enjoy it so. Relax. Your body wants this more than it has ever wanted anything. Open your thighs."

His breath against the sensitive corner of her mouth made her turn her head from side to side, seeking to get away from the tickling. Again before she was aware of her actions, her thighs had opened and she had half raised one knee.

"You see," her devil tormented her, his breath hot in her ear. "You see. You want this. You want me."

"No," Moira whimpered. "No."

"Ah, yes," he replied, nibbling down the side of her throat to take her nipple between his teeth. "Say it."

"No," she cried, pressing against him with her hands.

"Say it," he insisted, nipping her with his sharp white teeth.

Shaking her head wildly, she thrust her fingers into his tousled black hair.

"If you pull my hair, I will bite you until you let go," he warned against her breast.

Her fingers relaxed, then stirred convulsively. She felt wildly excited within herself. Waves of feeling coursed up from some central point inside of her to spread throughout her body which writhed as if it had a will of its own.

Rhiannon's left arm had slipped under her right leg bending it back up to her chest. Gently he slipped his right arm from under her head and began to play with the now open area between her legs. Tenderly he pressed against the spot which she had not known she possessed. She cried out in surprise and delight and arched her body up to meet him.

"Open your eyes," he commanded. "There will be no pretense between you and me."

Her eyes flew open to meet his gaze.

He swiftly moved himself to kneel between her legs. "Draw both legs up now," he ordered, again pressing his fingers against her and gently rubbing.

He positioned himself carefully at the entrance to her body. She was trembling now with passion and fear, all thoughts of mastery and submission swept from her mind by the sensations he was building within her. As she met his eyes, she realized that he was trembling, too, experiencing the same sort of feelings. Shocked, she realized Rhiannon felt for her as she felt for him.

"No pretense," she whispered and smiled timidly, her soft mouth curving, her blue eyes crinkling at the corners, her whole face reflecting her acceptance.

Smoothly he drove himself into her body, his eyes closed in the intensity of his pleasure. This time there was no pain, so carefully had Rhiannon prepared her. Curiously she watched him, observing the hard set of his jaw, the strained look of concentration on his face as he began to move within her. Perhaps her sensations were less because she was so in awe of the expression on his face.

Then she became aware of the fullness stirring tender sensations within her own body. She drew herself tighter around him, instinctively matching his moves with her own in an effort to achieve something. She knew not what.

Steadily he thrust, the cords standing out on his neck, the muscles rippling in his shoulders as he braced himself on either side of her head. Then suddenly, he seemed to lose control. He was moving wildly in her, gasping for breath, sweat standing out on his brow and dripping down onto her breasts. When he shuddered and gasped, she felt him thrust inside her with an almost painful force. Then he was slipping down, relaxing against her.

She felt vaguely disappointed. Was there nothing for her that could equal that?

In a few moments he seemed to regain himself and pull himself out of her body. He gathered her warm against him and arranged the pillow. "Sweet," he whispered in her ear. "Sweet. You will have your joy complete when you are more experienced. Be patient."

What could he mean? Could it be that she would suffer as he did? For he seemed to be suffering, gasping and shuddering as he did. And yet she felt she wanted something more.

Twenty

While Moira lay musing, Rhiannon roused himself and rolled aside, relieving her of the last of his weight.

"I must get you some breakfast," he murmured dreamily. "I was selfish to exact such a toll on your body, but oh, my lady, it was wonderful."

Not knowing how to react, she stirred restlessly.

With a last kiss and a sigh, he rose and sought his robe at the foot of the bed. Belting it around his lean middle, he crossed the room to the chest. Moving its contents carefully, he withdrew a folded garment. As he returned, he let it unfold. The robe he displayed was the twin of the one he wore except it was a rich rust brown, trimmed with gold embroidery and gold braid.

"Stand up," he commanded brusquely, "and get into this so we can eat."

Carefully she sat up in bed, holding the covers against her chin and reached for the robe.

"No," he said, softly holding it out of her reach. "You are mine; a slave should not be modest before her master. I want to see you this morning in good light. There may be hurts on your body that need tending to."

194

She bowed her head and pressed her doubled fists against her mouth. Her humiliation would be deep-scarring, she realized.

"Come," he commanded peremptorily. "'Twould be the work of an instant to strip the covers from the bed and see you at your barest. Do as I bid you and we can eat together in perfect charity. You know you must come to it sooner or later."

She raised her eyes to his. Deep blue met ice blue and clashed. Then she flung back the covers and in a single lithe motion slid from the bed to stand before him. What difference whether she stood or lay before him naked? Bravely, she clenched her fists and threw back her head. The long brown mane whipped around her shoulders; her breath was coming fast, causing her breasts to rise and fall. She sucked her stomach in tightly, trying to control her shivering as cold draughts played around her feet and ankles.

A grin of pure pleasure lighted his face. He reached out his hand to take her wrist, but shifted his grip when he saw its pitiful condition. Pulling her away from the bed, he loosed her and walked around her slowly. His hand rested briefly on her shoulders, brushing the heavy hair aside and seeing where black and blue bruises showed from the beating. He ran his hand down her spine and rested it for a moment on the curve of her buttock. As he came to a stop in front of her again, he gazed his fill at her breasts, small and lovely, the nipples standing erect from the cold air seeping through the shutters.

Shivering, she watched the play of expression in his eyes and about his lean mouth. Again, he put out his hand and gently passed it over her left breast. She steeled herself and clenched her teeth. He moved his palm against the nipple. Still shy at his touch, she nevertheless felt a peculiar sensation almost of pleasure rippling through her body.

195

Unable to understand the sensations that only increased her tension, she was almost at the end of her endurance. She must twist away if he continued for an instant more. Suddenly, he dropped his hand, sighed, and held the robe for her to slip over her head. Despite her height, it covered her slender figure like a tent from neck to floor. Still grinning again, he belted it around her and led her to the bench beside the fire.

"The water is probably only lukewarm," he apologized ruefully, "but wash your wrists carefully anyway. 'Twill sting a bit because I have placed a cup of salt in it. Sailors use salt water to wash their wounds and they never get the sickness that causes the muscles to go rigid and the mouth to clamp shut. We use it all the time in this keep for bathing wounds and we are all healthy."

Moira pushed back her sleeves and thrust her hands into the water as he instructed. As the warm saline solution touched her wrists, she gasped and moaned, but did not withdraw them. Gingerly, she laved them, rubbing at the chilblains and the raw skin. "Oh," she moaned through set teeth. "It hurts. Are you sure this is really the thing to do?"

Rhiannon sat down on the bench beside her. "Keep soaking them. As soon as we have finished here, we will go downstairs to the blacksmith and let him cut these irons off me." He raised his manacled wrists for her inspection. "Then we will come back here to the apartment and you can hear me yelp." He grinned at her in the way she had come to know.

"I am sure this is some new torture you have devised for me," she grumbled as he reached for his tankard of ale.

"Come! Drink it down in one gulp and come with me."

"I cannot," she spoke practically. "I have no shoes. My boots and all my clothes are gone. What did you do with them?"

196

He struck his forehead with his hand. "I sent them to be cleaned and polished and mended." He thought for a minute. "Wait! I have just the thing." He dove into his chest in the corner and came up with a pair of strange-shaped scarlet and gold embroidered slippers with turned-up toes. "Try these," he chuckled. "They are too small for me. A peddler brought them through here years ago. Mother bought pairs of them for Edain and me. Edain wore hers out, of course, but I could not feel comfortable in them and then I outgrew them. If Edain had known I still had these, she would have had them, but I forgot until just now."

Moira braced herself against the table and slipped one on her foot. It fitted after a fashion but felt strange. In what shop had this shoe been made? she wondered.

As if he read her mind, Rhiannon spoke, "I think he said they came from Outremer. The peddler came from there. Indeed, he had silks and velvets the like of which Mother had never seen. She went mad. Father had to drag her away. There may still be some of that stuff in the bower. We will see it later if you are interested."

She put the other slipper on her foot.

"Come now, let us go. Do not be afraid. Remember you belong to me." As he faced her, his hands adjusted the fillet so that the body of the bird rested in the hollow of her throat and the wings swept back around her neck.

His face was serious. "This may hurt like sin and I need my companion with me."

Walking beside him through corridors, down stairs, and out across the bailey to the blacksmith's forge, Moira was aware of stares and sneers from men and women alike. Holding herself proudly, she pretended to ignore the looks. They were, after all, her enemies, as she was theirs. If any one of them were in her father's power, he would treat them the same.

Inside the forge, the smith studied the manacles

thoughtfully. "Truly, my lord, I do not see anything for it but to saw them off. I could split them, but I might slip and split your hand, too. No. 'Twill be an arduous task, but that is the only way that is safe."

Nodding, Rhiannon bade him get on with it.

"Set yourself down here and lay your arm on the anvil. I will get my file and clippers. Mayhap when I get it through enough, I can clip the rest and hasten the task."

So saying, he fell to. Moira watched for some minutes as the screeching of the file played along their nerves. Rhiannon had set his wrist firmly against the anvil and grasped the manacle in his other hand, but it twisted back and forth, biting and abrading the already-raw skin. At the same time, the iron began to heat and soon the metal became too hot to hold.

Moira could bear the sight of his suffering face no longer. "Fool!" she shouted at the smith. "Pour water over it to cool it! If you have such little care of your horses, I am surprised that there are any who can walk without laming up."

Rhiannon slumped back as the smith went to get water. "I said I needed my companion with me," he smiled wanly. He raised his arm and flexed it where it had been stretched out straight so long. A ring of blood stained the bandage although the manacle was not yet halfway through.

After the smith cooled the iron, Moira placed her fingers around Rhiannon's. "Together we will hold this. Otherwise this fool will have worried your arm off before he gets the thing through. What an ill-equipped shop! Not even a vise to lock this into."

"My protector," he grunted, leaning his forehead against her shoulder. She could not jerk away because to do so would let the manacle slip. She stood bent over by his side while the file screamed and the iron heated.

Finally, the smith drew back, took his heavy metal clippers with which he clipped off the tips of horseshoe nails, inserted them between metal and flesh, and split the iron neatly. With tongs, he bent the manacle back enough for Rhiannon's wrist to finally slip free. Sweat stood out on the brows of all three as they braced themselves for the second ordeal.

Another half an hour passed before the second manacle fell away and Rhiannon rose. Grimly, he thanked the smith and throwing his arm around Moira's shoulders, stumbled from the forge into the pale sunlight.

"We must go back up to your room immediately," she told him. "The wounds in your wrists are open and the water he used to cool the iron was not clean. Do you trust me to care for you? Surely your mother and sister would have better heart for it than I."

"No," he shook his head, smiling down into her face. "I want you." Recovered somewhat, he removed his arm from her shoulder, but he carried his arms carefully in front of him as if they strained him, his left arm particularly.

Back in his apartment, Rhiannon slowly collapsed on the bed, his feet hanging off, his arms lying relaxed across his middle.

Sympathetically, Moira brought a cup of sweet ale to his side. He opened his eyes and smiled his thanks. Hunching himself up on one elbow, he drank thirstily.

"Come to the fireside and I will unwrap those wrists and see the damage," Moira directed.

There she uncovered the wounds. They were worse than he had imagined, terribly bruised and scoured, swollen from impaired circulation or from infection she could not tell. When the lackey brought the hot salt water, Rhiannon thrust his hands into the kettle with a quick grimace. A muffled yowl escaped him and she grinned at him. "Relax," she bade him, refilling his cup of ale and holding it for him to drink.

"That goes better," he said after a lusty pull. "Have some yourself, Moira."

She tilted the pitcher of ale, poured her own cup, and drank slowly. Moving to his side, she set down her cup and selected strips of linen to wrap his wrists. When she had laid them out neatly beside herself, she picked up a linen towel. He gave her his hands one at a time to dry and bandage with clean linen. When she was through, he called for his lackey to clear away the mess and bring broken meats and bread for a light meal.

As they ate together, she began to be aware again of his appraisal of her person. She could not meet his eyes, but kept steadfastly concentrating on her bread. To her relief, before the meal was finished a messenger knocked at the door, summoning Rhiannon to wait upon his father.

He stood up abruptly and strode to the door. "Do not leave this room while I am gone. Rest on the bed. Sleep in comfort and warmth. When I return, we will plan together."

She said nothing nor did she look at him. The door closed. Jumping from her chair, she ran to the window. Throwing the shutters aside, she leaned into the aperture some two feet thick. A drop of fifty feet yawned below her to a precarious slide of rock dropping farther to the valley floor, farther still to a clump of scant trees, and then farther still to the sea. Rhiannon's rooms were at the back of the keep. Her only escape here would be to death.

Sliding her body back into the room, she turned to the small door to the right and found, as she had suspected, a private room for the toilet stool. Blushing furiously at the implied intimacy of her presence in his private apartments, she backed from the room, closed the door, and pressed against it, looking around hastily.

In the main chamber, she knelt at Rhiannon's chest. Perhaps it contained a knife, something with which she could arm herself against her enemies.

Suddenly, her body slumped and she let the lid fall. What difference if she found a knife? She could not fight her way out of the keep with a knife. She could perhaps kill Rhiannon, but to what purpose? If she killed him, she must kill herself or be sure to die in a terrible agony of vengeance imposed by his father. She did not even have any clothing. Surely this brown cassock and scarlet silk slippers would not protect her from the cold. She might be able to slip down in the dead of night to the stable and steal a horse, but she would not be able to ride it past the guards and get out of the keep.

Disconsolately, she rose and moved to the bed. She would rest until he returned. Perhaps he would reconsider . . .

Her thoughts interrupted themselves. He would take her again tonight! Humiliation tormented her as she clenched her fist and gritted her teeth. He would climb into the bed with her and use her as he had done today. She could not bear it. She would not. Surely, death was preferable to this thing which she must endure not just once, but again and again until her father sent messengers with a ransom and an exchange could be arranged. Further, a sly voice whispered inside her that the humiliation would become worse each time, for she would become more eager for the gentle caresses, the physical pleasure of touch and kiss. The whole experience would insidiously affect her will.

She flew to the window. Let him find her body on the rocks below. Moira opened the shutters and gazed down. The door opened behind her and she spun around.

A lackey stood in the door, a smirk on his face. "I came for the tray," he announced. Ambling across the room, he gathered up the cups and remains of the meal.

Moira watched with caution as the man moved around the room, straightening and tidying, pulling the bed-covers in place, emptying the slops in the privy room. Finally finished, he left with his various burdens without a word or bow.

As the door closed behind him, Moira dropped down weakly on the bed. Her body shook. Would she really have had the courage to throw herself from the window? She lay on the bed with closed eyes.

She awoke with a start as Rhiannon entered the room. Her overstrained nerves had only allowed a light sleep. She sprang from the bed as if it were hot and stood beside it, swaying dizzily.

The room was dark and cold. Rhiannon knelt at the hearth and blew up the fire. Moira moved slowly across the room, stopping to take the branch of candles from the table and to hold them out to him as he pulled a brand from the fire.

When the candles were lighted, she returned them to the table and sat in the chair facing him.

"Father is upset that I have you with me in my room," he said. "Owen Llewellyn and others have been talking to him. They want to imprison you in the dungeon until a ransom can be offered. Owen wants . . ." he paused.

"What does he want?" Moira asked softly.

"Owen wants your eyes."

Moira drew in her breath and clutched the arms of her chair. "I have done nothing to him. Why this unreasoning hatred of me?"

"His wife and three sons were traveling with him in a company to make pilgrimage to Palmerston Abbey where his wife's kin were buried. A band of raiders fell upon them to steal the gold offerings they carried. The boys were struck down like so many rabbits in the field. The attendants, too. Owen was wounded so terribly that they thought him dead. His stomach was slit open. He lay in his blood and watched them rape his wife. She screamed for mercy, prayed for God's help. Finally, she prayed for death. Then she died."

Moira bent her head and shuddered.

Rhiannon raised his eyes. "To be truthful, no one really knows who perpetrated the raid. We found him, brought him back here. Somehow he survived. I think he lives on hatred and vengeance. He cannot die until he has cleansed his soul. He has sworn an oath to destroy all of Lorne. But no one knows whether your father's men did the deed or someone else. Owen is—" he spread his hands helplessly. "Perhaps he adopted our enemies as his own and little by little they became the murderers. He is berserk."

"What will you do with me?"

Rhiannon smiled and shook off his grim mood. "Why, you are mine! I have told my father that I won you and that I intend to keep you to please myself. I reminded him that I have never brought back a slave, nor have I asked any shares of the spoils that have been taken. He wants to see you at supper tonight. We will eat in the private family room in Mother's quarters."

He held out his hand to her. "Come, my companion. They may be a bit unfriendly at first, but they will get used to the idea that you are going to be with me wherever we go from now on."

Moira backed away. "I *will* be ransomed by my father," she averred. "He *will* send messengers. They are undoubtedly on their way." She paused, struck by an awful thought. "Unless he does not know that I am here."

"He does not know," Rhiannon's teeth flashed in his wolfish grin. "He thinks us lost or dead. He believes he bluffed my father at Lorne Rock, causing him to withdraw the attack."

Moira's shoulders slumped.

"Come," Rhiannon reached out and took her hand. She followed where he led.

Twenty-One

At the door of the bower through which were the private apartments of the Lady Branwen, Rhiannon paused and turned Moira to face him. With proprietary hands, he brushed her long brown mane behind her shoulders and adjusted the fillet around her neck. "I must get you a mirror," he said softly, "and I also must get something else for your throat." He ran his hands back through his black hair. "I need my band when I ride."

At his insistent handling of her, her ice blue eyes flashed fire at him. Ignoring her expression, he put his hands on her shoulders. "No one I have ever seen or heard of has a slave like you. Everyone will envy me . . . once they get used to the idea." With a delighted chuckle, he dropped his hand into hers and opened the door. Together they entered the bower and crossed to a small stairway, winding up into a curtained alcove which served as the antechamber to the private apartments.

The other three members of the family awaited them. Lord Gethin sat in a wide carved chair, a chalice in his hand. His brows were drawn together in a scowl. His lips narrowed in a hard line as Rhiannon led Moira into the room.

Lady Branwen sat at her embroidery frame opposite her husband. In the light of the working candles, her expression was impassive. Her face was framed by a white linen coif upon which sat a blue embroidered cap and veil. The decoration on the cap was repeated in the design around the neck of her overdress of blue wool. Her undergown, with sleeves extending to her wrists, was of white sendal, fine and shimmering. Her eyes of soft brown, so unusual in her pale face, lighted as Rhiannon entered the room.

Rhiannon's sister, Edain, was likewise dressed in blue, but of the plainer shade of woad. Her hair was brushed and hanging free down her back. She rose from her place beside her mother and came forward to greet them.

"Brother, you have kept us waiting. You know how I hate to be hungry. Is this your slave? Margwin said that you were bewitched and that she should be burned and you exorcised." She looked at Moira rather fearfully. "Are you a witch?"

Moira drew back, but Rhiannon answered for her. "No, Moira is not a witch, but she is a very brave lady who is going to be my companion." He spoke this loudly. His father showed no sign of having heard except to lift his chalice and drink deeply.

Rhiannon kissed his sister on the cheek and crossed to the embroidery frame to kiss his mother. Lady Branwen raised her mouth to her son and smiled. "We are blessed by God to have you safely returned to us. I have made prayers for you almost from the day you left on that venture. You are our dearest hope."

Rhiannon dropped to one knee beside her. "Mother, I was in great danger and near death many times and this lady saved my life. Moira of Lorne, come forward." He rose and led her into the light.

206

Lady Branwen regarded Moira coolly. "You have dressed her in your garments, Rhys. Is she really a woman?"

Coloring beneath her words, Moira threw back her head. Lord Gethin snorted. "Too tall. Like a man. A witch perhaps, or a warlock."

Edain drew near to touch Moira's hair. At the touch, Moira whirled around. Edain drew back in fear.

Lord Gethin sprang from his chair. "By God! You will return her to the dungeon. If we can get a ransom for her from Lorne, then perhaps I will send her back. Otherwise she can rot there or be sold as a slave. I say you will not make her your companion or whatever you call your whore and parade her before your mother and your sister."

Rhiannon was white to the lips with fury. "She is mine! I captured her! We rode together through hell. I would have been dead twice at least had she not helped me. Her nature is gentle and tender for a suffering human being. I will not throw her back in the dungeon to freeze and die!"

Gethin took a stride that brought him almost chest to chest with his tall son. "You would defy me?"

Lady Branwen spoke from beside the embroidery frame, "My husband, dinner is about to be served. I have gone to great pains to order your favorite foods. We will sit and eat and remember that we are a happy family and give thanks that we are all together." Smoothly she interposed her soft body between them and led Gethin to the small table erected in the alcove beyond the embroidery frame.

"Edain, bid the squire serve the first course. Rhys, will you sit?"

Only four places were set at the table beautifully draped with white cloth. Silver bowls, spoons, and knives shone under the soft candle glow.

Rhiannon took his place beside his mother. Gethin and Edain sat in the other two high-backed chairs. Lady Branwen indicated a small chair behind and to the left of Rhiannon. "Sit," she ordered Moira. When Rhiannon would have protested, his mother interposed smoothly, "By your own admission, she is your slave. You surely do not expect that she would share the table with your family."

The squire entered with a steaming kettle in his hand and ladled rich cheese soup into the bowls. Accompanying him was the small lackey that had brought the towels the night before to Rhiannon's room. He carried a plate containing the finest white bread Moira had ever seen. The family waited while Gethin blessed the meal and then began to eat.

Moira's mouth watered as she gazed with incredulous eyes at the table and the food. Never had she seen the like. Her father's board was never covered with cloth; they ate all their meals from loaves of black bread hollowed out and filled with whatever unappetizing mass of vegetables and broken meats the cook might have prepared that day. Her father drank wine from a silver chalice, but never had she seen such elegant bowls as well.

After dipping his thumb into the butter which reposed in a silver dish beside the salt, Rhiannon handed Moira a piece of the white bread, liberally smeared. She accepted it and bowed her head. Her humiliation was complete. Never had she thought to accept food from his hand like a pet dog. She could not take a bite. Her throat swelled with pain at the recognition of her humble position.

"How did a woman save your life, Rhys?" asked Edain, her bright blue eyes sparkling with interest.

"Why, we were set upon in the hut of an old woman," her brother replied, addressing the table. "We were sleeping and when we awoke six villains had us pinned with knives at our throats. They dragged us out and divided our clothes and were deciding who would kill me and dishonor the lady. I was chained and her hands were bound behind her. We were in a bad way. But I untied her hands while they drank themselves into a stupor. I told her to run while I attacked them with the chains, but she came off the floor, grabbed a rake, and smashed the skull of the one who was making for my back. That is why I would rather have her as my companion than some of the friends I know."

Edain's eyes grew big with admiration. "I would have been too afraid to even open my eyes. How can a woman be so brave?"

Her father grunted, "'Tis not natural. She was unwomanly."

"But our son lives. Perhaps she was too manly, but they are both alive and he has returned to us," said Branwen quietly, as she signaled the squire to clear away the bowls and bring in the next course.

"More wine," called Gethin. A second squire appeared carrying a large pitcher. Dark golden wine splashed into the cups and Gethin drank deeply.

A large platter was set ceremoniously in the center of the table. Small fowl roasted, salted, and spiced with marjoram, sweet basil, and pepper, were arranged on the plate with a few baked apples and pears, the last of the winter's crop.

Helping himself liberally, Rhiannon grinned with obvious enjoyment. "Pheasant!" he exclaimed. "Mother, you will make me fat and lazy." She smiled her pleasure.

Gethin and Edain helped themselves and the lord began a long comment about the political situation in South Wales now that the English king Edward I had named his son Edward Prince of Wales. "There is no more Wales in the south," he declared. "Only in the north, here on this coast, does Wales exist. 'Tis important that we remain strong. We must acquire more land to combat the power of the puppets in South Wales. With Lorne's lands and holdings, we could have a force to remain at peace. Too strong for the English to trifle with."

Tense, Moira glanced at him from under her eyelashes. That explained the raid by Rhiannon. A trial of strength. Proudly, she thought that her father had not been found easy.

"In a way, that one may be our key to success," he continued, chuckling. "Yes, I had not realized before. We will use her to bring Lorne to terms. Say you she is his only whelp?"

Rhiannon nodded quietly. He sliced a bit of meat from the breast of the bird on his plate and speared it efficiently with his knife. He was carrying it to his mouth when he changed his mind and passed it to Moira. Stubbornly, she turned her head aside, refusing to take the bite from the blade. Turning, he saw the bread in her hand uneaten. Shrugging, he ate the bite himself.

Gethin shook his head sadly. "But she is a woman. The best we can hope for is a ransom that will supply a few bowmen and the return of our own lads held captive."

The third course was a salad of cabbage and onion garnished with small black olives which had come all the way from Provence. Both Edain and Rhiannon picked the olives out and ate them first, spitting the seeds into the rushes on the floor. Rhiannon bade Moira open her mouth.

"What is it?" she asked curiously.

"An olive. Open your mouth. Have you never had such before?"

She shook her head and opened her mouth obediently, her curiosity overcoming her shame. When she bit into it, her teeth immediately encountered the rocklike center.

210

"Do not swallow the seed," giggled Edain. "A trader comes into Colwyn Bay every so often from the south of France. Mother goes mad buying the most amazing things to eat. He brings things especially for her now, knowing that she will buy them. One time she bought sugar from Levant. It was in lumps and so sweet. But I like honey better."

With the olive, Moira's appetite awakened and she felt dizzy from the lack of food. Surreptitiously, she took a bite of the white bread and butter. Never had she tasted anything quite so good.

Rhiannon's mouth curved into a smile as he toasted his mother with a raised wine chalice. "Mother, you have outdone yourself."

Smiling lovingly at them, Branwen signaled for the next course. The small filets of beef were served in a tureen, simmering in a rich sauce spiced with pepper in the manner of the Crusaders. A young lackey brought more silver bowls and the squire ladled the pieces into the vessels.

Rhiannon cut another piece and held it out to Moira. She reached for it with her fingers, but he withdrew it, shook his head. "With your mouth," he insisted.

Edain giggled again. "She will be like a favorite dog."

Gethin roused himself from his plate. "She should not be sitting here. She is either slave or prisoner. She should not be in the room with the family."

Branwen placed her hand on his arm. "Let him have his little pet for now, my lord. You can only fix his determination by this protest. He will tire of her in a few days."

Rhiannon scowled at his family. "She will be taught to serve me well," he insisted defensively.

He cut another piece of meat, sopped a piece of bread in the sauce, and topped it with the meat. Turning, he gave it to her again, making her take it with her mouth from his hand.

Moira's face was white to the lips. Her hunger was imperative, but her shame was profound. Suddenly, she could endure no longer. Defiantly, she spat the bite out onto the floor.

The four stared at her. Only Rhiannon did not seem surprised. He had tried her sorely, but his aim was to put her in her place, to make her acknowledge in front of his father who was master.

"Your pardon, Lady Mother," he said as he rose. "Down on your knees!" he commanded.

"No!" she hissed. "Enough of this play. Let your father return me to the dungeon."

"You will be my slave, as I have said. Down on your knees!" he thundered.

She sat stubbornly glaring her defiance, her eyes chips of ice.

His hand flashed out and grasped the fillet around her neck. Twisting it, he pulled her off the chair onto the rushes on the floor. He reseated himself at the table, cut another piece of meat, and offered it to her. She was now beside him on her knees, her face at the table level, for all the world like an intelligent bitch. She would not open her mouth, she vowed. Although hunger along with the tension of the struggle was making her faint, she refused the meat.

He set down his knife and grasped the fillet again in his left hand. With his right, he cuffed her across the mouth.

While Edain and Branwen stared fascinated and Gethin chuckled delightedly, Rhiannon transferred his hold to her cheeks and forced her mouth open by pressing in against her teeth. Then with her mouth open, he popped the bit inside.

"Do not spit it out," he commanded. "I shall replace it with hot pepper if you do."

Their eyes clashed. Blue sparks seemed to jump

between them; then Moira nodded her head slowly and began to chew.

The family relaxed. Edain laughed a bright, tinkling laugh. Branwen smiled and congratulated her son. Gethin's laughter roared out loudest of all. "Humility! God's bones! That will teach her."

When they had finished the meat, Lady Branwen signaled for the final course, a pastry filled with jelly and flavored with rosewater. As they ate, again Rhiannon dipped his spoon into the mixture and held it to Moira's mouth. His eyes met hers, threatening reprisal if she refused. With a sigh of acceptance, she obediently opened her mouth and he tipped the delicacy in.

She could never remember anything that tasted quite that good before. Her eyes closed as she savored it, allowing it to melt in her mouth. Nothing she had ever eaten could compare with the strange and wonderful bites of food she had been given from this table. She opened her eyes to find Rhiannon's eyes again upon her with a smile in them. Another bite was on the spoon before her lips. Without hesitation she accepted it, swallowing eagerly.

Rhiannon smiled again with a nonchalant wave of his hand. "You see," he said. "Tamed to my hand."

Gethin rose angrily. "You will not keep her in your room as your body slave. She will kill you if she gets the chance. You can never trust her."

"Your father is right, Rhys," said his mother softly. "She is not a bitch, but a woman. She is your most hated enemy."

"When she gets through with you, she could slip into our chambers and kill your mother and me, your little sister."

"She will do no such thing. She is mine, my slave." Rhiannon stood up. "Have I not shown you her obedience? She is but new to her state. Give her time."

"No!" Gethin's face was furiously red, his breath stentorious.

"I say yes! She has saved my life. I will not throw her back into the dungeon to rot or freeze. You have your slave in your chambers. What is Margwin? Who is she that you would parade her before your lady wife and your daughter?"

Lord Gethin's face went white. His anger was such that he clasped his hand convulsively against his chest. "You dare!" he gasped. "You dare to speak to me so!" Branwen sprang forward to catch his arm as he tottered back and to place her shoulder against him to help him into his seat.

"For pity's sake!" she exclaimed. "Go! Take that creature and leave us. He has had too much to drink and his head is too full of vengeance. You do not think of *his* brother and *his* father. Too much blood has been spilled by the kin of that one. Get her out of his sight!"

"She'll kill us all," muttered Gethin. "Your mother's blood will be on your head."

"By your leave, Lady Mother," said Rhiannon, bowing. Silently, Moira followed him across the room to the door. Together they walked across the dark bower.

Twenty-Two

"Help me to get away," Moira whispered. "You can see that I can never stay here with you as you want me to."

"No," Rhiannon said. "We will return to *our* rooms. To let you escape would be to no purpose. You heard my father. He needs Lorne lands to hold Wales in the north against the English. You are the key."

They walked in silence to the door of his room. Once inside, Rhiannon sat down in his chair. "Pour me ale, Moira, for I must think long and clearly. You must help me."

"I?" she gasped. "What can I do?"

"Why, together we shall plan what I shall do to keep you with me and pacify my father."

"The dungeon."

"You would die. I will not let you go. You could have run twice and left me. *I will not let you leave me.* You belong to me. What I take, I keep."

He quaffed the ale she handed him.

Suddenly he smiled. A wolfish grin curled his lips back from his white teeth. Moira glanced at him and then stared.

215

"What does the smile mean, my lord?" she asked warily.

"In the morning will be soon enough for you to know." His eyes narrowed speculatively. "Now for more pleasant things."

"What things?" She rose and backed away.

"Why, you and me, sweetheart."

"Oh, no," she whispered. But even as she said the words, she realized that she lied.

He came toward her matter-of-factly, as if their lovemaking were a normal thing. "No, sweetheart, do not fight me. My body craves your warm beautiful self in bed beside me. Come, take off your robe and let me ease this craving." He kissed her on the ear and nibbled down her neck. At the same time, his hands caressed her shoulders and gathered her against his chest. She moaned in protest, but his hand slipped down her back to tug upward on the skirt of the brown robe. In a swift movement, he pulled it up, stripping her efficiently with a naturalness that forestalled her nervousness.

A wave of anticipation swept through her. She could not be afraid that he would hurt her. The experience of the morning had been pleasant somehow. Further, his presence, the hard male body, had created a strange tingling excitement which she could not identify.

"Tonight, sweetheart, I shall take a long time to love you. You will begin to feel more of what it means to be a woman. Perhaps you will feel it all," he nuzzled her throat and then brushed her breast with his hard hand.

She could do nothing but twist in his arms as he pressed one hand into the small of her back while the other cupped her breast. His lean fingers played with her nipple until it stood hard and erect. Pressed against his body, she could feel his manhood hardening. Soon he would strip off his own clothes and take her. But for now, ripples of feeling were coursing through her veins and muscles in response to the insistent play upon her nipple. She threw back her head and gasped for air, for she seemed to require more as heat engulfed her body.

"Please," she gasped. "Let me go."

"Not yet, sweetheart," was the reply. His mouth replaced his hand on her breast. His lips closed over her nipple, sucking it between his teeth and nipping it.

She gave a little cry of anguish as she twisted and writhed in his arms. His hand slid down to splay over her firm white belly. He rubbed it too with the palm of his hand, allowing his fingers to tickle the tuft of hair at the base. In her desire to breathe, she tossed her head back and forth on her shoulders, emitting little whimpering cries and gasps.

Suddenly, he released her and she fell to her knees, unable to stand from the weakness engendered by his fondling. Her whole body trembled as he stood over her and removed his clothing. Her eyes were closed as shudder after shudder ripped through her body. She could not understand what was happening.

She felt his hands under her arms, raising her to her feet. She opened her eyes. Gently, he pushed her back into his chair and pulled off one of the strange embroidered shoes. Cupping her left heel in his hand, he trailed his fingers across her sole, studying her face closely with his wolfish grin lighting his eyes. She shivered, then jumped as she sought to draw her foot away.

"Ticklish," he observed with satisfaction. "'Tis well. The more sensitive your skin, the more pleasure you will feel."

At last, when she thought she could bear no more, he pulled off her other shoe and stood her on her feet. Leading her naked to the bed, he laid her face down across the coverlet. When she would have struggled, he placed his hands firmly on her shoulder blades. "You are not to resist," he commanded softly as he began to massage her back and shoulders. At first she did not respond, but he moved lower and gripped her buttocks in his two hands, alternately squeezing and releasing. Helplessly in response to his ministrations, she began to moan and press her body down and then up in the rhythm of his play.

"Does that feel good, sweetheart?" he whispered close to her ear. "Do you begin to understand why I want you so badly and why I wanted you so that I could not deny myself in that stable? Do you want me? Do you ache inside?"

She did not reply but sought futilely to quell her response to his fingers which were now parting her thighs and rubbing and caressing her inner parts.

He kissed her buttocks and pressed his mouth and teeth and tongue against first one tense white mount and then the other.

A little cry broke from her. "What are you doing to me?"

"Making a woman from a girl." He laughed and turned her over. "And making you understand how it will always be between you and me."

He straddled her and lowered his buttocks onto her upper thighs so that his weight held her legs and lower body immobile. The heat from his lower body penetrated her and surrounded her, joining between her thighs, adding to her increasing distress. She felt on fire, as if she had a high fever, and she could not catch her breath.

Gently, sitting up straight, he began to play with her breasts with both hands. Nervously, she gripped his hands by the wrists and sought to fend him off.

"No," he commanded her sternly. "Put your hands above your head or at your sides. You are not to interfere in any way. That is my command to my slave."

Hesitantly, she released his wrists and placed her

hands at her sides. He grinned at her and continued to squeeze her breasts and pinch and press her nipples. When she would have raised her hands involuntarily as she writhed in the most exquisite torture, he stopped and leaned forward slightly from his knees. "Slip your hands palm up between my thighs and calves," he commanded. When she did so, he again lowered his body, thereby gripping her hands and holding them tightly within his flesh.

Waves of thrilling feelings, heightened by her realization of how total her bondage was to him, swept over her body, leaving her weak and whimpering in their wake. She could scarcely move, except to convulsively fling her head from side to side and arch her chest under his implacable hands. "Stop! Stop!" she cried. "You will kill me, if you continue. You are murdering me!"

He laughed exultantly. "No, my dear, you have a long way to go before you die."

He eased himself forward slightly and began to press himself down against her with his hips while he continued the subtle ministrations to her breasts. As he touched her, he called to her, "Look, sweetheart, look what you do to me with your sweet body."

She looked at his protuberant muscle, raising itself erect above her flat white belly. Moaning, she closed her eyes, but he would not allow her to keep them closed.

Sharply, he pinched her nipple. "Look, I said."

She gasped and looked at him. Briefly, she struggled to free her hands, but desisted to stare fascinated as his hands left her breasts and moved lower to part and caress and feel her ever-moistening body.

In the same manner that he had done her breasts, he caressed her, squeezing and pulling and parting. He pressed his thumb over and over against the spot of flesh which throbbed and pulsated with a life of its own between her thighs. Until last night, she had not known such a spot existed that would seem to be the center of her being. It gave her such exquisite pleasure and pain as he rolled it between his thumb and finger.

She was almost insensible, writhing mindlessly beneath him when he finally raised himself off her. Her hands dropped from his thighs to grip the sheets convulsively as he raised her knees and doubled her calves back on her thighs. Carefully, he positioned himself at the hot, moist opening of her body now prepared to receive him. Catching her under her buttocks, he drove himself into her body, at the same time pressing his weight against her folded legs.

She could not move except as he did. Her cry of excitement was high and keen as he plunged into her expectant body. She could feel him inside her, filling her, making her feel complete and at the same time strained to the breaking point. Something would burst, she was sure. She could not sustain such pressure, such excitement, such sensation from her toes to her head. Gently, he withdrew from her and plunged again. She cried out as he seemed to press into her body more deeply and drive her breath away.

"Feel!" he commanded her. "Feel until you die. Do not seek to pull away." His voice was hoarse and rasping as he plunged against her compressed body again and again. With each stroke, he seemed to lift her higher and higher. Her body grasped his muscle and sought to hold it tightly within her. He cried out with pleasure when he felt her.

"Oh, God, Moira, you are so wonderful. You feel so good."

Wilder and wilder, tighter and tighter, the waves of sensation kept coming swifter and swifter until they were indistinguishable. She gritted her teeth to still her scream and then despite herself it was ripped from her body as he thrust himself more deeply it seemed than she

220

could receive. With that scream, her body seemed to dissolve in a wild flood of pleasure such as she had never known. Her limbs relaxed, her head fell back. For an instant, she lost consciousness and then recovered to open her eyes and see Rhiannon's face above her. His eyes closed as he shuddered, gasped, and cried out as piercingly as she had.

His body collapsed against her, and for a long minute she took his entire weight upon her compressed body, feeling nevertheless that she could have held him there forever. Her arms reached up and clasped him. Her hands smoothed his strong muscular shoulders, now wet with perspiration. His hair had fallen over his brow; she brushed it aside.

He roused slightly and rolled off her, slipping from her, and leaving her bereft. His eyes were closed as he lay on his back breathing hard from his exertions. Without opening them, he moved to gather her body against his own and bring her head to his shoulder. As he pressed her face against his neck and shoulder, she inhaled the strong masculine scent of him. It was sharp, yet very pleasant. Again she caressed him, allowing her fingers to smooth the hair on his chest, to explore his masculine nipples and to finally rest on his waist below his ribs.

For several minutes they lay together unconscious and yet each totally aware of the other.

Rhiannon spoke first. "Now, do you see?" he asked. "That sort of love is what made us and what makes us what we are. You now know what I can give to you as I knew what I could take from you. Except, oh, sweetheart, 'tis immeasurably better when you give to me. There is some pleasure for a man in taking an unwilling, frightened, fighting woman, but it is unsatisfying, a thing of the moment."

Her voice came in a whisper. "Then why did you take me so cruelly?"

221

"I could not help myself," he said softly. "All the tender acts of kindness you had bestowed on me, the bathing of my wounds, the touching of our bodies in sleep, the smiles, the glances, all had set about to inflame me. I had had the experience before. Every young man does, you know. There is always some willing wench around to experiment on."

She moved restively in his arms. "Easy," he soothed, "do not be jealous. For a young woman, it is different. She must wait until she is taken and then she may not know the feeling until she has experience. For a woman, the first time and sometimes even the second can be painful. I hurt you, sweetheart, when I took you in the stable. I am sorry I did, but I am not sorry that I took you. Never that."

"Will you continue to desire other women?" she asked softly.

He was silent for a moment, considering. "Probably not," he said wonderingly. "I am sure I will think them attractive, but I feel that I will only want you more when I gaze at them."

"Will I desire other men?" Her question was a bucket of cold water in his face.

He sat up swiftly and looked down at her. "No!" he growled. "You are mine. You will not want other lovers. Only me. I am your master. You will desire only me."

He lay back down abruptly and gathered her back into his arms. Never had he felt such a wave of jealousy as he felt at that suggestion. She was his. By right of capture. She wore the screaming eagle. She belonged to Hawk's Keep forever.

Twenty-Three

Moira awoke first to gray light filtering in through the shutters. The fire had gone out on the hearth. The bed curtains had not been drawn and the room was cold. She lay on her back under a welter of warm wool and fur coverlets. Atop the whole, was a dark blue cover embroidered with the gold insigne of the screaming eagle intricately and fancifully executed with many stitches. She was warm and comfortable, but as she tried to sit up, she felt a lightheaded dizziness. A fierce pang in her stomach made her moan. Her mouth began to water. Hunger. She must have food, she felt, or die. Drawing her hand from beneath the covers, she regarded it carefully. Before her eyes, it began to tremble uncontrollably.

Rhiannon stirred and opened his eyes beside her. His smile greeted her. "Good morning, sweetheart." She felt his hands on her thighs, caressing her, insinuating his fingers between them and touching her. "Are you sore, my lady?" he asked and chuckled when she blushed. His right hand with its strong lean grip gently massaged the flesh and muscle of her inner thighs. She felt her body begin to warm under his ministrations.

"Please," she whispered softly. "I am so hungry."

His hand moved upward across her body, resting in the hollow between her hip bones, moving further up to caress her ribs beneath her breasts. "Poor lady. I had forgotten. You ate almost nothing last night. Remain in bed. I shall serve you once more, but you will have to start doing this for me, as a good slave should." Kissing her ear, he jumped from the bed, protesting as his feet struck the cold floor.

She watched him as he sprinted across the room to his boots, drew them on, and stirred up the fire. His body was beautiful, she had to admit to herself, like a sleek, well-conditioned, well-bred animal. Perfectly proportioned, elegantly muscled. He slipped his robe over his head, corded it around his lean waist, and strode out of the room.

Was she truly to be his slave? Was there no way out of this hateful house where all hated her and wished her dead? He could not stand against them all for very long. He was probably being stubborn because he was being opposed. Of course, he *was* very stubborn.

She heard his voice in the corridor and then he was in the room again. Behind him, lackeys came scurrying, carrying wood and charcoal for the fire, the tub for bathing, hot water and towels. The silent man who was obviously his body servant brought fresh clothing. A kitchen scullion brought a large tray bearing bread, a steaming kettle of porridge, broken meats, and ale.

In a flurry of activity they prepared the bath, set the table, laid out fresh underclothing from the chest, and exited, bowing.

Moira found she could contain herself no longer, but climbed from the bed, grimacing as her bare feet touched the cold floor. She pulled a cover from the bed as she rose and wrapped it around her, enveloping herself in it from shoulders to knees. Padding across the room to the table, she freed one arm from the cloak. Greedily, she caught up a small loaf of fresh warm bread and bit into it. It was the same white bread she had been given a taste of the night before. She sat down in her chair and munched, swallowing with difficulty. Eagerly, she reached for the ale. Rhiannon poured her a cupful and watched her drink. Noticing her awkwardness in eating with one arm while managing the cover about her with the other, he picked up her brown robe from the day before and came to stand at her side. "Stand up and let me put this on you," he said.

Setting the ale down, she reached for the robe with her free hand, but he withheld it. "Stand up," he repeated. She did so. "Now drop the cover." His eyes were twinkling at her.

Solemnly, she met his eyes and dropped the cover. Smiling, he looked his fill at her slim tall white body. The chill air made her flesh prickle and her nipples harden. Regretfully, he handed her the robe which she hastily pulled on, then found the silk shoes where she had slipped them off.

"You eat your fill," he said, turning away, "while I bathe." Pouring water into the tub, he disrobed and stepped in. He did not sit but stood, ladling water over himself and scrubbing his skin with a small cloth until he was satisfied.

Moira turned her back on him and sat at table, eating some of everything before her. She could hardly believe that she was actually having a minute alone to eat hot, well-cooked food. To her horror, she realized that she could not eat very much of anything. Her stomach seemed full almost before she had begun. With only a small amount of bread, a spoonful of porridge, and some chunks of pork, she was filled. More would bring her discomfort, she knew.

She sighed and sat back.

"Trouble, sweetheart," came a voice behind her.

"My stomach has shrunk," she complained. "I want to eat more. It tastes so good, but I cannot."

"Wait a while." She heard him splash from the bath, but did not turn her head. "You will see." His voice was muffled by garments which he was pulling over his head. "In a few minutes, when I sit down, you can eat some more. You will be all right."

"The food tastes so good, too," she mourned. "I have never had bread like this. Sometimes on special days we had some light brown bread, but never white. Usually we just ate black bread, so hard we sopped it in wine or whatever we were drinking. Usually wine."

He padded eagerly to the table. His hair was damp and tousled and drops of water sparkled in his beard. Seating himself, he enthusiastically ladled food into his bowl. Moira poured ale into his cup and watched as he ate and drank. Once she picked up the spoon and tried again to eat a few bites, but set it down in disgust.

"Now, listen to me," said Rhiannon, grinning his wolfish grin when he finished his meal. "We are going to make this work. You will stay here with me. Through you, my father and I will control the whole of North Wales. Did you hear him last night? South Wales has sold itself to the English. Only with Lorne, can my father and I unite the north parts and keep it free. Father does not realize your worth. He has not seen you in action. You are your father's greatest prize, his son. He will pay anything, swear anything to get you back."

"You believe this," said Moira somberly. "But no one else does. Unless we can get word to my father to ransom me, I will never leave this place alive."

"No one will hurt you. You will stay here as my father ordered." He was grinning.

"What do you mean? He ordered you to chain me in the dungeon."

"You will not be in the dungeon." Rhiannon went to the coffer on a shelf above the chest. From it, he pulled a long gold chain. "This was made for me at my mother's request. The links are gold. I use it to belt my best tunic. We will have the smith up here to make a chain for your neck and wrists. Then when I leave with you, everyone can see you are a slave, but a very special one. At Father's command, when I leave without you, I can simply attach this chain to a long one and you can have the freedom of the room without any worries."

She stared at him open-mouthed. A grudging respect for his determination and at the same time his resourcefulness grew in her. Perhaps he really meant what he said. But she did not want to be his slave. Slavery was the end of freedom and her own will. A dim horror rose in her mind. She dropped her eyes from his triumphant face to stare numbly at her plate.

For a moment he was silent, nonplussed by her reaction to his great plan. "What is wrong?" he asked in alarm. "Are you ill? Do you have a pain?"

Her laugh rang through the chamber, high and hysterical. "No. Oh, no. It is just that you are so pleased at my complete humiliation. I am to be chained and imprisoned in this room, and you expect me to be glad. You expect me to be pleased that I shall be held helpless while Owen Llewellyn and your father and the jailer and who knows how many others wait ready to spring upon me and tear me to pieces, blind me, ravish me when your back is turned."

"But, Moira, you have everything you could want here."

"Everything I want!" she screamed at him. "I want to be *free*. I want to return home to my father. I want to ride my black stallion through the heather beneath the walls of Lorne's Rock."

She was shaking from the violence of her outburst as

he gathered her into his arms. "So you shall. We shall work this out together. We will be companions when our fathers have settled their differences and have called a truce."

"You are a fool," she sighed. "They will never settle their differences until one of them is dead—until the whole family is dead. Of the Lornes, there are only two remaining."

"And I hold *her* in my hands," said Rhiannon. "You see. This will work. Here. Sit down and eat. I go to summon the smith. Do not be afraid. When he has finished, I will find some clothes for you and take you riding. Would you like that?"

Her face brightened. "Riding? You dare not!"

"Well, maybe for a walk—on the headlands above the sea. You will like it there. Sit down. Drink another cup of ale. Eat some more."

While he was gone, her mind turned and twisted like a wild thing in a trap. Once she ran to the window and looked down again at the pile of rubble and rocks beneath the walls of the castle. Only a moment and she could be out from that window and smashed into oblivion on these cruel stones. With a sigh, she turned back into the room. Life was too sweet. Her father would surely find her and ransom her eventually. Lord Gethin was the key. He would not believe his son as to her value. He would consider that she had been further degraded by Rhiannon's defloration. Perhaps he could be persuaded at some time, if she could speak to him alone.

Rhiannon returned with the man who had removed the manacles the day before. He carried with him his tools for soldering the gold links together, as well as an iron staple to be bradded to the wall, a twenty foot length of chain such as dogs were chained on, and a common lock.

"The staple first," Rhiannon indicated. "Put it on the

wall just here." He indicated the wall about five feet from the floor beside the bed.

The man nodded and soon the apartment echoed and re-echoed with the deafening sounds of iron on hard wood. When the staple was in place, the man made a loop in the dog chain and began to heat his solder in the fireplace. His bellows pumped for a few minutes and then he carried the solder to the spot, dropping it on the two edges of chain link. The heat was sufficient to melt the edges and make a bond between them. He then splashed some ale on the spot to cool the chain and temper the metal.

"Now for you," said Rhiannon and Moira took a step backward. "If you misbehave or in anyway disturb this man while he is working, you could burn yourself very badly. Will you behave or must I tie you?"

Moira's throat was dry. The awful moment had come. She set her white face, drew her lips in between her teeth, and bit down hard. "I will obey you," she said. "Do what you will."

"Come, stand here and let me measure you," ordered Rhiannon. He took the fillet from her neck and drew the gold chain around in its place. "It need not be tight, you know," he reassured her. "Just so that it can be symbolic of your captivity. When father sees it, he will be satisfied." He measured off a piece of some fifteen inches in length and turned to the smith. "Cut here," he instructed.

"Do you want me to solder this link back together around her neck?" asked the smith.

"Yes," said Rhiannon softly, taking Moira's hand and leading her toward the smith.

The man shook his head doubtfully. "Milord, I do not think it can be done without injuring her."

"What do you mean?" Rhiannon said. "Irons are welded on condemned felons every day."

229

"Well, yes, they are, in a manner of speaking," the fellow hesitated, "but you see, sir, nobody cares whether they get burned or not."

"Explain."

"You see, sir, gold must be heated with the solder between the two edges. Otherwise it cannot be done neatly."

"Then do it commonly and then polish the gold to its proper shape," Rhiannon was becoming exasperated. "She will kneel with her head in my lap and you will place the gold edges on a block of wood upon my knee. I will hold her hair out of the way and prevent her from moving. You will solder the two pieces together with hot metal, cool it, and then polish it. Now."

"Aye, my lord," said the man doubtfully.

"I hope this lout drops solder on your knee," gritted Moira in Rhiannon's ear. "I can see you trusting me to him, but your knee—after what he did to your hands yesterday!"

"Quiet!" Rhiannon rejoined out of the side of his mouth. "Kneel down. Grasp my calves in your arms and rest your face on my thigh."

Moira was so provoked at his obstinacy that she forgot to be afraid. She did as she was bid, resting her right cheek on his left thigh. Carefully, he gathered her long hair and laid it over her left cheek. His hands placed the gold chain around her neck and she felt the small block of wood being placed against the back of her head.

The smith secured the chain to the wood with wires and likewise bound the links. She heard him moving to the fire, heard his bellows, heard him come back. There was the smell of burning wood. She felt Rhiannon's thigh tense under her cheek. Involuntarily, she grasped his legs tighter. Then a dry sizzle, and a warm wine trickled down the back of her neck and dripped onto the floor.

"Done, sir," the smith exclaimed proudly. "'Tis a fine

230

joining. When 'tis cool, I can take a little piece of soft cloth and polish it up, but in truth the lady can do it herself. It looks like a little gold bead on the link. 'Twill hardly be noticed."

"Thank you," said Rhiannon. His hand rested on her head, holding her in place when she attempted to rise. Gently, he stroked her hair. "Is the metal cool to the skin now?"

"Should be," was the reply. "No real problem once the flux is poured on it. It cools off quick like after that."

"Then gather up your tools and go," ordered Rhiannon.

Moira relaxed her clasp on his calves, but he continued to stroke her hair and hold her at his knee.

Quickly, the smith gathered up his tools, and wood block and his bellows, and left the apartment.

Moira tensed beneath Rhiannon's hands. He was planning something. Gently, he placed both hands in her hair and pulled her head back. His hands slid down the sides of her head and held her cheeks between his palms. He kissed her. Sapphire blue eyes met those of ice blue. "Give me your hands," Rhiannon commanded.

Moira felt compelled to obey him. His will was hers at that moment. Something strange was happening to her she knew, yet she had no will to stop it.

Rhiannon placed her hands palms together between his two palms. "Repeat after me," he commanded, "I, Moira of Lorne, enter into your homage and faith and become your man, by mouth and hand," he paused. "Say it," he prodded.

"'Tis the oath of homage," she protested.

"I know," he replied. "Say it."

Her face went white.

"Say it," he repeated. "You are mine. I want no other but you. We will become as brothers."

She straightened her spine. "I can do this only if I

never am asked to move against my father."

"You have my oath," he replied. "I, Moira of Lorne, enter . . ."

"I, Moira of Lorne, enter into your homage and faith and become your man, by mouth and hands . . ."

". . . and I swear and promise to keep faith and loyalty to you against all others."

". . . and I swear and promise to keep faith and loyalty to you against all others."

". . . and to guard your rights with all my strength."

". . . and to guard your rights with all my strength."

Still holding her hands, Rhiannon made the response, "I, Rhiannon ap Breannon, do promise you, vassal Moira, that I will guarantee you against every creature with all my power." Still holding her hands, he bent and kissed her upon the mouth.

Wonderingly, she rose to her feet. He stood, too. His hand slipped under the gold chain at her throat. "This is your investiture," he said. "You belong to me forever, for that chain can never leave your neck."

She sat down stunned in the chair opposite him. "Do you realize what you have done?" she asked. "Do you truly mean what you have asked of me?" Her eyes searched his face.

He walked across the room and opened his chest. "I meant every word."

"I have never broken a vow," she said softly. "I would not know how to do so. Believe me when I say that I hold hard by my word."

"How old are you?" he asked suddenly, pulling out hose and tunic from the chest.

"Twenty years," she replied.

"And you were yet a maid when I took you." He pulled out more garments and carried them across the room to her. "Your father was raising you to be his son. For good or ill, you are entitled to my respect for that reason. Put

232

these on. We will dress each other and go for that walk I promised you on the headlands."

"But these are your clothes."

"This afternoon, we will visit the bower and get Mother to sew some more suitable things for you," he grinned. "And we will also try to find what has been done with your gown and silk blouse that you came in. I sent them to be cleaned and they have not been returned."

He started to strip off his hose.

She looked at him. "Why are you changing your hose? Those were fresh this morning."

He grinned at her. "Because that damned fool dropped solder on my knee. Not only did he burn a hole in the wool but in my leg as well."

Against her will, a chuckle broke from Moira's lips. She covered her mouth with her hand, but could not suppress the ripple of laughter that escaped.

"By all the saints," he continued, "I'm afraid to trust my horse to him now. He might come up lame."

Her laughter burst from her. It felt so good to laugh. And he laughed with her, richly, deeply, at the pleasure shared and the pain ended.

Twenty-Four

Out on the headlands above Colwyn Bay, the icy wind blew their hair about and reddened their cheeks. Moira threw back her head and faced the blast, her long brown mane blowing back and up like a burnished flag. In the weak sunlight, her hair glowed with copper lights, an unusual shade of red-brown. Suddenly, she spread her cloak like great wings and stood on tiptoe, leaning into the gale. Her mouth opened and her eyes slitted.

Never had Rhiannon seen anything so beautiful. The wind molded her tunic against her body, so that her every shape and curve from breasts to knee was visible to his admiring eye.

"Oh, if I could only fly," she called to him. "I feel that I almost could."

He stepped in front of her and lifted her by her waist. She whooped in surprise and then in pleasure as he lifted her over his head to the length of his arms and tilted her forward. She straightened her body in his hands until she was lying in the wind. He held her that way for a minute, then gently lowered her, letting her body slide down his body, touching himself with every part of her. When she was on her feet, he folded his cloak around her and held her warm against him. He kissed her nose, her eyes, her cheeks, and last her soft mouth.

"Come, we must return. You will take a chill from all this icy air after being shut up so long and starved."

She laughed ruefully. "This air feels almost warm after the icy wet of that dungeon."

Nevertheless, they wrapped their cloaks around them and headed back toward the keep at a brisk walk.

In the bailey, they encountered Huw Llengaron putting his horse through its paces. Moira shouted without thought, "Huw Llengaron! Huw, come to me."

Heads in workshops and smithy rose to watch curiously as Huw Llengaron rode his stocky pony toward the pair and stopped. Moira stepped forward. "I must thank you, Huw Llengaron, for saving me and I do so in front of Lord Rhiannon. My lord, you must know that this man unbound my hands when the circulation was almost stopped, fed me, gave me a cloak to shelter in for the night, and, most important, after I was imprisoned in the dungeon sent furs to protect me from the cold. Without his help and intervention, I would not have survived. He obeyed your command in every way to bring me safe to the keep until you could claim me."

Her blue eyes smiled up at Huw, who knew himself to be her man for life.

Rhiannon's voice startled him. "You did well. She is my vassal now and will serve me well. Service and courtesy to her are service and courtesy to me."

"It is my pleasure, my lord," responded the horseman and bowed. "By your leave," he wheeled his horse and thudded off.

Rhiannon's eyes followed him. "A good man. I will remember him. There are many like him, but there are also many like Owen, who will resist any attempt we may make at peace."

235

Moira glanced at him. "You are serious about this. You really think that together we might hold a key to peace for a time."

"I believe so," he replied. "If so, it was a lucky day for me when you knelt down beside me to give me your sweet charity."

Moira flushed and ducked her head. He regarded her soberly. "Do you still blame yourself in some way for a weakness?"

When she nodded silently, he continued, "You are even as God made you. In many ways you are a man, except that your woman's heart would not be hardened to cruelty."

"I was weak," she said.

"You were natural. I tricked you. Any man with a spark of decency would have done the same as you did. Look at me. I am placing my life in your hands. You might be tricking me."

"But you know I am not," she said.

"Since this morning I know, sweetheart," he said and kissed her on the chin. Quick as a breath, her head tilted and her lips brushed his. Like the wings of a butterfly, they brushed over his lips and then drew away.

Abruptly, she jerked herself from his arms and whirled away to walk swiftly across the bailey and in at the sallyport. He had to increase his strides to keep up with her. Once inside, neither spoke for a long minute while they paused to allow themselves to become accustomed to the darkness of the corridor.

"Follow me," he said, leading her to the bower.

When they entered together, at least twenty pairs of eyes stared at them in unconcealed amazement. Twenty pairs of hands at first were idled as if the devil himself had entered the room. Indeed, one or two of the more timid maids crossed themselves at the sight of Moira in men's garments, her hair unbound and her gold chain gleaming in the hollow of her throat.

Lady Branwen came forward courteously to kiss Rhiannon's cheek and receive his kiss in return. Moira curtseyed to her. "How may I serve you, my tall son?" asked the lady.

"Lady Mother, Moira of Lorne has no clothing except that which was worn to the keep and has now been taken from her. First, if you could find what has happened to it and in what state it is and have it repaired."

"I will do so," Branwen replied formally. "Is there anything else?"

"By your gracious will, lady, I would have Moira outfitted as becomes a person of her birth."

Lady Branwen stiffened. "I doubt that we can find the time, my son. The Christmas livery is being prepared and we have very little time. Perhaps in a few months if she abides with us so long . . ."

"She will be with us, Mother," insisted Rhiannon.

"I doubt that, my son. Your father has sent messengers to Lord Lorne to demand ransom."

Rhiannon's eyes blazed. "It matters not. She will not be ransomed."

Branwen was silent.

Rhiannon moved farther into the room. "Mother, I very much desire that Moira have a gown and a tunic, blouse, hose, and cloak. Also, the requisite undergarments that women wear."

Soberly, his mother nodded her head and turned. She led them across the bower to a large chest built into the paneling of the wall. Opening it, she indicated materials, folded and waiting for use. "Select what you would have for her. Alys, come forward and take her measurements."

The woman came hesitantly and began to measure with cord which was then knotted at the proper lengths. When she came to the length from neck to floor, she shook her head and glanced up in wonderment at Moira's tall form. Moira glanced down in embarrassment at the length of herself, then raised her eyes to catch Rhiannon's amused look.

"My lord," she said, "I fear there is overmuch of me."

"Not too much for me," he replied. She blushed and caught the expression of distaste and disapproval on Lady Branwen's face.

"Choose what you would want made up for your slave's livery." Lady Branwen paused delicately over the word *slave*. She indicated again the cedar paneled chest.

Swiftly, Rhiannon stepped forward and chose a length of dark blue wool to be lined with common woad for a cape. A piece of tawny wool, fine spun and soft, was selected for a tunic with brown for stockings. He rejected a dark forest green wool but accepted a coarse purplish-blue wool, stained with blackberry. "Make this into a gown like the one she came in, split up the front and back, and *chausses* to match," he commanded.

He stood back from the chest and frowned. "Is there naught else to choose from?"

His mother stiffened, "Only the materials that I keep for the family's exclusive use remain."

Soberly, he faced her. "I would see them, too."

Moira tugged at his arm, "Please, my lord, it is enough. I shall have all I require."

He ignored her. Her mouth tight, his mother produced her ring of keys and unlocked a smaller chest within the chest and flung back the lid. On top, lay a length of shimmering peacock blue samite woven with heavy silver threads. "That is what I want for her gown."

Both Moira and Branwen gasped. "Oh, no, my lord," exclaimed Moira. "'Tis much too fine for a slave!" exclaimed Branwen simultaneously.

Rhiannon was insistent. "Make it into a gown like the one you are wearing, Mother, and embroider it with silver. And under it, some of that fine white stuff that you use for your chemise."

Branwen almost collapsed. "Cotton, my son. 'Tis too dear. We have no more of it."

Moira's hand trembled in agitation. "Please, my lord, do not dress me so. I am your slave. People will look at me and my clothing will be . . ." she swallowed, ". . . too fine. 'Twill put shame upon your mother and your sister."

At the appeal in her eyes and his mother's white face, Rhiannon retreated. He looked at them both and then let his eyes slide around to the staring faces in the bower which had suddenly grown quiet. "Oh, very well. Those three will be enough for now. But I beg you, Lady Mother, set women to these garments and complete them rapidly. She cannot wear my clothes forever."

Branwen drew herself up with a long sigh of relief. "We shall begin the tawny and brown today."

Rhiannon smiled. "Thank you." He kissed her cheek.

Moira swept the floor in a deep curtsey. She could not bring herself to speak, for the lady acknowledged her with an icy stare of disdain. Her eyes flashed a fiery hatred that brought Moira straight up from the floor with head held high.

Rhiannon strode toward the door. Moira's eyes clashed once more with Lady Branwen's and then she too followed after him with a proud stride. There could be no friendship between her and any lady in this house, she realized. Rhiannon was her only hope until her father sent for her.

After the visit to the bower, Rhiannon found himself growing more and more uncomfortable as they approached his bed chamber. The thought of chaining her to the wall, although little more than a ritual, embarrassed him. With her by his side, he felt whole. She had sworn the oath of fealty to him. With sensitivity unfamiliar to him, he realized that she would hate the chaining even as he himself would.

For her own sake, he reasoned, she must submit. His father was already angered by her presence in his apartments. Owen Llewellyn would snatch at any excuse to make trouble. If she were left free to roam, the soldier might seize her, hurt her, or even kill her on the pretext that he was protecting the family.

In Rhiannon's imagination, he could feel her nervousness and her dread. How he longed to leave her with a soft kiss! The door of the chamber was before them. Stiffening his resolve, he strode across the room to pick up the chain where it lay in a coil beside the bed. Carrying the end in his hand, he came back toward her, his eyes revealing nothing of the turmoil of his thoughts.

With a sinking sensation in the pit of her stomach, she watched him come. Her whole soul cried out within her. Desperately, she longed to flee, but where could she go? The fact that Rhiannon would fasten this chain hurt more than she cared to examine. The guard in the dungeon had chained her with heavier irons in the frigid darkness. Strangely, this bondage seemed immeasurably worse.

Grasping her by the shoulders, he turned her back to him. Roughly, he pulled the golden chain away from the skin on the back of her neck and circled it with the padlock which also held the end of the chain. Instead of being steady and sure, his fingers shook so that he fumbled badly, dropping the lock so that it struck her back just below the waist, causing her to jump.

"Sorry, my lady," he muttered.

Her reply was an inaudible murmur.

At last, he snapped the hasp into place and swung her back around to face him. His eyes searched her face for a sign of her feelings, but she was as expressionless as a statue.

"You must stay here in this room," he said. "I have work to do. My father needs me to see to the defenses and to drill the men."

Still Moira did not speak.

Rhiannon looked across the room at the fire. "I would have you at my side," he said by way of apology, "but there are too many who will not as yet accept you. You must school yourself in patience."

Her blue eyes looked up at him. Silver blue pools, cool and still, in her gaunt white face. Never had he felt such a wave of emotion as swept through his body at that moment. It was strange to him. She was his enemy's daughter, his slave, he had used her body to his pleasure three times and would make use of it again at his will. She was strong and tall, he knew, yet she seemed so vulnerable. Her shoulders under his tunic were delicately boned. He let his hands slide down to her shoulder blades and press her against him. Her soft breasts touched his chest and flattened, her head turned on his shoulder, and he stroked her hair with his right hand while with his left he traced his way down her spine and pressed first the small waist and then her buttocks against him. When they touched everywhere, he leaned back slightly from the waist and tipped her face up to meet his. Gently, he kissed her soft cool lips. "Sweet," he whispered, sighing as he turned away and left the room.

In a daze, she moved the several paces to the chair, his chair, with its heavy carved arms and back. Seating herself, she arranged the chain in her lap, pressed her head back against the carvings, and grasped the arms. Thus, surrounded by him, she sat with dry eyes staring into the fire that stirred fitfully on the hearth.

Twenty-Five

Owen Llewellyn opened the door to Rhiannon's chamber, his baleful stare immediately finding Moira where she sat dozing. As her eyes fluttered open, he calmly turned and slid the bolt home, barring the door to entry.

Heart thumping madly, Moira tried to assume a calm demeanor. This man she had marked as insane; any sign of her fear would only increase the danger to herself. Consequently, she sat perfectly still, regarding him coldly.

His eyes lighted as they took in the chain running from the bracket in the wall across the floor to the gold chain around her neck. A low chuckle broke from his lips.

Despite her fear, she managed to regard him calmly. "Lord Rhiannon is drilling his men." By a dint of will, she forced herself to speak in an even voice. "Did he send you for something?"

"That whelp!" Owen sneered. "*He* does not send *me* to run errands for him. As a commander of equal rank, I came to check on the presence of a captive slave in the family living quarters of the castle. Instead of being imprisoned in the dungeon, or put to work at hard labor in the scullery, I learned this . . . witch . . ." He spat the words from between froth-tinged lips, ". . . this witch was actually installed in chambers where Lord Gethin's womenfolk might be endangered."

When Moira remained silent, he strolled forward, each stride heavy with menace. "I had heard the cub had taken you into his bed, but thought he surely would have returned you to the dungeon the next morning."

Clearing her throat, Moira shook her head. "I am kept where my Lord Rhiannon pleases."

"He is a fool and his father is blind to leave you here in this chamber. You should still be in chains in the lowest dungeon."

"I *am* chained," Moira rejoined, lifting the metal links in her hand to show him. "I can do naught but pace this room. I am no threat to the peace of this castle."

As if she had not spoken, Owen crossed the room, grasping the bracket in the wall and giving it a hard pull. "As officer in charge of the security of this keep and all who live within, I recognize it as my duty to inspect this chain and see if it be strong enough and tight enough to hold you fast. I have already suggested to the good priest that you may be an evil spirit who has cast a spell on Lord Rhiannon. I have suggested an exorcism be performed, but Lord Gethin, who is too indulgent of his son's whims, has denied that."

As he spoke, he ran the chain across the palm of his hand. "The bracket seems solid enough, but the chain seems too light. Much too light." Hand over hand, he advanced toward her, sliding his hands along the chain, tugging harder with each step. His glowing eyes never left her face as he studied it closely for some sign of fear.

Suddenly, he jerked the chain cruelly, pulling her sideways out of the chair. She struck the floor on knees and hands, a tortured cry wrung from her mouth.

In a movement surprisingly quick in one so heavyset, he straddled her body, squeezing her ribs tightly between his knees. "Witch," he snarled.

Terrified, Moira would have screamed, but her sound was cut off by his swift upward jerking of the chain. One hand fastened in her hair, lifting her up on her knees. Laughing now, he moved around to the front of her, pressing her inexorably toward him, as he dragged her face up to stare into his malevolent eyes. "Beg!" His laugh was high-pitched. "Grovel! My wife begged. She pleaded and prayed, and still your father's men tore her apart."

"No! My father's men had nothing to do with it."

"I say yes!"

Nails clawing at his wrist, Moira tried to ease the pain in her throat. "I am my lord's slave," she ground out. Would nothing penetrate his hate-obsessed mind? "I am sorry about your wife, but my family had nothing to do with such as that."

"You lie!" he shrieked. "Liar! And you shall pay for that falsehood, as well as for the horrors your family committed." The hand fastened in her hair forced her face against his lower body.

Out of her newfound knowledge came the recognition of just what Owen intended. Hard, throbbing muscle burned through the man's clothing, burgeoning against her face as he pressed her against him.

Nausea rose in her throat. Please, she longed to say. Please do not. But her mind told her that he would be only more excited by her pleas for mercy. Instead she ducked her head, wrenching her hair from his fingers and lunging into him, trying to throw him off balance.

Delighted by her near helplessness, he staggered back only a step before recovering himself. Unfortunately, she fell forward, crashing into his knees and falling sideways to the floor. The chain slipped from his fingers and clattered about her head and shoulders. Released, Moira rolled out of his reach, knowing even as she did so that he could pull her back to him at will.

"I am the lord's slave," she panted. "Touch me and he will surely see you punished. You are damaging his property."

"That's good," he laughed, stooping leisurely to pick up the metal links. "I love to hear a once-haughty lady hiding behind her slavery. Listen to yourself! Reminding me of your degradation. Oh, it does my heart good. My wife and children must be smiling now at the sound and sight of you." Like a cat with its paw on the tail of a struggling mouse, he rattled the chain significantly. "Acknowledge yourself a slave if slavery will save your life. You are a true whelp of Lorne. They are cowards and bullies all."

His eyes glazed, as he remembered. "She was so young, so helpless. She begged, but they would have no mercy." He shivered with his memories. No longer did Moira struggle at the end of the chain. He was not seeing her, but another place, another day, another woman.

The only sounds breaking the silence of the room were the labored breaths of the two adversaries. Moira's eyes darted over the furnishings. Somewhere there must be a weapon. The spartan surroundings yielded not so much as a heavy candlestick to her desperate eyes. Barren of ornamentation, Rhiannon's quarters had been, until her arrival, a virtual monk's cell.

The poker!

Calculating the length of the chain dangling loosely in Owen's hands, she recognized the futility of such a move. He would simply tighten his grip on the links and bring her up short before she could reach the fireplace. How he would laugh! Helplessness and despair welled up in her. At any moment, he would break from his trance.

As if roused by her thoughts, he blinked rapidly.

Focusing on her tall figure, her hands closed around the chain beneath her neck, he laughed. "I've not had a woman since she died," he declared. "Love died with her." His face contorted. "But hatred lives. Revenge lives." He repeated the words. "Revenge lives."

Hand over hand, he dragged himself along the chain toward her. One cruel hand forced her to her knees again, while his other sought the lacings of his breeches. Horrified at what he intended, Moira's control broke. With a panic-stricken sob, she began to writhe, striking hard at his belly. Her fists struck the lower abdomen and the swollen muscle he fumbled to release.

Grunting in pain, he slapped her face, knocking her sideways against the end of the bed. Her panting ended in a gasping shriek of pain.

"Up on the bed," he growled, catching her by the shoulders and heaving her across it with the strength of madness. "I'll hear you plead for mercy yet."

Like a cornered animal that finally turns and bares its teeth, she spat at him. "Never. You will never hear me plead."

His hard hands ravaged over her breasts, pinching and squeezing, but she remained stoical. Her ice-blue eyes glared defiance at him.

"Scream!" he demanded. "Plead, damn you." He caught Rhiannon's robe and jerked it upward from the hem, exposing her long slim legs.

Fiercely, she kicked at him, but he laughed and flung his thigh across hers. "If you won't plead, at least fight."

He was so much heavier; his strength wore her down quickly. Despite her impassioned, desperate squirming and thrashing, he was able to ram his metal-hard, throbbing weapon between her tight-closed legs.

In another minute, she would be unable to summon up the strength to continue the fight. Already her weakened body was trembling and sweating. A low sob burst from her lips as her breath groaned between her teeth. Cursing her womanhood with its inferior muscles, she pushed with all her strength, futilely spending her energy against his heavy shoulders. Her hands slipped up to claw at his cheeks.

A blow from the back of his hand sent her senses reeling. At the same time, his hard knee drove between her legs. She was losing consciousness. Thank God! The worst would be over without her knowing.

A knock sounded at the door.

Owen Llewellyn shook his head as if a fly buzzed around it.

Had the knock been going on for some time? Certainly it was loud . . . determined.

"Help!" Moira's scream brought another knock, more heavy, more rapid. Insistent.

Owen levered himself up on one arm. Again she screamed.

"Shall I fetch Lord Rhiannon?" The voice of one of the lackeys, high-pitched, hesitant, sounded muffled through the thick door.

"Yes! For God's sake, yes."

"No!" Owen's roar almost succeeded in drowning hers out.

Her eyes locked with his as his face, dripping with perspiration, hung above her. "He'll kill you if he finds you here. Get out now. Leave this room immediately and I'll not tell him you were here."

"Who's there?" The lackey's voice was impatient, nervous.

"Get out now." Moira repeated. "I am as I was when you entered. Another minute and you will pay with your life. Lord Rhiannon knows how to defend his property." Privately, she doubted that her rape and death would cause more than a passing reprimand, but she dared not let her doubt show. A brave front was her only hope.

His face mirroring his torture, Owen raised himself on arms and knees. Sweat dripped from his brow onto her face, spattering stinging salty droplets into her eyes. Blinking rapidly, she dared not look downward lest she be shamed by what she might see. Instead she turned her face in the direction of the door as she flung up her hand across her eyes. Even though Rhiannon had forced her to accept his body into her own, she had never felt unclean. His ardor had been natural, free, joyous, like a healthy young animal. Somehow, he had made her accept him without shame or humiliation. But, this was achingly, terrifyingly different. Owen Llewellyn's demonic hatred blazed from his widened eyes, as he reluctantly, angrily straightened on his knees.

As the knock sounded again, this time a long imperative tattoo, he contemptuously stepped over her body and off the bed. With defiant movements, he restored his clothing to rights.

"We are not finished," he hissed, bending toward her ear, his breath bitter to her heightened senses. "You and I have a reckoning still to come."

Suddenly furious, she rolled across Rhiannon's wide bed and stood up, straightening her robe. Head high, not deigning to look at his contorted, perspiring face, she strode to the door, the chain rattling behind her. She threw back the bolt.

"Come in," she commanded imperiously of the oldest of the lackeys who had brought the bath two nights ago. His young face reflected his alarm, as he rubbed his bruised knuckles. To even the most obtuse of people, the atmosphere of disquiet was thick in the room.

Without another word, Owen Llewellyn brushed between them rudely and pushed his way out of the room. While the lackey stared after him, Moira tottered unsteadily to Rhiannon's chair, slumping down into it and clasping her hands to still their trembling.

248

"Milady." The lad's voice was uncertain.

With a slight shake, she raised her head and summoned a wan smile. "Be about your business, sirrah," she whispered.

Face serious, he collected the slops and paused at the door. "Shall I send for a woman, milady?"

"No, thank you," she replied. Her trembling hand sought her forehead. "But thank you for . . . everything."

Despite her command, the door opened within a very few minutes. The wench from the laundry appeared with the clothing Moira had worn. Her eyes glanced inquiringly around the room. "May I serve you, milady?" she murmured. "One of the boys said you might be feeling a bit under the weather." Her tone indicated a general lack of interest. Moira suspected that her status of slave made the other servants reluctant to aid her.

When Moira, white-faced, silently shook her head, the wench flounced over to the chest. Tossing her head, she neatly deposited the folded garments on its top. "Conal will be bringing your boots up when he brings Lord Rhys' things," she informed Moira, with a resentful look in the other's direction. "He said I was to bring your other clothes up here. I do what I am told. 'Twould be my hide I suppose if I failed to do my job."

Glancing toward the door to reassure herself they were alone, she took a step toward Moira and folded her arms across her bosom in evident disapproval. "I'll warn you not to put on airs. Free women don't have to fetch and carry for slaves. When you get sent down from the lord's room to the scullery, you best not have made enemies along the way."

With these words, she vanished into the privy room and returned with Rhiannon's discarded clothing which she carried away to be washed and mended.

Alone at last, reaction sweeping over her, Moira

shakily buried her face in her hands. She had never prayed before with any conviction. Now there seemed to her nothing but prayer left. Her father must get the ransom soon and rescue her. Rhiannon could not overrule his father who wanted the gold to fit and arm his men. More than that, Gethin wanted her out of the keep. She clenched her hands and sought to steady their trembling while she prayed silently for help now that she was in the midst of her enemies. The fire died on the hearth, but she did not notice. The room became chill and still she sat in the chair, trying to rebuild her disordered mental defenses.

Finally, Rhiannon came into the room, bringing with him his man Conal, who carried Moira's boots in one hand and a basin and razor in the other. With composed face, Moira rose swiftly from the chair and Rhiannon sank down. The three lackeys followed Conal. One stirred and rebuilt the fire in the hearth, one brought a tray of food and a pitcher of ale that he placed on the center table. The third carried a kettle of hot water and a basin for washing.

"Wash and eat, Moira," Rhiannon bade her, "while Conal shaves me. I must go down to the hall and eat with the household tonight, but I do not want you to starve and yet I do not want you to be hurt as you were last night. You will sit behind me as a good slave should and wait upon me as my own special servitor. Father and Mother will be pleased to see how well you have been trained and how well you submit." He chuckled gleefully.

Moira felt sick at his announcement that she must return to eat with the family. They would hate her the more, the more he thrust her upon them. Yet she was hungry and she knew she could not exist on just a few scraps from his hand at the table. She fell to with a good appetite and drank two cups of ale before she was through.

When she sat back, Rhiannon grinned at her. "That goes better, right, sweetheart."

She flushed and caught the look Conal threw her as he was gathering up the remains of the shaving equipment.

Bent over the basin, washing his hand and arms, Rhiannon did not notice her embarrassment. When he straightened up, Conal whisked the basin away and left the room.

Rhiannon regarded her critically. "Dress yourself in your clothing, if it is in good shape. I want everyone to get used to seeing you in that type of garb. When we ride out of the keep together, I shall want you with me dressed in that fashion. You are unique; every man will envy me. A man-woman." He threw back his head and laughed. Then he settled himself in his chair. "Strip for me, sweetheart. I want to see the woman part of you."

"No, please. It is not decent. Someone might come in," she begged.

"No one will enter this room without my permission," he averred.

"People have been entering this room all day without your permission," she argued. "You do not realize because they do not seem like people to you. The laundry wench, the lackey from the scullery, others."

"Then bar the door," he agreed amicably, "but hurry."

Miserably, she did as he bade. Her chain rattling behind her, she crossed to the door and barred it. Returning to the fire, she quickly stripped off her clothing. As she did so, she tried to ignore him, yet blushed despite herself.

When she was naked, she stood with her back to him, facing the fire, fists clenched at her sides.

"Come here and I will unfasten your chain," he called, pouring himself a cup of ale and drinking from it hastily.

With dragging steps, she came to stand naked beside his chair. Solemnly, he looked her up and down from her trembling lips and downcast eyes to her slender white feet.

"Kneel down," he commanded. He drew the key from beneath his tunic and pulled her forward until her white breasts touched his knees. His big hand closed firmly around her right shoulder and he held her against him while he inserted the key in the lock. "This will be our ritual," he said. "After you have eaten, we will dress for dinner or undress for bed. You will come and kneel here, leaning against me in this manner and I will free you. Do not wait for me to command you. Do it."

"Yes, master," she intoned with heavy sarcasm.

He grinned at her. "'Tis well you practice the word. I want you to use it before others in the hall every night." He opened the lock, pulled the chain free, and handed it to her. "Now place this under the staple against the wall and come back and dress before the fire."

Angrily, she rose and did as he commanded. As she pulled her clothing on over her body, she was pleased to find it smelling of herbs used in the soap. A rent in the skirt of the gown had been repaired. When it was in place over her body, she raised her eyes to look at him and saw his expression was tender.

"Very nice, sweetheart," he said softly.

She carried her boots to the chair that by mutual agreement had become hers and pulled them on over her *chausses*. They were cleaned and well-oiled. She was delighted with the sheen and ran her hand lovingly over one. These boots were her pride, for they had been made especially for her large feet and long legs and they fitted her well.

Then she sat, while Rhiannon dressed himself, and they descended to the hall. The servitors were already going through the motions of the first course when they entered. He took his place at his father's right at the head of the table. Moira stood at his back, her gown and silk shirt open at the throat to reveal the gold chain around her neck.

Servitors brought soup first to be served in the pewter bowls. Lord Gethin ignored her as did all, except from time to time when surreptitious looks were cast in her direction. She stood still, hearing the noise and bustle, smelling the tantalizing odors of the foods from the various courses, her eyes blank and fixed on a spot somewhere in the center of the fire.

She could not know that her pale eyes appeared almost luminous in her white face and that her fixed expression was disconcerting many of the ladies at the table.

The story of Rhiannon's captive had spread throughout the keep, propelled by Owen Llewellyn's malicious denunciations. The strange garb, the divided skirt over men's *chausses* and boots showing the division of her legs as she strode across the floor at Rhiannon's shoulder, had raised a wave of scandalized mutterings.

The threatening sound implicit in the atmosphere of hostility had stiffened Moira's resolve to show no fear. Now her icy composure, so unlike the grovelings of beaten and tormented captives, was unnerving to the company. Owen noted with satisfaction the resting of hands on dagger handles and the wary looks of the men. A small, timid lady crossed herself hastily before turning her face away. She refused to look toward the head table for the rest of the meal.

A pair of musicians tuned in the gallery and began plucking away at a lute and a recorder. A slight frown appeared on Moira's forehead. They were unbelievably bad. She turned her head and looked toward them.

Rhiannon, who had turned to offer her a bite of rabbit from his plate, caught her movement. "Is there something bothering you?" he asked.

253

"The lack of music," she replied softly. "Never have I heard a more unmusical pair."

"Can you do better?" inquired Lady Branwen, her voice like ice at the implied insult to her entertainment.

The challenge could not go unanswered. "By your leave, master." Moira bowed her head to Rhiannon.

"It is my command that you entertain us," he replied, hugely gratified that she should serve him and the company. "Which instrument will you use?"

"The lute, so please you."

"Bring the lute," he called to the musician in the gallery.

The man scrambled down and brought it. His face hardened when it was taken from him and handed to Moira.

The hall became silent as she slung the strap around her shoulder and strummed the strings. Wincing slightly, she adjusted the pegs and strummed again and again. Finally satisfied, she raised her head to Rhiannon, who had turned his chair half around.

"What will you, my lord?"

"A ballad, my lady." A mutter went up among those who had heard him address her in that fashion, but he did not notice.

"Bewitched him, she has," Owen growled to the couple sitting beside him. The man nodded with an obscene gesture, but the woman threw a look of horror in Moira's direction and leaned across the board to repeat Owen's words.

"Bewitched . . . Witch . . ." The words fled down the table.

"She wears those chains of gold, but they are not real. She magicked them herself."

"She wove a spell around the lord that drew him from the table to release her from the dungeon."

"She does not eat real food. At the Lord Gethin's table,

254

when Lord Rhys tried to feed her, she changed herself into a dog before she could eat."

"Witch . . . Black spirit . . ." The words flew round the hall.

Moira raised her voice to include all the occupants of the hall. "Being enslaved, I sing of freedom." Her voice was low and melodious. The tune circled up and around through the chords on the lute. A lady stood in a tower gazing out at the moors upon which her love had died. She belonged to the conqueror and would never see her home or family again. She would be imprisoned in the dark tower room in body, but her heart and mind would ever fly away from his cruelty. Never could she be free, and yet never could he enslave her.

When she finished, the room was silent. Then a muttering grew. No one applauded, but Rhiannon stared at her with his sapphire blue eyes.

"Play something a bit more cheerful," he commanded, "and do not sing."

"Yes, master," she replied.

He turned his chair back around and the trencher was whisked away to be replaced by a pastry tart filled with blackberries. He bit into it in a bad mood. Her obvious sincerity and pain bothered him. He had, against his will, grown very fond of her.

The lutenist stood fidgeting, waiting for his instrument to be returned to him. Finally, at the end of the meal, Rhiannon signed that Moira should surrender the lute to its owner, excused himself from the table, and paced from the hall. She followed behind him, her head bowed, her cheeks flushed with humiliation. Each time he forced her to exhibit herself before people as his slave, she felt more keenly the position to which she had been brought and the pain cut her most deeply.

In his chambers, he turned and hugged her. "You were splendid," he said. "Father said not a word when he saw

255

the chain around your neck. The lute was a good idea, too. It added just the right touch of humility and subservience. Except the song. I did not care for the song."

Moira pulled from his grasp and shrugged. "I did not intend that you should enjoy it. I sang it to you so that you might know its message."

He frowned, opening his mouth to speak.

"Hear me, Rhiannon ap Breannon," she said. "I want to be free. I cannot bear the thought that I shall stay here in this room chained every day. Indeed, I have opened the window and looked down. I would not pause an instant if I did not hold the hope that my father will ransom me."

"But you will ride with me when I go out of the keep," he argued. "I took you for a walk yesterday. You will not even consider jumping from that window," his voice rose, "or I will have it closed up."

"And yesterday I sat chained in that chair. My hands were idle, my spirit dying. There are many ways for me to kill my body, if I choose to do so. You cannot prevent me by boarding up a window."

"You swore your oath to serve me by mouth and hand, to obey me," he insisted stubbornly. "I forbid you to take your own life."

"How can I serve you locked in this room?" she countered. "Even your dog runs at your side."

He threw up his hands in disgust and turned to the table. Pouring himself a cup of ale, he dropped down in his chair and stared at her. Tall and proud, she stood before him, her hands clenched at her sides, her head thrown back, her ice blue eyes shining in the firelight. She was beautiful and her body was exciting to contemplate as she stood there, but it was not enough. He had seen her smile, had heard her laugh. Today, in front of the sallyport, she had kissed him. It had been just a breath on his lips, yet it had moved him as had nothing else. What would it be like to be loved by this woman? What would it be like to love a woman?

Morosely, he took another sip of ale and met her eyes, "What did you do in your father's keep that your hands were not idle?"

Moira paused, surprised. "Why I kept his house, oversaw his meals, and directed the preparation of clothing, even as your mother does so efficiently here. But more. My father's keep is small in comparison to this place. I rode and practiced with a sword. I trained and exercised my horse, the black that I have not seen since I came into this place. He is a good horse. Is he well cared for?" Her eyes questioned Rhiannon and he nodded.

"I have placed him in the care of my groom who cares for all my horses. He is like you, a prize of war," he grinned.

"I practiced my lute when time permitted. I had a good teacher."

"You did indeed," he said. "You played beautifully. Everyone would have applauded, under different circumstances."

"And I cast my father's accounts."

"You can read and write?" He stared at her in amazement. He could scarcely sign his own name and here this man-woman could read and write and cast accounts.

Moira hesitated. He might be angered at this knowledge. "It is an important skill," she said defensively. "My father did not care and there was a priest in our keep for my early years. My brother would not learn, but I heard my father talking to another man about a fellow who had been cheated by his seneschal. My father was angry, but could see no way around the trouble. The other man said that if a man could read and figure, he could never be cheated by little black marks on a page."

Rhiannon incredulously acknowledged the truth of her argument.

"So I decided that I would be more than my brother in my father's eyes. I could learn it without appearing undignified. My brother would have been lowered in my father's eyes. So this way I can never be cheated, and neither could my father," her voice trailed off. She shrugged tiredly.

Her captor recovered from his surprise with a doubtful grin. "Well, at least the knowledge did you no injury."

She winced at this remark, but said nothing.

Setting his ale aside, Rhiannon rose from his chair. "Tomorrow we shall walk and ride. You shall have a lute, if there is another one in the place. A book . . ." He spread his hands doubtfully.

Tensing, she raised her head to stare at him, alert to the sudden change in atmosphere in the room.

His eyes glittered in the firelight as he surveyed her. The very sight of her pierced him like a dagger in his vitals. The knowledge of how her soft body clasped his, the memory of how her sweet voice responded to his thrusts with cries of passion she could not repress. He was sweating, rock hard and ready.

He knew if he spoke his voice would be unsteady. Instead, he motioned her to come to him.

She flung up her chin at his imperious gesture. Defiance sparked in the blue eyes at first, then died as his sardonic grin reminded her of her position.

Determined to remain cold and reveal nothing to him, she stiffly moved to stand before him.

"Undress me."

Drawing in her breath sharply, Moira clenched her hands. Even knowing what he would do to her could not prepare her for it. To be his body servant now on top of the humiliation she had already suffered added a crushing weight to her already wounded spirit. A plea for mercy trembled on her lips. They parted, her tongue touched the lower one, moistening it so that it glistened in the firelight.

Rhiannon felt his body tense as if for battle. The moment between them was electric. If she did not obey in another second, he would strip them both and . . .

Her head dropped. "Yes, master," she whispered.

Her trembling hands raised to the heavy torque of gold around his neck, unfastening it and laying it aside. Next came his ring and the leather belt from his middle. The velvet tunic and soft linen shirt beneath were each lifted in turn over his head. Standing so close before him, she could not help but inhale the sharp aroma of his body. As before, the scent set loose strange uncontrollable tremors in her lower belly. She became aware of the heat and a sudden embarrassing moisture at the joining of her thighs. Without thinking, she shifted her body slightly.

With a slow smile, Rhiannon recognized the significance of her movement. Pouring himself more ale, he seated himself in his chair, long legs sprawled, his eyes slitted as he watched her neatly fold his clothing on top of his chest.

When she turned back to him, she could not control the embarrassed blush that rose in her cheeks. His position revealed all too clearly beneath the tight woolen *chausses* his burgeoning desire. Rooted to the spot she stared at him.

"My boots," he reminded her huskily.

Shaking herself dizzily, she knelt at his feet, her hands trembling, her head bowed, seeking to turn her eyes away from him. Her will deserted her! Try as she might, she could not control her eyes. Ever they kept returning to his body, his wide shoulders, his chest with its dark mat of hair narrowing down to a vee which disappeared into the top of his only remaining garment. Again unaware, she licked her lower lip. Before her very eyes, the muscle seemed to swell and strain against the fabric.

Hastily, she directed her attention to the boot in her hands, missing the knowing grin that spread across Rhiannon's face. Delighted at her reactions, he drained the ale.

The boots set aside, she waited trembling on her knees, her damp palms pressed against the tops of her thighs. Shivering as if she were freezing, she sat with bowed head.

"My *chausses*," came the inexorable voice, hoarse now and almost unrecognizable.

Slipping forward between his knees, her hands reached for the tie at his waist. Where her fingers touched, his skin burned. The tankard clanked loudly against the table, startling them both.

He seized her wrists, guiding her hands as he stood. His movement pulled the material over the tops of his thighs. His eyes were like midnight blue lakes searching, staring down into her white face.

Her lips parted slightly as her excitement required more breath than her slightly flared nostrils could draw into her lungs. Studying her, for sign of fear, he slowly raised her hand to his chest. When her fingertips touched his flat masculine nipple, it erected. The acute sensation drew a gasp from him as his eyes closed in ecstasy.

Of its own volition, her other hand slid through the black hair on his ribs to find the other nipple. Assailed by her questing fingers, his eyes closed, his head thrown back, he swayed forward slightly. His thighs came in contact with the soft mounds of her breasts. A deep groan escaped him. His hands clenched painfully around her wrists as he searched for control.

Despite the embarrassment of her position, Moira shuddered uncontrollably as wave after wave of desire wracked her body. The feel of him beneath her fingers, the heat from his body, the scent of him enveloping her made her dizzy, but the dizziness created in her longings that she would never have believed she had. Instead of longing to fling herself away from him in horror and distaste, she found herself longing to fling herself against him, to press even her face against the throbbing muscle before her eyes.

Wild with frustration, her nails clawed at his nipples, inflicting tiny daggerlike stabs of pain. Rhiannon growled with pleasure. Still holding her firmly by the wrists, he hauled her body to her feet, stretching her along his own naked length until they were face to face.

Breathing heavily, they stared at each other, their faces flushed, their lips parted. Between them, she could feel the hard-throbbing muscle pulsating against her belly.

And she wanted it! She longed for it inside her. Moisture stood in her eyes, as the ache in her body grew to savage pain. Her own body throbbed as mercilessly as his. Like a bow, she arched her hardened breasts against his chest.

"You want it, slave girl," he snarled.

His words hurt. Deep within her being, her cringing soul recoiled at the truth of them, but she could not deny them nor herself.

"Yes." Her voice was a sigh of resignation which changed to eager pleading in the next instant. "Oh, yes."

With a growl of triumph, he released her wrists, allowing her to coil her arms tightly around his neck. His hand clamped hard over her buttocks, fingers digging into her flesh, grinding her against him. His mouth savaged her lips, her throat, his teeth closing over the gold chain and tugging it. Dizzy with desire, he lifted her off her feet and carried her, hugged tightly against him, to the bed. There his hands tore her clothing from her body and divested himself of his *chausses*. Both fierce

261

with passion, they faced each other beside the bed. Her fingers spread toward his body, then clenched themselves into fists and dropped to her sides.

A hoarse laugh of triumph rumbled from his throat. Proud as a devil, he swung his long frame onto the blue spread and stretched out, hands cupping the back of his head. A wicked smile curved his lips. "Now you will serve me, slave girl," he chuckled.

Humiliated beyond reason, she could only stand beside the bed, her eyes bound to his recumbent figure, her breath panting, her heart pounding. The steady throbbing between her legs, the pain in the lower part of her belly reduced her pride to dust. Only ignorance of the method of pleasure he wanted her to employ prevented her flinging herself upon him.

Her hesitation amused him. "I shall have to teach you many things to make you a satisfactory woman," he laughed. "As a companion, you are as good as any man, but as a woman you lack skill."

Her eyes flew to his face, reading there a teasing, laughing demon who was enjoying every minute that she died a thousand deaths.

Pitying her, he held out his hand. "Mount me," he commanded, his voice gentle. When she hesitated, he patted the edge of the bed. "Put your knee here . . . please."

It was indeed like mounting a horse, she decided later when she thought about it. Except that instead of the smooth saddle back, she was compelled to lower herself onto the stiffness of his passion, to literally impale herself, engulfing him within her while he cried out in delight and gripped her hips, roughly holding her in place. The ecstasy of his rough handling coupled with the ache inside her caused her to twist her hips, a movement which relieved the ache only to build another more urgent one in its place.

"Move as you will," he whispered through set teeth. His hands released her hips and fell limply to the sides. Her fingers splayed across his belly, digging themselves into his thick black hair. Gingerly, she raised herself slightly, then sank back.

"Oh, yes," he moaned. "Oh, yes." His fists clenched around handfuls of the spread.

Rising and falling, she rode him as she would her black horse, except the sensation was beyond anything she had ever thought possible. Her own excitement was breathtaking. She flung her head back then forward, as she drew in deep breaths and released them in hoarse gasps. Her loose brown hair swirled around her shoulders. Strands of it whipped across her lips and cheeks and stuck there, adhering to the dew of perspiration now covering her body.

"Dear God," he gasped. Within her, his muscle stabbed upward, hurting her for the first and only time. Hot liquid flooded her when she cried out as his upward thrust released the tension and pain within her at the same time. Head thrown back, spine arched, breasts offered to the canopy above their heads, she accepted the spiraling whorls of sensation as the world went black before her eyes. Unconscious, she slumped sideways, her body slipping away from his and sprawling half across him, half on the bed.

When she awakened, he was cradling her in his arms, soothing her with his hands, petting her body, whispering in her ear. Gradually, the meaning as well as the intent of the words penetrated her consciousness. She had done well. Never had a woman done so well. She was a peer among women as well as among men and she was his. At last she was his!

Moira curled herself away from him, her knees drawn up high, her hands clasped beneath her chin. She felt drained as she had never thought possible. Her body floated in its total relaxation. Dimly, she felt his hand lightly caress her shoulder.

"Sweetheart," he whispered against her ear. "Why do you turn out of my arms?"

"I am ashamed. I have never been so humiliated."

"Why?" He sat up, looming over her, trying to read her expression in profile.

"Because I could not withhold anything from you. Not a single thing." Her voice shivered at the memory. "As long as you took me, I could maintain some claim, some small feeling that I was still alone, still me, that at the core I was still resisting. But now . . ."

"It was meant to be," he assured her, turning her into his arms again and pressing her against his shoulder. "*We* were meant to be. Believe me when I tell you the sensations you arouse leave me no core of resistance either."

"But I do not hold you prisoner," she whispered sadly, her mouth opening in a yawn she smothered against his shoulder.

"Do you not?" he chuckled. "Perhaps you do not know your own power."

He waited for her comment, but her even breathing told him that she slept. So sweetly and quietly had she relaxed that he had not known. Probably she had not known either, merely passed from waking into sleeping as a child among her toys.

Her protest and her unhappiness bothered him. She should be settling down now. Accepting her slavery. Accepting the fact that she would be his companion as he had envisioned. The time was close when he wanted to take her with him. In a few weeks after the Christmastide, he would be riding again, protecting his father's lands, making plans to get back the men imprisoned in Lorne Rock. She must accept her station, for he wanted her with him.

He shook his head, stroking the soft brown hair as he did so. What more did she need to make her realize that she was bound to him for . . . He stopped suddenly in his musings. She was bound to him for life. He felt that now. He knew it. She was his companion, his man-woman, his bedmate, his vassal. But an idea dawned upon him. One other bond was possible to them. One that would be forever. He would *marry* her. When there were children, they would be the union of himself with this strong, beautiful, unconquerable girl.

He was so pleased with himself that he shivered. How simple! How silly that he had not thought of marriage before! He placed his hand tentatively on her shoulder, thinking he would tell her of his great idea. Her even breathing stayed his hand. He would tell her in the morning. How happy she would be!

Twenty-Six

"You are mad! I have known for a long time that you saw things the way you wished them to be, not as they were. But this is above all." Moira was almost breathless with exasperation. "You are truly mad. We cannot marry."

"Why not?" he argued, irritated that she had not melted into his arms at the suggestion, as he had expected her to.

"Because of who we are," she cried. "Our fathers, our kin, our people are at each other's throats. We are enemies! You think because you are stronger, I accept your domination with good will."

"You did last night," he reminded her.

"I cannot see the point of resistance," she rejoined. "I would only injure myself."

"You did not resist. You responded," he reminded her again. "I will marry you. I am sure it will be the first time in history that a lord has married his vassal, but we will set the new fashion. It is the perfect solution. Our fathers will be pleased once they have time to think about it. And you as my wife will be accepted here. You can do as you like. Ride with me. Take over the accounts. Practice your lute in the bower. When the children come, you can bear them and resume your activities with the assurance that they are being well cared for as the heirs to Hawk's Keep."

She was silent, her fury smoldering at his presumption.

He patted her shoulder. "You will like the idea when you get used to it. For now, rise and we will dress and go for a ride."

His suggestion of a ride cleared her face and thoughts for a few minutes. To ride again would ease her troubled mind. She could always think better after a brisk gallop with the wind.

Swiftly, she sprang from her bed and as swiftly sprang back in as Conal entered the apartment with water and a basin for washing. She squeaked in alarm, but he ignored her with studious concentration as he deposited his burden. Impassively, he shaved Rhiannon's face, gathered up his razors, and left.

Rhiannon washed his face and hands and dried himself with the towel. She followed suit after wrapping herself in the robe Rhiannon had given her yesterday and which she now tacitly appropriated for her own. Together they dressed quickly and headed for the stables at a good pace.

Her joy at seeing her black gelding was evident. She buried her face in his dark mane and he whinnied and nuzzled her. The grooms saddled him for her and a fine bay, cherry red with gleaming black mane and tail, for Rhiannon. Swinging up simultaneously, they cantered out of the bailey and onto the headland, shimmering in the frosty morning. Neither spoke as they galloped their horses along the cliff.

Moira's lungs expanded as she drank in huge gulps of icy salt air. Out they galloped through the barbican gate and onto the downward slope that led into the valley.

Ahead lay freedom. She glanced at Rhiannon riding tall beside her and her heart sank. She could not hope to escape him. Besides, she had given her word. She was his vassal. He had given her the admiration and status of his friend. He stood against his parents for her. He deserved more than her attempted desertion now. Whatever was to happen between them, she knew must be worked out to their mutual satisfaction.

The black's stride was longer than the bay's and Moira pulled ahead slightly. Rhiannon had a chance to admire her beautiful seat upon the horse, her blending with it as if they were one. Her brown hair whipped behind her as the horse galloped into the wind.

They rode to the floor of the valley where Rhiannon called a halt. "To the north and west lie Colwyn Bay and the little village beneath the keep. To the east lies more of our lands as far as Connah's Quay and the River Dee. To the south . . ."

She interrupted, "To the south lie the disputed lands over which we have fought for so long."

"But no more," he insisted. "We will change all that."

She bowed her head, then raised it and looked toward the south. A shudder coursed through her body as she wheeled her horse and cantered back along the way she had come.

He turned to follow her and caught up. "Why are you turning back, Moira?"

"Because I am hungry," she replied. "And because I would be riding with all speed in that direction if I looked for one more minute. And because I promised not to."

"Then, by all means, let us return to the keep since you are hungry," he smiled. They spurred their horses up the trail together. She rode ahead of him, but as the trail twisted and turned she looked ever toward the south with longing in her eyes.

They returned to the hall where the main meal to break

the fast was in progress. He seated himself in his accustomed place and indicated the place beside him for her to sit. She hesitated, but since most people were finishing, no one seemed to mind. Quietly, she seated herself at his right as a servitor came forward to ladle porridge into large bowls. Pieces of salt pork were added to the top and the meal was washed down with ale. Again the hot crusty bread was set on the table before them with pats of butter to be spread on with their thumbs.

With each new item of food, the servitor handed everything to her and she in turn served Rhiannon. It was a serivce required of a slave or private body servant. Her status was known to everyone; no questions were asked.

When their meal was finished, he returned her to the room and locked her chain in place around her neck. Without speaking, he left her alone in the room. Again she seated herself in his chair before the fire and braced herself for the long day.

To her surprise, he returned in less than half an hour carrying a lute, a book, and a needle with several skeins of thread. "You have no excuse to sit idle now," he informed her gleefully. "You can practice and you can read. I do not know what the title is and to my knowledge 'tis the only book in the keep. 'Twas left here by a fellow who traveled this way many years ago. I think he left it by mistake. 'Tis a pretty thing," he opened it to display the carefully copied and illuminated pages. "And finally," he finished triumphantly, "if music and books do not fill your time, you can mend my clothing. Start with that hose with the burn hole in the knee." He grinned and was gone.

Moira bent to the book immediately. Never had she seen a one such as this. Her reading had been from the Bible in the Latin of the Church and the Welsh dialect of the Rock's accounts and daily lists and doings. The book before her was a new and exciting mystery to her. Many of the words were strange and the drawings so fanciful as to be almost frightening in their implication of the unknown. The title was the *Mabinogion* and before Moira had laboriously read far into it she was caught up in the fascinating beauty of the stories of gods and heroes, of deeds unparalleled.

The shadows lengthened and still she read, her pace increasing with practice. From time to time, the servants had come in again to do their usual chores and still she read on, ignoring them as they cast suspicious glances at her and privately labled her strange, addled, and probably a witch. Only witches and priests and sometimes clerks could read. No lady ever read, they believed. When Rhiannon returned shortly before dusk, she leaped up, greeted him, and poured him ale. Together they ate their evening meal of bread and broken meats. As he had commanded, she knelt before him, pressed her breasts against his knees, and waited while he unlocked her chain. As she raised her limpid eyes to his, he kissed her gently with rising passion, but allowed her to draw off his boots while she was down before him. With her help, he disrobed and climbed into the steaming bath. He sat in the tub, allowing the warm water to ease his tired muscles while she watched him. At his command, she poured him more ale.

When he was settled comfortably, he cocked an inquiring eye in her direction. "What did you do today? Did you find the day better than yesterday?"

"I read today from the book you left for me. I have never known anything like it. It is the story of knights in search of the cup from which Jesu the Christ drank at the Last Supper." Her eyes sparkled with pleasure as she lifted her eyes to his. "I had heard that it was possible for a book to tell a story, but I had not ever seen such a thing."

270

"Read a portion of it to me," he commanded.

She opened the book to the first page and began, "Lords: Now listen in the name of the Virgin Queen! May Almighty God who distributes all rewards look to receive you too into angelic glory!" She read slowly and carefully, her voice low and pleasing. Rhiannon sipped his ale and the bath water grew cool. Finally, they both realized that the light was gone and that she was reading hunched over the hearth by the light of the dying fire.

Hastily, he rose out of the bath and dried himself while she undressed and climbed into bed. That night he drew her to him and made love tenderly to her, preferring himself the gentle arousal and quiet completion.

Afterward, they lay side by side in the dark while she told him some of the events of the story. "Will you read more of it to me tomorrow night?" he requested.

"It will be my pleasure," she said. "I will do mending tomorrow on your clothes and practice on my lute and when you return to the room at nightfall, I will read for both of us."

He drew her against him to kiss her neck beneath her ear. "I am coming to believe that the best thing I ever did was to trick you into freeing me."

She made no answer, but she was not asleep. Her body quivered at his words.

"Sweetheart," he sighed against her neck, shaking her gently.

"What?" she whispered, exasperated.

"Do you think that you might come to say that the best thing you ever did was to offer wine to a suffering enemy?"

She refused to answer him, but turned out of his arms and presented him with her back.

He chuckled softly and curled his body spoon fashion around hers, his arm across her. In a minute, his even breathing and his relaxed body told her he was asleep. For

271

her, however, his words had disturbed a part of her that she could not bear to look at. She ground her teeth silently in a sort of nervous anguish. Finally, she relaxed in his warmth and slept.

In this manner, they passed their days for the next week. They woke together, rode or walked together, and ate together. In the afternoon, he chained her to the wall and left her to herself. She mended his clothes and practiced her lute. In the second week, he brought a dusty pile of scrolls and parchments into the apartment and set them on the floor beside the table. A small lackey followed with a bundle of tally sticks, a checker board with counters, and an inkhorn and quills.

Rhiannon grinned wolfishly. "I told father that you could read and cast accounts. At first he was unimpressed, but I reminded him how long it had been since the priest had even looked the mess over. On further consideration, he decided that you could do what you would with it and then he could have it all checked by the priest when he returns."

Moira viewed the dusty pile with disgust. "I think I would rather play the lute."

Rhiannon shot her a look and saw that her eyes were downcast and her hands were crossed demurely in her lap. He chuckled and lifted her chin with his dusty fingers. "No doubt. 'Tis the first time I have seen you looking so maidenly. I think you suddenly seek to play the soft and innocent, as well as ignorant, maiden to avoid a nasty job. Remember, sweetheart, it cannot be both ways. If you are my man-woman, then you must play the man's part as well." He kissed her on her pouting lips.

"I was but trying," she smiled.

"Looking at that mess, I cannot blame you," he agreed. "But you said you could do it. So have at it. I would not want your hands idle nor your spirit dying."

He jumped back in time to avoid her well-aimed foot. At the door he turned, chuckling.

"'Tis well you are chained. We can bring you all manner of interesting and unpleasant jobs." He slid around the door and closed it after him while she searched vainly for something to throw.

By noon, Moira had cursed Rhiannon roundly. The dust rose into her nose each time she opened one of the scrolls. Her eyes itched; ink stained her thumb and third finger. But she was making headway. A tiny thrill of satisfaction accompanied the action of re-rolling each yellowed scroll to lay it aside and turn to another. And the columns of figures grew on the fresh sheets of paper.

Bent over a particularly indecipherable set of figures, she did not hear the door open quietly behind her. The sound of Rhiannon's sister's youthful voice startled her so that she broke the nub off the quill.

"'Tis true! She must be a witch!" Edain's voice was high and shrill. "Look, Margwin, she is casting spells, just as Owen said."

Twisting her body around on the bench, Moira frowned at the two women who stood at the door. The chain rattled against the wood, reminding all three of Moira's status.

"See how Rhys has her chained," Edain nodded smugly. "He must know that she is dangerous."

"Or that she is useful," the blond woman, whose name Moira remembered from the conversation between Gethin and Rhiannon, shrugged knowingly.

Rising, again with a disconcerting rattle of the chain, Moira inclined her head. "How may I serve you, Lady Edain? Lord Rhiannon is about the business of the keep. Usually he does not return to these rooms before nightfall."

Pointing rudely, Edain chattered to Margwin as if Moira had not spoken. "So tall! Did I not tell you she was

273

so? She is built like a man."

Margwin's frank appraisal made Moira's cheeks feel hot. Edain's youthful thoughtless rudeness was far more tolerable than the knowing smirk of the other.

"She does not seem very beautiful," Edain sniffed. "That must be another proof that she is a witch. She must have cast a spell over my brother so that he thinks he sees her as beautiful."

"I am no witch," Moira denied softly. "I have no spells to cast."

"Oh, you could not admit if you were one," Edain laughed. "The priest has said that a witch can never tell the truth. And then, sitting there looking at all those black marks and making more yourself. You are just as father says. A witch."

The blond woman Margwin shifted her weight from one foot to the other. Her heavy bosom under the finely woven wool shivered. Placing one hand on her wide hip, she yawned delicately. "I really have to agree with you, Edain. She must use witchcraft to attract Lord Rhys. He has always liked his women to be womanly."

One eyebrow rose quizzically as Moira regarded the one who had spoken. This woman belonged to Lord Gethin, either as slave or mistress. So much she had gleaned from the conversation around the table the night of the family meal. Did Margwin look elsewhere as well? She longed to ask when Rhiannon had confided his preferences to his father's mistress, but held her tongue. Her ice blue eyes stared hard, appraising the other.

As if she read Moira's thoughts, Margwin flushed. Angrily, she tossed her head. "Shall we be gone, Lady Edain?"

Oblivious to the undercurrents in the room, Edain blinked in surprise. "Oh, I suppose so. I could not believe that we had such a creature in the keep, but now . . ."

The two women left, closing the door.

Shaking her head, Moira sank down on the bench again. Although her father's position and her status had kept her a solitary person with few women friends, she wished that Edain had at least spoken to her directly rather than talking about her as if she had not been right there. Still, she could expect no better as the body slave of the lord and enemy to the rest of the keep. Added to those humiliations was the taint of witchcraft. No one would come near her. She sighed, passing a hand across her forehead.

Over her shoulder, she made a face at the work yet to be done. She would have liked a friend.

For three days more, she struggled with the accounts, discovering shortages, mistakes, overcharges, and overpayments. Finally, she prepared a list of all materials which should be in the environs of the keep according to the accounts and a statement of the errors she noted. Rhiannon took it to his father and returned with the message that the priest would be grateful.

"I doubt very much that he will be grateful," she replied. "He is not well trained. There were many errors which he should not have made."

"I only hope they were honest errors," Rhiannon remarked dryly. "Father does not like to be cheated."

On an evening of the second week of her enslavement, Rhiannon was sitting at her side, their chairs drawn together, and she was reading to him, pointing out the words as she spoke each one. He repeated them in a monotone. Very quickly, he was getting the idea. Words were all composed of letters and each letter represented a certain sound. He was amazed at the ease with which he could pick up the words after he caught the idea.

He had never really understood his own name, until she had explained to him about the letters that represented the sounds. Then he could see that his name was really a combination of the sounds of it. He could read hers more easily, for hers contained fewer letters and therefore fewer sounds.

The sight of Rhiannon's dark head bent over the book, his face intent, his black hair more disordered than usual where he had run his hand through it impatiently, moved Moira. Her fingers itched to push the unruly locks back from his forehead.

He looked up at her, catching her staring at him. The eager expression in his eyes changed to one of inquiry. Hastily, she blinked, catching herself up and supplying the word he needed to read further.

Again, the reverie caught her. So peaceful, so alone, the two of them. His knee touching hers as they shared the book, their bodies so close together that she could smell the herbal soap Conal used to shave him, could feel the warmth emanating from his body.

What would he do, she wondered, if she were to reach out to take his face between her two hands and kiss him full on the mouth? Excitement pricked her.

A knock sounded at the door of the apartment. Without waiting for an answer, the door swung open and Owen Llewellyn stood framed in the doorway. "Lord Gethin requires both of you in the hall immediately," he scowled.

Moira sprang to her feet. "My father has ransomed me," she cried.

Rhiannon rose behind her, putting his hand on her arm. His face was scowling. "And that pleases you, does it?"

She turned to face him. Her voice trembled with the depth of her emotion. "To be free!" she exclaimed. "To be among friends again. To be the mistress of my own body. To be able to ride when I choose and to walk where I choose. To see smiling, friendly faces at table rather than ones filled with hatred and fear." She drew in her breath sharply. "Yes! Yes, I want to be *free!*"

His face set in hard, cold lines. "Moira of Lorne, I will give you anything else in the world. I swore that to you. But I will not set you free. I have spoken with you again and again. You belong to me. School yourself to the idea, as I have schooled myself to the idea that I am no longer one person but two."

She bowed her head. In icy silence, they walked from the room and presented themselves in the hall before the dais. Lord Gethin sat in his high chair. To his right and down on carved chairs and benches sat Owen Llewellyn, Henry Fletcher, Huw Llengaron, as well as others she did not recognize. An argument had been swirling among them.

Gethin ap Breannon raised his hand for silence. "My son, I summoned you to the council where the disposition of your property is being discussed. We are uncertain what course to take. Some say to accept the ransom which Lorne is offering. Others," he indicated Owen, "insist that she be kept as hostage for Lorne's continued quiet. What do you say?"

"He should not be consulted. Of course, he will want to keep her," sneered the heavy Owen. "The bitch has whored herself upon his body until he is besotted with her. He cannot be expected to make a wise decision. She should be kept all right, but not by him. She should be kept under close guard. If her father so much as stirs along our borders, we should send him a finger; if he lifts his hands against us, a tooth. That is the way to keep the hound at bay."

"No," spoke up Huw Llengaron. "We are not beasts. She is an innocent girl. She has not killed nor burned nor looted. Let her return to her father. His ransom will pay many men to defend us. We will be too powerful for him to attack. We do not make war on innocent women."

"In truth," Lord Gethin spoke, "I agree with Huw. She is a woman and can be of little value. I am surprised at the amount of ransom offered for her return. One hundred marks is a great amount of gold."

"Hear me!" Rhiannon stepped forward. "My solution to the problem is a good one which offers peace and security." They all stared at him. Moira tensed at his side. "She is her father's only daughter and only child. All other members of her family are dead. She has told me this herself. Her father grows old."

"Kill her," demanded Owen Llewellyn. "With her gone, he will die swiftly."

"She will marry me," Rhiannon announced. A mutter of consternation and surprise went up from the men. "She will unite with me by blood. When her father dies, I will inherit his lands through her."

"No!" Moira protested. "My father will gladly pay the ransom. Lord Gethin, I beg you."

"Silence!" Lord Gethin was on his feet. Clearly, such a possibility had not occurred to him. And clearly, too, much was to be gained by this singular offer from his son.

"I will not marry you," she spat at Rhiannon.

"Was she a virgin when you first mounted her?" Gethin spoke as if she were not there.

"A pure and innocent maid," Rhiannon affirmed, grinning broadly.

"Has any other had her?"

"None."

"Girl, has any but my son touched your body?"

For a full minute Moira thought, weighing the consequences. Such a declaration made in a council would be a statement that would forever brand her. Although she longed to lie to shame Rhiannon and make him withdraw his proposal, she dared not. Fearful and confused, she bowed her head, her cheeks scarlet. "No," she whispered.

Lord Gethin rose and paced back and forth on the dais studying her. "Her blood is tainted," he said. "For years

278

we have fought these people."

"Let it end here," said Rhiannon. "With her father's death, we would be overlords of all of North Wales. Before his death, we could call upon him for peace and aid. The blood would be binding on him as well as on her."

"I will refuse at the altar," Moira argued. "You cannot force me to marry against my will."

Rhiannon turned her to face him and shook her savagely. "You will do as I order you. If you refuse to obey my commands, there are ways. A simple drink laced with poppy and you would do exactly what I say."

She shuddered and lapsed into silence.

"Is she with child?" Lord Gethin asked.

The room fell silent as all seemed to lean forward to hear the answer.

Rhiannon shrugged. "Whether she is or is not is unimportant. She is my slave and will soon be my wife. She will be treated as the lady she is from this time forth. From the time of her marriage, she will be allowed the freedom of the keep even as my mother and sister, whose sister she will then become."

"She is a Lorne! An enemy!" howled Owen Llewellyn. "She will murder us all."

"She will serve us all and honor us all." Rhiannon retorted. "She holds hard by her word, for her father raised her to be his son as well as his heir. She understands the duties of a woman and the loyalties of a man. If she takes her oath, she will hold by it."

"Not if she were drugged at the altar," Gethin spoke. "There is not a man among us who would hold with the value of those words."

"She will not be drugged," Rhiannon said quietly. "She will obey my command because she holds by her word. Is that not right, my lady?"

Again, the expectant silence.

Finally, Moira lifted her proud head. Her face was white as death, her eyes great luminous pools in the light. Her right hand rose to grasp the chain around her neck. "As you will, my lord," she said.

His eyes met hers in a long embrace. "Then my will be done," he said. "Congratulate me, my lords," he turned to the waiting room. "For in three days time we shall be married."

Twenty-Seven

"Were you really younger than me when you learned to ride a horse, milady?" The youngest lackey Jenk paused in cleaning the hearth, to stare admiringly at the brown-haired woman who had captured his heart as well as his imagination.

The other two brothers were still standoffish, inclined to do their tasks and leave without a glance in her direction. Jenk, on the other hand, had instantly taken to her pleasant smile and quiet manner. She was not haughty like Lady Branwen, impatient like Lady Edain, nor rude and abusive like Margwin. When he had discussed her with his brothers, defending her with those arguments, they had jeered at him.

"She's just a slave, dolt!" Higg the oldest had declared. "Why shouldn't she be nice to you? You're better than she is."

"I ain't," Jenk had argued. "She's a lady through and through! But so nice."

Now from over her embroidering frame, she smiled at him, her blue eyes warm and encouraging. "My father gave my brother a pony and was teaching him to ride. I was watching from the garden wall. Father told Matthew to turn the pony's head with the reins, but Matthew got it wrong. He was left-handed, you see, and had a problem with directions all his life. 'I can do it,' I said. Father said, 'Let us see.' He plopped me up on the back of Matthew's pony and slapped it on the rump. I was determined not to fall off, but to do it the way Father had said. And I did.'' She chuckled. "Matthew was furiously angry, but Father only grinned. The next day he brought me a pony, too.''

Jenk's eyes were like stars in his round tanned face as he pictured the scene. "Your brother must have been a long time forgiving you. Higg and Wat get mad as fire if I try to get too big for my breeches.''

"Serves them right," Moira replied. "The older ones need to remember that you are a person, too. You will be a man before they know it.''

The door flew open without a knock, slamming back against the wall. Suddenly, the room seemed filled with hard-faced men with clenched fists.

"Resist and you draw your last breath here and now, witch." Owen Llewellyn stabbed his finger at Moira as she rose from her chair, tipping over the embroidery frame. In his other hand, he carried a drawn sword.

"The priest has sent for you, Moira of Lorne, to be exorcised," Owen continued grandly. "If he finds that exorcism is not possible, then you will be handed over to the church court to be burned as a witch. Either way, the Lord Rhiannon will no longer be held in your thrall.''

"I am not a witch. I cast no spells," Moira protested, her hands outstretched to ward off the men who formed a menacing circle around her.

"Tie her hands!" warned one burly fellow. "The witches have the power in their hands. Fasten her, Jock.''

Lunging backward to escape them, Moira tipped over the chair as she made for the dagger she knew Rhiannon kept in the chest at the foot of the bed.

Like wolves, they were upon her. One wrenched her hands roughly behind her while another pulled a piece of leather cord from his jerkin and bound her wrists tightly. A third stuffed a greasy wad of unprocessed wool in her mouth and tied it in place.

Her legs were seized when one man went back across the chest with her foot in his stomach. Two men wrapped heavy leather cord around her slender ankles.

"Now for the hood," Owen snarled, satisfaction tinging his voice as she was hauled to her feet, panting yet defiant. "Cover up those witch's eyes that might steal a man's soul." A black sack was thrown over her head and the drawstring pulled uncomfortably tight around her neck.

Through the muffling terror-filled darkness, she heard their voices.

"Where's the scullion?"

"He's run. Shall I get him?"

"What matter? He's too stupid to know what's gone on. Besides, who would he tell?"

"Here! Hold yourself still." A heavy fist slammed into the side of her head.

The sound of someone praying penetrated the throbbing pain in her head. She was seated upright in a hard chair. Groggily, she stirred, seeking to raise her head. The hood had been removed, but a hard hand pressed against the back of her skull, holding her head bowed. She tried to draw a deep breath, but was prevented by tight cords encircling her chest. A slight flexing of her muscles informed her that her hands were still bound tightly behind her.

The hand shifted to grasp her hair and jerk her head up. "Now," Owen's voice snarled in her ear. "Now raise your face and reveal your demon to the good priest."

283

Candlelight cast flickering shadows over the faces of the priest and the men whom Moira recognized as the ones who had kidnapped her from Rhiannon's apartments. Implacable hatred gleamed from their eyes. A thrill of fear shivered up her spine.

"Release her mouth," the priest intoned piously. "She must answer for her immortal soul whether it be the property of Satan or of God."

With a quick flick of his wrist, Owen pulled the tight kerchief down around her neck and plucked the wad of wool from between her lips.

"Speak, daughter. Say what you are for your immortal soul."

Fighting nausea from the taste of the gag as well as the dryness it had caused, she could only shake her head. Wisps of wool clung to her teeth and tongue. Forcing some moisture into her mouth, she gathered the rough, irritating stuff and spat it to the side.

"Sacrilege!" Owen noted with satisfaction.

"I could not speak with that disgusting wool in my mouth," Moira protested hoarsely. "I am not a witch. I have never cast spells. I am a helpless captive of the Lord Rhiannon. As such, I am his property. *You*," she faced the assembly defiantly, "are the ones who are jeopardizing your own lives by mishandling me." Her eyes sought Owen Llewellyn's in the yellow glow. Angrily, he flushed.

"Father Ambrosius, this woman is too far gone for exorcism. She should be tried here and now for witchcraft."

"Agreed, my son." The thin priest stepped upward into the stronger light to seat himself in a carved chair on a raised platform.

Her mind working frantically, Moira stared at him. The richness of his robes, the gold crucifix swinging at his side belied the poverty of a simple parish priest.

Rhiannon had said Gethin did not like to be cheated. Could this be the man responsible for the abysmal condition of the keep's books?

"Let the trial begin! Let justice be won! Let the Lord's will be done!"

Sensing the futility of protest, Moira stared into the dimness around the chair to which she was bound. Where had they carried her? She was not in the church. No cross nor altar sanctified these deliberations. Could Rhiannon find her? Would she be tried and burned before he could rescue her?

Never once did she doubt that he would claim her. A small grim smile curved her lips. He did not like to be robbed of his property. She was sure that whether he cared for her as a person or not, he would not allow others to take that which he regarded as his own.

"Who comes first to bear witness against her?" The priest Ambrosius raised his hand and gestured toward a spot behind and to the right of Moira's chair. A burly figure shuffled forward. The guard of the dungeon!

He threw her an uneasy glance as he stepped into the light.

"Odo, the warden," Owen Llewellyn announced in a grand voice.

"What did you witness that made you suspicious that this woman might be bewitched?"

Blinking blearily first at the man in the high chair then at the bound woman, the guard cleared his throat. "Well, your worship, she was brought to me by Lord Owen here to be imprisoned, her being a Lorne. But right away, things begin happening wrong."

"What things?"

"One man, Huw Llengaron, sent her furs to keep herself warm." He shook his head in a puzzled fashion. "Never had nothing like that happen before. No one cares about prisoners nor sends them furs. Usually they just stays there in their cells until they dies. Then I takes them out and throws their bodies in the lye pit."

Despite her intention to remain unmoved by this charade, Moira shuddered. Such would have been her fate, as Owen intended, had Rhiannon not returned to bring her forth.

The warden droned on, describing various instances of prisoners living and dying.

"Get to the point, man!" Owen snarled. "This prisoner, Moira of Lorne."

"She was different," the warden nodded. "She never begged for mercy, always glared at me from the back of her cell. I put her in the lowest cell in the keep," he explained to the priest. "Icy cold it is. She should have froze to death, but she didn't. Always her eyes kept glittering at me like the fires of hell was burning in her, you understand."

A mutter from the crowd encouraged him. He grinned foolishly. "She never cried a single tear, your worship."

"Never wept?" The priest leaned forward at the statement.

"No, your worship. Never. Not a single tear. Oh, I beat her hard one day. She tried to bite me. Punished her I did with no food, but something fed her and kept her warm and she never cried for mercy. 'Twas like she knew she had nothing to fear from poor guards like meself."

Father Ambrosius nodded sagely, his eyes meeting Owen Llewellyn's. "'Tis well known that witches cannot weep. Their tearducts, as well as other womanly aspects, are dried up." He motioned the warden away.

"Mair, the laundress," Owen called.

Nervously, the scullery maid sent to Moira's chamber after Owen's attack stepped from the shadows. "Always has a candle lit beside her, she does," the woman blurted in a shaking voice. "I never thought nothing about it. I just come in daily for the soiled clothing. That one. She never goes near the bower with the rest of the womenfolk. Always sits alone with that candle burning beside her."

"Why should the candle be there?" The priest pronounced the question to draw attention to the importance of the answer.

"For her to read that book that Lord . . ."

"To read from a book?" The priest interrupted the wench's testimony excitedly. "To read from a book?"

"Oh, yes, your worship, she always reads from the book and she was teaching Lord Rhys to read from it . . ."

"Teaching the lord." The priest's sonorous, scandalized tones—those with which he harangued his parishioners—thundered in the room. "Teaching the lord. Dear blessed saints preserve him. Worse and worse. A witch who would bewitch others and lead them into the snares of the devil. She is Satan's own."

His voice rose in righteous wrath as his face flushed and his eyes swept the room to see who dared to disagree. None spoke against him. None cared to dispute words of condemnation against this enemy. The angry mutterings died in silence.

"Owen Llewellyn," the priest nodded to his chief supporter.

"Oh, aye, your worship." Owen stepped forward into the light. "She and all her kin are spawn of the devil. Demons from hell who murder innocents. My wife and babes . . ." He paused. His eyes rolled insanely as they widened, showing the whites all around the iris. "They were foully slaughtered by the men of Lorne."

Father Ambrosius stirred restively. "But that was long ago, Lord Owen. How did she bewitch the lord to bring her into the keep?"

"Cast spells," Owen snarled. "*Spells!* If my men and I had not arrived when we did the day we found them together, Lord Rhiannon would have been spirited away.

They stood side by side. She was supposed to be his prisoner, but she had entrapped him. When he returned to the keep, he took her out of the dungeon where she belonged. Called him right out of his meal, right away from his table she did. With witchcraft!" Spittle had collected in a white foam at the corners of his lips.

"You say the lord left his meat to release her from the dungeon?" The priest's voice carried the proper tone of amazement.

"Yes, your worship. Lifted him right out of his chair she did. His mother and father could not stop him. He released her and took her directly to his apartments where she worked her will on his body." Here Owen's voice lowered malevolently. "He has been besotted ever since. What evil, lustful practices did she engage in with him no one in this company will ever know."

A mutter of voices swelled behind her chair. Had this not been so terrible, Moira would have laughed out loud. She could not help but think of Rhiannon's deliberate initiation of her into the rites of love despite her protests, her resistance.

"She taught him!" Owen thundered. "Oh, the witch instructed him well! What filthy practices of hand and mouth and body did she use to bind the young lord to her side and to the devil? I shudder to think what his young body might have been subjected to."

A woman's voice in the assembly, suspiciously like Margwin's, rose in condemnation. "A terrible witch indeed!"

"'Tis certain he wants to marry with her now," the priest agreed piously. "Further profanation of the Lord's sacred rites. If this marriage should be performed, the whole of this keep would be placed in deadly danger. Excommunication would be the fate of all who sanctioned this unholy alliance."

His glittering gaze sought to pierce Moira with his

288

righteous fury. "Speak, witch. What can you say to defend yourself against the honest and lawful testimony given here against you?"

"False," Moira replied calmly. "All false. A base of truth, priest, from which false conclusions have been drawn for the purpose of revenge for a madman." She nodded in the direction of Owen Llewellyn. "All know the great tragedy which blackened this man's life. All know of his obsession for vengeance."

"Do not speak of obsession and vengeance here," Ambrosius warned. "You are on trial for your soul. Defend yourself."

"The warden says I did not weep. What good would weeping have done? My tears would only have made him laugh, as would my pleas for mercy. Huw Llengaron pitied me because I was an innocent woman wretchedly imprisoned. His own tenderness and mercy prompted him to the act, not my so-called spells."

"Deny, if you can, the charges that you have bewitched the Lord Rhiannon."

"I do deny them. Lord Rhiannon has kept me a political prisoner. He and his father Lord Gethin planned to use me first as a hostage against the release of men taken prisoner by my father in Lord Rhiannon's raid. Later, when I was found to have worth in my father's eyes, Lord Rhiannon determined to marry with me in the hope of forcing an alliance with my father to unify all northern Wales against the English. I have had no say in this. Certainly, I have not bewitched Lord Rhiannon. He is a man as any other." Her voice trailed away to a whisper. But she had said too much.

"Slut!" The woman's voice rose from behind her.

"All these words may be true," Ambrosius agreed solemnly, holding up his hand in silence, "but the damning knowledge is there for all to see and cannot be denied. The devil's own skill is invested in you, woman, his handmaiden."

"I have no skill," Moira's voice was even. Her eyes never left his face. Puzzled, she shook her head.

"You have. You have sold your womanhood at an early age for this ability which only the devil would bestow upon a woman. God himself gives this ability to some few men who are His chosen keepers of His word. But never to the daughters of Eve, who betrayed us all. The black words on the pages of evil works condemn her." The priest rose from his chair, his hand upraised. "Vile witch. Thou didst make the devil's pact, which I doubt not an inspection of your body will reveal. By this terrible knowledge he gave you, you seek to discredit God's servants in their appointed tasks as well as to seduce the righteous from the path to heaven. Your ability to read and to write betrays you to us all."

Angered, Moira surged forward against the cords that bound her upright in the chair. "Now the reason for this travesty is clear, priest. You did not keep Lord Gethin's records as you should have done. Your carelessness was revealed to him at Lord Rhiannon's instigation. Perhaps you were not merely witless," she suggested angrily. "Perhaps you were stealing . . ."

"Silence her!" Ambrosius thundered. "Her accusations prompted by the devil befoul this assembly."

Owen's hard right hand whipped round his body and cracked across Moira's face. Her denunciation ended in a shriek of pain.

"Strip her, so we may see the devil's mark upon her body," the priest commanded, his face red with anger at the accusations which galled him in the spots already touched by Gethin's angry words.

One man knelt at the back of the chair, fumbling at the knots.

Moira licked her bleeding lip. "I am innocent," she insisted thickly, turning her head away from Ambrosius and Owen. "I am Lord Rhiannon's affianced bride. You condemn yourselves . . ."

The cord fell away. Owen's rough hand on her shoulder hauled her to her feet. His other hand sought the neck of her gown to rip it away.

"I would not do that if I were you, Owen," Rhiannon's voice lanced through the proceedings. "I would very gently remove my hand from her throat and set about in quickest fashion to free her, else this arrow will find your heart and end your insane quest for vengeance once and for all."

"My lord," Ambrosius descended from the platform, his hands fluttering in agitation. "My lord . . ."

"Father Ambrosius." Lord Gethin followed his son into the room. "I trust you have an explanation as to why my son's apartments were broken into, his intended kidnapped from them, and her body brought to this place to suffer this indignity. Your power is within the church, not in this keep."

"My Lord Gethin . . ." Ambrosius fell back. The sound of scuttling footsteps could be heard. A door opened in the wall behind Moira's chair. Silhouettes of departing figures could be seen in the rectangle of light. Alone to face the powerful man he had cheated, Ambrosius bowed his head. "Mea culpa, Lord Gethin, I only sought to protect all my sheep."

"When I want your protection, pastor, I will ask for it," Gethin declared. "Could you not minister to the soul of this wretched man?" He indicated Owen Llewellyn, who stood white-faced, the froth flecking the corners of his mouth.

Ambrosius bowed his head. "I am heartily sorry, milord."

Rhiannon uncocked the arbalest and stepped forward to place an arm around Moira's shoulders. Trembling with weakness, she leaned against him, massaging her wrists awkwardly. "Can you walk, sweetheart?" he whispered against her hair.

"I think so. I cannot feel my feet, but doubtless they are down there on the ends of my legs just below my ankles." She gave a nervous little laugh tinged with hysteria.

He cursed softly, passing the weapon to the small lackey, who stood wide-eyed but grinning behind him. "By your leave, Father." He swept Moira up in his arms, despite her embarrassed protests.

"You have it, my son," Lord Gethin nodded, his eyes never leaving the priest's cowering figure. "Take your lady to your apartments and see to her hurts. I shall deal with this with the help of my good *page*, Master Jenk."

As Rhiannon turned with her in his arms, Moira's fingers stretched out to caress Jenk's blond head. "My thanks, good friend," she called as her lord bore her away.

Twenty-Eight

The change was almost too much for Moira to bear.
From captive she became honored guest. Before she and
Rhiannon had risen from bed on the morning following
the abortive witchcraft trial, Conal had delivered a
message, uttered in most respectful tones, that Lady
Moira was to present herself to Lady Branwen in the
bower at her earliest convenience.

Rhiannon laughed as Moira fretted through the small
meal that Conal had brought to their table. "I suspect
that Father has instructed her to make you a gown to be
married in. Do not forget the blue silk that I liked so
much but you were reluctant to have. I should have
insisted, but the idea had not occurred to me that you
would need a wedding dress at that time."

Only two lackeys, glancing enviously about at the lady
whom Jenk had succored, brought bath water, tub, and
towels. Moira sank into the warm water and bathed
carefully. Since she would be scrutinized by all the ladies
of the bower, she wanted to be at her best. Finishing
quickly, she stepped out and Rhiannon took the towel
from her to rub and pat her dry. While she dressed, he

bathed himself.

Brushing her long hair, Moira began to braid it, but he stopped her. "Wear your hair loose, in token of your virginity," he instructed her.

"I am no virgin, as well you know, and so does everyone in this keep," she protested.

"You were a maid when I took you. No other man has possessed you. I would proclaim to all in the church that you bring to my bed a body that has been known by no one but your husband."

"I have too much hair. It will never stay smooth down my back."

"Then get Mother to make you a band or something to tie it back from your face, but no braids or knots," he grinned. "It is my command."

Suddenly, she smiled and swept the floor in a deep curtsey. "Aye, my lord. Your will is mine."

"'Tis well," he grinned his lupine grin. "Go now. You are free to roam wherever you wish within the keep today. But do not go outside. I trust you, but you know those who would harm you and say you were trying to escape. Do you obey me in this?"

"Yes," she responded. "I will be too busy at any rate." She marched resolutely to the door, but paused before it, her hand on the handle to look back at him. Her face was troubled. "I feel torn apart," she said softly. "I am my father's daughter. He taught me to keep my vows. At the same time, he taught me to hate and to make war. I cannot do both. I cannot unsay my vow to you. I have, I fear, destroyed my peace."

Rhiannon regarded her soberly. "Do as I command. In war, when knights are captured they are given their parole on their word of honor. You have done nothing more or less than they." He came to her and took her in his arms. She laid her head against his shoulder. "I have vowed to you that you will not be called upon to fight

294

against your father."

In a muffled voice she spoke, "But I am marrying with the enemy. I am joining my flesh with his."

He smoothed her hair. "You never had a choice. I would have had you against all the world."

With a sigh, she pushed him away, turned, and glided out the door.

As she entered the bower, the buzz of conversation stopped, then rose again in an ominous hum. Lady Branwen and Edain were sitting before twin embroidery frames beneath the windows on the east side. Where the tapestries had been drawn back, a hazy sunlight filtered through the skins scraped thin and oiled and stretched on frames to protect the room from the December chill.

Lady Branwen rose from her chair to meet her son's intended bride. Her face was cold as stone. Her sky blue gown and white wimple made her brown eyes appear hard as topazes. As the woman approached, Moira curtseyed. Branwen returned her obeisance with a stiff inclination of the head.

"The purple wool and *chausses* are ready for you to try," she said without preamble. "If you will follow me."

When she saw the garments, Moira realized they were meant as a slight, for they were the most inexpensive materials chosen, being coarse native wool dyed with cheap common stains. Lady Branwen had expected that Moira would be ransomed from the castle, or perhaps that Rhiannon would forget his orders.

In one corner of the bower, a small screen had been set up behind which ladies could disrobe. Moira flushed with embarrassment before these hostile eyes because she had no shift. Shivering, she stepped behind the screen and began to undress. First, her tawny gown and then the slippers and *chausses*. She looked ludicrous, she knew, and her humiliation was total when Lady Branwen, who had followed and stood regarding her critically, said in a loud voice, "Come! Come! Strip off that shirt as well for we have a linen shift and shirt that matches the outer garments."

Stripping off the shirt and flinging it defiantly over the screen, Moira bowed her head before the stare that Lady Branwen directed at her. "Turn sideways," she directed in a loud voice. Moira did so and Branwen sighed. "You show no sign of childbearing. Can it be that you have not conceived? As thin as you are, you should be giving some indication at this point."

Laughter rippled through the bower. Moira blushed to the roots of her hair. "I do not know, milady, but I do not think it possible to know so soon."

"Why does my son wish to marry you and with such unseemly haste? I fear he has taken leave of his senses or, perhaps worse, become bewitched. They say you are a sorceress. Turn around. Turn all the way around and hold your arms out from your sides." Gritting her teeth, Moira did so. The feeling of shame was leaving her to be replaced by cold anger. "I see no evil mark upon your body," Lady Branwen continued. "Alys, bring the garments."

With a sigh, Moira lowered her arms to her sides and gratefully accepted the linen underclothes and wool gown and *chausses*. Swiftly, she put them on. They fit well enough, but were distressingly plain and obviously carelessly sewn. The contempt for her was evident in the rather large, uneven stitches in the seams. Furthermore, the embroidery and fine finishing of the hems and facings that characterized the garments of the other women in the bower were absent.

No one expected me to stay, Moira thought.

"Come this way," Lady Branwen commanded. Moira put on her slippers which clashed hideously with the purple wool and followed Rhiannon's mother to the chest against the wall. In silence, Branwen opened the chest and then unlocked the inner chest and flung back the lid. On top lay the precious blue samite which had caught Rhiannon's eyes. Tenderly, the chatelaine drew it out and held it across her arms like a baby. "My son wishes you to have this. I assume you would be happy to accept it as a bridal dress."

"Mother!" Edain protested, darting forward, "oh, no, Mother, that was promised to me for my betrothal gown."

"Hush!" the mother exclaimed sharply, "your brother has first choice in these matters. He is the eldest and will marry first."

Edain's eyes filled with angry tears. "Why must I give up *my* betrothal gown to that creature? Margwin says that she is nothing but a slut."

Branwen's eyes flashed fire at this outcry. "You will go immediately to your room, Edain."

"No, I beg you. Let her stay," Moira's voice was low and gentle. "I would not take her dress. Let us look further in the chest. Surely there will be something that would become me as well."

Edain flashed her a look of disbelief. "Take it if you want it," she said angrily. "I would not have you beg for me to my mother."

Lady Branwen flung down the precious stuff onto the lid of the chest and slapped Edain across the face. "You, my girl, will comport yourself like a lady and not like a spoiled child. Twice now, this one whom you have insulted has refused this material. She has done so with creditable charity and sensitivity. You have been ungracious and uncharitable. She has conducted herself far better than you."

Edain was too surprised to cry. Now she looked from her mother to Moira with shame and amazement on her face.

"Soon she will be your brother's wedded wife and as

297

such your sister. Your *elder* sister. She will be my daughter. School yourself in grace and manners so that I can be proud of both of my daughters."

Edain's face flushed beet red and the mark of her mother's hand disappeared from her cheek. She hung her head and clasped her hands tightly together in front of her.

Moira turned to the chest, conscious of the oppressive silence in the room as all watched the domestic drama interestedly. Beneath the silk lay another piece in a soft apricot hue. Scattered over the cloth were exotic flowers woven with gold threads. Moira picked it up and draped it over her shoulder. With her bright brown hair, the color would do very well.

She said as much, then asked if there were a piece of fur to trim the neck and sleeves.

Edain sniffed and then smiled timidly. "There is some dark brown. It is marten, not cony," she added, by way of reassurance that it would be of elevated rank. "I'll fetch it." She darted off.

Her mother bent over the chest and extracted another bolt of material. "Here is some cotton for shirts and chemises. It is very dear, but you are my son's choice." She signaled to Alys to come forward and take the material.

Moira smiled slightly, remembering that there had been no cotton in the keep when Rhiannon had requested it for her last week.

Finally, Branwen drew from the chest a piece of finest, sheerest sendal. It was only a small piece, but she tossed it over Moira's head and adjusted it. "This will be for your veil. Gwyneth," a short woman rose from her seat, "bring shears." Securing the sendal to Moira's hair, they trimmed the edges and created a soft, floating veil that reached to the waist in back and to her chin in front. The sendal was a whisper of a cloth, beautiful and very expensive. No one would criticize the garments that Lady Branwen ni Rhiannon was providing for her son's bride, however unwelcome and undesirable his choice might be in her eyes.

Removing the veil and giving it to Gwyneth to sew the tiny stitches required to roll a hem on such fine stuff, Branwen looked again at Moira. "Will you wear that chain for the wedding?" she inquired.

Moira touched it. "I am certain that I shall. Leave the neck of the gown low enough to reveal the chain above the fur."

The other woman nodded. "You will need slippers other than those which belonged to my son." Another woman was summoned and Moira's foot was drawn off onto a skin which had been tanned soft. "We can make you slippers of the same material as the gown and lined with heavy linen." She drew back the hem of her gown to reveal her slippers which matched her gown. "They have become a part of each woman's dress here in our keep, but not I think in other holds. We like them very well."

"They are lovely," Moira agreed.

Branwen smiled a faint, chilly smile. "Let us now cut the dress and we can begin to sew. You do sew, do you not?"

Moira nodded. "My father did not always expect that I should be so different from a woman. Before my brother was killed, I was destined for marriage even as Edain is. When he died, my life was substituted for his."

"How did he die?"

"He was injured in a riding accident. The wound became inflamed and he died of the sickness which causes the jaws to clamp together."

Branwen was silent for a moment. "It is good that you do not have a vengeance to overcome. Too many in this keep despise the name of Lorne with undying hatred."

"Do you, my lady?"

"I hate no one. I want to see the end of the Lornes before my son is killed and I am widowed. When Rhys did not return, I prayed with all my might. When they brought me word that he was alive, I gave thanks upon my knees." She spread the apricot silk out on the table and began to pin. Alys came forward with the knotted strings that had measured Moira's body. When all was ready, Branwen cut the cloth into the desired pieces.

Meanwhile, Edain had returned with the marten skins. "Here," she said, thrusting one into Moira's hand, "are these not soft and beautiful? Mother had promised me ermine to go with the peacock blue. I love furs and these will go perfectly with the apricot silk." She laid one across the material. Her chattering seemed to come from a different person than the hurt, angry girl she had been before. She is a child, thought Moira. She bears me no ill will. Perhaps she could be my friend.

"Ermine will go beautifully with the blue which in turn will match your blue eyes," Moira said.

Edain laughed her tinkly laugh. "You are a very agreeable person. I was so sure that the silk was gone forever that I could not forbear to strike at you. And you gave it up for me. Mother was right. I behaved badly and you behaved well."

"I would have been disappointed and angry, too," replied Moira.

Together they worked through the day. In the mid-afternoon, a repast was brought by servants. All the ladies rose to eat cheese, fruits dried and preserved with honey, small slices of bread, and a mild wine. Moira had never tasted such liquor. Seeing her obvious enjoyment, Edain volunteered, "Mother has made a deal with a merchant from France who puts in at Colwyn Bay. He brings her casks of fine French wines."

As the light began to fade, the ladies departed to their rooms in the keep and outlying buildings. Moira returned to Rhiannon's apartments, an ache between her shoulder blades and fingers sorely pricked by the needles. There had not been a thimble in the hold to fit her finger.

The apartment was warm, a fire blazed in the hearth, and Conal had brought a light supper. Quietly, she sat down in her chair to await Rhiannon's coming and promptly fell asleep. When he entered, he found her curled in her chair, her head dropped to one side, one foot drawn up under her.

He smiled, his feelings warm and tender. He had not seen her today and he had missed her. She had filled his life so completely that he had hurried to get back to the apartment to tell her about what he had done that day. Tomorrow, he thought, he would take her with him and show her his part of the keep: the stables, the bailey, the armory, the fields where they practiced their swordplay and their riding. Let other women make her dress. She was his man-woman.

During the morning, he had dropped in at the smithy and gotten the man to make a second gold chain, this one with a clasp, to go around her head over her veil. It would be a chaplet, but in fact more like a little gold crown holding her veil in place. She had complained of her hair being too wild. This would keep it calm. Other brides wore chaplets of flowers or holly, but she would be crowned with gold. He had also bade the man make chains of gold for her wrists. These were like the others and all were made from the same long gold chain that he had had as his own belt.

To him, the chains were symbolic of her vassalage to him. Whenever he thought of her hands between his palms, together repeating the sacred words, he thrilled. To own someone so completely pleased him mightily. Especially to own someone so worthy and so far superior in his eyes to others.

As he mused, he picked up the pitcher of ale, clanking

it accidentally against the plate. She opened her eyes and smiled at him in a bemused fashion. Slowly, she sat up straight, unfolding her lithe form, stretching her arms above her head, and rising from the chair. A languorous expression curved her lips. His heart leaped at her beauty.

"I fell asleep," she said huskily. "Shall you eat now?"

"Come sit beside me," he said. "I have something for you."

She sat at his side. Then he pulled the gold chain from the pocket of his tunic. "This is for your head, to hold your hair and your veil in place," he said. "See! It has a clasp so that later you can wear it around your neck or loop it twice around your wrist."

She held it up before her and her face was a study of conflicting emotions. Her hand unconsciously clasped the mate soldered forever around her neck.

How she longed to scream at him her hatred and shame for what they symbolized to her. He had enslaved her, made himself her master, put the chain around her neck, and now sought to add another to it, one that would weld her to his side for all time. She was marrying him at his command. She had no say in the matter. Never by choice would she marry this arrogant, thoughtlessly cruel, insensitive, determined man.

Afraid to show him her true feelings, she bowed her head, clasping the new chain tightly in her fist. "You are too generous, my lord."

"Not at all," he said. "Not at all. I am having bracelets made for you out of the rest of the chain. It was my belt. You cannot expect me to wear it with fifteen inches cut out of it. So I had him take the other twenty or so and make these things for you. You see, when you get through wearing this for a crown, you can fasten it around your neck. It is shorter than the other one and should do very well. You will set the fashion."

She gulped and could not take another bite of food.

He ate on without noticing, delighted with her acceptance of his gift, oblivious to her distress and her subsequent lack of appetite. Polishing off two cups of ale, he retired to the fire, prepared to listen as she read to him.

"Could we forego the story tonight?" she begged, still so angry that she could not bear to think of sharing anything with him. "I am rather tired." He looked at her narrowly. She had never complained before. The thought struck him that perhaps she was with child.

"Of course, sweetheart," he said. "You have had a busy day with fittings and sewing. Tomorrow will be less tedious. I intend to take you to my part of the keep. Let the women make your gown. I want you with me at my side." He beamed at her. "Actually, the thought had occurred to me to have the wall chain attached to a belt around my waist. That way you could never stray farther from my side than . . ."

Where she might have strayed was lost in her scream of rage. Her right hand flung the gold chain across the room directly at his grinning face. Only the trained reflexes of a warrior enabled him to knock it down with his hand. The empty tankard whizzed after it, clipping the top of his head as he ducked. "Sweetheart . . ." he shouted, "what . . . ?"

"Idiot!"

"Wait . . ."

"Stupid . . . boasting . . . callous . . . insensitive . . . damnable . . . hateful . . ." Her words rose to a shriek as she flung herself across the table toward him, her fingers curved like talons, thirsting for his blood.

He caught her wrists as the two of them went down under the weight of her lunging body. Sprawling on his back, both hands busy, he stared up at her in amazement as she straddled him, spitting and hissing.

"Stupid! Stupid!"

"You are repeating yourself, love." His voice was the gentling tone of a father to an overwrought child.

"Only because words fail me. You . . . you are so proud of yourself. You shame me, strip me, make free with my body, with my mind. Put the name of whore and witch on everyone's lips . . . and now wife . . . chattel . . ." She writhed ineffectually above him. Her breath came in agonized gasps as she twisted one wrist free and lashed at the side of his head.

He did not reply. Lightning quick to avoid her nails, he rolled over, pinning her body beneath his. The urge to laugh at this tigress was drowned in the shock of her violent attack. He grunted in pain as she brought her knee up between his legs, jolting him, but doing little damage as his hardened thighs caught her before she reached her goal.

"Vixen!" he grated.

"Yes," she snarled. "Call me animal now. Let me warm your bed like any good female. Chain me as you would a hound." She tossed her head wildly, as he imprisoned her wrists in one of his fists and caressed her cheek and shoulder with his fingertips.

"Be still," he commanded. "Damn you! Be still!" His mouth imprisoned hers, ravishing her lips.

Sweet fire leaped in her body at the contact with his. Beneath him, he felt her body subside. His tongue thrust itself into her mouth, caressing now wherever it moved.

She felt him shift his weight slightly, rolling his hip onto the floor, so she was not so hard pressed. At the same time, his hand found her breast, cupping it, molding it, expertly arousing the nipple. She drew in a sobbing breath as her body melted in the heat of desire. Her rigid limbs relaxed and opened to him. Drawing up his leg, he rubbed his knee against her ultra-sensitive mound until she moaned uncontrollably. His hand released her

304

wrists, allowing her to clasp his shoulders. He kissed her again and again on her cheeks, her eyes, her throat, the lobes of her ears. His hot tongue thrust inside her ear, causing her to writhe frantically at the tickling and teasing. Again she cried out, not knowing what she said.

Suddenly, he drew off, pulling himself up to a kneeling position beside her figure which had instinctively cupped itself around his body. Knees bent, thighs open, chest arched, mouth agape, her arms reaching for him, he left her. Her eyes flew open to stare into his own.

"Look at me," he commanded, his voice a hoarse rasp. His hand trembled, his breathing was labored as if he had fought a life-and-death battle. Against the material of his hose, his manhood thrust itself, throbbing with the force of its demand. "Look at me!" he repeated. "And look at yourself." His voice dropped to an agonized whisper. "You are all I have ever needed or desired in a woman. *Never*, never say that I have whored you again. I captured you, yes. I enslaved you. I made you my vassal. And our marriage will be the final bond. I do it for you, so that you will feel that we are one, that neither of us is subservient to the other." He paused for breath. His eyes, like glittering sapphires in his face, looked suddenly drawn with the force of his emotion. "By this I am enslaved. You did it to me. I cannot do my work without thinking about you, without wanting you beside me. The idea of the chain to bind you to me was spoken in jest, but it was half serious. Remember, Moira. A chain has two ends. The one is just as irrevocably bound as the other."

Her anger faded at the torment he revealed. From his own point of view, he perhaps had been just as shamed as she over this attraction he could not suppress. He had defied his father, had set himself against friends and allies whose advice was ever to set her apart from him. With awakening understanding, she closed her eyes momentarily. A shiver of desire wracked her, stirred by some other deeper emotion she could not name.

Her hand sought the chain she had flung at him when she had attacked. Drawing it from under her hip, where its gold links had pressed themselves uncomfortably, she looped it twice around her wrist. There it glittered as she raised both hands to the lacings of her blouse. As he watched, hypnotized, she stripped the strings from the eyelets, baring her hard white breasts to the firelight. Breathing deeply, she arched, cupping them in her palms like offerings to the god.

"Yes, my lord," she murmured. "Yes, Rhiannon."

Twenty-Nine

The day of her wedding broke cold and bleak with light flakes sifting lazily out of the gray sky. As soon as light streaked through the shutters of the apartment, a knock sounded at the door. Rhiannon emerged from his bed grumbling. Conal had been sent with the message that Alys was waiting to conduct Lady Moira to the private apartments of Lady Branwen to be robed for the wedding.

Rhiannon turned back scowling. "I do not get to see you bathed or dressed. What kind of nonsense is this? I have been bathing and dressing you now for two weeks. Why should I not have the pleasure of dressing my own betrothed on her wedding day?"

Moira did not answer him, but sprang from her bed, slipping into his slippers and robe. From his casket, she selected her jewels—the chaplet and the two bracelets which the smith had brought to the apartment yesterday afternoon. Hastily, she brushed her hair, avoiding Rhiannon's teasing embrace as she skittered toward the door.

As she started to leave, she caught his look of disgruntled disappointment. No sense angering him. After today, I will belong to him in the eyes of the church.

With her heart thudding irregularly, she turned back from the door and crossed the room. Gently, she placed her hands on his shoulders. His eyes were like sapphire lakes in which she could drown herself and lose her soul. Caressing him, she moved her hands along his broad shoulders to his neck and then up to his cheeks. Taking a deep breath, she raised her face to his and kissed him full on the mouth. Their lips clung for an instant, then she stepped back before his arms could close around her.

In their passion they had kissed, and he had kissed her often against her will, but never had she purposefully raised her mouth to his to kiss him out of affection. He touched his hand to his mouth and then his smile broke. It was a different expression from any she had ever seen, as different from his wolfish grin as could be possible. He looked like a young boy who had been given a much desired toy for Christmas.

She smiled back and then she was gone.

Alys silently conducted her along the corridor to Lady Branwen's apartment. Outside Moira paused, braced her shoulders, and nodded to the woman. Alys opened the door and ushered her in. Several ladies as well as Branwen and Edain were waiting. A bath had been drawn. Delicate lavender perfume rose from the steaming water. As Alys assisted her to remove her robes, the others looked at her with such cold, accusing expressions that Moira shivered.

"Step into the bath, my lady," Alys murmured. "You must not catch a chill on your wedding day."

Alys and Gwyneth then descended upon her, bathing her and washing her hair, first with soap scented like the bathwater with lavender and then with vinegar. Finally, they rinsed it with clear water again and again until Moira was sure they intended to drown her.

Finally, when they were satisfied, they allowed her to

step from the bath and to be toweled dry under the critical eye of Lady Branwen. No part of her body escaped the scrutiny of the assembled ladies and Moira was blushing to her hair when they had finally finished and allowed her to don her shift.

"I can detect no fault in her body," pronounced Lady Branwen to the assembled group.

A tiny lady with a high, piping voice spoke up. "She seems well made and unblemished."

Her cotton chemise was slipped over her head and she stepped into soft linen hose which were pulled up carefully and smoothed to fit her legs and hips. Then she was seated on a curule chair next to the fire where Alys toweled and dried her hair. Next, she brushed it until it shone and then began to arrange it.

"No," Moira protested. "My Lord Rhiannon has commanded that it be left loose under my veil."

Edain giggled and Lady Branwen pursed her lips. "'Tis an affront," she said. "All know that you are no virgin, having shared my son's bed these past two weeks. Has your flux come upon you at the appointed time?"

"I do not know the time," Moira replied. "Indeed I have forgotten, but I think it is not yet. Also, I was so starved and hard-used for a fortnight earlier this month that I may be late."

"I doubt that," replied the lady coldly, "but it shall be as my son wishes."

Moira was then allowed to rise from the chair as two other ladies brought forth the apricot gown trimmed with marten at neck, sleeves, and hem. It was slipped over Moira's head and laced tightly at the back. The sleeves were long and flowing; the skirt had a small train which fell behind Moira as she walked. Finally, the veil was brought and placed on her head.

At that point, Moira freed herself from their hands and took the chains from the pocket of her discarded robe.

"These are Lord Rhiannon's gifts to me," she said. "He bids me wear this one as a chaplet to hold the veil in place and these around my wrists."

The assembled ladies gasped. Edain squeaked, "Why he is actually proud to be marrying a slave!"

Other comments, some made under breath but some made loud enough for Moira to hear, were equally as biting. Moira's breath came short and she felt that she might faint. They had laced her so tightly and had given her no meat nor drink, since she was to go to confession before her wedding mass. Sternly, she pulled herself upright and faced them proudly. "Everyone will know that I do not marry him of my own free will, but at his command. There is no shame in being forced to yield to a stronger power. I cannot kill myself, for God forbids. My Lord Rhiannon has acted with great understanding of my feelings and my state.

"Come!" she snapped to Alys. "While you dawdle, he awaits me."

Alys jumped and glanced at Lady Branwen for confirmation or reproof, but none was forthcoming. She ducked her head and hastened to obey, placing first the bracelets on each wrist and then pinning the gold chain around the crown of Moira's head, letting the veil sweep down from it to cover her face with sheer, shimmering sendal.

When she stepped back, all gazed at Moira. Her face was pale and unhappy, but her dress on her tall graceful figure was elegant.

Coldly, Lady Branwen stepped forward as Edain came to her side. "Alys, the cloak," she rapped. "My daughter," she addressed Moira, "you are my son's choice. Honor your marriage vows as you honor your name. Honor your husband's body as you honor your own." For an instant, she hesitated. Alys came with the cloak, a beautiful garment which Moira had not seen before. It was rich brown velvet lined with soft brown fur. Branwen placed it carefully around Moira's shoulders as Edain lifted her veil. "This is your gift from us to keep you warm on this day and on all the days to come."

Moira was speechless. No one had ever given her such a priceless gift. The cloak was of the heaviest and finest velvet made. Moira was not to know that the material had come all the way from Italy, purchased at great price for a special occasion for Lord Gethin. "My lady," she stammered making a deep curtsey. Lady Branwen extended her hand for Moira to kiss. She felt the hand tremble under her lips. Lady Branwen might make the grand gesture, but she was far from accepting her daughter-in-law with anything beyond the most formal courtesies.

Moira rose and bowed to the ladies in the room. "My thanks," she said.

Edain ran to the door. "I shall send the lackey to tell Conal to have Rhys ready," she trilled.

Moira rejoined Rhiannon in the great hall. Lord Gethin came forward, bowing to her formally. As she curtseyed deeply, he took her hand and placed it in Rhiannon's. Behind them, the procession formed to walk to the chapel. Because of the unusual winter wedding, no flowers were strewn upon their path. No musicians preceded them to pipe them to the altar.

Moira had no time to do more than glance around her at the unfriendly faces glaring at her. Her eyes were caught by Rhiannon's. He grinned at her, his determined wolfish grin, tempered by gentleness as he glimpsed her face beneath the veil. Fortunately, the cloak covered the apricot dress, so he did not know she was not wearing the blue samite he had requested.

She could not help noticing that he was the most handsome man she had ever seen. His lean, wolfish face was clean-shaven, his sapphire blue eyes sparkling above

311

a rich blue tunic lavishly embroidered with gold at neck, sleeves, and hem. His lean waist was belted by a wide jewel-encrusted belt of soft black leather. His legs were covered in fine wool hose, also blue but of a deeper shade. From his shoulders hung a magnificent blue velvet mantle lined with gray fur. His shoes and gloves were of very fine black leather.

Her eyes widened under the veil as she beheld the back of his black head as he turned to stand beside her. On his thick curling hair was set a gold chain the duplicate of hers. What could this mean, she wondered. Swiftly, she faced front, but her mind was in turmoil.

An icy blast hit them as the door of the hall opened and they walked out and down the steps. The path had been cleared of snow, but the wind had drifted it a bit so that sometimes her feet in their thin leather slippers were covered. She shivered and her teeth began to chatter. The wind from the sea was bitter cold, ruffling the veils of the ladies and cloaks of the gentlemen as they walked along the path. The tiny chapel was built halfway down the side of the slope to the village and the bay beyond.

The procession took less time than would have normally been required, for the way was so cold. At the door of the chapel, the priest appeared and Rhiannon and Moira made their vows at his command, while the procession stood on one foot and then the other and huddled and hunched their shoulders against the bitter wind.

When they were ushered into the church, the building itself seemed warm by comparison, although it was unheated except for the tapers burning in every sconce and candelabrum. Two elaborately carved chairs were drawn up before the altar and Moira and Rhiannon were seated in these. All the other members of the procession sat on the benches and chairs in the various pews and enclosures.

Cushions had been placed before the chairs, so Moira was able to lift her feet from the icy floor. Nevertheless, she shivered and wrapped her new cloak more tightly around her. Only dimly did she realize that a priest other than Father Ambrosius began the ceremony. By the time she was called upon to make her vows, Moira was so miserable that all thoughts of refusing at the crucial moment fled from her mind in her haste to escape the biting cold. As the words escaped her mouth, binding her to Rhiannon forever, she felt only a sense of the inevitable crashing down around her. For a moment she swayed, but his hand, tightly gripping hers, steadied her. She glanced at him from under her veil to see his eyes, bright and possessive, daring her to do other than his bidding.

I am marrying this man, she thought. Correction, I have married this man. My father will never understand. My home is lost to me forever.

The mass began, but she could not hear it. "Dear God, Heavenly Father," she prayed silently, "help me to comport myself with dignity. Never let my courage fail me." Her eyes were closed, but suddenly they flew open as Rhiannon touched her arm.

"Let this woman be amiable as Rachel, wise as Rebecca, faithful as Sarah," intoned the priest.

"And courageous as Deborah," prayed Moira silently, her lips moving beneath her veil.

The mass was over. Rhiannon advanced to the altar to receive the kiss of peace from the priest. Turning, he extended his hand to Moira, as the congregation muttered in amazement and the priest stood slack-jawed. Without question, she rose and approached him, until she too stood beside him at the altar. She knew as well as he did what he was according her here. No woman approached the altar. If he had done as he should have according to custom, he would have returned to her chair

313

and embraced her there. By bringing her up beside him, he had awarded her an equality unknown.

With a smile of pleasure on his face, he lifted her veil and folded it back over her head. Solemnly and with great dignity, he bestowed upon her mouth the kiss of peace. His lips were warm and tender against her own. Gently, they moved and opened as his tongue caressed her lips. Answering him, she opened her mouth and allowed him access to her.

Finally, they drew apart, both shaking at the intensity of emotion which each felt and transmitted to the other. "Mine," he whispered triumphantly. Then he turned her and they faced the congregation together. A beautiful smile split his face. Glancing at him, she could not help but respond with a timid smile of her own. A sigh went up from the congregation. Then they all began to chatter and to laugh nervously as the tension of the day was released.

Rhiannon led her from the chapel, but on the front steps he stopped. "I should carry you," he said. "Your feet are too thinly clad to walk in this snow."

"You cannot, my lord," she begged. "I am too heavy and the path is steep and slippery. But we can run together. We need not wait and walk in a dignified procession." Suddenly she laughed, flinging back her head in the wind. "We have defied the world on more than one occasion. Let us defy it one more time." Her hand shot out from the folds of the cloak to grasp his and they were running down the steps and being blown by the wind up the hill. Their cloaks billowed around them. Her unbound hair and veil whipped around her face.

He laughed aloud for joy when they reached the bridge over the trench in a matter of minutes. They turned to look back, as she leaned against the palisade to catch her breath. Her cheeks and lips were red and her mouth open, breathing in great gulps of the icy air. He waved to his

314

father and mother and the party struggling up the hill from the chapel, then swooped back around and kissed her full on her cold open mouth, tasting snowflakes on her lips and tongue.

"Only a little farther, love, and we shall be within the hall. I will have you warm in just a minute."

She nodded agreement. Together they ran across the lists, through the bailey, and into the main court. Here he picked her up in his arms, kissed her soundly on the mouth again, and carried her up the steps into the warm, lighted hall. Her arms encircled him as she laid her head against his neck.

Feeling her heart beating furiously against his chest, he held her longer perhaps than was necessary before he set her feet down on the rushes beside the great fireplace. Moira looked up at him and felt a thrill of pride at his dark face flushed from the exertion, his blue eyes sparkling with joy.

Reaching for the ties to her cloak, he pulled it from her. As he did so, his brow wrinkled. "I thought you were to have a dress made from the blue silk," he said.

"Hush!" Moira said softly, looking around and seeing only servants. The wedding party was still toiling up the hill. "This apricot silk goes better with my coloring and my gold jewelry. The blue was shot with silver threads. But most important, that material had been set aside for Edain's betrothal gown. I could not deny her. Rhiannon, she is young and it had been promised to her. Lady Branwen said it was your right as the elder, but I knew you would not really mind."

He was scowling still.

She pirouetted in front of him. "Is this not attractive? The fur is marten. Edain got it for me herself when she found I would not take her dress."

He smiled at her. "You are kind." He grabbed her around the waist as she stopped her twirl. "The courage

315

and wisdom of a man with the heart and soft body of a woman." His caress was bold. Hot and flushed, she pushed him away as the first of the wedding party burst in the door.

Dafydd and Huw Llengaron were among the first to step forward to shake hands with Rhiannon and to bow cordially to Moira. Huw smiled at her and bent to take her hand. "My wishes for your happiness, Lady Moira. You are a most worthy person."

"Thank you, Sir Huw," Moira responded, dropping a curtsey to him.

Lord Gethin came across the floor to take her formally by the shoulders and bestow the kiss of peace upon her cheek. Formally, he held his arm for her to conduct her to the dais to the seat of honor usually occupied by Lady Branwen. Rhiannon followed with his mother, conducting her to the right of his father's accustomed chair. For the feasting today, the bride and groom were given the places of honor on the dais.

Servants brought a heavy chalice and placed it between them and a heavy plate of silver.

Lord Gethin waited until all were seated and all had been served the fine wine. "To my son and daughter! Rhiannon ap Breannon and Moira of—," he paused and shook his head angrily, "Moira," he repeated. "To Lord Rhiannon and Lady Moira!"

Rhiannon drank from the chalice first, then handed it to Moira and she finished the wine.

And so it went throughout the long feast. Course after course of meats and pastries were served. Each was placed on the plate between them, with Rhiannon taking the first bite and then giving Moira the best portions.

Moira lost track of the food that was presented, tasted, and then taken away. Her head whirled from the wine, the rich food, and the close proximity to Rhiannon's lean, hard body which more and more pressed itself

316

against her arm and shoulder. He held the chalice for her to drink. His fingers touched her cheek as his arm encircled her shoulders. The musicians began to play. Under the table, his knee pressed hard against her own.

A circle of men and women formed on the floor as the round dance began. Rhiannon drew her to her feet. "No," she whispered. "I do not know how. We never had dancing in our hold."

"Then I will teach you, sweetheart. 'Tis not hard."

Pink with embarrassment, she allowed him to draw her to the floor. The other couples were dancing with hands touching, but Rhiannon took both her hands in his and placed one arm around her shoulder so that he guided her more strongly. The steps were truly simple. In a matter of a few turns around the circle, she had learned the dance and smiled hesitantly at the new experience.

At the end of the dance, they remained before the table on the dais. He drank from the chalice, then offered it to her. "To my beautiful bride," he called. "Much happiness to you both," called Huw Llengaron, raising his chalice. "A long life," came another voice. "Many children."

"I say, *no!*" roared a voice. Owen Llewellyn rose from his chair, pitching his body over the table into the center of the floor. He staggered crazily, righting himself with an effort. Clearly drunk, he was beside himself with fury. "Witch!" he roared. "Fool!" he shouted at Rhiannon.

He swung around and faced the room. "Do you all forget so soon?" Tears flowed down his cheeks as drunken sobs punctuated his next statements. "She killed our kin. So many brave lads. How many did not come home from the raid that fool led against her father? What was the price of this joining? She killed my wife, my little ones." His face changed. "She is a witch! Burn her, I say! She has bewitched the lord's son."

Huw Llengaron stepped forward, signaling to two

footmen who stood at the door of the hall. "Come, Owen," he said softly. "You are tired!"

"No!" The face contorted with fury. The brute launched himself straight at Moira. The two footmen caught him by the arms and hauled him back struggling and screaming.

At his first words, Moira had spun around within the circle of Rhiannon's protecting arms. The cursing, flailing man drew her attention only for the moment required to see that he was restrained. Her eyes, scanning the table, seeking out the mood of the crowd, found the envious dark eyes of Margwin. Lord Gethin's mistress stood with one hand clenched over the back of the chair Owen had flung himself from. Her mouth was arched, baring her teeth in an ugly grimace. Moira could not help but think the woman hissed at her like an angry cat.

In her ear, Rhiannon spoke, his lips brushing aside her soft hair. "Do not be alarmed, sweetheart," he said softly. "He is a drunken madman. When he is sober, he is better controlled."

"But he hates me," she whispered. "All in this company dislike me. Look at their faces. Especially Margwin."

"What of Margwin?" Rhiannon's voice sounded puzzled.

"Why, see . . ."

No one stood behind Owen Llewellyn's chair. Indeed, most of those seated at that section of the table were either dancing or slumped back in lazy pleasure.

Moira faltered. "Only Huw Llengaron feels any charity toward me at all. Look around you. The feasting is over."

"It shall not be so," he said. "Music!" he ordered. The recorder began to play a gay tune. "More wine for everyone!" The lackeys and servitors scurried forward to fill everyone's cups.

318

Fortunately, so many were drunk that the interruption had not created a strong impression. So many people became disorderly from time to time that little notice was really paid to their words.

The dance formed again, but when Moira refused, Rhiannon put his arm around her to lead her back to the dais. At the table, he continued his attentions to her. Below the dais, the men were becoming noisier and more boisterous. One man, abandoning all sense of decorum, openly fondled and kissed the rather pretty plump lady sitting beside him.

None of this behavior was a scandal to Moira, raised as she had been at Lorne's Rock where few ladies actually lived. The majority of feminine companionship there was furnished by wenches from the kitchen. However, Rhiannon's wine-warm kiss in public before his father and mother was an embarrassment. She pushed him away.

"Come, sweetheart," he said huskily. "Kiss me in token of your affection for your new lord."

"Cool your ardor, my lord," she pleaded. "Your father and mother are watching."

"What difference?" he asked thickly. "We are married. I may have a kiss from my bride." So saying, he grasped her firmly by the shoulders and twisted her in her seat to plant a warm, wet kiss on her protesting mouth. Although his kiss was passionate, she could not respond as she wished. He drew back, looking puzzled.

His father spoke, his animosity ill-concealed. "Is this the wench that you sought to marry with? Bah! She seems cold comfort." He banged down his chalice on the table. "Give me a plump, soft female anytime. What say, girl?" He wagged his head at Moira. "Will you warm my son's bed as a good woman should? Bah! Not likely. Lemme show you a real woman. Warm. Passionate. Give a man a real pleasure in his bed."

319

Moira's eyes flew to Lady Branwen, but her mother-in-law was staring straight ahead. Only the twitching of her lips and the convulsive grasp of her hand on the chalice betrayed her feelings.

"Margwin!" Gethin bawled. "Where's Margwin?"

The voluptuous blonde stepped forward from the shadows behind the tapestry at Lord Gethin's back as if she had been waiting for his call. Surprised, Moira raised her eyebrows, letting her eyes purposefully shift to Owen Llewellyn's vacated chair and back again. Did Margwin slink behind the tapestries and hangings like some prowling feline?

For an instant, hatred flared in the woman's dark eyes, then the expression changed completely, as if a mask had covered the truth. A vacuous look of gentle amiability spread over Margwin's face. The tight-pinched lips loosened and became soft and inviting. Giggling shrilly, Margwin ducked first to one side then to the other of Lord Gethin's chair, making him look for her twice.

With a roar of pleased laughter, Gethin caught a hank of the long, blond hair she allowed to float over his shoulder and pulled her down by it into his lap. Shrieking, she tried to get out of the chair, but he would have none of that. Grabbing her around the waist, he pulled her down. Fondling her big soft breasts beneath the thin wool gown she wore, he kissed her noisily. "Here is a real woman," he informed his son. "Got children off that one," he jerked his head back over his shoulder indicating his wife, "but when you want a good loving and a lusty tumble, you need a girl with soft curves. Right, wench." Margwin giggled. Her eyes rolled as she twisted her head to look at Lady Branwen, white-lipped and staring straight ahead. Margwin giggled again. Her back arched as she thrust her breasts, now partially exposed by Gethin's fondling, into his face. He chuckled drunkenly as he bent to rain his kisses on them.

Moira's eyes flew to Rhiannon's face, but it was carefully closed. She could read nothing of his feelings about the humiliation of his mother before his sister as well as the assembled men and women of the keep. Instead, he lifted the chalice and drank deeply. "Come, sweetheart." He set down the empty cup and led her to the floor once more.

Seldom did they return to the dais after that. They danced until they were tired. Between dances, they sat in chairs drawn up for them next to Huw, Dafydd, and Henry. Henry was an Englishman, husband to Alys, the woman who had helped Moira to dress. From time to time, Moira glanced at the dais where the essentials of the tableau remained the same. A drunken man, a giggling wench, and a shamed wife.

As the evening came and the priest appeared, Moira and Rhiannon followed him to the apartment. There he blessed the bed as was the custom, after which the gentlemen withdrew. Branwen, Edain, and the other women who were still sober enough to stand on their feet undressed Moira for bed. All her clothing was taken from her, her hair was brushed, and she was invited to climb into the big bed which had been strewn with lavender. Only her gold neck chain, glowing in the light of the candles, remained on her body.

The men came laughing and jesting down the hall. Rhiannon was thrust into the room half undressed. He grinned his wolfish grin at the group as he quaffed the last of the wine from his chalice.

"My friends," he said, swaying slightly as he righted himself from his drinking pose. "I bid you good night. May your rest be as pleasant as I am sure mine will be."

Laughing, murmuring, and making many coarse suggestions, the men and ladies withdrew. Rhiannon turned back to the bed. "I said I would do it and I did," he said grandly, gesturing with his cup.

321

"Have you counted the cost, my lord?"

"I have counted the gain, sweetheart."

"You have married a woman whom all hate and despise. Your family cannot bear the sight of me."

He waved his hand as if he would brush away such small details. "When they come to know you as I have come to know you, they will love you as I do."

"Do you love me, my lord?"

"Can you doubt it, sweetheart?" Stripping off his tunic, he came toward her bare to the waist. The scars on his torso gleamed whitely in the firelight. The scar on his shoulder had faded to a bright pink. "I have loved you every night since I have taken you to my bed."

"That is not my meaning." She shook her head. "I know you use my body. Gethin uses Margwin's. But Margwin is not pleased. She would not be faithful to him. Certainly, there is no loyalty between them. Am I the same as she? Do you count my body as he counts hers?"

"That is all there is to love," Rhiannon replied. "I admire and respect you as a man for the strength and courage you have shown. What is more, you are heir to your father's lands. At his death, you will inherit all his holdings and at my father's death I will inherit all that he owns. Together we will rule the north of Wales."

"A great dream," she nodded, "but my father may very well disinherit me so great is his hatred of you. You are a marked man from this day. He had planned your death by torture, you know. He may even include me in his vengeance now. I am sure he feels that I have been rendered unworthy."

"Ah, but you are still alive," Rhiannon stripped off his boots and *chausses*.

Moira regarded him steadily. Her pulse began to pound in her ears. Ripples of intense desire coursed through her veins. She took a deep breath in an effort to counteract the breathless feeling she was coming to know so well.

"He may offer a bounty on my head as well as yours."

Rhiannon drew the covers from her and knelt with her body between his legs. He caught the back of her head with his hands. "Such a beautiful head," he said, caressing her hair and cupping her skull. Gently, he brought her lips toward his thighs. "Kiss me, sweetheart."

She clasped her hands around the twin trunks of his thighs. The black hairs tickled the surface of her palms. The tips of her fingers dug into the backs of his legs as he pressed her face against his hard, flat belly.

A chuckle rippled from his lips as he reached the pinnacle of pleasure given only to the conquerors of the world.

Beneath him, her body went rigid then relaxed into a slough of despair. As great as was his arousal, as burgeoning as was his manhood against her breasts and throat, so was her defeat. She had married with the enemy. Until death. By the bond of blood she was now one flesh with Rhiannon ap Breannon.

His hands moved through her hair, caressing her cheeks. His fingers looped themselves into the gold chain around her neck and pulled her back onto her elbows, where she lay staring up at him, her eyes blue pools of pain in which he could have read her defeat and despair had he been so minded. But only joy filled his consciousness.

Clenching his jaw, with one hand in the chain around her neck, he passed the other around her waist and hauled her upward. The action dragged her flesh roughly across his heated body. Voraciously, he kissed her forehead, her cheek, the corner of her mouth, her throat that arched before him as her head fell backward. Realizing that she was limp in his arms, he trailed his hot mouth down across her breast until his teeth closed over her nipple. At first, the momentary pang barely penetrated her consciousness, so buried was she in her depression.

His hard hands pressed more strongly against her shoulder blades, lifting her insistently to his mouth. Then he bit her. Not just a soft love nip such as he had bestowed countless times, but a true hard punishing bite.

The pain wrenched her from her lethargy. How dare he! Furiously angry at him, at her reduced state, at herself for giving in to despair, she struck out wildly, catching him on the side of the head with her forearm. The blow, delivered on the arc of a wild swing, overbalanced them and sent them sprawling on the bed.

Violently angry at the man she considered to be her tormentor, she continued to pummel him, rising on her knees above him. He raised his arms, to defend his face and head, allowing the blows to rain harmlessly about him, while strangled sounds issued from his throat.

He was laughing!

Breathing hard, she sank back on her heels, her clenched fists pressed against the tops of her naked thighs.

"Feel better?" he inquired gently, warily lowering his arms.

Oddly enough, she realized that she did. Grimly she nodded.

"Wine has that effect more times than not," he announced placidly. "I have had the feeling myself. Things look black and getting blacker. Takes a good night's sleep or a stiff jolt to get you out of the mood."

She passed a trembling hand across her forehead. He rearranged himself more comfortably on his back among the tumbled covers. His self-satisfied grin flashed. In some ways, he knew her better than she knew herself. At least with him around she would never be allowed to sink into useless self-pity. A faint smile quirked the corners of her mouth.

He extended his arms; his smile turned warm and inviting. For an instant she hesitated. Nothing was resolved. And yet everything was. No matter what she felt, she was his wife. She remembered Lady Branwen sitting at the table while her husband fondled another woman. Shamed, true, yet proud. There were always victories. Always defeats. And always compromises.

Her fingertips touched his, slid into his hands. Her body warmed to the sensual touch that the simplest contact between the two of them transmitted. No longer stiff with apprehension, she swayed forward, undulating her body across his thighs, pausing to plant a warm, moist kiss in his navel, caressing the skin around it with her tongue before continuing upward. Her nipples rasped across the hot skin covering his ribs and they expanded in a mighty intake of breath.

"Oh, God," he whispered. "Dear Moira."

Her kisses feathered the dark curling hairs around his nipples, then trailed lightly across the ultra-sensitive skin that formed the scar on his shoulder.

"Sweet wife." He writhed, moaning, his hands clasping and then seeking to release hers.

But she would not allow him to let go, to use his hands as he willed. If she was a slave, then so was he. Insistently, magically, she continued her exploration while he twisted and groaned, all control broken. As his muscle prodded her belly, she rubbed herself back and forth across him, feeling the perspiration on her skin mix with his.

Sliding farther upward across his body, she pressed the throbbing core of her desire against his engorged tip. Her own daring and the sensation she created within her own body drove her almost mad. Tiny whimpering sounds escaped her as she kissed him over and over. With her mouth open, her tongue tasted the sweat of desire on his face.

With a howl, he forced her hands behind her back and rolled over on top of her. Now she was beneath his weight, pressed into the mattress, moaning with desire, his muscled hardness bruising the most delicate and sensitive spots on her body as sensation after sensation spiraled within her.

She wanted . . . she wanted . . .

He drew back, then instinctively, blindly, thrust forward. Her cry of ecstasy mingled with his own. Hard as steel, he pierced her while her eager flesh closed around him, caressing him, undulating along his entire length.

The moment was sublime. Triumphant. Like gods, they clove together, exploding into a million pieces of star-bright sensation.

Then clasping each other tightly, they floated gently back to the reality of warm covers scented with lavender and their own particular scent comingled. With her eyes closed, she pressed her lips against his temple. He stroked her hair back from her face where its long strands tickled his lips as well. Exhausted, he turned on his side, pulling her with him, careful not to disturb his sword couched so firmly in her sheath.

Thirty

Christmas morning Moira awakened with a distressing nausea which caused her to hastily quit the bed she shared with Rhiannon and dash to relieve herself. She returned dizzy and drained to be helped by her husband to the bed again.

"The fish from last night," she managed to gasp. "I am sure the piece I had was tainted."

"Perhaps," he agreed. "We will eat in Mother's apartments after mass this afternoon. There will be meat. I confess I grow tired of the continuous fish. 'Twould sicken a goat."

He poured her ale and she drank it slowly, wishing he would stop regarding her so carefully. Finally, he turned away and began to dress himself. The ale did much to settle her stomach and she began to feel normal.

Conal entered with the bath water and shaving equipment. A screen had been set up in the room at Moira's request, so that she could bathe with some privacy while Conal shaved Rhiannon. Moving behind it, she slipped off her robe. As she lowered herself into the tub and began to sponge herself, her hands touched her breasts. They were unusually swollen and tender this morning. As she washed them gently, her puzzlement grew, for her nipples seemed puffy and unusually dark pink.

Dubiously, she cupped her firm breasts in her hands and looked down at herself, wondering how she had bruised them. When she looked up, she beheld Rhiannon staring at her. He had walked around the edge of the screen and now regarded her with satisfaction.

"I believe, my lovely wife," he said, emphasizing each word, "that you may be quickening."

Moira was stunned. She simply sat in the water, her knees drawn up, her hands cupping her tender breasts. True, she had had no flux, but she could not bring herself to admit that she was not merely late from the effects of her imprisonment and the mental and physical anguish she had endured for more than a month before her marriage. Indeed, she had truly not relaxed since she had been married to him.

"Oh, no," she whispered.

"Oh, yes," he replied, swooping forward to kneel beside the bath. His hands lovingly caressed her nipples which responded with extra sensitivity to his tender ministerings. He bent to kiss each one in turn, then ran his hand down her rib cage onto her flat belly.

He patted it gently. "Soon you will have a lovely little stomach growing here."

She covered her face with her hands. "I am to have your child," she said softly.

"Mine and no other's," he replied.

She was silent, her head bowed. At last, she clenched her hands on the edge of the tub and pushed herself up. Catching her under the arms, he helped her stand. Throwing a linen towel around her shoulders, he grasped the ends and held her facing him.

"You are so beautiful." His eyes moved up and down

her figure lovingly. She crossed her hands in front of her, but his words stilled her movement. "No, sweetheart, do not cover your beautiful body. Your breasts are like ripe fruits, your waist still so small that I could almost span it with my hands."

She blushed and hung her head.

"Look up and smile," he commanded. When she obeyed, he gathered the ends of the cloth and pulled her into his body. She could feel him hard and urgent against her. "God, how I want you!"

Tremulously, she responded to his impassioned kiss. A discreet cough sounded behind them. "Conal is waiting to shave you," she whispered against his mouth.

"Damn!" he exclaimed against her teeth. Reluctantly, he drew away. Her body had dampened his robe in front. He plucked it away from his body but not before she had seen the bulge of his awakened desire. "You are cruel, my lady!"

She gathered the linen towel around her and completed her drying. "I, my lord? No, I merely stood still at your command."

Groaning, he moved around the corner of the screen where Conal waited to shave him. "Wear your warmest garments. The tawny wool and your brown velvet cloak. Also your heavy leather boots. We will walk to chapel for mass."

"My lord, you need not coddle me." She came around the end of the screen at last, swathed in her brown robe.

Conal had finished with the shaving and Rhiannon headed for the bath. "My pleasure, Moira."

After the Christmas mass, Branwen held another dinner in her apartments. This time the table was set for five. For the first time, Moira entered her mother's apartment as a guest.

The old enmities had not died, but lay beneath the icy politeness and extreme consideration exercised by both

329

Branwen and Edain in Moira's presence. Gethin was seldom seen. He kept to his man's pursuits and winter was especially hard on him. With the unusually hard and cold weather, no hunts had been organized and even the exercise of horses had been left to the grooms who were ordered to take the mounts out of the stable and ride them. No one cared to ride for pleasure. The icy gale that blew from the sea brought on its wind, snow, and icy pellets of spray.

At the sight of his daughter, Gethin scowled and tossed a swallow of wine down his throat. Moira had chosen to wear her wedding dress of apricot silk with Rhiannon's gold chains around her throat and wrists. Her color was high and with the wine she and Rhiannon had shared in their apartment, her eyes sparkled.

When she entered the apartment on his arm, she was struck by the contrast to what had been her lot at last appearance in this room. What humiliation had she suffered that night when she had been forced to kneel beside his chair and take food from his hand! Did they all remember that night? she wondered.

The room was as she remembered it. The same beauty of appointments and of service, the same warmth and richness of color and light were everywhere. In her own mind, she longed to make the apartment that she shared with Rhiannon an even more beautiful place. Now with her child coming, the apartment must be expanded. She would have to have the child with her. A warm smile lit her face as she contemplated the baby and the joy it would bring. Something of her own in the midst of these strange, cold people who, with the exception of Rhiannon, treated her coldly or ignored her completely.

At Rhiannon's insistence, she had brought her lute. Seating herself on the curule chair where she had sat before, humiliated, treated like a dog, she quietly began to play a soft, soothing melody that wove in and out of the traditional chords of the Christmas season. As her fingers wandered idly, she found the simple tune to a Christmas lullaby.

At the conclusion of the song, Branwen signaled to the servitors and the family moved to the table. Rhiannon solicitously seated his wife at her place at his side and then waited for the other members of his family to sit. He gestured to the boy to fill his cup and the cups of the others.

"My father," he addressed Gethin, "some weeks ago against your wishes, I took a wife. She was one who was an enemy but who had sworn her allegiance to me. I said at that time that I took her because she was as good as any man I had ever known. She is brave and resourceful. She could ride and shoot and do all that a man should do. Now she has proved to me that she is also a woman. She will soon present me with a child."

Gethin sat quietly. His son's smiling face mocked his own feelings of discontent. He turned his head to regard Moira from under his brows. She sat with downcast eyes, her hands clasped in her lap for all the world like a gentle maid.

"She will bear you a changeling," he growled. "She was unnatural from the beginning. Too tall. She bewitched you."

Edain looked from father to brother with big, frightened eyes. Then she looked at Moira. "You do not look like other women that I know," she agreed. "Could a witch conceive a child?"

"Nonsense," Branwen broke in, laying her hand on her daughter's arm. "You are being foolish, child. This woman has not bewitched your brother. She has attracted him with her body and her ways. Just as Margwin attracted your father with her body and her ways."

Rhiannon stared at his mother. No emotion showed in

331

the cold, pale face surrounded by the cowl and cap which concealed her hair. She stated what to her was plain fact. Moira was of the same breed as Margwin, his father's bedwarmer.

Moira too knew exactly what she was being called. She flushed and raised her eyes to her mother. "I am married to Lord Rhiannon, my lady. He chose me over the arguments of many. He could have received a fair ransom for me and purchased many luxuries that would have given him much pleasure."

Tightening her lips, Branwen sneered, "Perhaps you did bewitch him." She signaled to the servitors who were listening impassively to this family quarrel. "We will now eat in peace. Sit down, Rhys. You can toast your coming fatherhood at the end of the meal at the appropriate place. 'Tis Christmas and there should be peace and good will in your heart, my lord husband."

The meal was nevertheless a torment to Moira. She could hardly eat from the choking loneliness in her heart. Rhiannon's family had brought cruelly to her mind that she had no one but her father and husband who cared about her in the world. No one but Rhiannon could protect her and if she displeased him or he tired of her, there would be no one. She would be among enemies. Her baby would be born despised.

Her hand trembled at the thought. In despair, she laid down her knife and sat back in her chair.

"Are you ill, Moira?" Rhiannon asked solicitously, bending toward her.

"A little, I think, my lord," she replied.

"'Tis sometimes thus," Branwen spoke. "The meats are too rich with all these sauces." She gestured to a servant. "Bring the lady a bowl of cream soup and some custard. Take away the meat, but leave the bread. I am sure you will find this more the thing. Since you are now quickening, you must be careful of your foods."

"I place my wife in your hands, Lady Mother," Rhiannon spoke.

Moira shuddered. "I shall be quite well in a moment. I would not think of troubling Lady Branwen."

"But, sweetheart," he insisted, "Mother has borne children and she oversees the bearing of the children in this keep. She will send for the midwife when you are near your time. She will take care of the nurse and the preparations after our son has arrived."

"Remember that she might be a daughter," Moira said. "Will you accept her?"

"So long as she is like you," he kissed her on the cheek and turned to the table. "Here comes your soup. Come! Eat up. We want the little one to be strong."

"My Lord Gethin, eat your food and stop glowering," Branwen sighed. "You can see that he is pleased with her. You must accept the fact of his marriage and look forward to the child to come. After all, it might be your first grandson."

By the end of the meal, Gethin was drunk. He muttered and scowled so that no conversation was possible between him and his family. Moira's face grew colder as she felt acutely their displeasure. She picked at her food until it cooled and sent it away untouched.

Rhiannon rose from his chair. "Merry Christmas, Mother." Rhiannon kissed her pale cheek. "A gift from us to you." He pressed into her hand a small wooden box, carved with fantastic birds and leaves. She opened it to discover a lovely gold brooch in the shape of the birds on the box.

"My dear son," she exclaimed. "You have pleased me. Whence came this gift?"

"Oh, I purchased it from a peddler who came here from the Holy Land many months ago. I was sure you would like it." He turned to his sister. "And this, Edain, is for you." He presented her with a package wrapped in rough cloth.

"Oh, for me. Rhys, you are a dear brother!" Edain kissed him enthusiastically, unwrapping the covering to reveal a length of blue silk as fine as mist and embroidered with strange designs. "Oh, 'tis lovely. I can hardly wait to wear it." She flung it around her shoulders. "Does it become me, Mother?" she squealed, preening.

"It is a joy to behold on you, my love."

"Father, these are for you." Rhiannon gave his father a pair of heavy gauntlets with chased leather cuffs. Gently, he laid them on the table beside the older man, who made no move, but merely nodded his head.

"And this, my Lady Moira, my dear wife, is for you." He produced a small sandalwood box. Opening it, she beheld a ring the like of which she had never seen. It was of heavy gold. A pigeon-blood ruby flashed fire from the center of five golden prongs cast to resemble the talons of a hawk.

He knelt beside her and slipped it on her hand. "The ruby is you, your life. I hope it is your heart someday. It flashes with all the fire of your proud spirit. To me, it is like your courage, bright, undimmed, everlasting. And I hold it in my hand. I will protect it and guard it and keep it safe." He stared into her eyes as he said these words.

For a long minute, she was silent, not knowing what to say. She believed him. From that moment on, she knew that he would hold hard by his word, as he had held by it from the first with her. Everything he had vowed to do he had done. He had vowed to make her his companion and then his wife and he had done so. That she saw a different meaning in the ruby clutched in the cruel gold claw did not alter the fact that he had meant it as a pledge of his sovereignty over her.

"But, my lord, I have nothing for you," she protested.

"You have given me the child," he whispered. "I could

not ask for a better gift." His lips caressed her palm, closing the fingers over his kiss.

His mother, father, and sister had all prepared gifts for him. Moira sat quietly with head lowered. Still unsure of herself in the keep, she had not asked for anything. Therefore, she had had no materials with which to prepare rich gifts for them. They in turn had pointedly ignored her presence. But, of course, they had given her the magnificent brown velvet cloak for her wedding present, she reminded herself. From time to time, she admired the magnificent ruby glinting on her finger in the candlelight. The more she looked at it, the more pleased she was.

While she was staring at it, she heard Rhiannon speak to her. Rousing herself from her dream, she saw him offering her his arm. She collected her lute and bowed to his parents. Branwen coolly inclined her head, but Gethin turned away in anger and refused to acknowledge her. Edain kissed her brother on the cheek, but took her cue from her parents and only smiled distantly at Moira.

Outside the apartments, they both heaved sighs of relief and then laughed at the similarity of their feelings. "I do not believe they will ever accept me," Moira sighed. "They hate me too thoroughly to ever smile at me. They will grow to hate you too, I fear."

"Nonsense." He put his arm around her waist and balanced his gifts in his free hand. "They are already unbending. Mother was instantly concerned when she saw you were not feeling well. She is the kindest person in the world. Father has put great shame on her, but she still treats him with love and courtesy. She will come to accept and even like you. And when you present her with a grandson with blue eyes and dark hair . . ."

"We might present her with a granddaughter and she might be six feet tall."

"Not when she is born. And by the time she grows to

that height, they will love her so much she could be a giant."

"I hope you are right, my lord."

"Call me Rhys," he commanded, smiling.

"If you wish, my lord Rhys."

"No," he swung her to face him. "Just Rhys! Now I want to be thanked properly for my gift."

"What do you want?" she hesitated.

"Say it," he prompted.

"R-Rhys?"

"Kiss me of your own free will, passionately and lovingly, the way you do when we make love and you forget yourself." His blue eyes bored into hers.

"Here in the hall," she protested. "Someone will see us."

"I want whoever is about to see us, but more I want you to kiss me without me holding you to do so. Instead, I want you to hold me."

Carefully, she set the lute down on the stones of the corridor. Turning back to face him, she found him grinning his wolfish grin. He was really a teasing, selfish beast, she thought, but he was her lord.

Cautiously, she approached his body as if it were something with which she was not familiar. Her arms went to his shoulders and then around his neck. Her left hand cupped the back of his head while the right pressed against the small of his back. She pressed her breasts, her belly, and her thighs against him, moving them slightly to fit their bodies together.

He gasped as he felt the warmth of her kindling him into flame. Still, he did not put his arms around her, but let one hang idly at his side while the other still balanced his gifts.

She turned her head to one side and placed her lips against his, softly and experimentally. Her lips moved. Her mouth opened. Her tongue flicked out to caress his lips, then his tongue. She felt him quiver and drew back from his face.

"Do not move, Rhys," she commanded. "I have not finished kissing you."

"Dear God, madam," he said breathlessly. Her lips stopped his comment. She pressed them firmly and passionately with her own and then thrust her tongue into his mouth and tasted the interior. She could feel him grow hard and eager against her as she sucked his tongue into her mouth and nipped it lightly with her teeth. Finally, she drew her face away and stepped back. "Thank you for my Christmas gift," she said demurely. "The ring is quite the most beautiful thing I have ever seen."

"You are very welcome," he said hoarsely.

"Come," she said huskily, for the kissing had held surprises for her, too. Picking up the lute from the corridor, she leaned warmly against him as they continued to their apartments.

Once inside, he set down his burdens, took her lute from her, and stored it away. Drawing her to the fire, he gently and deliberately stripped her of her clothing. As he took each piece away, he kissed the flesh he exposed, delighting in the smooth white skin and the warm blushes spreading over it as his mouth caressed and nipped her flesh.

Finally, when she was naked, he stood back and admired her, caressing her body and laughing in pleasure as she quivered and twisted, unable to remain still under his hand. Again and again, he commanded her to stand still, not to move a muscle, but then he kissed her until to obey him was impossible. "Lie down," he ordered, pretending to be stern with her. "Not on the bed, slave. Bring the furs from the bed and spread them in front of the fire."

Trembling, she obeyed him and stretched out on her

back at his feet, her long unbound hair fanned out on the furs. She wore only the gold wrist chains which she had seldom removed, the neck chain which she could not remove, and the ruby ring blazing in the firelight.

"I have one other gift for you which I did not like to give in front of my family," he laughed.

She watched as he went to the casket where he kept his ornaments and returned with another gold chain in his hand. "What are you going to do?" she tensed and half sat up.

"What it pleases me to do," he replied as he knelt at her feet. Before she could protest, he had grasped her right foot in his hand and fastened a gold chain around her ankle. "This is for us to play with together. I want you to wear it for me. Here," he held up another one, "is its mate. Put it on yourself."

Shivering with fear and sexual excitement, she did as he commanded. He laughed, "My companion, my wife, my slave." He flung off his clothes. "You are the most beautiful and most perfect of women. You are what every man dreams of having for himself some day."

As he caressed her before the fire, her excitement built until she could scarcely breathe. She tossed her head from side to side, making a flag of her hair. He seemed to be holding back, waiting for something. She did not know what he waited for, only that he was slowly driving her insane.

"Please," she gasped.

"Please what?" he inquired pleasantly, caressing her breasts slowly and deliberately, drawing his fingertips out to the very tips of her swollen nipples.

"Please . . ." she whispered urgently.

His teeth were clenched in his most evil of wolfish grins. "Tell me what you want me to do. Name it. Beg for it. You must beg for it, slave girl."

"No," she gasped and sought to pull away, but he

338

pinned her to the furs. Her weak hands and loosened thighs were no match for his hard strength.

"Yes," he ordered. "Beg for it. Say, 'Please, master.'"

"No," she hissed.

"Then we will go on just as we are."

She tried to fight him and her rebellious body, but she could only lie beneath him and writhe and shiver helplessly as the sweet torture increased. A groan of mortal anguish was wrung from her lips.

"Say it, slave girl," he whispered insidiously in her ear.

She could endure no longer. No pride, no sense of person was left to her. "Please, master," she gasped.

"What is it you wish, slave girl?" he chuckled.

"Take me now."

He parted her thighs and knelt between them. She raised her legs to encircle his back and draw him into her. When he pierced her body, she cried out at the savagery of his thrust and arched her body to accommodate him. Again, he thrust and she shuddered in ecstasy. Her mouth opened, her eyes closed, she endured such a wave of pleasure that she thought she would die and then was sure that she would live but would from that moment on be a different person. As she cried out again, he joined her in his own climax and they collapsed into the furs.

Much later, he smiled and caressed her shoulder. She stirred lazily and turned her face to his. "Was that so hard, sweetheart?" he inquired.

"Yes, Rhys, it was like dying. I feel that I shall never be the same."

"We all change," he said softly, rolling over and sitting up. "I have not been the same, since I met you. I have lost my independence, my freedom, my heart. 'Twas only fair that you lose yours also." He bent over her and kissed her.

Her arms crept up around his neck and held him down

while she kissed him sweetly and gently over and over, until he swept her up and carried her to their bed. He returned for the furs, spread them over her, and climbed in beside her.

"You are my master, Lord Rhiannon, and I am your slave," she whispered against his neck.

Wrapped in each other's arms, they fell asleep. Unbanked on the hearth, the fire leaped up once more before dying away to ashes. In its light, the ruby clasped in the golden claw blazed with unmatched brilliance.

Thirty-One

From the window of their apartment, Moira gazed out at the rubble of stones falling away from the wall below. What had been bare, gray rock in the winter when she had first looked out this window and thought to throw herself from it was now dotted with tiny clumps of green plants with white flowers. The air felt cold still, but the sky was clear and blue and the wind carried a different scent on it.

For three full months after Christmas, the weather had been so foul that riding was impossible. Snow and sleet had fallen for days and then had not melted but had been covered with more. Now, looking out of the window, she could see blooming snowdrops and her nostrils quivered with the scent of spring.

Behind her, Rhiannon placed his hands around her to clasp her belly. As she straightened and swelled out her chest, she pressed her shoulders back against him. For two days now, she had felt tiny fluttering movements in her slightly protruding belly. Rhiannon pressed her tightly and again she felt the tiny movements. As she turned her head, he met her lips with his own.

"Can you feel him, Rhys?" she asked.

"No," he replied. "Is he moving?" She nodded and he kissed her again. "He will be strong and hearty."

"He might be a girl," she reminded him.

Again her husband nuzzled her neck, chuckling. "Then she will be almost six feet tall."

Turning in his arms, she pushed him away. "'Tis too beautiful a day to stay indoors. Today we must ride." She headed for the chest to get her boots, divided gown, and *chausses*.

"You cannot ride, sweetheart, in your condition."

Blithely ignoring his statement, she continued to dress. "I cannot stay in this hold one more day without going mad."

"You will injure the child."

"Rhys," she turned to him, "I will be more likely to injure the child if I am mad and cannot properly care for myself. Come dress and we will ride together. Saddle the gray and the black and let us ride out into the clean, green air."

Shaking his head with many mutterings and growlings, he dressed himself. She hurried ahead of him in the corridors, past the bower, and out into the bailey to the stable.

Together they trotted sedately out through the barbican gate and down the winding road to the valley beyond. By common consent, they turned their horses' heads to the north and rode toward Colwyn Bay. Suddenly, she spurred her horse and galloped headlong along the road.

Cursing, he laid heels to his gray and followed her. She pulled her horse to a rearing halt at the crest of a small rise. Rhiannon, hot on her heels, had to pull his gray back to avoid crashing into her. By that time, he was livid with rage.

"Have you no thought for yourself, madam?" he

shouted. "By God, I shall put you on a lead rein and take you home."

"Rhys," she laughed at him, "I wanted to gallop and I did. Now I want to ride leisurely and enjoy the beautiful spring day. My lord," she reached her hand out and laid it on his, "the child is firmly attached by now. I am healthy and strong. I have ridden all my life. My muscles are holding him as firmly as if he were in my arms. Please let us enjoy this. It is my first day of freedom as your wife."

He smiled at her. They leaned together and kissed.

The small village on the slope was stirring with life. A great-breasted woman stood at the door of what was obviously an alehouse and nodded in a friendly fashion at Rhiannon.

"Anglesey Gwen," he hailed her. "Could you bring my lady and me a cup of your finest ale? My mouth has been dry for your brew for six months now."

"Your mouth is not too dry to spread out the soothing syrup, I hear," she cackled as she disappeared into the house.

"She is from the far north isle," he explained, "and a finer hand at brewing ale we have never had."

The woman rolled out of the door with two large leather tankards. Stepping back, she folded her arms with satisfaction. 'Tis a fine day for a ride, my lady," she spoke pleasantly to Moira, who smiled in response. "'Twould be right brisk down by the water, if that is where you go." Rhiannon nodded. "Mayhap you would like to stop back in for some bread and meat before you ride back up to the keep. You could warm yourselves right well in front of my fire."

"We will do that, Gwen, and gratefully," Rhiannon said, handing her down the tankards.

"'Twill be a pleasure to look forward to," said Moira, smiling.

They rode through the village and out onto the beach.

Past the shingle, they galloped down the sand. Spray splashed from their horses' hooves. Moira's cloak blew back in the wind and her hair came unbound.

Rhiannon had never seen Moira look so bright and alive. Her cheeks glowed, her eyes with their ice blue irises shone like diamonds. Finally, she pulled the black up to face the ocean, her breath fogging out of her mouth as she drew in great gulps of the cold air and expelled them with sighs of pleasure. Grasping her belly, she patted it lovingly. "He is awake and moving," she said to Rhiannon. "He loves the ride. I knew he would." She laughed with pleasure and Rhiannon drew his horse in beside her so that their knees touched. "Feel him, Rhys. I know you will be able to now." She guided his hand in through her layers of clothing until it lay cold against her warm skin.

Although he protested that she was going to be chilled, her gesture delighted him. When she pressed his fingers against her, he indeed felt a tiny vibration. His face broke into a grin. "'Tis wonderful," he cried. He pressed harder now, forgetful of his cold hand, but only wanting to feel the life that they had created together. "I never realized. He is already alive. How does he breathe and eat?"

"Through me. I breathe for him and eat for him, too, and drink fine ale from Anglesey Gwen's." She chuckled. "I wonder if he will be tipsy. He is very little and not used to such as that."

"Let us take him in and see," laughed her husband, adjusting her clothing with loving fingers before he headed the horses back up the beach.

Inside the warm and smoky, odorous alehouse, several fishermen sat at a trestle before the fire. A couple of villagers sat at a smaller table farther back. When Rhiannon and Moira entered, they too sought a small table, but the alewife would not allow them. Instead, she insisted that they sit close to the fire while she set before them the very best her house had to offer.

Moira attacked her meal with the precision of a woman eating as if life depended on it. Watching in amusement, Rhiannon remembered her statement about eating for the child. Finally satisfied, she pushed herself away from the table. The fishermen raised their tankards in salute to the couple. Rhiannon fished a couple of coins from his purse as he rose. "Let us go, sweetheart," he said. "You will need your rest. Not too much on the first day out."

"Go with God, my lady." Gwen dropped an awkward suggestion of a curtsey.

Moira inclined her head. "My thanks for this hospitality and the well-prepared food. We will come here often."

When they turned into the road that wound up to the castle, a horseman was clearly visible halfway up the trail to the barbican gate. Moira pulled up her horse in some surprise.

"That man ahead of us!" she exclaimed. "He is Thomas Tech Duinn, my father's man."

"The swine who nearly drowned me in the mud and then burned my shoulder?" Rhiannon inquired sharply.

"He was but following orders, Rhys."

"He was very enthusiastic," he observed sarcastically.

"Not so enthusiastic as Owen Llewellyn," she countered drily, spurring her horse forward.

They entered the hall only a minute behind Thomas. Moira saw that in his hand he carried a pine bough. Gethin ap Breannon was seated on the dais, his lookouts having informed him early that a stranger was coming. Flanking him were Henry, Owen, and Huw. Thomas' eyes slid nervously round the room till they came to rest on Moira. When he saw her, richly dressed and walking freely beside the young lord, his eyes narrowed and a smirk crossed his face. He bowed slightly to her, his smile knowing and evil.

"Approach and say your piece," Gethin commanded.

Thomas shuffled forward, the pine bough waving in his hand. Fumbling at his belt, he drew forth a fur-trimmed glove which he flung down at the foot of the dais.

Moira gasped, for the effect of the challenge from her father could mean her death. Instinctively, she moved closer to Rhiannon who encircled her with his arm.

"Gethin of Hawk's Keep, my master Peter of Lorne demands that you return his daughter to him. He has offered a fair ransom for her return and you have refused. Now he declares that he will take her from you by force of arms."

Owen Llewellyn snorted. "He can try," he muttered.

Lord Gethin's eyes were icy. "Return to your kennel and tell your master that his daughter is the slave of my son. That we do not give up slaves, especially those that have been tamed so easily and now labor for us so pleasantly."

Thomas let his eyes slide round to Moira. "Aye," he said slowly, "I can see she is easily tamed." He spat into the rushes on the floor.

Moira's face was white as she realized the full extent of what Thomas would return to tell her father. As he turned, she started toward him, but Rhiannon held her back. Flashing him a look of anger, she tried to struggle free of his encircling arms.

"No," he whispered in her ear.

"Let me go," she said, "I must explain to Thomas. He will tell my father lies."

"Will he, sweetheart?" Rhiannon turned her struggling body in his arms and dragged her into an alcove partitioned off by a tapestry. "What can he tell but the truth?"

"What do you mean?"

"You know what I mean," he said, tipping her chin up. "He will tell that you were enslaved and that you have been tamed to perform labor for us pleasingly. This is true."

"Oh, God!" she exclaimed in horror. "But he will not tell that I am your wife, that I am your vassal who swore loyalty to you in honor, that I carry your child which will be his grandchild."

"Your father would not want to believe that you have been treated well and nobly," Rhiannon continued. "Let him think that you are in danger. Then he will be more easily reasoned with when we talk face to face."

"He will never talk face to face," Moira said positively. "His hatred is too great."

"Then he will take you back if we are defeated, if he thinks that you were enslaved and mistreated."

She was shivering now, all pleasure in the bright day destroyed. She started to draw aside the curtain. Her hand touched the tapestry. Then she swung around to fling herself against Rhiannon's body. He clasped her tightly in his arms as she buried her face in his shoulder. Nervous tremors shook her body until her teeth chattered.

"Easy, sweetheart, easy. I have you. Cry if you want to, dear love. No one will see but me."

At his words, she steeled herself. "I never cry," she said and walked out with her chin up to face the men of his father's retinue. Their antipathy was apparent from the first step into the room. Seven days from now, they might lose their lives fighting over her. Lands on which they depended for livelihood would be sacked and burned by raiders led by the men of Lorne. Peasants who were just beginning spring planting would have their crops burned and their huts destroyed. The food would be in short supply next year. Some would be sure to starve.

Owen Llewellyn brandished an accusing fist in her

347

direction. "I say, hang her in a cage from the wall. Let the dog see what we do to bitches. He will either turn tail and run or lose his reason and charge into a trap."

Several men nodded in agreement and a mutter of assent rose, but neither Huw Llengaron nor Henry Fletcher made a move either to approve nor disapprove. Rhiannon stepped in front of her, but Lord Gethin rose from his chair on the dais.

"Silence!" he commanded in his deep voice. "She is my son's wife; she carries his child. As such, by the bond of blood, she is my daughter. We will not discuss what will be done with her as if she were an enemy. She has proven herself a loyal wife in the four months she has been in his apartments in this keep. She has had her chance to escape and do us all harm.

"We will delay no more. Henry, old friend, send messengers to the villages and to the small holds of each man to warn them to withdraw nearer to Hawk's Keep and to arm themselves to be ready to fight in seven days should the need arise.

"Son, you will command the patrols to ride daily out of the keep and along the frontier and road in the west. Take Dafydd Hopcyn to ride as your courier."

Dafydd jumped forward eagerly and Rhiannon grinned at him. They were good friends after the ride across the country to intercept Gethin last year.

"Owen Llewellyn," Gethin continued, "you will take a like force and ride south." The man bowed and he drew back his lips in anger when he realized that he was being sent into an area where confrontation was less likely. He opened his mouth to protest, but Gethin raised his hand.

"Huw Llengaron, you will be in charge of the garrisoning of this keep. Be sure that every possible preparation is made, every precaution taken. We may have all our people behind the palisades before the forty days are over.

"Are there any among you who can find fault or objection?"

In the electric silence, each man thought through the very simple yet effective plans for defense. As no one spoke, gradually a more relaxed atmosphere seemed to grip the assembled vassals. Lord Gethin signaled for his squires to bring forward cups of ale and pass them among the men. The eagerness for battle began to manifest itself. A man toasted Lord Gethin of Hawk's Keep. Another proclaimed death to the men of Lorne.

The winter was over; the spring was breaking. At the same time, the men, like little boys, saw this challenge as many things besides actual war and bloodshed. Here was a chance to display the training that many had worked to acquire; here, too, the chance to break out of the monotony of the winter and ride around playing games with life and death as the stakes. Perhaps there would be a duel to fight and certainly there would be chances to taste the ale and wenches of the countryside.

In disgust, Moira watched her husband and Dafydd joyously planning strategy and discussing which weapons to take, which horses would be needed, which supplies would be needed, which done without. So were her father's men behaving at this very same moment, she knew. A kind of philosophical calm settled over her. At least, she reasoned, none of this was really her fault. She was an excuse; if she had not been captured, another reason would have appeared. War by common consent had nothing to do with higher objects and large stakes.

Silently, she left the hall. In the apartment, Alys waited with her hip bath and Moira sank into it gratefully. She did not feel well.

"Bring me some soup, some bread, and some wine while I sit here and relax," she commanded.

When Alys left the room to obey, Moira was alone with the fire, the warm water soothing her lower body, and her thoughts. The baby kicked strongly within her and she jumped.

"I am not really alone," she said aloud. "You are here with me, my dearest one." She felt a strong stirring and smiled happily. I will not go with Rhiannon this time, she thought. I cannot be used against my father. He promised me that. But, oh, I shall miss him.

The horrifying thought struck her that he might be injured or killed. She shuddered.

When Alys returned with the tray, Moira had dried herself and was sitting in her brown robe before the fire. "Do you hate me, Alys?" Moira asked the little woman who was Henry Fletcher's wife.

For a moment, Alys stared into the fire. "Lady Moira," she replied, "you are a woman who has come through this circumstance far better than might be expected. Instead of being raped and passed from hand to hand as would have been the lot of most women, you have been given a soft place and perhaps a good life. Now the men say they go to war for you. Henry has already left with his troop. But, truly, my lady, we who have any wisdom at all know that they would have gone out to get into trouble without you as an excuse. They have done it every spring and every fall. They need no excuse."

"Thank you, Alys," Moira said, leaning her head against the high back of her chair.

"Now you eat this good soup and drink this wine. I will put a hot pan in your bed. When you finish, you climb right in. You did more than you should have today. You are the center of the storm again. Too much excitement is not good for the baby."

Moira shook her head irritably. "I am not tired. The babe kicks so strongly when I lie down that I can scarcely rest anyway."

Alys grinned and nodded sagely. "When you lie on your back, my lady, the babe within you lies on your

350

knobby backbone. It wakes him up and he wiggles and twists within you."

Moira's hand pressed against her mounded belly. "Really? I never thought of that."

"'Tis true. I will fetch you a small down pillow for you to put under him and you can lie on your side. That way both mother and babe can rest easily."

Alys departed, leaving Moira staring down at her body, contemplating the life that burgeoned within her. A real person with likes and dislikes, a complainer, to be sure, at the slightest discomfort. She smiled thoughtfully. How like Rhiannon! "If the world is not as I like it, I will make it over!"

The door to the apartment opened, admitting both Alys and, to Moira's utter astonishment, Lady Branwen ni Rhiannon.

"My daughter, Alys tells me you suffer from some discomfort and sleeplessness." A faint frown of concern marred the skin between the cool brown eyes.

Moira rose, hastily, dropping a deep curtsey. "Lady Branwen. Alys has already assured me that my problem is easily corrected. There was no need . . ."

A brief, wintry smile curved the lady's lips. "I was concerned when I heard that that foolish son of mine had taken you riding. How he could do such a thing is beyond me," she scolded.

Coloring faintly, Moira demurred. "I fear that I was the one who insisted that we ride. I had been in these rooms so long. The spring air smelled so fresh. Oh, but 'twas no danger, I am sure," she hastened to add. "I am used to riding. The babe was perfectly safe."

The smile faded from Lady Branwen's lips. "Careless, foolish girl. How can you who have never carried a child before know whether 'tis safe to ride or not? Do you care nothing for the babe you hold within you? It is your husband's. You should not jeopardize his heir."

"I am accustomed to riding," Moira protested.

"Indeed, Lady Branwen," Alys interceded, "Lady Moira was not at all tired nor uncomfortable. It is good for a woman to keep up with the activities she is accustomed to do. She will exercise her muscles and make the babe come the faster and safer."

Faced with arguments from two sides, Branwen relented with a tired wave of her hand. "You younger women will do as you please. In my day, we heeded what our mothers told us." She stood uncertainly, gazing around her at her son's apartments which she had never seen.

"Alys, will you fetch wine for the three of us?" Moira asked hastily. "Lady Branwen, will you sit yourself and join me? I doubt that Rhiannon will be returning for quite some time. He is preparing for the campaign."

On the point of refusing, Lady Branwen raised her hand to halt Alys, who quitted the room with a smile and a nod of her head. Sighing, the older woman took the seat Moira indicated. "I worry too much about babes," she admitted. "Rhiannon was my first born and Edain my last, but between them . . ." She stared into the fire. "I was so small," she explained. "Gethin was disgusted with me after . . . but I should not tell you these things. They will make you afraid." She looked at her daughter, who had not reseated but stood beside the table, hand on hip. "You are so tall and no doubt strong. Your body carries the child well inside you. You should have no trouble in bearing. I guess you will labor less than a day." Her voice trailed away. The fire leaped and crackled.

Alys returned with the wine and only two goblets. "I shall be on my way, Lady Moira, by your leave. You have finished your bath. You have pleasant company."

Moira smiled. "You are welcome to stay, Lady Alys." But Alys shook her head and slipped away.

Pouring the sweet, pale liquid, Moira handed her

mother the goblet.

"Thank you." Lady Branwen lifted it in salute. "To my new grandson or granddaughter."

Moira joined her and they drank companionably.

"It is fortunate that you are quickening," Lady Branwen continued, taking another sip. "The battles and skirmishes will go on unabated this spring as they have gone on every year since I was a little girl."

"Alys said that I was really not to blame," Moira interposed.

"You?" Lady Branwen made an indelicate sound through her nose. "Not at all. You are merely this year's excuse. No woman is *that* important." Her voice had a bitter tone as she drained her cup.

"So Alys told me," Moira remarked drily, refilling her mother's drink.

"A woman's main office in life is to bear sons to get killed in these wretched wars. For some women who can have many, 'tis not so bad, but for me . . . After Rhiannon, I had three sons more in quick succession, but they did not live. They were born d-dead." The chatelaine clutched the stem of the goblet as if her fingers would crush the metal. "They were too big, the midwife said. And turned the wrong way and I so small." Her face went white at the memory of her labor.

"If you would rather not talk about this . . ."

"I have *never* talked about it. How do I know whether I would rather not?" Branwen snapped. She stared at the liquid in the bowl of the goblet. "*In vino veritas*," she muttered. "There have been no women of equal rank here in the hold with whom I could discuss my problems."

"You were very brave to have Edain."

"Not brave, just very lucky. My labor began prematurely. I slipped on the stairs. 'Twas shortly after Margwin came to the keep. I was upset. Gethin had replaced me. He tried to make a secret of it. But I could not abide ignorance. I had to know. I was attempting to spy on them. I heard them, but they found me. I tried to flee, but I was clumsy." She shrugged, accompanying the movement with a pathetic travesty of a philosophical smile.

"How terrible!"

"Edain has been a great comfort. Gethin has been kind to her. And to me, I suppose. But he has not come to my bed since then."

"Who is Margwin?" Moira asked suddenly.

Lady Branwen shrugged again. "Some slave Gethin brought home from a raid with him. No one of importance, I should imagine. Why do you ask?"

Moira shrugged. "I think she dislikes me."

Again the indelicate snort. "Margwin dislikes everybody who has more than she does. She has sought to turn my own daughter against me. I am sure she has begged Gethin to set me aside and make her more than she is. I expect your elevation by my son galled her sorely. She imagines that Gethin should set me aside and make her chatelaine of Hawk's Keep."

"I think she envies me more than that."

"Surely you do not think... Surely she never imagined..." Lady Branwen took a healthy sip of wine. "Such an idea is too laughable. You mean, she is jealous of you? But Rhiannon never gave her a look. He resents her for her presumption of my place."

"She has been at Owen Llewellyn's ear," Moira declared. "I am sure of it."

"That poor, insane soul," Lady Branwen waved her hand dismissively.

"He is dangerous to me and through me to the lord's heir."

Lady Branwen did not answer. Her hand containing the goblet wavered. "I should not have drunk so much, so fast," she observed, her voice slurring slightly on the word *fast*.

"Sometimes drinking helps a little to dull the pain," Moira soothed. "My father always said it did."

"In this case, he was right," Lady Branwen agreed. "I—I cannot understand why I feel happy and sad at the same time, as if I had unburdened my soul at the same time I have taken on a great sadness."

"Rhiannon got me drunk once," Moira remembered with a smile. "It helped. There was darkness and cold all around us."

"You must go to bed," Lady Branwen rose determinedly, staggering slightly to the side. "Shall I help you to disrobe?"

Surveying her mother's swaying figure, Moira doubted very seriously that Lady Branwen could find the lacings on the blouse. Nevertheless, she did not want to refuse the generous offer. "If you like."

"Oh, I can do it. You think my hands are clumsy. But 'tis not so. I am a bit weepy and a bit dizzy, but otherwise I am . . ." She shook her head slightly and smiled distantly, ". . . fine."

True to her words, within minutes Lady Branwen had efficiently helped Moira off with her clothes. Wearily, now, Moira slipped between the covers.

"Here is the small pillow Alys brought for your stomach. You lie on your side and slip it under . . . so. My grandson will then lie quietly and rest when you do."

Lady Branwen arranged the bed to her satisfaction, then pulled the cover over Moira. "Good night, my daughter." Lady Branwen patted Moira's hand where it lay across the mound of her stomach.

"Good night, Lady Branwen."

"I think I will take the rest of this wine with me," the chatelaine remarked with something suspiciously like a chuckle as she doused the candles and departed.

Moira stared into the warm heart of the glowing fire. Strange and stranger! As the weeks and months of her captivity passed, she was drawn more and more into the doings and the lives of these people until they seemed to become more and more family to her. Her own father and the people she had left behind became as shadows from a time gone by.

On her finger, the ruby rested benignly in the claw. Musing, she touched her index finger to the top of the stone. Daily, it became more the symbol Rhiannon had conceived when he bade the smith make it. His wife and now his child held safe within the talons of the hawk.

She put her hand on her belly. The babe lay peacefully still. She could imagine him, curled around himself, his tiny hands under his determined chin. Demanding his own pillow! She smiled and patted him lovingly.

When Rhiannon came to bed hours later, she was still asleep.

Thirty-Two

The flames rose out of the thatched roofs of the peasants' huts at Ffestiniog at the foot of Snowdon. The prevailing winds carried the smoke from the damp thatch toward the west. Rhiannon rose in his stirrups and sniffed the wind. With Dafydd at his side, at the head of a troop of twelve of his father's best, he had been riding back and forth along the border from Tremadoc Bay to the river which emptied into Colwyn Bay. For eight days, he had ridden this route without sign of Lorne.

"Smoke on the wind!" Rhiannon remarked.

"Aye, my lord," Dafydd agreed.

"Could be he has crossed the border in the night to start his raiding as he moves toward Hawk's Keep."

"More than likely," Dafydd said. "Shall I ride south and then circle to get the warning to the hold?"

Rhiannon thought a moment. "No, not yet. Lord Gethin knows he is coming. He does not know with what force and how armed and mounted. We will investigate his forces, scout behind him, and then you can ride with information that can help the keep prepare."

"Right, my lord," Dafydd responded.

357

They galloped their horses northeast. Within the hour, a haze of smoke was visible on the air. The vegetation thickened. At Rhiannon's signal, the men strung out single file behind him as they wound through the woods. The afternoon was beginning to wane and the only sounds in the stillness were the soft pacing of their horses and the creak and jingle of saddle leather.

Rhiannon felt the prickle of tension at the back of his neck. Strung out with the end of the line out of sight of the front, they were in great danger. A favorite trick of Peter of Lorne was to send small groups of men to harry a larger force by picking them off one at a time. Rhiannon swung in the saddle to speak to Dafydd. "Pass the order back to close up tight. Keep each man with his horse's nose to the tail of the mount in front."

"Yes, sir," Dafydd's young, unbearded face was pale in the gray hazy light. His voice cracked slightly. Rhiannon grinned. The boy was brave. No man could ride better than he. When he had watched Dafydd practicing in the bailey, he had been amazed at the skill with which the boy sat his horse, controlling with his knees alone and maneuvering between obstacles. Rhiannon realized that Dafydd might very well come to be his right hand man as Henry Fletcher was his father's.

The trail widened ahead and the darkness began to fall. The main group could bed down in that clearing, Rhiannon thought, posting one man out ahead and one man back along the trail. At daylight, they could ride into Ffestiniog and see which way Lorne's men had taken.

As the gray's head broke from the trees, Dafydd spurred his lighter, faster horse to the left and jumped it into the clearing. Simultaneously, a heavy body dropped with a blood-chilling cry onto Dafydd's back. The knife flashed in the heavy hand and the attacker and the boy rolled from the saddle together.

Cursing, Rhiannon grimly jerked back on the reins,

causing his horse to rear. Towering over the man on the ground who had rolled free of Dafydd's bleeding corpse, the gray plunged down. Both ironshod hooves sank into flesh, and blood spattered the chest of the horse as the death scream rang out.

Behind him in the forest, Rhiannon could hear similar curses and screams as his troop fought for their lives. Drawing his sword, he swung down from his horse and knelt beside the boy's body. The knife had buried itself to the hilt in the left side of the chest. No power on earth could help him. The only blessing was the quickness of the death. He could have felt no pain, only a momentary stunning blow before darkness closed in.

"Ride!" a man screamed behind him. "For the love of God, Lord Rhys! Mount and ride!"

Men were filling the clearing, turning it into a melee. Rhiannon could count perhaps nine mounted men who had made it into the clearing. His other men must be dead or captured. Rhiannon sprang for the saddle, as from the corner of his eye he caught a dark figure lunging at him. Swinging his sword, he heard a satisfying yowl of pain. His left foot found the stirrup. As he swung his right leg over, a stunning blow struck his left thigh close to the groin. He fell forward on the gray's neck as his momentum pushed him astride. Almost face to face with him was the leering face of a man-at-arms with a short spear. He had gone for the groin rather than disemboweling the horse as he should have done. Rhiannon's sword hilt smashed into his face. The man fell back with a gurgling shriek and Rhiannon righted himself in the saddle.

All was suddenly quiet in the glade. Only Rhiannon and his nine remaining men lived in the gloom. Wheeling their horses, they finally formed a circle facing outward.

"Are they gone?" came a hoarse question out of the semi-darkness.

"For the time being," Rhiannon replied, "but we must move out of here quickly and quietly."

"Which way, milord?" a tired gruff voice spoke out of the dark.

"Northeast," Rhiannon replied. "We know that they are behind us."

"We know that they are in front of us, too. And, like as not, they know how many we are and what we are about. They'll be back to get us all."

"Make for the road that leads under the shoulders of Snowdon. It is in the clear and we can make good time," Rhiannon commanded, his voice coming in light gasps as his leg began to throb and burn mightily. Wheeling his horse, he rode to the side of the clearing opposite the trail they had entered. The blackness was deepening now, but he continued to search doggedly until he found the exit. "Follow me," he called.

They rode for miles, until finally the trees became less dense and the stars broke through the treetops. At the end of perhaps an hour, Rhiannon called a halt. He had stuffed a strip torn from his tunic into the hole in his leg and the bleeding seemed to have lessened. Nevertheless, he knew he had to stop to get help.

"Pass the word to halt and report," he commanded.

Nine men joined him in a circle. Exhausted, they crouched on the ground, holding their horses' reins.

"Who's hurt?" Rhiannon questioned.

"Pwyll Hobcyn, sir," came a hoarse voice. "Got a knife slit in my side. Not deep, but I cannot stop the bleeding."

"See to him," Rhiannon said, "and help me down. My left leg is cut."

Two men sprang to his side, supporting him from the saddle. His pain wrung a moan through his set teeth as he had to bear the weight on his left leg to dismount. Sweat dripped down his face even though the night was chill. He stretched out while a pair of rough hands wrapped a tight cloth around the wound, *chausses*, and undergarment, too.

With no light and no fire, the only possibility of help was to bind the wound tightly to stop the bleeding. The niceties of washing and bandaging would have to wait till morning.

"We will rest here for a couple of hours. Two watch one hour before us and behind us and two relieve them. The man behind must be extra careful. They could have followed us."

"'Tis not likely, sir. They did not have horses."

"Nevertheless, every man must be careful." Rhiannon clenched his teeth against the pain as he settled back on the cold ground. Cursing himself for letting men be trapped in the wood, he lay sleepless, listening to the soft, moaning, sighing breath of Pwyll Hobcyn. He heard the sentries change in an hour and observed the stars as they swung above him. At the end of the time, he called the men up.

His leg had stiffened considerably as he lay on the cold ground. When his two men came to lift him into the saddle, he could not bear his weight. He could scarcely stifle a scream as they jarred him against the saddle bow. Cursing roundly, he gave the order to move.

As dawn began to pinken the sky before them, they came to the smoking ruins of the village whose destruction they had smelled from afar the day before. A few people stood about in grim silence as Rhiannon's men limped into the street where the huts had stood closely pressed together for security and warmth. No livestock bawled a welcome, no dogs barked, no pigeons cooed.

In the usual manner, Peter of Lorne had begun his war by systematically stripping the countryside of its wealth. By pitilessly ravaging the villages of the peasantry,

361

Hawk's Keep could be impoverished and stand in danger of starving in the winter months because the villeins would have neither money nor victuals to supply the keep.

A spokesman stepped forward. "They came from the south, Lord Rhiannon. Lorne's men for sure."

"How many?" Rhiannon gritted. His wound was making him dizzy, but this burned-out shell offered him no place to rest or even to eat or drink.

"About three score. Howling they were and killing everything they could not carry away."

"Did they take any prisoners?"

"No, just killed those that tried to resist, burned the houses, and drove off the cattle." The man's voice broke. "What shall we do now?"

"Gather up whatever you have managed to save and come with us to Hawk's Keep. You will be welcome there. When this thing is ended, we will return you to your land and help you to rebuild."

The man nodded, touched his forelock, and moved away. Signaling the man to dismount, Rhiannon waited patiently while two came forward to help him from the saddle. Gazing around, he realized that these people really had nothing at all. No food, no clothing except that on their backs, and no shelter. Carefully, he studied his men and finally gestured to a lightly built young fellow with a dark face and dark, tousled hair.

"What is your name?" Rhiannon asked when the young man had come forward.

"Cei Aberdyfi, my lord."

"Cei, you must ride to Hawk's Keep ahead of us. Report to Lord Gethin the news that the raiders have entered our lands and burned Ffestiniog. Three score men are in their number for sure, possibly more if the ones who ambushed us in the woods are another party. Tell him we are returning at a slower pace to bring the villagers and the wounded. Tell him also that we will send scouts out from the main body to gather more information." Rhiannon rubbed the top of his thigh to ease its aching. He closed his eyes, sighing for a moment. "Can you remember that?"

"Yes, my lord." Cei repeated the message as Rhiannon had given it to him.

"Good, man! Take the strongest horse. Take that one of Dafydd's." Rhiannon bowed his head as his stomach knotted with the pain of Dafydd's death.

"Yes, my lord." Cei bowed and was gone.

While Rhiannon ate and rested his leg, the villagers gathered their few remaining belongings and congregated around his men. The wounded man Pwyll Hobcyn was better this morning. In a way, Rhiannon supposed he had been lucky to have gotten his men away with so few losses.

Within an hour, the little troop moved off. Rhiannon led, with two of his men behind him. The others dispersed themselves in twos among the villagers. A pair of scouts rode out ahead of the troop to report back at various intervals or to leave sign that nothing had been seen.

As the day wore on, Rhiannon and his men ate in the saddle. Battle-hardened, they gnawed bites of beef, salted and dried and causing aching thirsts, but nevertheless easing the pangs of hunger. The villagers had a few victuals which they passed among themselves. Even so, their progress was geared to the slowest ones.

The procession came to the river, swollen after weeks and months of icy rain and snow now melting down from Snowdon's mighty shoulders. The ford was broken away. The further bank appeared undermined and fallen.

Evidently, it was passable, for the scouts had not returned. Rhiannon urged his horse into the stream which swirled around his mount's knees, then belly, and

363

finally to his chest. In the icy water, Rhiannon's teeth set up a chatter, for his body was feverish from his wound. The water came no higher than the gray's chest and then began to recede with each step. Finally, with a leap the horse gained the opposite shore. Rhiannon turned in the saddle to wave the others through. Suddenly, on each side of him rose a man-at-arms. Unceremoniously, he was dumped from the saddle. One leaped astride and spurred the animal into a run. The other knelt on top of him with a dagger at his throat.

Rhiannon's eyes opened wider as he recognized Thomas, the brute who had burned him. "Peter of Lorne takes back his horse!" Thomas grated. He glanced up to see two of Rhiannon's men charging as best they could through the swirling water, their horses slipping and losing their footing in their haste.

Thomas chuckled gleefully as he watched, then he turned his attention back to Rhiannon's prone, tensed body. "Then he takes back his daughter." Thomas punctuated his statement with a stiff jab of his knife under Rhiannon's ear, cutting the earlobe deeply. "And then he takes your life."

So saying, Thomas reversed the knife and slammed his fist into Rhiannon's jaw. With speed belying his burly size, Thomas made for a stand of trees where he sprang to his own pony and spurred it savagely.

When he returned to his senses, Rhiannon's anger and pain evidenced themselves in a long howl. The villagers who had crossed to the other side of the stream beheld him with blood streaming down his cheek from his ear. The wound in his thigh was broken open and bleeding. He was almost too weary to move after twenty-four hours without rest.

Only the common sense of his soldiers prevailed upon Rhiannon to prevent him from taking the horse that had belonged to Cei Aberdyfi and riding off in hot pursuit of the gray horse that he had stolen from Peter of Lorne. As night darkened, he rested morosely beside a tiny fire built for him by one of the men. He would not eat, but merely gazed into it, staring at the flames, his eyes glowing red like a wolf's as he contemplated his shame and allowed his wounds to heal.

Thirty-Three

In the week which followed the departure of Lord Rhiannon and his men, Hawk's Keep prepared for war. Siege was thought inevitable. Large stores were brought in and added to the supplies which had been diminished to their lowest point by the winter.

For Moira, the week was the most painful since the time she had spent in the dungeon. She was left alone most of the time. Only Alys came from the bower to see to her needs daily. When she descended to the hall to eat in the middle of morning, she was pointedly ignored by one and all. The servitors, taking their cue from their masters, served her the last of the food, always greasy, congealed messes on the heels of the loaves of bread.

Finally, Alys spoke to Lady Branwen about their treatment of the expectant mother of the lord's grandson. The food improved, but the service was rude and frequently done under duress. Every woman and child was made painfully aware that she was the enemy's daughter and that her presence was causing the entire conflict. The fact that this conflict had been in existence every spring and fall for longer than anyone could

366

remember made no difference. Moira was the one at fault.

Edain took particular pleasure in speaking to her mother in Moira's presence of the danger that Rhiannon was in, the cruelty of the cold nights. "I saw Rhys in a dream last night, Mother," she cried. "He was wounded and shivering. 'Tis over a week and we have had no word."

"Edain, you are overimagining things. Try to be a little cheerier," Branwen urged.

"But how can that creature sit there at table with us when my brother is suffering and starving, probably hurt somewhere." Edain's voice rose shrilly. "She should be sent back to her father, then this would all stop."

"Hush, Edain," her mother admonished. "Moira is your brother's wife and as such is your sister."

"Sister! She's no sister of mine," Edain cried. "She's a witch. Margwin says that only a witch could have cast a spell over my brother so that he lost his reason and fell madly in love with her. She says that the child she carries is not my brother's child at all but the spawn of the devil himself."

The mutterings at the table grew loud at this. Many women cast their eyes on Moira, then looked away quickly and crossed themselves. In some haste, Moira rose from the table and quit the room. Alone in her chamber, she lay prone on her bed, her lips drawn in between her teeth, trying to control the nervous shivering that racked her. The baby kicked and tumbled within her as if in agony for her.

Finally, she rose and drew on her boots. She would ride along the headlands on her black and blow the terrors of her mind away. On impulse, she turned to Rhiannon's chest and opened it. Inside, under some of his clothing, she found what she was seeking. Her dagger, the one he had taken from her in her bedroom months ago, lay still in the sheath which had been made for it. Carefully, she attached the sheath to her belt. She was alone in this castle of enemies with a helpless life stored within her body. She would be prepared.

In the bailey, she waited while a groom reluctantly saddled her black. His insolence grated on her nerves already frayed from the morning's encounter. Icy-eyed, she stood, striking her boot with her whip.

Huw Llengaron approached her. "Pity the poor horse to be ridden by one so impatient." At his comment, she relaxed and smiled.

"You are right, sir." She ruefully tucked the whip under her arm and clasped her gloved hands together. "I am but worried."

"Madam, you need not be. We are all worried, but Lord Rhys is the least of our problems."

"Why so? He is on the border. He could be fighting at this very moment."

"'Tis not your father's way, my lady. He will raid the villages and burn the seed that is just now to be planted. He will drive off the livestock that will shortly reproduce to provide food for the summer and replenish our depleted winter supplies."

The groom came with her horse. "If you wait one minute, I will ride with you," Huw said pleasantly. "I am sure you can have my horse here within one minute," he addressed the groom. The fellow vanished into the stable with a bow and a tug at his forelock.

Moira grinned. "I see that he knows the voice of authority."

"You will have that authority someday, my lady. Do not fear. What you were will be forgotten in the face of what you are."

"What am I?" Moira's face sobered. "I am the enemy."

"No, my lady." Huw was interrupted by the return of the groom with his mount. Without waiting for the groom's help, Moira swung into her saddle. Huw Llengaron swung up beside her.

Out on the headland, with the wind blowing in their faces, Moira felt that she was free for the first time in days. A friend rode at her side.

Smiling, Huw continued their conversation. "My lady, you are the friend of these people, although they do not know you yet. You carry the lord's heir. Moreover, you are stronger than any of them. Many of the women in the keep envy you. You are the wife of the man they hoped to marry. Oh, yes, several girls were considered possibilities for marriage to him. They are all jealous and disappointed. Their mothers are resentful.

"Moreover, Rhiannon loves and honors you above any woman. And why should he not. You behaved honorably in every way. You have the distinct advantage over every man in this keep in that you can read and write. You are teaching your lord to read. Within you lies the means for peace in this northern land."

"Rhiannon has talked of peace to you then," Moira said.

"Rhiannon has talked of nothing but peace for you. He does not say he loves you. He may never say that. What he says is that you can ride, that you can read, that you can write, that you can sing and play the lute. When he works, he sometimes hums between his teeth. He hums the tunes you play of an evening in your rooms."

Moira was silent, her head bowed. She had never in her wildest imagining believed that Rhiannon even gave her a thought after he rose from their bed in the morning. Now Huw Llengaron, his friend, was telling her that he spoke of her constantly. "He never leaves my mind," she whispered softly. "Our child constantly reminds me of

369

him. But even before it stirred, I could not escape my thoughts of him."

"Exactly, my lady." Huw Llengaron smiled at her. She raised her head and met his eyes. "I think you love him, too."

She was speechless. Her eyes flickered. Quickly, she turned her head away to gaze out across the bay.

"Enjoy your ride, my lady. I must return and resume my duties. But do not let the slurs at the board distress you. Every one here knows that you were the excuse for war. If it had not been you, something else would have set it off."

He bowed over the saddle bow and wheeled his horse back toward the keep.

"Thank you, Huw Llengaron," Moira called. "You have warmed me again."

He spurred his horse. It jumped forward. "My pleasure!" he shouted.

Moira sat with a smile on her lips, gazing out at the headland. Finally, she sighed and moved the black forward at a sedate walk. Within her, she was aware of the stillness of the baby. "Have you gone to sleep?" she spoke aloud. "Rest easy. All is well."

When she returned to the bailey, she saw several refugees already seeking the shelter and security of the keep. There were no men in the groups, but women, children, babies with their animals. One very irate woman was belaboring a tall girl who seemed unable to cope with a cow and her calf. The girl had evidently allowed the animal to get loose and it was unconcernedly eating hay from the rick reserved for the keep's horses. The angry groom screeched at the woman, the woman at the girl.

Swinging down unassisted, a smile on her face, Moira led her black into the darkness of the stable. In his stall, she unsaddled him and began to rub him down with dry hay. When the groom returned, she had finished and nodded to him pleasantly as she strode by him. He gazed at her open-mouthed and then turned away, scratching his head.

At breakfast three days later, Cei Aberdyfi limped into the hall to report to Lord Gethin of the attack on the troop and the burning of Ffestiniog.

"How did my men fare in the attack?" was Gethin's first question.

"Well, my lord. Four men killed, two wounded, one of them Lord Rhiannon." His next words were drowned out. Branwen cried out and Edain burst into tears.

"Witch!" she screamed at Moira, springing to her feet. "My brother is dying and 'tis all your fault!"

Alys hurried to Edain's side. Her face grave, she grabbed the hysterical girl, pulling her firmly in against her shoulder. "There, there, my pet. Lord Rhys is merely wounded. Hush!" She pressed her hand against the back of the girl's fair head, muffling the noisy sobs and imprecations.

Gethin rose to his feet and pounded on the table. "For the love of God! We will have quiet while the man makes his report!"

Edain stopped her noise abruptly and Alys released her hold.

Gethin glowered menacingly at his daughter and then resumed his seat. "Are his wounds serious?"

"No, my lord. They seemed not. He bade me report to you that some three score men were in the group that attacked and burned Ffestiniog. If a different group attacked us in the woods, then the force might total four score or less."

"'Tis most likely that Lorne comes with a force of some hundred or so fighting men," Gethin remarked.

"Did they loot the village before they burned it?"

"Yes, my lord. They drove off all the livestock and left the people to starve. My Lord Rhiannon comes at a slower pace behind me to bring the people to Hawk's Keep and to further scout the country for more information."

"He does well," nodded Gethin. He raised his head and measured Cei. "You are a good man. If your report is true and well spoken, you will be rewarded beyond the commons when this battle is done." He gestured to a servitor. "Take this man to a private alcove in the hall and see to his comfort and his rest. When he awakens, wait upon him as you would me."

Gethin rose from his chair as Cei followed the servant. "Madam," he spoke to his wife, "I trust you will speak to our daughter about this unseemly and undisciplined display of emotion. Edain, you have disgraced us with your lack of control. Go to your room and await your mother there." He turned to Moira who sat quietly, her hand tightly clutched around the stem of the chalice. "You are cool, madam," he observed.

"'Twill do no good to scream and cry, my lord Father." She faced him, white-lipped. "I was taught from the earliest years that such commotion interferes with thinking and planning."

He snorted, "You were instructed well. Tell me, what will Lorne do now?"

Moira rose calmly. "When I married your son, he promised me that I would not have to take arms against my father. I cannot tell you, even if I knew."

Gethin exploded, "By God, woman, 'tis your own husband out there. Will he be attacked or will he be allowed to get those people to safety?"

Inwardly, Moira trembled with the force of his words and the fear she felt for Rhiannon wounded, in danger. Outwardly calm, she faced Lord Gethin. "I can only

372

repeat that I cannot help you."

With a foul oath, Gethin stalked from the hall followed by his men. The women gathered in clumps, staring and whispering. Lady Branwen faced her across the dais. Her face was white, her eyes angry. "Unnatural!" she spat and swept from the hall.

Thirty-Four

Gathering her strength, Moira calmly withdrew to her apartment. There, she frenziedly began to dress in her tawny divided gown and *chausses*, her boots, her warm vest.

In such haste was she that she did not hear the door to the apartment swing open. Only the deliberate thud of its closing caused her to swing around, her hand on the dagger she had just belted at her waist.

"'Tis good you are going." Margwin stood triumphant, her shoulders and the flats of her hands pressed against the oak panel, her breasts thrust out in their thin wool coverings. Her long blond hair brushed against the tips of her nipples, clearly defined by the tightly drawn material. "Gethin is even now giving the order for your imprisonment."

Her blue eyes chips of ice, Moira regarded the voluptuous figure. "How dare you enter these private apartments? You were neither commanded nor invited here."

Silenced for a moment by the cold contempt she read in Moira's eyes, Margwin hesitated. "I came to warn you," she said, half apologetically.

"I thank you. Now you may go."

Margwin straightened away from the door. "You should go now. Do you hear me? Lord Gethin is ordering your imprisonment."

"You sound very sure." Moira had not moved. "I cannot imagine that you were privy to his council's deliberations."

"I overheard. He made no secret of his decision."

"What reason did he give for imprisoning the mother of his first grandchild?" Moira smiled icily. She tilted her head to one side and regarded Margwin steadily. What motive had this woman for coming here to persuade Moira to leave Hawk's Keep?

"He is too angered about the wounding of Rhys to be concerned about the unborn babe."

At the familiarity Margwin assumed in calling Rhiannon by his nickname, Moira stiffened and threw up her head. The gesture was not lost on the other woman who swayed forward into the room, hands on hips that seemed in danger of dislocation at every step. "Rhys," she smiled, licking her lower lip suggestively, "is *so* important to his father, as well as to everyone in the keep."

"*Lord Rhiannon* would be enraged at any insult or injury done to his wife and unborn child."

Margwin shrugged delicately. "That is as may be. In all likelihood, the babe is not the young lord's anyway. All know you were with child when the lord married you. But the father of the babe is in doubt. After all, did not Huw Llengaron send furs to you while you were imprisoned? Owen says that Huw protected you and spent long hours with you when they were bringing you back to the castle."

Shocked at the calumny heaped upon the head of her one friend by this slut, Moira's breath hissed out of her throat. Her hand flew instantly to the hilt of her dagger and drew it from its scabbard at her belt.

"You will never say those words again!" Blade held before her like a small sword, she advanced toward Margwin. Death looked out of a face white with anger.

At this outburst, Gethin's mistress realized she had gone too far. Confronting her was no hapless servant girl nor docile lady, trained from childhood in unquestioning obedience to authority or those who usurped authority. Instead, she faced a woman more like a man than any she had ever seen before. Indeed the hissing of Moira's voice seemed harsher and more masculine than she had ever noticed. The one whose menacing posture brought her steadily forward was one who held her honor as her life and faced any insult with blade.

With a squeal of pure terror, Margwin whirled for the door. Moira's movement to intercept her was too slow, burdened as she was with her gravid body. Margwin jerked the door open and fled down the hall, her shirts hiked up past her knees.

Moira stood in the doorway, dagger in hand. Her first impulse was to hunt her quarry down. However, the thought of Rhiannon wounded and in danger filled her mind.

Margwin could wait; the confrontation with her could easily be resolved at almost any time. And would be, she promised herself. For now she must find Rhiannon. Carefully, she made her preparations: knife, warm furs, her heavy brown cloak.

The oldest lackey was coming down the corridor toward her, but she strode past him with only a brief polite nod. Once she turned the corner, she quickened her pace, feeling nervous that someone might question her, or worse, try to stop her although she knew there was none to know except Margwin.

At the door to the bailey she paused. If Huw Llengaron

were abroad, he would surely stop her. While the lackey might ignore the bundle, the sharp eyes of a person who cared might recognized it as supplies for a journey.

Fortunately, the bailey was empty of all but a few serfs who went about their daily routines. While the groom saddled her black without comment, she approached the flimsy wooden shed that served as the kitchen. Poking her head in the door, she beheld the cook and several scullions engaged in preparing the main meal of the day. At the sight of her, one scullion nudged the cook and pointed in disbelief.

Waving his long wooden spoon, the cook waddled forward. "What can I do for you, my lady?" he asked pleasantly enough.

"Why, I have a mind for a long ride past the palisades. I thought you might fix me some victuals to take along for a light meal. I feel hungrier than I used to." She grinned knowingly, glancing down at her body.

The cook chuckled and winked at her in an agreeable conspiratorial fashion. "Why, I be glad to fix it up for you." He pulled out a clean white cloth. Slicing bread into generous pieces, he laid each piece down with a huge chunk of meat on it, added some pepper and wrapped the whole up in the cloth. "Would you be wanting some wine, my lady?"

"Oh, yes, please," Moira was delighted to find another friend.

He fetched a small jug from the floor behind the table leg where he had undoubtedly set it for his own private use. Again he winked at her in a knowing way.

"Thank you so much," she said.

"My pleasure, lady." She turned to leave. "If you ever need any special thing for that special hunger, you just send word by one of the lackeys. I fix good clean food." She smiled at him and left the shack, buoyed up as she had not been in days.

As she cantered the black out of the bailey and across the barbican, she smiled. She was free, riding out alone on her horse, putting the hatreds behind her. Ahead of her lay Rhiannon, a man whom Huw Llengaron said would never say he loved her.

She stirred uncomfortably in the saddle. Why was she leaving the keep with its warmth and comfort to ride with her quickening womb across the north of Wales? She refused to answer herself.

She rode and walked periodically for hours. Whenever one seemed to hurt her back, she did the other. Carefully, she paced the black and herself, so that she came to the end of the day having covered many miles and feeling surprisingly fit.

As the darkness fell, she camped well away from the road in a warm huddle of fronds and moss under a thick tree. With her furs wrapped around her and the black horse chomping grass not far away, she snuggled down to munch her meat and bread and drink her wine. Almost before she had satisfied her hunger, she was asleep.

By noon of the next day, she had been sighted by Rhiannon's advance guard. They approached her warily at first and then shook their heads in puzzlement at the sight of her when they recognized who she was. One offered to ride back with her, but she refused to allow him to do so and spurred her horse into a gallop.

Topping the rise, she beheld the little group not far down the valley. At its head she beheld Rhiannon, drooping in the saddle, his body slumped over the bow. Farther back, another man too slumped over his horse. The peasants were walking, limping, dragging their burdens. The whole group appeared to be sick and dispirited.

A pang of pity swept through her at Rhiannon's posture in the saddle. With a sharp dig of her spurs, she drove the black over the crest and into the valley. She

378

cantered down the slope and her cloak and bright brown hair blew out behind her in the wind.

Through his muffled consciousness, Rhiannon became aware of the approach of another horseman. Feverish and in pain, he had been concentrating on taking the weight of his body on his arms and allowing some ease to the painful wound on the inside of his thigh. Every step the plodding horse took rubbed his leg, and blood had been seeping through the bandage for about half an hour. He knew he must call a halt soon. His burning eyes raised themselves from the ground and beheld his wife cantering toward him, her hair and cloak and the horse's mane and tail flying like banners.

He closed his eyes and shook his head. When he opened his eyes, she was even closer than before. His mouth opened. He gulped fresh air. From his cracked, feverish lips a hoarse croak issued. And then she was beside him. She was leaning out of the saddle. Her arms were around him. His feverish hands grasped her, pressed her to him. He would have lifted her out of the saddle had not his thigh sliced bitter pain through his entire body.

"You!" he croaked. "You are real!"

"Of course I am, Rhys," she whispered softly.

"What are you doing here?" His voice was unsteady. In weakness and pain she seemed so precious that he felt tears prick at the backs of his eyes. Oh, God, he thought, am I going to weep against her? Briskly, he pushed her aside and straightened in the saddle. "Answer me, madam. What are you doing here, with child, placing yourself in danger and depriving yourself of—of—" He faltered.

She was smiling at him. He could not belabor her when she looked at him with those limpid blue eyes. "Rhys, I came to be your companion. 'Tis what you said months ago that I was to be. Remember. You said, 'Together we

379

can face and best anything.' I could not remain in the keep when I heard you were wounded. Who would care for you as you should be if not me?"

He tried to look at her sternly, but he was too glad to see her. His leg hurt abominably and his throat felt dry and hot. He knew he was feverish and he could taste a brassy sharpness in his mouth. He merely nodded his head. "Eh, well, turn your horse around and ride beside me. How far did you come alone?"

"Just yesterday. I left after breakfast. I slept out last night just as you and I did. Fortunately, I had sufficient clothing and furs this time."

He tried to concentrate on what she was saying, but his body was too weak to hold the thought. In a few minutes, he was slumping in the saddle again.

Beside him she rode, more concerned than she had ever been. She had felt that heat of his body, the dry crack of his feverish lips. She saw for herself the blood oozing through the rough bandage on his thigh. His ear and face were also slashed but scabbed over. High spots of color rode his cheekbones.

Wearily, the procession wound on for four more agonizing hours. Finally, they reached a small pond in a meadow. The children were exhausted; the women and men who carried babies were staggering.

"We will camp here for the night," Moira said coolly, after she had called a halt. A couple of the men grumbled, but a glance at Rhiannon's angry stare silenced them. "Dismount, you two. Help your lord from the saddle. Drag that miserable saddle off that creature and place it on the ground. Spread furs for a bed. Where is his own saddle? Surely, if his horse were killed someone would have saved the saddle. Were you running for your lives?"

"No, my lady," one man volunteered. "Lord Rhiannon was attacked and his horse was stolen."

An angry growl from Rhiannon warned him to keep his mouth shut. Ducking his head, he hastened to make the bed and help Rhiannon to it. As Rhiannon sank onto the soft furs, it took all of his courage to keep from crying out in pain. Instead, he allowed himself a groan wrung from between clenched teeth.

Briskly drawing her dagger, Moira cut away the clothing and the bloody bandage to bare the slash. "Holy Mother," she breathed. "You fool! You were among enemies the last time you were hurt and yet Thomas and I did a better job on you than these idiots."

"It was dark at first," Rhiannon protested. "Then, later, things kept happening and interfering."

Moira rose to her feet and went off to fetch some water from the pond. When she returned, his eyes were closed and his breathing had evened. She could scarcely believe it, but in truth he was asleep. She smiled fondly. Tomorrow she would get him home, but tonight she would bathe his wound and care for it and snuggle down beside him in his furs just as he had said she would.

In actual fact, two days were required to bring the bedraggled little troop to within the palisades of Hawk's Keep. With Moira as their actual leader, they walked for shorter intervals and rested longer. Rhiannon's wound was painful and when she would observe him gritting his teeth and leaning on his arms in the saddle, she would proclaim a need for a stop to ease her back.

The women in the troop were fully aware of her condition before more than half a day and from time to time came up beside her to inquire about her and to offer bits of homely advice. The men-at-arms stopped grumbling. The whole procession took on a holiday air from time to time.

Rhiannon was no longer feverish after Moira had carefully cleaned and dressed his wound, but slept through the second night without waking.

A day's ride from Hawk's Keep, the guard on the watchtower spied the procession. At his challenge, the identifying banners were unfurled and the party rode forward. Passing before the man, Moira realized that he started with surprise, his mouth dropped open.

The skin on the nape of her neck prickled in warning. Her passage along this road only three days before had drawn no more than a bored glance.

At the barbican, the sergeant whom Moira had seen only once before stepped forward, laying a rough hand on her horse's bridle. "Shall I bestow her safely in a cell, milord?" he addressed Rhiannon.

Rhys' black brows drew together in a fierce frown. "What mean you, 'bestow her safely in a cell?'" His voice was low so the words did not carry to the party behind them.

"Your father's orders, milord. Lord Gethin gave us strict instructions regarding this one."

"I see." Rhiannon glanced across the lists toward the door. "No," he replied softly. "No. I think not. Rather send ahead to announce our arrival. I myself will conduct my lady where I will."

The man saluted and turned to a lad standing some paces behind him. After a few rapid instructions, the messenger darted away at a dead run ahead of the slow-moving party. The sergeant turned back to Rhiannon. "Glad you caught her, milord. Her with all our secrets and such."

Not trusting himself to speak, Rhiannon merely nodded; his jaw clamped tight on what he might have said.

The refugees from Ffestiniog began to scatter to areas of the bailey where they might find shelter or erect some temporary cover. The soldiers of Rhiannon's troop separated also and urged their mounts into trots to hasten to their families.

"My lord Rhiannon," Moira spoke softly at his side. "Do not be angry. Be glad that we are home and safe. Look! Your father and mother already stand on the steps to greet you."

"If you had not been with me," Rhiannon's voice was acid with anger, "you might have been injured by some fool trying to 'capture' you."

"But I am with you, my lord. No harm was done."

"You are too generous with the family by half." He bared his teeth in a feral snarl.

"My son!" Lady Branwen could no longer bear to remain in haughty dignity on the steps. Picking up her skirts, she hurried toward the riders, her veils floating behind her. "How do you? How is your wound? Is it serious?"

Dismounting, he swept her into his arms, hugging her close. "Not serious, Mother. See, I can walk almost as well as ever." He limped a couple of steps to demonstrate, then turned her in his arms to face Moira. "Thanks to my lady wife who came to fetch me. Her careful nursing of my wound drew out the fever and eased me almost by the first night we were together."

Branwen's brown eyes encountered Moira's pleasantly smiling blue ones for only an instant, before the chatelaine dropped hers in shame and embarrassment. Vividly, her bitter words to her daughter returned to gall her. Instead of being unnatural as Branwen had accused, Moira had dared the dangers of the open country to reach Rhys' side and help him. The fact that to do so would never have occurred to Branwen made the woman exceedingly ashamed of herself.

"Once more you have cared for my son," Branwen acknowledged humbly.

"'Twas my duty to my husband," Moira replied briefly.

Huw Llengaron sprang forward to give his shoulder to

Rhiannon as he mounted the steps with difficulty. "My thanks," Rhiannon said and turned to embrace his father and Edain heartily.

Moira sat her horse in quiet dignity until Huw came to her side. "Will you dismount, my lady?"

"Yes, Huw." She swung her leg over and he caught her around the waist. When she put both hands on his shoulders, he lowered her gently to the ground. The child kicked strongly against his hands and his face lighted with pleasure.

"My lady Moira, you do me great honor by allowing me to help you down," he smiled softly.

"'Tis an honor to be helped by such a gallant gentleman," she replied, a bright smile lighting her face.

Gethin came forward stiffly to offer her his arm to lead her into the hall. The gentle touch of his hand under her arm and the courtesy with which he led her first into the hall gave the lie to his scowling features.

Around them, a muttering rustle of sound grew among the men and women assembled to celebrate the return of the lord and heir. In the company of the right of the dais, Moira caught sight of Margwin's flushed face, the eyes burning angrily. Owen Llewellyn, flecks of white foam at the side of his mouth, snarled furiously in the ear of the man standing beside him.

"Father," Rhiannon addressed him loudly when the pair reached the dais, "why was my lady greeted with the news that she was to be imprisoned as though she were a captured spy?"

Gethin turned around, his back to the dais, at the same time turning Moira to face the throng. "Through a mistake in judgment, for which I am heartily sorry, my son," he replied, his scowl fiercer than ever.

"My lady is my vassal," Rhiannon declared loudly, including all the group in his announcement. "She has sworn the oath of homage to me and I trust her with my life."

The words brought gasps of amazement from the women and appraising stares from some of the men.

"She would not cooperate with the council," Gethin defended himself stoutly.

"She could not do so in honor," Rhiannon countered. "She owes allegiance to her father as well. I have pledged her my sworn word that she can never be used in battle against him."

Gethin hesitated. Then he smiled a bit sourly. "It is well," he nodded. "Come, Lady Moira." He led her up the steps of the dais. Behind the table, he called for wine, then seated her at his right hand. Rhiannon sat beside her and Branwen sat beyond her son.

Bending over his daughter in the posture of solicitude, Gethin made his apology, his face serious, his voice gruff. "I thought you unfaithful. I believed you had deserted my son and returned to join your father with your knowledge of the keep's fortifications and strengths to present him to regain your status in his eyes." He drew a deep, shuddering breath. "I placed a reward on your head for your recapture."

"Will you withdraw it now?" Moira stared at the table before her.

He glared at her bent head. "To be sure. My son shows the effect of good care."

"He was feverish and in great pain when I reached him. No one had properly cared for his wound." Moira regarded her husband fondly where, head turned to his mother, he laughed and joked with her. "He is one who will not allow himself to be coddled. He fears to show weakness of any kind. Neither will he show love. He married me for expediency. You were justified in your concern."

Gethin seated himself, shaking his head. "I received bad council from two quarters that I foolishly accepted."

His mouth tightened meaningfully. "The one, I should have discounted at outset, knowing the condition of the councillor. The other, I shall have to look more carefully into. Perhaps there is motive here beyond the obvious." His steely eyes searched the assembled company while his fist tightened around the stem of his goblet.

Privately, Moira wondered if Margwin might have widely overstepped her privilege. If so, the woman was to be pitied. Gethin was not a man to overlook such presumption.

The servants brought bowls of warm water perfumed with lavender and other pleasant-smelling herbs. Gethin dipped his hands ceremoniously. "You are a surprising woman," he said at last. "You have strange and unnatural skills. I know of no other wife who would have ridden out of the keep to find her husband and see that he was properly cared for. Particularly one so newly married and under such difficult circumstances. Furthermore, you carry his heir within your body. My experience with women has led me to believe that they are generally weak and unhealthy during the periods when their wombs are quickening. Forgive my plain speaking, my daughter. I but seek to excuse my blunder."

"Your frankness is understood, Lord Gethin," Moira replied. "But remember also, and pardon my frankness, I am as nothing in this keep without him. I had understood from a source close in this household that you doubted my loyalty as well as the father of my babe. I felt compelled for many reasons to bring my husband back. Perhaps I too believe in expediency." Moira looked straight into Gethin's eyes.

"Who would dare to say such a thing?" His voice was hard and unusually flat, as though he controlled his anger with some effort. "Never mind. I think I see the beginnings of something more than ordinary here, although the motive I do not see." He drew a deep breath.

"But to the point. If you were merely expedient, you would have left the keep and made your way to join your father's forces."

"But I had given my word, both before man and God."

"Some men break their word."

"I have been taught to live by mine." Moira's resentment rose at this turn in the conversation. "A woman may have as much honor as a man. Sometimes more and sometimes she has more difficulty maintaining it and keeping it unstained."

Suddenly, Gethin laughed, a short amused bark. "Wine!" he shouted. A servant scurried forward. "I toast the safe return of my son and my daughter, who carries within her body, the seed of the future of all the Breannons." He raised the chalice to his lips, drank, and offered it to Moira to drink also. "Come, my daughter, drink."

In amazement at this unlooked-for turnaround, Moira lifted the chalice to her lips. Her eyes swept the room wherein many at the tables applauded courteously. They lighted on Huw Llengaron as he nodded with a grin and raised the chalice to her.

Thirty-Five

The month of April was one of great strain on the inhabitants of the keep. Stragglers by the dozens appeared at the gates with word that their homes had been burned and their livestock scattered. The men of Lorne's Rock were striking without pattern, riding from place to place destroying as they went. With the spring rains, the bailey was a morass of mud and the situation of the people huddled there trying to survive was precarious. The coughing sickness had attacked several of the children and all were now subject to fluxes from the bad water. Within the hall, food was monotonous and of poor quality: fish from the sea, brown bread, and ale.

Five days after Moira and Rhiannon returned, they were summoned to the hall by Gethin. A council was sitting. Henry Fletcher, Huw Llengaron, and others presented grim faces. Rhiannon took his place beside his father on the dais. Gethin spoke, "This man has a message for us."

Sitting hunched over on a stool before the dais flanked by a soldier sat a shaggy, unkempt figure. His fur tunic and trousers seemed to blend with the wild and tangled hair on his head and face. At first, his head was bowed, but as Gethin spoke, he raised it, his burning eyes sweeping the room to rest on Moira. Hatred shone out of their gleaming black depths. With a growl, he lifted his hands. Both thumbs had been hewn off. Only blood-stained bandages wrapping misshapen palms thrust out accusingly toward her.

"They did this to me," he snarled. "Me. I am a forester, a hunter. How can I grip a bow or an axe now? The one who did it, the big one, grinned."

Moira covered her eyes. Rhiannon placed an arm around her shoulders.

"The tall one with gray hair, he said, 'Tell them to return the daughter of Lorne before all are mutilated or killed!'" The man's voice was a sobbing, gasping groan. "What will I do? What will become of my family?"

Gethin ap Breannon rose. "Your family will come here and become part of the household of this keep. You will be given work to do, herding and caring for livestock, after the times are settled. You need not fear."

The man groaned again and shook his head. "No axe, no bow."

Someone led him away at Gethin's signal. Rhiannon rose angrily from his place. "Why did you summon my lady wife to this meeting? She has no say in whether she returns or remains. Punish me with these scenes of pain and torment, but leave her alone." His rage was almost overwhelming him. "Such sights are not good for a woman in her condition to look upon."

Gethin faced him. "We need to ask the question again. Does she stay or go? The situation is extreme. Half the forty days are gone, but half remain. Food is scarce. There will be no more game from the forest. Can we ask these our people to live on fish and roots and bad water when we have the means to end this?"

Rhiannon went white. "She is my wife. She carries my

child. By the bond of blood, she is your daughter. This is not the first time we have fought these people. This is merely the first time that you have huddled in your keep and not ridden out to lead the attack."

"He keeps his men moving. We cannot keep riding out after them, exhausting our mounts and leaving the keep defenseless. We must split our forces while he can ride and forage as he wills." Gethin was angry and defensive against this criticism from his son.

"But he must come to do battle soon. There are fewer and fewer people to harass. They are mostly in the vicinity of the keep now." Rhiannon spoke excitedly. "Let me have a troop to ride out at intervals during the day. We can . . ."

"Waste your energy and your horses' and arrive too late in every case," Gethin finished for him. "Peter of Lorne has been my enemy too long. He will do what he will do with great skill. He has outriders and spies watching this hold even now. The minute you ride out, the information will be speeding on its way to him along with the direction in which you ride."

Rhiannon sat back in stubborn, glowering silence.

"You are determined that the woman stays. You do not renounce her." Gethin regarded him narrowly. At his son's angry silence, he finally heaved a sigh. "I was sure you would not, but I had to be convinced, as did others in this room. If we fight, we should fight for something that is sure."

He turned to his men. "We will wait two more weeks. Let every man rest himself, sharpen his skills, put his business in order in case of the extreme eventuality. At the last, Lorne will close with us. The forty days of service will be over shortly and he will have to move. We shall meet him rested and strong while he has tired men who have been traveling constantly for five weeks. Let every man take heart in that thought." With a nod, he dismissed the men and quit the dais himself. Rhiannon excused himself to Moira and strode after his father.

Moira looked sharply around for Huw Llengaron. She saw him deep in conversation with Henry. She stared at him across the room until he felt her gaze and glanced in her direction. Their eyes met in silent communication. Abruptly, he excused himself from his conversation and hurried to her side.

"My lady," he said.

"Huw Llengaron," she responded, "sit here beside me and help me to work out an idea that may become a plan."

Startled but curious, he glanced around to see that most of the men had moved off on affairs of their own. The hall was empty but for servitors. He shrugged and sat down in Rhiannon's chair on the dais.

"Is it true that my father and his men are living in the forest within a few miles of the keep?"

"Aye, my lady. But we cannot catch him. He has spies stationed in sight of the gate even now. We could not stir a troop of men out without him getting wind of the move."

"Could a message be gotten to my father?"

"A message?" he looked at her speculatively. "Aye, my lady."

"I wish to meet with him." At his exclamation of surprise and protest, she raised her hand. "I know what you must think, but know you that I fear for the lives of all. I do not want one man killed because of me."

"If he could get you within arm's reach, he would take you with him," said Huw. "My Lord Rhys would have my head."

She smiled. "At least you do not tell me to behave like a natural woman and not think of meeting my father in the woods to try to secure peace."

He smiled in his turn. "You are a woman of your word.

391

More than that, your word is your deed. More than once I have seen you act with great determination and valor. Do you think your father would listen to you and not try to take you away with him?"

"I think the effort would be worth the result. Whether he would do what I say or not, who can say? I think he might. And if he would not, then he is still my father. I have not seen him in six months. He might die in the battle. He does not know that a grandchild has been conceived. He thinks I have been tortured and ill-used, for when he had Rhys in his hands, he tortured him. Had he kept my lord, he would have killed him slowly and painfully. My father measures all by himself."

"My lady, I fear you make a grave mistake."

"Huw Llengaron, give me the chance to do this one thing. Will you not be my man?" Moira's ice-blue eyes gleamed out of the hollows of her strained white face. Her pregnancy had not brought plumpness to her frame but instead had refined it. Her hand lying on his arm was delicate with blue veins and thin, tapering fingers.

He lifted her hand and as he did, he felt the softness stretched like velvet over the fine strong tendons and bones. He pressed his lips to the back of it, feeling its warm smooth skin. He inhaled the clean fresh smell of lavender. "My lady, it is my pleasure," he said smiling.

Within hours, a man slipped out of the bailey and up onto the headland, carrying a message for a secret parley in the woods at a certain time and place. Peter of Lorne should come alone and meet that which he longed to see.

"I tell you I heard them," Margwin insisted, her voice a hoarse croak. "They were plotting together even as I told you."

"Even as you told me before, sweet Margwin?" Gethin's voice was even, his question not a question.

"Yes! Even as I told you before."

"But your report was not the truth."

"I am sure I was not mistaken," Margwin insisted brazenly. "Who knows what that creature intended once she was outside the keep? No doubt she was riding to her father and encountered Lord Rhys' force accidentally. Once identified and trapped, she probably brazenly lied to her lord." Margwin thrust her full breasts impudently against the purple wool of her dress. Her nipples clearly outlined against the material, she smiled coquettishly at the lord of Hawk's Keep.

"'Rhys,' Margwin?" Gethin's hawk eyes were hooded.

Starting guiltily, she tried to judge his reaction to her slip of the tongue. "Lord R-Rhiannon," she stammered.

"Indeed," Gethin agreed smoothly. "One should not forget one's place."

"No, my lord." Margwin trembled before the coldness of his tone. The interview was not going as she had envisioned.

Casually, Gethin poured wine into chased silver goblets and presented one to the woman who had shared his bed for almost a dozen years. At his courtesy, she smiled again, moistening her lower lip with the tip of her tongue in a motion he had seen her do hundreds of times. He had found it sexually arousing before, but tonight he merely regarded her coldly. What was her game? Despite her impassioned words, he knew she had purposefully lied to him about Moira's leaving the castle. Moira's report that someone had impugned the paternity of the child she carried had further angered him.

He knew his son even as he knew himself. Never would Rhiannon have married the girl had there been a particle of doubt in his mind as to her loyalty and chastity. The ugly rumor he felt sure Margwin had spread struck deep at the family solidarity and reputation of Hawk's Keep. Such reports might be called forth in years to come to

393

discomfit and perhaps to disinherit rightful heirs. For that reason alone, he had already decided to dismiss her.

But her motive for such plotting eluded him.

"My son is very handsome," he said at last in a neutral voice.

"Not so handsome as you, my lord Gethin," was the quick rejoinder.

"But younger," he prodded.

Margwin swayed forward, her breasts almost touching the velvet of his tunic. "I care not for younger men, my lord."

"Do you not?" He stared at her as if he had never seen her. She had been very young when he had taken her to his bed. A scruffy girl with a smudged face and tangled hair. Her clothes were torn, her feet bare and dirty to the ankles. Yet a rare beauty and a touch of ancient lore had gleamed in her dark eyes. Rather like a Norn from the old myths, she had risen from the rocks and rubble beside the trail. On impulse, he had extended his arm to her and she had caught it.

Like a stray dog, skinny and starving, he had brought her home, not really having any idea what he might do with her. Now her clothes were of the finest. She had learned to imitate the speech of his wife and her ladies. She had learned to clean her body and her hair. She had taken on an air of breeding and quality with a speed which now surprised him as he remembered it.

He suddenly realized he did not know her age. "How old are you, Margwin?"

The question caught her offguard. What was his reason for asking? "Twenty-six, I think. I have forgotten."

"So much younger than I. I am almost twenty years older than you. While Rhys . . ." Suddenly, he knew. The idea was so preposterous, but many ideas that women got in their brains were. "Did you think to seduce my son?" His voice so soft that she could scarcely hear the words. Her whole body strained slightly forward to catch them, then reeled back visibly when they were uttered.

"I know not what you mean, my lord. Surely you do not accuse me . . ."

"My son has married, Margwin. He is beyond you. Indeed, he never was possible for you."

"My lord . . ." Her dark eyes were wide with agitation. Both hands clasped the goblet as if life depended on it.

"Is that why you parley with Owen Llewellyn, pricking his madness constantly, rather than allowing it to subside and fix itself on some other object than my son's wife?"

"I do not . . ."

"Take care that you do not lie to me. I have seen you with your mouth at his ear. I discounted the sight. Now I begin to see some sort of plan emerging."

Margwin set the cup down on the table. With both hands freed, she slipped them up across his broad shoulders and around his neck. Her slender fingers threaded themselves in his graying hair. With accustomed skill, she pressed her voluptuous body against his, allowing him to feel her curves from knee to chest. Drawing a deep breath which pressed her breasts hard against his chest, she kissed him on the mouth. Her tongue probed his firm lips, seeking entrance into the interior.

He was like a statue. Finally, she drew off, staring at him with big, hurt eyes. The pout on her lips had charmed him for a decade. Now it appeared merely petulant and a bit boring.

Nervously, she stroked the skein of pale yellow hair that lay across her shoulder. "I swear, my lord, I merely passed the time of day with the man. I speak to many. If my doing so displeases you, I shall leave off."

He shook his head sadly. "Margwin, I fear you have

dreams above your station. I cannot have the peace of my keep and of my family disturbed by you. My son has married with a chaste woman. She was not my choice, true, but she has proved herself to be more than worthy. Furthermore, she carries my grandchild within her body."

Her eyes narrowing coldly, Margwin tossed her head. "How can you be sure of that, Lord Gethin?"

He stared at her appraisingly. "What mean you by that question?"

"Simply that she might have had knowledge of any one of a number of men."

"Lord Rhiannon says not."

Margwin laughed a bit too shrilly. "A woman may fool a besotted swain if she be clever. Any man so enthralled by such as she would be easy to fool."

Gethin raised an eyebrow as he lifted his cup to his lips. "Do you think my son is under some spell?"

"Why else would he defy your wise council and his mother's pleading, not to mention the disapproval of the whole of this court?" She picked up the cup from the table and drained it. "She has tricked him into claiming another man's bastard."

"Do you have any idea who the father might be?" Gethin's voice remained calm, but a hectic color began to tinge his cheeks as his anger began to build.

"Owen Llewellyn has an idea on that score."

"Which he imparted to you."

"He makes no secret," she excused herself sullenly.

"But he is a madman. His word is discounted by all. He mutters outrageous things at all times. We tolerate him here and care for him because we pity his terrible loss. Furthermore, he is a brave and fierce soldier. None better in battle if he feels the cause is right."

"His word in this case is based upon observation,"

Margwin averred staunchly.

"And who does he name?"

She hesitated. The man was also a trusted soldier. But no blame would fall upon him. Moira had been merely a captive whose body was the property of all. "He names Huw Llengaron."

Gethin gritted his teeth. "Why?" His voice was the rasp of steel sliding from the scabbard.

"He spent time with her. He sent her furs when she was imprisoned. He has even been seen riding with her." Margwin laughed. "Rhiannon has been tricked by the witch of Lorne. She should be exorcised and set aside, or sent back to her people. The young lord should look elsewhere for a loyal wife."

"To you?" Gethin's mouth dropped open incredulously.

Again she hesitated. "I am ever loyal to you, Lord Gethin. You took me with you and raised me to be your companion and your love. I would do as you command me."

Astonished beyond anything he had ever heard in his life, Gethin dropped into a chair, regarding the woman who stood before him now with downcast eyes, hands crossed modestly before her. Suddenly, he began to laugh. His mirth came rolling out in a great explosion of sound. Once begun he could not stop. Even when Margwin's face changed from its normal color to a dull red of anger and disbelief. Still he laughed.

"I see nothing in our conversation to arouse mirth," she declared haughtily.

"Do you not?" He threw back his head and roared again. Laughed at the wench he had lifted from the dirt of the roadbed, laughed at her presumption, laughed at her aping of the grand manners of his wife. Suddenly, he saw by comparison his wife's slender body, still straight as a lance, still fragile, still delicate with its fine bones and

397

pale, smooth skin. Was it still as wonderful as he remembered when they were first married? The thought sobered him.

"I will send you to the abbey of St. Dunstan-in-the-Field, if you desire to withdraw for a time." He rose to his full height. "I will dower you, if you wish to marry and can arrange a union with a man of good character from any one of several neighboring manors."

Margwin's face went white. "Oh, no," she gasped. Her hands clasped together beseechingly. "Do not send me away."

"I must." A muscle spasmed in his jaw where it clenched. "You have spread untrue and malicious rumors about my house. Your false sense of your own worth has led you to sick fancies about your future." He shook his head sadly. "I am to blame. I allowed you to assume the position of a lady which you believed to be real."

"I am a lady," Margwin protested, her eyes flashing. "I talk like a lady. I dress like a lady. I behave like a lady."

Gethin held up his hand. "Say no more, I command you. You have shown yourself to be a danger to this keep. For the good companionship you have shown me, I will provide for you handsomely."

"But I . . ." she began, screwing her face to burst into tears.

"Leave me."

At his implacability, her mouth arched in a snarl. Margwin clenched her hands in fury. "*You* . . . you . . . you would turn me out with nothing but a few coins. I have been like a wife to you. If you had but asked, I would have borne you strong, beautiful children, many fine sons."

"I want no bastards to cloud the issue of inheritance." Gethin suddenly felt very tired. "Be gone. No one will know of our conversation. You will be allowed to depart

398

with dignity and grace. Do not spoil your chances with useless ravings and rantings."

Her breath coming hard in her throat, Margwin backed toward the door. "You are not through with me," she promised. "You will never be done with me. Will you crawl back to that whey-faced wife and try to worm your way back into her bed, now that she is past the age to bear children? Bah! She will not take you back, I'll warrant. She will scorn you. You will remember me. I swear. *You will remember me!*" Her voice rose as if she uttered a curse. The door slammed behind her.

Gethin stared at it for a moment then poured himself another goblet of wine. The cool, pale liquid swirled in the bowl. His wife loved fine wines. Solely through her efforts was the keep provided with the luxurious food and drink, the soft decor of hall and bower, to which he had become accustomed. The years had been hard on them both, particularly on her, yet she had never reproached him. Had she accepted Margwin as his right because she could not have more children? Yet Margwin knew how to prevent babies. Many women did. Perhaps his wife did also, but she had never protested.

The memory of her warm brown eyes and soft brown hair stirred him. He longed to touch it again and to see her eyes cloud with passion. She had always been a passionate little thing. Had she missed the excitement and pleasure of his lovemaking? He had never once considered that she might. His conscience gripped him with steel claws. Angrily, he tossed the dregs of the wine hissing into the fire and rang for his valet. He would bathe himself and shave his skin smooth before he approached her.

Margwin's precipitous entrance into Owen Llewellyn's room roused the man from a daze. Since no one ever visited him, he spent long hours staring into the fire. His dreams both waking and sleeping were nightmares, bedeviled by visions of men whom he recognized as Peter of Lorne killing and raping. For almost a minute, he could make nothing of the creature who flung herself on her knees before him, wailing and tearing her hair.

Finally, her words repeated over and over in the most impassioned tones of hysteria forced themselves into his mind. *"She has bewitched Lord Gethin!"*

"What say you?" he managed at last, his eyes widening until a white ring appeared all around the iris. "What say you, woman?"

Sure that she had his attention at last, Margwin began to sway back and forth on the floor before the fire, moaning and writhing. "The house of Breannon is doomed! Doomed!" Her sobs rose and fell as tears streamed down her face.

Wildly, she grasped her dress at the neck and tore it from her body, baring herself to the waist. As her nails raked across the white skin, red scratches appeared.

To Owen's disordered mind, the sight was enraging. "She must die! She must die! The witch must die!" He sprang to his feet, drawing his sword from its scabbard where it lay on the table beside him.

Margwin flung herself against his legs. If Owen ran from the room to attack Moira in the apartments of Rhiannon, he would in all likelihood be killed. Furthermore, Gethin would lay his sudden violent act at Margwin's doorstep. "No!" she cried. "You must not kill her where the lord can know. He is bewitched, I tell you. He has fallen under her spell and will hear no word of warning against her."

"She must die!" Owen repeated, struggling ineffectually against Margwin's clinging arms.

"Gently, gently, my friend. Stop! Stop! Owen! Listen to me. Listen." Finally, he looked down at her. His eyes became puzzled as if he could not for a moment remember from whence she had come.

"Sit down," Margwin coaxed, her drowned brown eyes staring up into his face, pleading with all the coquetry of which she was capable. Her breasts pressed against his thighs. "Please, Owen, please, sit down. We must plan." Her voice became soothing as she sought to quiet his wild-eyed frenzy.

He subsided into the chair, his eyes fixed on her. Her right hand brushed the long fall of blond hair back from her face, raising her breast from behind his knee. He licked his lips, his wild eyes focused on the lush white fruit, its nipple brownish red and erect. He had known no woman since his wife's death. His passion had been channeled into his thirst for revenge. Now here was a woman whose passion matched his own. He licked his lips again, running his left hand over the lower half of his face, wiping away the moisture that had collected around his mouth.

"We must watch and wait. Our turn will come." Margwin watched his eyes. "Our turn will come, my lord Owen," she crooned. Breathing deeply, she straightened herself on her knees. The palms of her hands, she rested on his thighs, her long fingers flexing slightly, gently kneading the knotted muscles she found there.

"Watch and wait," he repeated in a trance. His left hand reached out almost tenderly to touch the scratches across the top of her breast. "Who did this to you, my love?" he whispered. "Who would hurt you so?"

"The witch caused him to do it," Margwin lied, drawing a deep breath as his fingers brushed against her nipple. "The witch is to blame for everything."

Owen let the sword rest gently on the floor at his side. His other hand covered her other breast, cupping it, weighing it, rolling the nipple gently beneath his hard, calloused thumb.

Her fingers kneaded the flesh of his thighs, moving closer and closer until they rested against the muscle erect beneath the *chausses*.

His eyes closed in intense erotic pleasure. He spoke a name. Gasped it from his gaping mouth. Tears trickled down his cheeks. The woman he named was not Margwin, but she did not care. Her fingers were busily moving aside his clothing. Her own passion had been roused, also. Now his touch made her flesh burn as he fondled her nipples with increasing assurance.

He spoke the name again. His eyes flew open. Margwin's face was very close to his. "You are not she," he whispered.

"No, Owen," she replied, raising herself so her mouth was only inches from his. "We cannot have the ones we love. We must love each other."

"I will kill the witch," he vowed. "I will avenge our loss." The violence of his emotions at his vow made him squeeze her breasts cruelly. At the same time, he brought his mouth down on hers crushing her lips to plunder her mouth. Her whimper as she writhed in pain was tinged with a strange overtone of pleasure.

Thirty-Six

For two weeks, Moira anxiously awaited the return of the messenger sent to her father. Each day Huw Llengaron's sad shake of his head cast her spirits lower. Peter of Lorne was moving constantly. The messenger might be unable to find him. Or more likely, the messenger had found him without being allowed to deliver his message. In which case, the messenger had simply disappeared.

"Shall I send out another man, my lady?" Huw suggested tentatively. Moira sighed and shook her head.

"No. 'Twas a foolish dream. Thank you, Huw."

And then the following day the man returned. He had been taken captive and moved from place to place with different men until finally he had been brought into the camp of Peter of Lorne. When he had been brought to the man to relay his message, he had been released the next day with the reply.

"Peter of Lorne will meet that which he has longed to see at midnight one mile south from the twin rocks beside the Colwyn Bay road."

"I shall accompany you, my lady," Huw Llengaron insisted.

"Only to the twin rocks and I will be glad of your company," Moira smiled, "but no farther. He is, after all, my father, Huw. He will not harm me." She smiled ruefully. "At least not very much."

So she thought as she slipped from Rhiannon's side and dressed quickly. In the light from the fire, she could see his dear face looking peaceful, youthful, his sweet mouth firmly closed. His arms and shoulders were sprawled outside the covers, for he was always warmer than she who liked to snuggle down under piles of furs and sometimes was accused by him of sleeping under him. She longed to plant a kiss on his lips, but knew that she would probably waken him and then she could not get away. Only for a minute more did she feast her eyes while he stirred restlessly, flinging his arm to her side of the bed. Sighing regretfully, she turned and left, closing the door silently behind her.

Noiseless as a night creature, she sped down the twisting corridors so familiar to her now and out through the sallyport into the bailey. Huw Llengaron was waiting for her there with her horse. In one swift, graceful movement, she swung herself into the saddle and they were off. He passed her without question through the barbican. Beneath the night sky, black and partly overcast with scudding clouds and frightened stars, they galloped down the road toward Colwyn Bay.

At the twin rocks, she dismounted and Huw showed her a path which led directly south into the woods. "Go with God, my lady," he whispered. "I will wait here until you return."

"No, Huw. Return to the keep. I shall be safe enough coming back. You need your rest. Be sure to leave word that they are to let me in."

"My lady, please . . ."

"Huw, I go to meet my father. Not some monster. Return to your duties. I would not have you in any

404

trouble for aiding me in the venture."

He sighed and turned his horse back up the hill. She steered hers into the darkness of the rocks and trees beside the road.

The forest was still and a soughing wind blew at her back. The trees were not thick. From time to time, the clouds parted to let the moon out to light the way. The only sound around her was the creak of her equipment and the soft hooffalls of the horse as it walked through the thick carpet of fallen leaves and mosses.

Once she thought she had lost her way, but then the path opened up ahead of her and she rode into the clearing. At first, she thought it empty and feared that she had come too late. She dismounted from her horse, dropping the reins. Her eyes slipped round the area and beheld nothing but a small pile of rocks and a bare ground illuminated by the moon.

Suddenly, she was startled to see one of the rocks move and detach itself. A man dropped his fur cloak and placed his hands on his hips.

"Moira?" her father's voice spoke to her. "Moira, is it you?"

Moira realized that she had not seen Peter of Lorne in seven months. He looked older than she remembered, his grizzled hair whiter than ever. His once heavy girth seemed shrunken, as if he had not eaten and drunk as had been his wont. In the dim light of the clearing, he held out his arms to her. With a glad cry, she ran into them.

He bent his head and held her tightly, kissing her cheeks, his white beard tickling and scratching her. His hands gripped her shoulders painfully and then moved over her back, pressing her against him.

"Are you all right, my little one?" he whispered hoarsely. "Are you injured in any way?"

"No, Father," she drew back and smiled. "I have been well treated except for a few bad times at the very first."

"They tortured you."

"No, only imprisoned me until the son Rhiannon returned."

"And you are not harmed?" He could not believe his eyes. His daughter was beautiful in the light of the moon. Her eyes sparkled and her body was as straight and tall as he remembered it. Her mouth curved in just the same way when she smiled. "I feared. I feared for you so. All the long winter, the house was cold and desolate without you. I missed you over and over again. At Christmas I thought my heart would break.

"I offered ransom, but when it was refused, I was sure that you were dead or badly hurt."

"No, oh no," she hastened to reassure him. "I have been well-treated."

"Why?" His voice was suspicious.

"Father, let us sit down and I will tell you all that has happened to me." She tried to draw him back to the stone.

"No! We leave now." He took her arm to lead her away.

"No, Father, I cannot go. There are many reasons, but the most urgent one is that I gave Huw Llengaron my promise that I would not leave. 'Twould go very hard with him if I disappeared and they learned that he had brought me here."

"You owe none of these swine anything."

"Father," she began softly. "I was captured and made a slave. I was imprisoned in the lowest dungeon in the keep for three days. I had no food nor water except what I could lick off the walls. Huw Llengaron sent furs to me to keep me from freezing to death."

Peter of Lorne growled a string of curses. "Come with me. That will all be a bad memory."

"Listen, Father!" she grasped his arms urgently. "You must listen and understand what happened to me.

406

Rhiannon ap Breannon captured me and brought me away from Lorne's Rock. He opened the dungeon for me and then he enslaved me." She bowed her head; even now six months later, her pride suffered.

"I will kill him. I have vowed to on the grave of your mother, on everything I hold sacred that I will . . ."

She put up her hand to stop his vow. "When your offer of ransom came, some wanted to accept it, but he would not allow me to leave his side. At that time, I was chained in his room for many hours of the day."

She felt his muscles bunch in anger. "And at night . . . what did he do at night?"

"He is as other men and yet not like others," she said softly.

"May he burn in hell."

"Father, the reason why he would not accept the ransom was because he has a great dream. A dream for a union of North Wales against the English. He wants your friendship and your aid." Peter of Lorne drew in his breath sharply in fury. "Father, he married me."

With a snarl, the lord of Lorne's Rock struck her across the mouth with the full power of his mighty right arm. She was flung sprawling on her back half a dozen feet away from him. "And you, you bitch, you accepted him. You said the words that bound yourself to him." He tore his hair. "The shame! Had you no more strength than to crawl to him like a whimpering bitch to a heinous wolf?"

Stunned, she lay struggling feebly to move while he raged and cursed her. At first, she thought he would kill her as he lunged after her body and straddled it. His thonged whip dangled from his wrist and he raised it threateningly.

She extended her hand palm up, pleading for his understanding, begging him to listen. At the same time, within her heart, she knew she could expect no love nor

407

understanding from her father. She had failed him in every way. He had taught her to be strong and defiant and she had been weak and pliable in the arms of the enemy.

Expecting no mercy, yet hoping for it, she raised her voice as he drew back to strike her. "Do not strike me! I am with child!"

Her cry was the wrong thing. Peter of Lorne screamed with fury. His whip beat down her suppliant hand and then drew back and lashed her prone body again and again. She curled herself into a tight ball around the child in her belly and endured with clenched teeth. At least he would not have the shame of making her cry out.

"You are no daughter of mine! You are not even human in my eyes! You are a bitch! I was a fool! To think that I could change a woman into a man! You are a shame upon our house!" With each exclamation, he let the whip fall upon her unprotected back, shoulders, and head. Finally, he could no longer stand. He dropped to his knees beside her, gasping in exhaustion.

Through a haze of pain, her back flaming so that she could scarcely breathe, she was dimly aware that he had stopped his lashing. Still she could hear him cursing her through the gasps for breath. She screamed in agony as his heavy hand grabbed her shoulder and turned her over.

"Oh, Moira," he whispered. "Why did you do this thing?"

"Father," she sobbed. "Father, I was a captured knight. He treated me as such. I was given my parole if I would swear vassalage to him. He always respected me and recognized that I was his equal. That I had been reared as you had taught me with all the virtues of a man. In the end, he married me because he saw in me the chance to make a union for our people."

"You should have killed him!"

"I gave him my word."

"What about your loyalty to the family?"

"Father," she pleaded, almost fainting as the pain in her back grew worse rather than subsided. "I swore only on the promise that I should never have to raise against you or yours. He swore to me that I would not."

"And you married with him?"

"He had already claimed my body, but he married me as if I were a virgin. We were married in church."

"You could have refused at the altar."

She slumped down on the ground, almost unconscious from the pain. "He was my liege lord and I his vassal. I had sworn to obey him."

Peter of Lorne rose to his feet. From his full height, his words fell on her like stones. "I will kill him if I can. But I will never take you back." He turned on his heel and started away.

Moira raised her head. Blood trickled from her cut lips. She panted like a hurt animal. "Father, please," she called as loudly as her strength would permit. "I am with child. It will be your grandchild."

The tall, cloaked figure halted abruptly at the edge of the clearing. She saw his shoulders quiver, then he straightened and marched determinedly into the forest. A shiver ran through her body. The ground was cold. A stillness as on the eve of battle permeated the atmosphere. She lost consciousness.

Rough hands grasped her under her arms and dragged her upright. When she moaned and would have slumped again, a swift, sharp blow across her cheek did much to clear the dizziness from her mind. Opening bewildered, aching eyes in the dimness, at first she could not make out the face of the figure who held her. The saltsweet taste of her own blood nauseated her. A convulsive shudder racked her, communicating itself to the hard hand grasping her upper arm.

"Here! Straighten up!" A man's harsh voice snarled in

her ear.

The cruel grip transferred to her wrists, grappling them together and binding them tightly behind her back. The sensation was so devastatingly familiar that Moira's heart sank and cold horror settled in her stomach. "Owen Llewellyn," she whispered, her voice only an agonized breath of sound.

A hard cackle of sound jarred her ear as her captor again grasped her shoulder and hauled her back against him hard. "Right you are. Oh, yes. You thought to run away, to escape me and my vengeance, but I watched. I waited until you made an unguarded move."

"You could not have followed us," she denied. "We rode in utmost secrecy. There was no one to observe us. I am certain."

Owen chuckled delightedly. His once clever mind realized that sometimes people discounted what he said. The thought that he had completely fooled not only Moira but also Huw Llengaron pleased him mightily.

"I am the lord's wife!" she cried. "Beware! You dare not hurt that which is his. The hawk's talons are sharp as death and his range is wide."

When she would have said more, a thick wool scarf was tied round her mouth, effectively gagging her. When he stepped back, she darted forward, hoping to lose herself in the darkness between the trees. Her plan might have succeeded had an exposed root not tripped her. Unable to use her hands at all, she was only just able to twist her body to the side to avoid falling on her belly on the hard ground. As she fell, her head struck the trunk of a tree, dazing her. Owen recaptured her in an instant, drawn in the dark by the hard thud of her body colliding with the wood.

"We will take some of the fight out of you," he muttered, pulling her upright and scooping her unprotesting body up in his arms. "Oh, yes, witch, we will take

410

all that viciousness out of you. You will be meek and tractable before we are through with you."

Her head throbbing with pain, Moira could not struggle. Vaguely, she wondered who "we" might be. The child kicked within her, a living reminder that she must fight not only for her very life, but for the life of Rhiannon's child as well.

He carried her for what seemed like hours through the woods. She could feel the laboring of his breathing after several minutes. His whole body became wet with perspiration at the great effort he was expending. Twice he lowered her to the ground, leaning above her, breathing hard. The first time he rested, his curses rained down on her defenseless body as he vented his spleen, but the second time he was too out of breath to do more than cough in great whooping bursts of sound.

Evidently, they were far from any human beings who would hear the sound and come to investigate. He muttered again, his words groaning out of his mouth. "Witch. Heir of the devil himself." His grim chuckle brought on another fit of coughing. When he recovered his breath, he scooped her up again.

Thanking God that he did not attempt to sling her over his shoulder, she kept her eyes firmly closed, nurturing the hope, however faint, that exhaustion and strain would bring on some kind of seizure. Unfortunately, with the tireless strength of the mad, he ignored his body's demands and bore her onward.

The woods thinned. The ground became more uneven as he stumbled and cursed. Suddenly, she became aware of a faint, monotonous sound which she recognized to be the sea. If only he could put her down again, she would make another attempt to escape. Better to run in the darkness, risking a fall and unconsciousness, than to be carried down to the shore and drowned like a pathetic, unwanted animal.

"Halloa!" His voice strained from his throat, his shout merely a hoarse shadow of its former strength, but it was answered.

Her eyes flew open. The stars tilted overhead. The moon sailed by on her left. Then a door swung open near her head, creaking as its hinges protested after long disuse.

"Who calls?" a woman's voice whispered nervously.

"'Tis I," he groaned. "Let me in. I die."

The door cracked farther. He stepped through and she heard it close behind them. An instant later, the room was lighted by a smoky pale glow. Someone must have uncovered a lantern.

"Let me see. Let me see!"

"'Tis her all right. No need to fear. We have her now."

Ungently, she felt herself lowered to the ground, rather like a sack of meal. "Why does she not move?" the woman's voice continued. "Is she dead?" A disappointed tone crept into the petulant whine.

Owen Llewellyn cursed as he struggled to draw breath into his heaving lungs. "Damned . . . witch . . . better not . . . die."

The light came close, so close that Moira could feel the heat and see the red glow through her eyelids. A woman's cold hand fumbled for the pulse under Moira's clothing. "Warm and beating," came the satisfied voice. "In fact, I would make assurance . . ."

A tip of fire touched Moira's cheek, causing her to jerk involuntarily. Her eyes flew open.

Margwin laughed maliciously as she brandished a twig with a glowing, smoking tip. "Playing dead. I thought so." Waving it at Owen, she jeered, "She made you carry her all the way I warrant, in the hopes that you would lose consciousness."

The madman's eyes burned with their wild white light as he stared at her, his face contorted, the perspiration

412

trickling from his disordered shock of greasy gray hair. His teeth were bared in a feral growl.

The horror of the tableau flashed in Moira's mind. Helpless she lay, her hands tied tightly behind her, prone on the dirt floor of some hut miles from the keep perhaps, yet somewhere close to the sea. At her shoulder crouched the merciless, jealous Margwin, her eyes glittering in the light from the lantern, a wisp of smoke curling upward around her head from the brand with which she had burned her helpless captive. Crouching on the other side of her body, his sour smell rank in her nostrils, his face drawing ever nearer to catch every flicker of pain in her face, was mad Owen.

She drew a deep breath. Ignoring the man, she hunched herself up on one elbow to face the woman. "Gethin will murder you for this," she said coldly.

"He will never, *never* find out," Margwin hissed.

"You know he will. Nothing that occurs in Hawk's Keep escapes his notice. You will both be discovered. Rhiannon will not rest until he finds me. Remember, I carry his child."

Margwin chuckled again. "I will tell everyone that you left with Huw Llengaron. Who will deny it?" She glanced significantly at her cohort. "Perhaps Huw might meet with an accident."

Shaking his head back and forth like a bedeviled bear, Owen groaned. "Huw is a good soldier. He was bewitched by her beauty. He will come to understand and forgive and forget."

"How did you follow me?" she demanded. "We were very careful. I am certain I was not observed."

Owen chuckled again. "The messenger you sent to find Lorne reported to me. He saw no reason not to. Especially after I persuaded him that the security of the keep was at stake."

"Then he will know whom he told," Moira insisted.

"You must see, Margwin, that Gethin will find out. He may already have been informed. You can never return. Furthermore, you will lose your place. You will have nowhere to go. Release me now and I will return and say nothing. I will tell them that I got lost."

"My place," the woman snarled, snapping at the word. "My place! You took my place. I was being prepared to be the wife of the young lord. I know it. Gethin had trained me carefully. The time was almost ripe. Then you appeared and bewitched Rhys."

Moira could not repress a start of surprise. A cold frisson of dread rippled down her spine. The woman was as mad as Owen.

"Besides. No one will associate your disappearance with us two. You went to parley with your father. Huw Llengaron knows this. When your body is discovered, it will be believed that he killed you." Owen slapped his thighs in evident pleasure.

Like two evil children, the two grinned at each other across Moira's body.

"When you are discovered to be missing . . ." Moira faltered. Her fear for her life made her weak. Death, her death, stared at her from their glittering eyes.

"Kill her now," Margwin breathed like an incantation. "Kill her, Owen. Kill her. Let her blood run and avenge the deaths of your wife and children so long ago. Free my love from her spell."

His blade slithered out from its scabbard. The point pricked her side, just below her ribcage.

She drew a deep breath, steeling herself to accept it as her last. At least she could die well. She would not give these two the satisfaction of begging.

The madman hunched himself forward on his knees, moving the blade from her side to her throat. He bent so close to her face that his fetid breath made her stomach heave. "Beg!" he commanded. "Cry! Plead! Scream for mercy!"

His face in the lamplight was a demon's countenance straight from hell.

Her ice-blue eyes met him fiercely. "Never!"

The point of the dagger pricked her throat. "Beg," he demanded, an hysterical note in his voice. The point pricked her skin, stinging her and making her flinch despite herself.

"Do it!" Margwin pushed the lantern closer. A strand of blond hair sizzled as it wafted across the flame. "Do it!"

The silence was pregnant. Within Moira's body, the unborn child kicked strongly. She set her teeth. She might die anyway. But the longer they could be delayed, the more chance she would have to save herself. Help would be more likely to come. Rescue in the form of Rhiannon or Huw became more imminent with each passing minute.

She stared up into her tormentor's eyes, her expression never faltering even when her blood traced a scarlet stream down the blade of his knife toward the hilt. For just an instant, something gentle flickered in his eyes. Then it vanished in the glaring anger.

"You *will* beg," he vowed, ripping the dagger away and stabbing it viciously into the floor to cleanse it.

Margwin sprang up. "You must kill her now," she commanded. "We must dispose of her body and get back to the keep before we are missed. Otherwise, she is right. People will become suspicious."

Owen climbed wearily to his feet. A reaction to the superhuman exertion he had demanded of his body caused him to tremble now that his rage had abated. "I will not have it over and done with like the slaughter of a chicken. I want her to suffer. I must hear her beg. The souls of my wife and children must hear her beg."

"She will never do so," Margwin argued, shaking the lantern at him until the flame danced. "She fears not as a woman should. She is like a man. She bewitched Rhys, remember. She will bewitch you, too."

Llewellyn snorted sarcastically. "She can try!" Drawing another leather thong from his tunic, he bent to tie Moira's ankles together. Behind him, Margwin railed in helpless frustration. "Leave her here for twenty-four hours without food or drink. Return tomorrow night. She will beg then. Alone, cold, and deserted by her father. That swine beat her. She is a witch and he a devil." A thought struck him, interrupting his monotone of spoken thoughts. "Why did your father beat you?"

Unwilling to satisfy the man's curiosity, Moira closed her eyes. Her fingers were numb, her throat stung and burned where his blade had pricked her. The realization that the most pressing danger was past left her deathly weary.

"Unnatural," he grunted after a moment. "Father beats his own daughter and she with child." He shook his head as he heaved himself to his feet again. There he turned to face the haggard face and burning glare of his partner.

Margwin looked twice her age. Since Gethin had dismissed her, she had lost weight, refusing to eat in the hall now that her status had been reduced. The maids whispered and laughed behind her back and gloated on her discomfiture. Margwin had never been considerate. As most people when elevated to a station through no work or effort of their own, she had enjoyed playing the grand lady to those whom she considered inferior to her exalted station.

"She must die!" Her voice rose to a shriek. "If she escapes . . ."

"She will not escape," Owen's voice was an attempt at placation. "How could she? She is bound hand and foot. We will bar the door when we leave."

"If someone comes . . ."

"No one will come here. This is the watchtower above the sea. All the watchmen have been pulled off to guard

416

our front. No enemy attacks us from the rear. She will lie here until we come for her," he chuckled. "And she will think of her fate. And that of her unborn child. When we return, she will cry for mercy." He rubbed his hands together in anticipation.

"We cannot be sneaking from the castle night after night," Margwin objected. "We dare not be suspected."

"We will not be. Come. Calm yourself. You must put on a fair show of concern in the morning, if anyone should ask what might have become of her." Owen Llewellyn's rage seemed spent as he yawned widely, almost in the face of his frantic companion. Stretching wide his arms, he shrugged his shoulders, rubbing one tentatively. "I fear I have strained myself carrying her so far." He nudged the still body with his boot. "I should have realized she was pretending. She is crafty. A witch in truth."

Moira did not respond. Indeed, her senses were dulled almost to the point of unconsciousness. Tomorrow would be time enough to mourn her luck or her foolishness in going to meet her father. Only her deep and sincere desire to prevent more bloodshed between the two men in the world who held her love and absolute devotion had moved her to the act which might now prove to be her undoing.

She heard the protests and the arguments only faintly. Her senses faded completely. She was deeply asleep before the door to the hut swung closed.

For long hours, she did not move. At the first rays of dawn, she stirred, rolled over, flexing her fingers, shuddering at the pain. The child stirred and kicked strongly within her.

"You will not leave me," she whispered to the unborn one. "You are my very own." Determination surged through her. She doubled her legs under her and struggled to her feet. Swaying perilously, she nevertheless stood erect. "We shall survive," she declared.

Thirty-Seven

Rhiannon ap Breannon raged like a wild man when he awoke to find Moira gone. Like the wolf Lorne had named him, he flung back his head and howled. Those within the keep stirred in their sleep or sat bolt upright in their beds. Throwing on his clothes, he loped along the corridors and out through the hall to the gate. The darkest part of the night—just before streaks of dawn stained the night sky—cloaked the surrounding land in inky blackness.

Seizing the drowsy guard, he wrung from the alarmed lips the story. "Yes. Two riders rode out at midnight. Huw Llengaron and another with hood drawn over head and face concealed."

Releasing the guard with a feverish curse, Rhiannon swung back toward the keep, encountering Huw Llengaron on the steps of the hall.

The man's face gleamed whitely in the darkness. His voice faltered. "She has not returned, my Lord Rhys?"

"Where did she go, Huw? By God, man, you are one second from death if you do not answer me truthfully and swiftly."

"She went to talk with her father, to try to reason with

him to put off the battle which we knew must soon be drawn. She hoped to prevent bloodshed among those she loved. But she should have returned long ago."

Rhiannon spun away in agony with a wild curse. "She would! She would! Brave, foolish vassal! I should have chained her to my bed. Courage of a lion in a woman's body! Moira!" His voice was a moan of pain and loss.

Huw Llengaron vanished into the darkness toward the gate. "Has no one returned other than myself?" he questioned hopefully.

Thoroughly alerted, the guard answered quickly. "Two riders returned an hour ago, sir. Owen Llewellyn and a companion whose face also was covered. I passed them through." His young face wrinkled in a frown. "But those were all, sir. Did I go wrong? I swear I have kept good watch."

Huw patted the boy's shoulder. "You have kept good watch, sirrah. Lord Rhiannon! Owen Llewellyn has been out of the keep tonight with a companion!"

"We must rouse my father." Rhiannon led the way into the hall. "He is the only one to whom Owen will answer."

Pounding on the door of Gethin's bedchamber roused only his sleepy valet who informed them that the lord was visiting the Lady Branwen in her chamber.

"My mother?" Rhiannon's voice was tinged with incredulity. "Say you my mother?"

The valet shrugged. "So he said in passing."

By the light of guttering candles, Gethin roused his wife from sleep. His hand toyed delicately at the warm joining of her thighs where he had delved deeply only a few hours before. Kissing her shoulder before allowing his teeth to softly pinch her nipple, he smiled in remembrance of their meeting a fortnight ago.

419

He had presented himself at her chamber with some uncertainty. "Wife." His voice sounded a trifle unsteady.

"My lord. Gethin?" She sat in a high-backed chair before the fire. Her hair waved smoothly from her crown down her back. It was the same rich brown he remembered, except that now streaks like liquid silver fell away from her temples. A robe of deep green velvet trimmed with dark brown fur revealed her white throat and dipped to a point between her breasts.

Suddenly, he realized that he had not seen her in deshabille in years. He had not seen her white throat nor her long hair. She was his own wife, yet he knew himself almost a stranger to her body.

She rose to come toward him, alarm in her eyes, her hands outstretched to clasp his own. "Is something wrong?"

Gathering both her hands in his, he raised them toward his lips. "Yes," he replied, his eyes drinking in her beauty. "Very wrong. Very wrong indeed."

"Oh, what, my lord?"

Instead of answering, he kissed her hands before turning them over palm up. When she had been a young bride, he had discovered that her fingertips were extraordinarily sensitive. Now he kissed each one in turn, feeling tremors begin as she drew in her breath sharply.

"My lord?"

"Branwen." His sapphire blue eyes sought her face.

She blushed. From between her breasts, the color rose into her throat and then into her cheeks. How charming to be a woman of forty years and still blush like a girl.

He hesitated. He could claim his rights as her husband without further conversation. She would not object. Her gentle nature coupled with her sense of inferiority at her own inability to bear children would forestall any

420

reproaches. Still, he felt a need to somehow apologize. Yet how did one apologize for a decade of neglect. He drew a deep breath. If she protested or looked askance even once, he would withdraw. She should have the opportunity to turn him away if she chose. He had wronged her too long to pour salt into the wounds. He studied her expression.

Her brown eyes searched his face before slipping down to take in his nightrobe, open to the waist. Her lips parted. The tip of her tongue traced her lower lip nervously.

"Branwen," he repeated her name. "May I please come into your bed?"

The tears shimmered in her eyes, one escaped down her cheek. Another tremor shook her body.

"Gently, love." His hand sought the tie on her robe, pulling it loose, parting it. The sight of her aroused him mightily. Now it was his turn to shiver. Her body was even as he remembered it. Except for faint silvery lines wavering horizontally across her belly below her navel, she might have been his bride of almost a quarter of a century ago.

His hands caressed her hips, her trim waist, and finally rose to cup her breasts, palming her nipples which turned hard beneath his touch.

"Oh, Gethin!" She caught her lower lip between her teeth.

He pulled apart his own robe and lifted her to him. Unable to wait even for an instant, he held her small body along the length of his own, felt her fire as she moaned in tortured ecstasy.

"Oh, Gethin!" she cried again.

His hands clasped her buttocks and lifted her. She parted her thighs and wrapped her arms and legs tightly around him while he guided himself into her. Her cry was high and keening.

"Dear God!" he gasped. "You are like a virgin. So tight. So hot."

"Oh, do I please you? Oh. I never thought to feel you inside me again. Oh, Gethin. I die." Her head fell back as shudder after shudder coursed through her body, transmitting themselves to him. So hungry was she for him that almost as soon as she had begun, she slumped limply in his arms.

With their bodies locked together, he had carried her to the bed and flung himself upon it, her body beneath his. There he completed the pleasure for himself and brought her to a climax again.

Her sobs of pleasure and love had soothed the guilt he was feeling. He had gathered her into his arms, pressing her body against his from toe to chin, feeling her slight frame with every inch of his skin as she had drifted off to sleep, her fingers twined in the curly gray hairs of his chest.

Each night now for two weeks he had come to her bedchamber. She had greeted him with eagerness that matched his own and sometimes surpassed it. He told himself that she was making up for all the long years without him, but sometimes he doubted himself. His memories of her unbridled passion in their youth returned. When they were quiet together, sometimes guilt pricked him still. She loved what he could do for her body. How terrible for her to have been deprived of such joy for so many long years!

A knocking at the door disturbed him. Patting his wife's hip familiarly, he reached for his robe.

"This interruption had best be important," he muttered as he carefully replaced the covers around Branwen.

The knocking came again, louder, more insistent.

Gethin's face wore a dark scowl when he finally opened the door to his son and heir. Rhiannon's fist was poised to knock again. The look on the youthful face gone quite gray with worry caused Gethin to relax his features somewhat into questioning lines. "What has happened?" He pushed his son back out into the hall and closed the door behind them.

"Moira has disappeared. Huw and I suspect foul play but know not where to turn. That is . . . We thought to come to you."

"Tell me what happened." Gethin drew his son back into the chamber and reached for his *chausses*.

Rhiannon started in some embarrassment at the sight of his mother sitting upright now in her bed. Her long hair was tangled; her shoulders were bare behind the blankets which she clutched to her throat. Although faintly bluish smudges under her eyes bespoke a sleepless night, her face wore a relaxed and loving smile.

"'Tis your mother," Gethin remarked drily. "My wife."

Flushing slightly, Rhiannon turned his back and strolled to the fire, stoking it and extending his hands to the flame.

"Son." Gethin reached for his boots. "You have a fire in your room."

"My fool of a vassal persuaded Huw Llengaron, a man who fell under her spell almost from the first moment he met her, to arrange a meeting with her father in the hopes of persuading him to make peace." Rhiannon faltered. "Huw said she hoped to prevent bloodshed on both sides and end the war forever." Staring into the flames, Rhiannon mutely measured the depth of his loss. Moira had become all in all to him. He had never spoken to anyone about the deep flood of emotion that threatened to unman him now. Until he could speak to Moira herself and confess his feelings, he would not confide them to anyone else.

"Lorne, of course, laughed in her face."

"She did not return."

A soft exclamation from the bed together with his father's quiet curse, brought Rhiannon around, his face white. "She sought only the best for us, for all. We must do something, everything possible to save her."

Gethin rose, his face troubled. He handed Branwen her robe and shrugged himself into his shirt and tunic. The very distinct possibility existed that Moira was dead. If so, he sincerely mourned for his daughter whom he had come to respect and, on occasion, to actually exchange a pleasant word with. She had made a man of his son, bringing home to him responsibilities and duties that he shouldered gladly for her sake. The harum-scarum raider was fast turning into a sober leader. Good women brought out the best in a man. He smiled at his wife reassuringly. The look in her eyes echoed his own feelings.

"There is more," Rhiannon came to the foot of his mother's bed. The scene was strangely intimate, the two men and the woman returning to the place where they had all begun. Each felt the tension in the others in an extraordinary manner. "Owen Llewellyn was abroad last night."

"Owen Llewellyn?" Gethin frowned.

Rhiannon nodded. "He and another rider whom the guard could not identify rode in less than a couple of hours ago."

"How was the meeting between Moira and Lorne arranged?" Gethin's mind worked fast. The seeming non sequitur made Rhiannon blink.

"By messenger, I suppose."

"Let us find this messenger and discover whom he delivered his messages to." Gethin put his arm around his wife who had managed to clothe her shoulders and now would have risen. "Go back to sleep, Branwen. We will return and report to you when we ascertain what has

424

happened. Lorne may have taken his daughter, in which case we can negotiate for her or win her." He smiled at Rhiannon. "On the other hand, if Owen Llewellyn heard ought of this meeting . . ."

Branwen shook her head. "I must be up anyway, my lord. I shall question Alys whether Moira gave any indication of her plans."

Gethin nodded with a smile. "Come, son."

Owen Llewellyn's mouth worked nervously as he clenched and unclenched his hands. At first, he had denied all knowledge of any messages or meetings. However, at Rhiannon's furious snarl, he had muttered reluctantly that his duty was to oversee the security of the keep. Of course, the messenger had reported to him. Beyond that, he knew nothing.

Angrily, he retaliated at the insult. "You come and question me?" His voice rose petulantly. "She is a Lorne. A Lorne. A witch," he assured Gethin. "She has bewitched this young man. She will bring down her father upon us now that she knows our secrets. You would not believe me. She is . . ."

They closed the door on his rantings. "Put a guard on him," Gethin instructed Huw. "I do not hear anything new in what he says, but he is crafty in the ways of the mad. Since he rode out last night, I am suspicious."

Rhiannon spun on his heel. "I will not wait. He will speak about where my lady is."

Gethin caught his arm. "He truly may not know. Would you torment someone already so tortured that he cannot reason properly? We will watch him. If he knows of your lady's whereabouts, he will seek her out soon and we will follow him."

Rhiannon's eyes glittered. "And what then?"

They had arrived at the door of the hall. Gethin faced

his son soberly. "I will send him away. Moira has proved herself a loyal mate to you. If he cannot see that, he also might not see that my grandchildren are precious to me."

"My lord Gethin." Branwen hurried down the corridor toward them.

"My lady," Gethin took her hand. "What news?"

"Alys says Lady Moira gave no hint that she planned anything different last night. She is as amazed as any of us. I have instructed her to tell no one that my daughter is missing, but to pretend as if nothing has happened. She is to listen to all gossip and report anything suspicious in the talk of any." Branwen reached out with her other hand to touch her son. "If any have stories to tell, they will not escape the scrutiny of the bower."

Despite his worry over Moira, Rhiannon could not resist staring at his mother. Her face was younger somehow, the deep lines that had seemed permanent at the corners of her mouth and down the center of her forehead had softened. She smiled up at Gethin ap Breannon like a happy child who has done well and knows with certainty that she will receive a reward in the near future. The lord of Hawk's Keep in turn smiled down at his petite wife as if he could scarcely restrain himself from her lips.

Huw Llengaron coughed lightly.

Shaking herself, Branwen turned to Rhiannon again. "There is one more thing," she began hesitantly.

The men looked at her expectantly.

"I cannot think how this would be of importance, except that it is unusual. The wench who lights the fires reports that Margwin was not in her bed last night. In fact, she was not in the keep. She returned before dawn this morning." She looked timidly at her husband, half expecting him to frown. Her report of Margwin's conduct might be construed as hope of discrediting a rival.

Instead, he clenched his fist. Leading the way down the

426

hall, he ushered the three of them into his private chamber. "Seat yourselves, gentlemen. My lady wife, sit here." He indicated a smaller chair with a cushioned back and seat. "I begin to scent a plot. Both Margwin and Owen Llewellyn have imagined grudges against your wife, Rhys. Owen knew Moira's plan from the messenger, and Margwin has been at Owen's ear in recent weeks. Both were away from the keep last night."

"Margwin?" Rhiannon's voice conveyed his amazement. "I can see no reason for her to harbor a grudge against my lady."

Gethin nodded. "'Twould amaze you more if you knew her reason. I fear your lady may be in danger from them rather than from her father. Huw, you must set guards to both of them. If they move from the keep, follow close. Indeed, although I should hate to fight without you, if battle be drawn, I place you in full charge of them until Lady Moira is located."

Huw Llengaron rose to his feet. "I will find her, my lord, if they have her. Neither of them shall get by me."

A frantic knocking began at the door. The boy Jenk burst into the room before Gethin could respond. "There's horns in the forest, m'lord! Horns! Three times! Horns!"

"Lorne!" Gethin exclaimed. He glanced at Rhys' white face. "Evidently she did not make an impression on him." He bent over his wife who clutched the arms of the chair as if she would imprint them with her fingerprints. "My love. I must go." Regardless of his son and his minion, he grasped her by the shoulders and pulled her to her feet. Pressing her body against him, he devoured her lips. "Keep you warm until I return," he whispered fiercely.

Turning from her, he faced the men. "Huw, you have your duty here at this keep as I have charged you. Rhys, I need you beside me. Jenk, summon Henry Fletcher. We will gather in the great hall as swiftly as possible."

"Yes, m'lord." Jenk dashed away.

Gethin followed him, pausing only to press his wife's hand to his lips.

After him in the hall, when they would have gone their separate ways, Huw Llengaron caught Rhiannon's arm. "My Lord Rhys, be comforted. She sought to bring peace to avoid the deaths of those she loves."

"Aye, those she loves. Her father," Rhiannon growled.

"And her husband."

"She never loved me. She promised herself to me because I had enslaved her. She accepted vassalage with honor. Never love." Rhiannon's voice was a bitter whip lashing himself.

"She loves you, my lord, and believes that you do not love her. She believes that you married her for her lands." With these words, Huw hurried away, his steps quickening into a run. A heavy bell began to toll and confusion answered in the bailey. Rhiannon stood stunned by all he had heard. He shook his head. Only one thought was clear. Moira was gone and she had loved him. He felt a stab of pain through his vitals.

Thirty-Eight

Margwin burst into Owen Llewellyn's room to find him girding himself for battle. Furiously, she flew at him, pulling his hands away from his middle, so that his sword clattered to the floor.

"We must go to the hut," she hissed. "I told you last night to kill her, but you refused. Now we must slip away again."

He faced her angrily. "I go to fight Lorne," he snarled. "She will stay till we return. The longer she waits, the hungrier and weaker she will become."

As he bent to pick up his sword, Margwin sank her claws into his shoulder, hauling him upright with surprising strength. "You fool! *After* the battle will be too late! Scouts will be combing the area for stragglers. They will find her. She will tell!" Margwin wrung her hands. "We will be exposed." She studied her man carefully as he hesitated. As his face softened, she covered her face with her hands and began to weep. "You will be safe, for you are a knight. They will forgive you. But I . . . I am only a weak woman. They will send me away. I have no place to go." With a soft sob, she pressed herself against his side, slipping in under his arm to bury her face in his shoulder.

"Do not cry!" he protested, patting her awkwardly.

"We must go," she insisted, "or we are undone." Turning tear-filled eyes up to him, she raised her lips and kissed the corner of his mouth.

It was enough. "Meet me at the side door to the bailey," he directed. "We will go before they come for me. I can join them on the road and say they could not find me. You will not be missed in the confusion of preparation." When he stooped to pick up his sword, he missed the sly smile of satisfaction that curved her lips as she darted out the door.

Huw Llengaron barely had time to flatten himself in the doorway of the room next to Owen's. The sight of Margwin hastening away seemed almost direct confirmation of Gethin's suspicion, Huw paused. Their meeting had caught him unprepared. Planning to watch Owen himself, he had not thought to bring a guard with him. Now the guard sent to Margwin's room would not find her there. He cursed himself as he stepped out into the hall, hands on hips.

Abruptly, Owen's door swung open. The two men stared at each other across the intervening space. Each knew what the other was there for. Yet each preferred to play the game for a moment, feeling out the opponent.

"Good," Huw spoke heartily. "You are ready. I am come to get you. Lord Gethin is assigning the men in the hall. You heard the horns?"

"Aye!" Owen swept his hand down the hall. "Lead on."

By force of habit, Huw obeyed. Stepping in front of Owen to lead the way, he staggered beneath a sharp blow across the back of his skull. Fighting blinding pain and dizziness, he sank to his knees, clawing for his sword. As his hands closed over the hilt, Owen's great fist caught

430

him against the temple, slamming him sideways into the wall.

Panting slightly from the excitement rather than the effort, Llewellyn stood over the body of his unconscious friend. Faint stirrings of regret already tingled in his nerve endings. He had crossed some sort of bridge. Unless he disposed of this man permanently, he had no recourse but to flee.

So be it, he thought angrily. He could not murder a friend. With a snarl, he grasped Huw under the shoulders and dragged him out of the hall. With swift, efficient movements, Owen bound the unconscious lieutenant hand and foot.

At the side door to the bailey, he waited impatiently. He must be away. That witch of Lorne had caused all of this. His mind fixed on her. She had taken his family and now she had taken his place. He could never return to Hawk's Keep, but he would dispose of her before leaving. Perhaps he would take Margwin with him to share his exile. The thought was cold comfort.

Even as it occurred to him, Margwin came rushing toward him. "Hurry," she cried breathlessly, as she flung herself against him. "Branwen confronted me as I was leaving, wanting to know why I carried a bundle. I think I convinced her that I was merely taking some clothing to some poor family, but I fear . . ."

"Owen Llewellyn," Lady Branwen's smooth voice interrupted them from the top of the short stairs at the head of the hall. "Lord Gethin requires your presence immediately among the men."

"Run!" Margwin gasped.

Without further thought, Owen flung the door open and dragged her with him into the bailey. There, the preparation for war had turned the place into a mass of confusion. With his hand under her arm, Owen led Margwin to the stables where already grooms had saddled mounts. Without preamble, he flung her upon one and selected one himself.

"Here! That horse is for . . ." a groom bawled. His statement was lost as Owen heeled the destrier away. Finding itself loose, Margwin's horse followed at a gallop. None stopped them as they rode out over the palisades.

As they galloped down the Colwyn Bay road, the horns sounded again from the forest. Owen pulled the mount to a halt. "I should go to battle," he insisted stubbornly. "Hear you. Lorne calls. My men need me." He shook his head dazedly and looked around him as if he expected them to be following.

Instead, Margwin rode up beside him, her blond hair streaming out behind her, her face contorted by the intensity of her frustration. "Get on!" she screamed. "We must kill her and be away! She has destroyed us both. My soul cries for revenge!"

"My men!" Owen protested.

Another long mournful blast rang from the forest below.

Angrily, Moira swung her whip down on the haunches of Owen's horse. "Ride for the coastguard's hut!" she commanded. "Then you may go and get yourself killed for all I care. More fool you!"

His mind slipping in and out of awareness of reality, Owen rode beside the crazed woman. Once he glanced at her in a puzzled fashion. Her face was a mask of fury, her eyes wide open, her lips parted and drawn back from her teeth as if she bared them to the wind. A frisson of dread prickled the hair on the back of his neck.

Tethering their horses on the leeward side of the hut, Owen drew his sword as he approached the door.

"Good," Margwin crooned. "Kill her quickly and we can be away. You to your battle if you choose and me to the east. Gethin ap Breannon will not shut me up in a nunnery to grow old on my knees with a lot of filthy, half-crazy old hags."

Unlocking the door, Owen entered, his eyes unused to the dimness. A faint movement behind the door warned him. Even as he half turned to meet it, a stick of wood came crashing into his temple, its bark tearing open the skin. With a curse he reeled sideways, dropping his sword as his hands clapped to the side of his head.

Moira caught up the sword and ran, careening into Margwin, knocking herself off balance as she sprang through the door. The older woman's hands, grasping her skirt brought her up short. Swinging around, Moira faced the blonde where she had fallen to her knees. "Release me instantly!" Moira's ice-blue eyes threatened death. Margwin fell away as she heard the howls of rage and pain behind her in the hut.

Free of the clinging hands, Moira spun away, running clumsily, trying to put distance between herself and the two in the hut. Out onto the headlands she sped, one hand clutching the sword, the other supporting her protruding belly.

Too late she saw her mistake.

The cliffs stretched out into a narrow promontory of land at this point, a small peninsula along which she must retrace her steps. When she turned panting, her heart sank.

Margwin led Owen, half blind with blood from the wound Moira's blow had opened in his head. When Moira sought to dash by them, they separated. Owen straightened himself, his trained fighting instincts exerting themselves. The weakness lay in the older woman. But Moira could not hope to evade her before Owen was upon them.

At bay, she hefted the sword. Laying the blade to rest across the palm of her left hand, she shifted her right to a firmer grip on the hilt. That done, she slashed it across in front of her body and flung back her head proudly. The ruby on her finger flashed into a hundred blood red splinters of light in the rising sun.

"You cannot hope to escape," Margwin called, her voice strained against the rising wind that blew ever from the sea. "Surrender yourself."

Moira's only answer was a slight smile.

"Beg for your life," Owen snarled, advancing a couple of steps almost to the head of the promontory. His practiced eye had taken in the authority with which Moira had handled the sword. She was no amateur for all she was a woman. "You cannot escape. Come to us and pray for your life or die on the rocks below."

Moira cast a hasty glance behind her, then shook her head. "Come and take my life if you can, Owen Llewellyn. You are the one whose sword was taken; your talk is nothing but air."

"What are you waiting for?" Margwin screamed. "She is only a woman. So she has a sword? What woman knows how to use a sword? You are a trained knight. Surely it would be but child's play to disarm her and slit her throat."

"Leave me, Owen," Moira called, her eyes never leaving his face. The tip of the sword was directed toward a spot some six inches below his heart. By straightening her arm, she would drive it home if he charged her. "I carry the lord's child. The battle is joined. I can hear the horns. You are missed."

"All in good time," he muttered, shifting unconsciously in his uncertainty. "My wife and children . . ."

"You would murder me," Moira challenged. Her sword trembled slightly in her hand as she felt the weakness in her muscles from the lack of food. A thought struck her. "Is this the way your wife died? Did she cringe helplessly? Or did she fight so long as she could to defend her children?"

The look on his face was answer enough as his

434

eyes dropped.

"She fought, did she not?" Moira smiled. "Did she catch up this very sword and make for the thieves and murderers who would take her little ones' lives? Did she try to defend you?"

"What difference?" Margwin screamed. "Kill her! Make an end! She is not a woman. She is a witch. You are a knight." Abandoning her position, she flung herself at Owen, trying to thrust him forward.

He shrugged her urgent hands off his arm and shoulder. "I am a knight," he nodded. "She is a woman." His eyes were calm for a moment as if the memory of his wife's bravery and sacrifice had soothed him for a moment. "I am a knight sworn to protect the weak and helpless."

"Go fight men, Owen Llewellyn," Moira commanded. "I shall never beg. You will get no pleasure here from me. Only shame. And if I die, your wife and children will still be dead." She shifted the heavy blade in her hand. Her shoulder was beginning to ache. The hilt was too big for her hand, but she could see the doubt in his eyes. "You may die yourself," she reminded him. "I will fight till all the blood drains from my body to save the babe I carry."

"It is a bastard!" Margwin cried. "And she is a witch!"

"It is Rhiannon ap Breannon's heir," Moira declared. "Owen, you cannot destroy the lord's child. Gethin has been good to you. He cared for you while you were wounded. He has given you food and drink and a warm place."

Owen straightened from his crouch. He shook his head as if emerging from a dream.

"She is a witch!" Margwin hissed frantically in his ear. "Witch!" she screamed at Moira. "Now you seek to trap Owen within your spell. You have destroyed my hopes."

"What hopes?" Moira spat angrily. "You were a bedmate to the Lord Gethin. He would never have given you to his son. You lie to yourself."

Her face contorted with rage, Margwin started forward. "You lie. Witch! I was even as you a captive. I was to be the young lord's wife. Gethin captured me for that purpose."

"Rhiannon seeks his own wife!"

"You bewitched him. Already he was casting looks in my direction." The half-crazed woman lunged for Moira. Her hands arched like claws. Her hair swirled and twisted in the wind like snakes. Her jaws arched like a wild beast's in its spring for the kill.

Fending off the madwoman, Moira thrust with the sword. Margwin sidestepped, circling, her back to the sea.

The sounds of the horns winding from the forest sounded faint but clear in the teeth of the prevailing wind. Despite her need for concentration, their dire call made Moira turn her head in their direction.

At that moment Margwin sprang again, lunging for the sword arm. Moira was quicker. The sword slashed at the woman's grasping hands. With a shriek of pain, Margwin's hands closed over the blade and came away dripping. Droplets of bright blood spattered Moira as well as Margwin, who flung her injured palms up before her face and turned to Owen accusingly.

Llewellyn stood mesmerized with the horror of his own visions and the sight of the blood on the two women. Catatonic in the face of his guilt at his desertion from the battle, crippled by his own memories, stunned by the sight of the women fighting, he could do nothing but stand like a stone.

"Men!" Margwin screamed. "Not a one is worth ought. You draw back! All of you!" She shook her bleeding hands again at him. Her breast heaved to draw in the breath to speak above the pain and rage. "You plot and plan, but 'tis all for nothing. You cannot carry through. Even your battles are nothing more than

436

exercises in futility. No war is ever won. Now you refuse to dispose of this witch. I threw myself on the sword, so you might take her from behind. You stand there like a lump with your hands hanging at your sides."

Snarling, spitting, frothing, hurling incantations of hatred and damnation against all men, Margwin lunged away from Moira to stagger wildly across the intervening space to Owen Llewellyn, who backed away as from a gorgon.

"No!" She snarled. "You will not escape. I command you to carry forth this office. I speak as Gethin has taught me to speak. I am his favorite. You will obey me."

With bleeding hands, she grasped his shoulders, tugging frantically at his tunic, staining it with bright scarlet streaks. Her tormented sobs and gasps for breath rent the air.

"Release me," he commanded feverishly. His face paled beneath the drops of blood that spattered it as he grasped her wrists and wrenched them away from his clothing.

"Kill her!" Breast to breast, they struggled for an instant before he flung her from him with a shudder of disgust.

With a sobbing scream, Margwin staggered back toward Moira, who sidestepped her reeling progress easily. Her steps carried her toward the edge of the cliff. A stone lay in her path. Turning, her foot slipped on its polished surface and she fell heavily.

A grating sound, then a rising rumble! The portion of headland on which Margwin sprawled slid downward. The rotten escarpment undercut by centuries of waves crumbled beneath her. The roar, clear and ominous, rose above the pounding of the waves.

Moira's eyes locked with Margwin's terror-filled ones only for an instant. Then the woman's piercing shriek was drowned in a veritable explosion of sound as rocks

437

and soil alike gave way and tumbled hurly-burly into the sea.

The cliff face was shortened by some dozen feet. Almost at Moira's feet, the new edge began. Shuddering, hypnotized by the sight, she stared downward into the boiling, churning mass.

Of Margwin's body, she could see no sign. The breakers leaped in great geysers of white water. Spray wet Moira's white face. As quickly as they exploded, they fell back, washing the rubble away, leveling it into the shape of the beach until nothing remained.

Thirty-Nine

Moira moved carefully a couple of steps before turning to face her last opponent. The man who had vowed she would never leave Hawk's Keep alive stared at her from only a few feet away. A push from his powerful arms and she would plummet to her death in the depths below land's end. All the horror of this man's treatment of her came flooding back as the glittering eyes regarded her. She thought of his abuse of her body: slamming her to the ground with her hands bound behind her; locking her in the darkest, deepest dungeon in the castle at the mercy of a beast; threatening to rape her in Rhiannon's own apartments; bringing her to trial for witchcraft when the extreme penalty he knew was burning; and now threatening not only her life but the life of her unborn little one.

Determinedly, she clutched the hilt of the sword stained with Margwin's blood. The drops on her face and the bosom of her gown were already darkening so that she looked more dangerous than ever to the confused man who now regarded her. Drawing in a deep breath, she feinted lightly with the blade. Again the ruby set in the golden claw caught the light.

One of her enemies lay crushed on the rocks and sand of Colwyn Bay; before her stood the other one. She would not surrender now. Lifting her eyes slightly, she filled her vision with the towering keep—dark and gray in the brightening day. She would return. They would not keep her from her home and her love.

The battle horns sounded again.

Owen Llewellyn faced her with his fists clenched. "My wife and children died because of you," he repeated as if his words were a litany once learned now repeated so often that it had lost all meaning.

"You lie and you know you lie," Moira replied calmly. "Your eyes betray you. You see me as I really am and know that I am innocent of their blood." Her voice dropped to a soothing, even tone. "I am only a woman, Owen. And a very young one at that. I have not yet lived a full score of years. I was only a babe myself when your family were beset."

"'Twas your blood. Blood will have blood."

"My father never attacked helpless pilgrims on the way to a chapel." Behind her, the sea roared ominously. Her scalp prickled as she felt the ground vibrate under her feet. She must get off this promontory or join Margwin in her grave at its base.

"We were on the way to chapel," Owen acknowledged. "She was always religious. Wanted to give thanks for my safe return and for the health of all our children . . ." His voice broke. His eyes glazed again.

Moira took a step forward and then another.

Suddenly, he threw back his head and howled. *"She died because of me!"* His confession rang to the very heavens. Dropping to his knees, he clawed at his hair. "She died because of me. *I* did not plan. *I! I!"* Collapsing forward, he pounded his head again and again into the unforgiving earth. Raising it at last, blood trickled down

440

the center of his forehead and between his eyes and along the sides of his nostrils to drip off his matted beard. Hideously bruised and bloodied, his features contorted with suffering. He resembled nothing human. Had a friend seen him at that moment, Owen Llewellyn would have been unrecognizable.

Staring at him in horrified fascination, Moira felt her stomach turn over at the sight of his self-inflicted torment. She had seen men tortured by others, but far more horrible was the sight of one punishing himself with no chance of expiation.

"She begged me to take an armed escort, but I scoffed at her. We were only going to the chapel in the woods. *I* would be her escort. *I* would disperse any persons foolish enough to attack *me*. *I* was strong. *I* was a great warrior." His face stared into hell and his eyes reflected the sin he had lived with for all those years.

"Some damned creature dropped on me from a tree. His first slash opened me up all across my belly. I was paralyzed. Went out of the saddle like a stone. My eldest boy . . . He tried to help me. Another chopped him down."

"Who were they?" Moira cried, appalled.

He strained the air through his teeth. "Churls? Villeins? Thieves? The scum of the earth? Who knows? They were whatever slimy beasts lie in wait to waylay travelers on their way to give offerings and thanks." He covered his face in his hands. Rocking back and forth, he groaned the names of the wife and children long dead, muffled by the great, heaving sobs that wracked him.

"You were right," he quavered, throwing up his eyes accusingly at Moira. "She caught up my sword. She was not a big thing like you. So small. Like a child. She could stand under my arm. These two hands could span her waist."

"She fought for her children and her husband." Tears

441

moistened Moira's cheeks at the thought of the valiant, futile effort.

"She killed one," Owen sobbed. "She ran him through, but she could not pull my blade from his body. The wound closed around it and she had not the strength to wrench it out. They were on her in a second." He could tell no more. The excruciating pain of his memories rendered him dumb. Only panting sobs issued from his gaping mouth.

Moira moved forward. Now was the time. The ground shivered beneath her feet. The sea crashed ominously behind her. The wind lashed her hair forward across her face. She must slip past Owen while he huddled sobbing, beaten by his own guilt, the lone survivor whom fate had punished with life for his crime of pride.

Now or never! Moira took a step. Did the ground shift downward? Or was the movement engendered by the oncoming tide and her own weakness. Another! Gasping in terror, Moira lunged forward as, with another ominous rumble, the cliff fell away beneath her feet!

The sword dropped almost at Owen's knees. Her hands clutched at the ground and rocks as her feet dangled over the edge of the abyss. With fingernails digging into the soft loam, she pulled herself forward on her belly, until she could get a knee over the lip and then roll to safety. Her body came to rest on top of the sword under Owen's very nose.

Only inches from the man's gargoyle visage, she caught her breath in terror. Had she survived the slide to be delivered into the hands of her murderer?

Their eyes met. His were tear-drenched yet calm, compassionate in the face of her terror. As if his confession and self-condemnation had cleansed him for the moment, he stared at her as if he did not know her, but felt only a mild interest in her form so awkwardly sprawled before him.

"How do you, pretty lady?" he asked in a quiet voice. He was oblivious to the surroundings or the times.

His question lifted her off her back and sent her scrambling for dear life past him and back from the edge. He was truly mad. She had no way of knowing when his sick brain might return to his ancient plot for revenge. He had no grasp of reality. Although he seemed lucid, his face gentle, his manner calm, revealing in that moment the man he had once been, she realized it would not last. Indeed, she doubted whether he would ever again see clearly. This moment would be replaced by the red rage again whenever he remembered his own guilt. Then he would cast around desperately for a scapegoat.

Climbing to her feet, she ran as fast as she could weave her way around rocks, through low bush, toward the trees on the Colwyn Bay road. Her breath came hard and raspingly into her throat. Her heart pounded. In her imagination, she felt his hot breath on her neck, but she dared not turn around to locate him or see if he indeed pursued.

Stumbling, falling to her knees, heaving herself up, she at last flung herself into the shadow of the trees on the other side of the road. Dodging behind the thick bole of an evergreen, she collapsed, gasping for breath. Her chest heaved. Both hands clasped her belly, holding the firm mound of her most precious treasure.

Dimly, with some surprise, she noted the stillness within. "Gone . . . to sleep?" she panted, her voice only a thread of sound. "Fine son . . . you. Let . . . Mother do . . . all the work."

She let her head fall back against the trunk of the tree while she dragged in long, painful breaths and her babe slept soundly, sweetly within the cradle of her hips. Once a slow movement caught her attention. Dropping her head forward, she watched one side of her stomach distend in a leisurely stretch at the same time the

443

opposite side flattened visibly. A warm feeling of love spread over her as she smiled delightedly. "Turning over, to get more comfortable," she giggled slightly.

A shadow moved in the forest some distance away. A dim figure detached itself from one tree and disappeared behind another. The man moved furtively, slipping from cover to cover glancing ever behind him. A straggler!

She had heard the great horns. The battle must be joined by this time.

Swiftly, the thought took shape. She must hide! A battle between the armed men of Lorne and Breannon could be at any moment sweeping through the forest and she could be caught in its path.

Still as a statue, as if she were a carved part of the tree itself, she watched the man until he disappeared from view. Then, heaving herself up on her hands and knees, she peered around the tree and up the slope.

Owen Llewellyn was on his feet, striding toward the horses he had left tethered behind the hut. Seeing them now, Moira cursed her luck. She had run the wrong way. Once in the saddle, he surveyed the countryside, his face covered with dried blood, his eyes wild like an animal's. Did he remember his companion with whom he had ridden to this spot? Somehow Moira doubted that he could even recall that such a person as Margwin had ever existed. As she studied his stern features, Moira shivered. How soon and how completely would the mistress pass from the minds of the men who had lain with her.

Again the great horns winded.

Gathering the reins of Margwin's horse, he galloped across the slope slantwise toward the road some distance from where Moira crouched. As he jumped the horses onto it, he looked neither to right nor left, but only spurred the quicker toward the battle. He had forgotten Moira completely.

Trembling now that she was momentarily safe, Moira slumped down on her face, almost unconscious, her body curved protectively around her child. How easily she could have allowed herself to slip into oblivion, but her mind rebelled. Her unborn child must be preserved. If she could retrace her steps toward the clearing where her meeting with her father had taken place less than twenty-four hours ago, Huw Llengaron might come for her. At least he would know where to start looking after the battle was over. To climb the hill to the keep with armed men everywhere was beyond her powers.

The babe weighed heavily on her nearly exhausted body. The force of the beating administered by her father, the privation of the night without food or proper rest, the intensity of her emotions aroused as death had been so near so many times, left her dazed. She looked around her, disoriented, before starting off in what she hoped was the right direction, weaving her way through the trees. Her stumbling steps carried her over the rocks with their sharp crevasses where tree roots had broken them. Once her foot caught in a tentaclelike vine twisting over a huge gray boulder. She tripped often, slipped sideways into trunks, was torn by the outstretched limbs. Her face was slapped more than once by a whipping branch.

Once she thought she heard a heavy movement in the woods behind her. Holding herself still, her hands cupped protectively around her belly, she waited, hardly daring to breathe. She had indeed heard someone. A muffled curse came to her ears as someone lost or strayed tried to find his way.

Fearfully, she sought a hiding place as a hurt animal goes to ground. Though she could not be sure, she thought the clearing where she had met her father lay somewhere to her right. A fall of boulders interrupted the forest before her. She must hide.

445

Moving almost by instinct, she found a declivity formed by two granite faces on one side and a fallen tree and undergrowth on the other. Although the rough surfaces tore her hands and branches scratched her face and pulled her hair, she doggedly wormed her way into the narrow space as a vixen finds a hole. There, panting and gasping, with only the bright sky visible above her, finally she allowed herself to relax.

Lying on her back, she felt the movements of her unborn one begin almost immediately. "Wondrous," she sighed woefully. "Now that I want you to rest, you want to play." Folding her hands across her belly, she settled herself to wait and gather strength. Her body burned, her lungs and throat felt raw from the icy air. The sleep that claimed her was the deep well of unconsciousness.

Forty

Gethin ap Breannon found a group of men, among
them Henry Fletcher, already gathered in the great hall.
Before he had a chance to call them to order, their excited
conversation was interrupted by the sound of a horn
winding from the forest. As it had before, three times it
sounded, a dire and mournful sound, a challenge as from
one great primitive beast to another.

Gethin leaped up onto the dais, his arms uplifted. "By
God, he calls us, lads. Lorne's challenge! Henry Fletcher!
Sound the alarm bell in the bailey! Every man up now and
forward! Arm and ready to ride! We will fight without
breakfast. Summon the priest and he will say mass and
offer confession as we ride past the chapel." He clapped
Rhiannon on the shoulder as he sprang down. "What say
you, son? 'Tis a great day. The Lorne will be defeated."

Rhiannon's heart was heavy. Always before, he had
gone eagerly into battle. Now he could only think of her
who was missing. His lady. His love. For what purpose
should he fight? He was struck by the futility of it all. The
terrible frustration of not knowing where she might be,
of not knowing if she might be cold or hungry or in pain.

He clenched his fists at his side to control a shudder of dread. Did she lie dead in some dark part of the forest?

With dragging steps, he returned to their apartments where Conal waited to dress him for battle. When he returned to the hall, his agony was further compounded by the presence of a much-shaken, white-faced Huw Llengaron.

"My apologies, my lords." Huw bowed his throbbing head over his knees. "He struck me from behind."

"A lackey sent to summon Owen Llewellyn found him," Gethin reported.

"My lord." Lady Branwen hurried into the hall. "They have gone. Owen and Margwin. Through the side door into the bailey."

"I must follow." Rhiannon bolted for the door.

"Your men need you, my son." Gethin's words brought him up short. "They cannot ride into battle undirected."

"My lady needs me," Rhiannon insisted.

"You do not know which direction they ride in. They may be fleeing rather than fighting," Henry Fletcher pointed out sensibly.

"I do not believe that Owen Llewellyn would ever run from a chance to confront Lorne," Rhiannon pointed out.

"Still," Gethin commanded. "Your duty is to your men and to me." He turned and hurried from the hall. Henry Fletcher vaulted out at a run. A heavy bell began to toll and confusion answered in the bailey.

Mounted, they passed beside the chapel where the priest stood at the door to bless them as they rode by. His hand marked the patterns of the cross in the air and his lips, moving ceaselessly, intoned the words of comfort and assurance. At the head rode Gethin with Rhiannon at his side, his youthful face pulled tight into a death mask by the intensity of his emotions. Directly behind the leaders came Henry Fletcher, a calm expression on his face. He had seen too many battles and survived too many to waste energy at this point.

In the rear guard rode Huw Llengaron, who had seen almost all from the beginning. Despite his throbbing headache, he insisted that he was well enough to accompany the troops into this last battle. That this was the end, he well knew. What was done here today would decide much in the way of peace and prosperity for the countryside. Today two rival forces that had swayed backward and forward against each other for generations would meet to decide which would yield and which would hold sway. The battle was now to the death. Rhiannon ap Breannon and Peter of Lorne would make it so.

Scouts had returned to report that forces of Lorne had gathered in the rocks and forest lands beyond the bayhead. A shiver of dread went through many seasoned veterans in the troops as word spread. If the scouts were correct and Lorne chose to fight there, this would be no stand up and charge fight, but duck and cover, strike and run. Every man must ride into the trees, knowing that clinging to at least one of them high up in the branches was a man of Lorne with a dagger in his hand. And yet, each rode, feeling that peculiar quality that men feel before they go out to kill, unquestioning obedience to a higher authority who orders that they do foolish or dangerous things with perfect reasonableness. And so they do.

The column turned from the road and angled off down into a wooded ravine which led to a level valley floor. Breannon's spies had reported that Lorne's last camp had been in the grove of trees on the opposite side of the valley floor. If he intended a pitch battle, here would be the logical and ideal place. His men would be rested for several days and the floor of the valley would provide good footing.

"Spread out!" The command was given back along the line. The men fanned to each side of the leaders. The horses moved up to form a line abreast. The footmen closed in behind as the line emerged from the trees.

"The sun's well up," Henry Fletcher observed. "Good! 'Tis no trouble from the sun today. No one gets blinded. Not too hot, not too cold. I hate to fight in the cold. When you get knocked down or hurt, sometimes you nearly freeze to death before someone comes to help you or pick you up."

Young Cei Aberdyfi at his side shivered. His information had proved useful and he had been rewarded. Now Henry's quiet pessimism made him wonder if he were going to live to enjoy his reward.

As the first horse breasted the bush at the edge of the forest, a line of horsemen appeared on the other side of the field. In the center of each glowered the two old leaders. Each was consumed with hatred and yet each grudgingly admired the other.

Peter of Lorne spurred his gray forward to caracole wildly. "See the horse, Breannon!" he shouted. "I said I would have him back. Last night I saw my daughter. I will not have her back. Her I leave with you. But you have shamed my house. Today I am here to complete the last part of my vow." At the mention of Moira, Rhiannon started forward, but his father restrained him.

"She is not with him," Gethin noted significantly. "She may be gone to ground somewhere between here and the keep."

"I pray so." Rhiannon nodded grimly.

At that moment, a sudden scream of rage echoed from somewhere to the left of the line. Owen Llewellyn's flying figure charged across the field. His face was streaked with dried blood, his sword was already stained. With his hair standing on end, he looked like a soul escaped from hell with the demons in hot pursuit. From

450

his open mouth, a string of foul imprecations issued as he brandished his sword. His spurs sank into his horse's flanks and raked backward, urging the animal to terrifying speed. Straight for Peter of Lorne he galloped.

Between Lorne and the maddened man charged another figure on a sturdy brown pony. Owen Llewellyn's terrified mount could neither halt nor turn. The rider of the brown raised a boar spear and Llewellyn's horse took the weapon to the guard in the chest. Both mounts went down as Llewellyn's yell of rage rose with his mount's dying scream and the cheers and cries of excitement from both sides.

Owen Llewellyn was up on his feet, his great sword swinging as he rounded his mount's thrashing hooves to get at the enemy who had brought him down. Late in scrambling to his feet was Thomas Tech Duinn, Lorne's messenger and right hand, leering like death himself.

As demigods or demons, both burly, cruel men met with a joy of battle in their fierce eyes. No quarter asked or given, they hacked and spun away from each other. A white foam flecked Llewellyn's beard as his emotions drove him farther into the red world of madness. His great sword flashed lightnings in the air as it thudded against Thomas' bearhide shield. The force of the blow drove Thomas back to one knee, but Owen had overreached himself to deliver it and could not draw back to aim the killing stroke until Thomas was again up and circling.

The stunned men-at-arms on both sides of the fight sat paralyzed at the red light of true rage. They could only watch dumbly from their horses or peep out from between the mounts as the two adversaries, evenly matched in cruelty, stalked each other. Again, like monsters from some bygone age, like the old bear-sarks of the ancient Vikings, they crashed together, Thomas' sword meeting and catching Owen's in midair. The grinning snarl never left Thomas' face while Owen's eyes flashed lunatic fire.

For several minutes, they crashed and circled, snarling at each other. The only sounds in the valley were their harsh grunts of effort as they swung their swords and the clang of the weapons against shields. At last, Thomas seemed to weaken. Barely did he manage to catch the madman's crazed sword on the boss of his shield. The men of Lorne released a groan of apprehension as their champion staggered back from the encounter.

With a scream of triumph, Owen threw his whole weight behind the swinging arc of his sword. Too late, he saw the shield deflected upward to catch his stroke and send it harmlessly over his opponent's head. Down below his knees and out from under the shield came Thomas' right arm, stabbing upward with a disemboweling stroke which Owen's own unchecked weight made all the more deadly.

In stunned silence, all forces watched as Thomas coolly righted himself, shook his sword free and raised its bloody blade above his head. Turning to Lorne who had watched from his spot, he grinned evilly. "My lord," he panted.

"Mount your horse, Sir Thomas!" Lorne called.

His words were almost drowned by the howl from the men of Breannon. As one, their enthrallment fell from them and they spurred across the field. The men of Lorne responded with cries and spurred to meet them past the bodies of horse and man and past Thomas, who swung himself into the saddle and galloped after them. In the melee, each man fought his opponent and prayed that a friend and not an enemy moved off his blind side.

As the mounts circled one another, the footmen were able to dash in and begin their deadly work of hamstringing the horses and gutting the horsemen by slipping their spears in between the saddle bow and thigh.

Lorne's gray unarmored head beckoned to Rhiannon as he slashed and hacked his way through a tall dark horseman. Lorne too had singled out the black tousled hair with the gold fillet binding it back from the dark face.

Meeting seemed impossible. The lines of men struggled and swayed, staggered back and lunged forward. The turf was chewed and torn. Blood spouting from ghastly wounds in men and horses wet the ground and added to the instability of the soft field.

Such violent effort could not long be endured by men and animals. Unhorsed riders sought to drag themselves off the field and riderless horses dashed for the forest, neighing wildly. As footmen were wounded, they limped from the area, trying to avoid the horses' ironshod hooves. Here and there a friend would pause to help another man off or drag a wounded brother or cousin from the area. Finally, the numbers decreased noticeably until a clear path opened up between Peter of Lorne and Rhiannon ap Breannon. With a howl, Rhiannon spurred his horse toward his torturer.

Lorne heard him and turned in the saddle barely in time to catch the sword on his shield. Both men swung their swords, aiming at their opponents' heads as their horses spun and reared. Neither man could gain the clear advantage.

Behind Rhiannon's plunging mount lay the carcass of another horse. As Lorne's big gray pressed hard, Rhiannon's smaller mount went down, falling over the belly of the dead animal. Rhiannon sprang free and stepped back as Lorne laughed.

"The moment of reckoning, eh, dog?"

Rhiannon stood his ground, waiting for the blade to fall, hoping to leap aside and then seize Lorne's arm and drag him from the saddle.

Surprisingly, Lorne backed his horse and dismounted, coming toward the younger man on cat feet. The field had grown still, except for the cries of the dying and the wounded calling for help. All awaited the outcome of this single combat.

Rhiannon lunged first, but Lorne parried with ease, returning the thrust. They circled each other as Rhiannon moved out of range of the dead horse and his own flailing mount's efforts to right itself.

Again Rhiannon lunged, his sword tip ripping the material of the tunic as Lorne's hilt turned the blade away.

"You are slow, old man," Rhiannon crowed.

"Slow, am I?" Lorne jeered. "Or are you overconfident and am I leading you in as Thomas did that madman?"

Rhiannon lunged again and locked hilts with his wife's father. Chest to chest they strove.

"Where is my wife?" he gritted.

"She were better dead," Peter snarled, throwing him off.

Rhiannon stepped back, his face white. For an instant, his point dropped. "You did not kill her," his voice was barely more than a whisper.

Lorne was amazed. For an instant, he too faltered at the drain of color from the younger man's face. "She's safe enough. Look to yourself!" Lorne shouted those words and lunged in to tear Rhiannon's tunic from the left shoulder and cut him in almost the exact spot where he had speared him before.

Only Rhiannon's reflexes saved him from being killed as he tardily side-stepped the blade.

Riposting with an anger born of pain, Rhiannon drove Lorne back until the man's feet tangled in the uneven slippery ground and he went down. Rhiannon's sword was at his throat in an instant.

"Where is she?" he snarled.

"In the woods somewhere off the Colwyn Bay road at

454

the two rocks. I left her there last night."

"You left her there! Did you not care that she was with child?"

"'Twas your child, dog."

"'Tis hers and yours, too."

Peter of Lorne's eyes flickered. "Kill me and make an end."

Rhiannon tensed his arm and then stepped back. "Pull yourself out of the blood and come again. I kill no man through an accident."

Without comment, Lorne righted himself and lunged hard at Rhiannon. Again, the clashing sparks of thrust and parry rained down on the field. Rhiannon was gasping now, as was Lorne. Blood ran from the younger man's left shoulder and his face grew whiter. The end came.

Rhiannon retreated and his back foot turned in the uneven ground. He dropped down to the back knee and could not force himself up. His swordpoint wavered.

Lorne straightened. His ice-blue eyes bored into Rhiannon's, testing, measuring. For Rhiannon, the moment was an eerie one. The eyes were Moira's. He felt as he had when she had sworn loyalty to him.

Then Peter of Lorne sighed. Resignedly, he stepped forward with sword raised. He tapped Rhiannon on the shoulder and stepped back. "I give you your life," he said softly, "as you gave me mine a few minutes ago."

Rhiannon struggled to his feet. He tried to raise his point, but his ears roared and black specks whirled in his vision.

Peter of Lorne turned on his heel, strode away, and caught the reins of the gray horse. He returned, leading it. "Take the horse, boy," he grumbled. "You will need a mount to get to her."

Without another word, he turned away. Rhiannon stood stunned, watching him as he walked rapidly toward the trees. Before Lorne reached them, Thomas Tech Duinn detached himself from their shadow, leading forward two horses. Peter of Lorne clapped the man on the back and together they swung up and rode into the dimness.

Rhiannon heard the thud of horses' hooves behind him and then his father and Llengaron pulled up beside him.

"I cannot believe it," said his father.

"The war is over forever," Rhiannon said. "In our own time, we have each given the other back a life."

Gethin shook his head. Huw Llengaron hastily bound Rhiannon's shoulder. "'Tis not deep."

"He could have killed me," Rhiannon said.

Henry Fletcher came riding up. "Shall I gather the men for another attack?" he asked Breannon.

"Aye, gather the men." Rhiannon opened his mouth to protest, but his father raised his hand. "We will go home, Henry. 'Tis all over."

They rode away together.

Rhiannon relaxed and then straightened wearily. "I must find my lady," he said. Huw Llengaron assisted him to mount.

"Go with God. You will find her safe. She is too cunning to be caught off guard," he grinned.

Forty-One

Rhiannon lifted his hand in salute toward the trees across the valley. Wearily, his body aching from various wounds, he settled himself on the gray. Patting its lathered neck, he spoke softly in its ear. Then he urged it out across the field where men lay in the rocks dead. From time to time, the horse snorted and jibbed as a spot of torn earth in its path gave off the sweetish odor of blood. Up the side of the valley he trotted and mounted the Colwyn Bay road.

The winds of evening struck his face as the sun began to descend behind the trees. He was the keeper of the peace of North Wales if he could only find the key. He prayed urgently that she did not lie somewhere dead, killed by some stragglers or some wild beast. Her father had implied she might be hurt. Pray God she had not been so hurt as to miscarry.

He turned his horse at the two rocks on the trail and took the path that showed faintly in the trees. Presently he came to the clearing. Softly he called her name. No answer.

She must have gone to ground somewhere near, he

reasoned. He began to search the clearing, looking for sign. In the center, he came to the spot where she had lain last night. Bloodstains dried and brown on the crushed moss caused him to curse softly. Carefully, he searched for tracks. She had been lifted and carried away toward the rough country. "Owen Llewellyn," he muttered fearfully. "Pray God his presence meant he had not killed her." With a shudder, he remembered the blood on the man's blade.

He followed the tracks through the woods for perhaps a dozen yards, calling her name softly as he walked. Then he heard her.

"Rhiannon?" a soft voice trembled.

"Moira," he spoke aloud. "Where are you, my love?"

"Over here." He stared in the direction of her voice, but all he could see was a dense thicket of blackberry brambles growing from menacing gray rocks. The bushes shook.

"Rhiannon, help me. I am caught. I cannot lift myself out." Her voice was weak and panting.

He sprang to the bushes and parted them, heedless of the thorns which ripped his hands. She lay in a crack in the rocks barely large enough for her body. With her right arm, she had managed to haul herself half out, but she could not get her legs under her to push and was consequently left hanging helpless.

She was bloody, bruised and scratched; her hair was amassed in tangles and snarls by the cruel briars. Altogether she presented the most woeful and unattractive picture. As she stared up at him with her ice-blue eyes pleading, she caught her lips between her teeth to keep from crying out in relief.

Suddenly, he grinned his wolfish grin. "How did you get yourself in there?" he asked, pushing the brambles further aside, but making no move to help her out.

458

With an exasperated glance in his direction, she struggled to lift herself out. Her efforts were futile. Her bruised arms were too weak to lift her body without the help of her legs, now too numbed to operate properly. "I hid here to protect myself and the baby from the battle. Please, Rhys. I am so cold and tired."

"When I have extracted a confession and a promise from you," he replied, grinning more widely and placing his feet on the rocks beside her so that he straddled her, his left boot by her right hand. With a start of pity he saw the dark welts across the back and the bloody, torn finger, but he realized that she could not be in great pain, for she was struggling and using the hand to grasp the rock face.

"What do you want me to confess?" she asked suspiciously.

"Tell me that you love me," he demanded softly, squatting down above her.

Her eyes fell and she slumped back into the hole. "Why do you want me to tell you that?"

"Because I love you and I want to hear you say it to me. Huw Llengaron said you love me, but I want to hear it from your own lips."

"Please lift me out, Rhys. I am so tired I think I will die in another minute." Her voice was so weak that he could not torment her any longer. Reaching down, he placed his arms under her shoulders. Despite herself, she cried out as he lifted her. He could only guess the condition of her back and shoulders to make her break her silence. Carefully, he set her on her feet on the rock at his side. Guiding her steps, he helped her down until they stood side by side on level ground.

"Now will you tell me what I want to hear?" he whispered, placing his arms around her waist and drawing her in against his heart.

459

A soft whimper broke from her lips. "I love you, Rhys."

As if those words had released a torrent, she could control herself no longer. The pent-up pain and anguish of long months burst within her. Deep, racking sobs choked her, bending her under the force of them.

"Do not cry, Moira. Please do not." Rhiannon grasped her shoulders, attempting to straighten her. "You are safe now. You will hurt the baby. Love, do not." His voice became husky with his pain. "Moira, I love you. Please do not cry."

She slumped to her knees, unable to bear the weight of the emotion which tore her to pieces. Her father, the terrible beating, the kidnapping and near death by Owen and Margwin, the shame and humiliation of the past months, the fearful guilt she felt because of her uncontrollable love for Rhiannon and then the realization that he knew about it, all combined to drive her to an emotional depth she had never experienced before.

On his knees beside her, Rhiannon felt his own tears begin to fall. He loved her so much and he had caused her so much grief and pain. Settling himself on the ground, he pulled her onto his lap and held her, rocking her as a father would a hurt child. His own tears stained her hair until her grief quieted and she could draw an even breath.

Trembling, she tilted her head back. Her eyes stared into his with incredulous wonder. "You, too," she whispered huskily.

He kissed her tear-stained eyes and cheeks and lips. "Me, too."

"I did not know men cried," she said at last.

"The bravest people cry," he reassured her. "You and I have brought each other to a change again."

"Margwin and Owen Llewellyn sought to kill me," she whispered. "Margwin went over the cliffs above

460

Colwyn Bay."

"Owen Llewellyn died on Thomas' sword."

"My father rejected me and our child," she continued, her voice sharp with pain.

"He has had second thoughts, my love. Look!" He pointed to the gray horse peacefully tearing grass from amongst the rocks.

"His mount!" Moira cried in amazement. "He said he would have it back and then he would have me and then he would kill you."

"He gave the horse to me as a wedding gift," Rhiannon smiled wryly.

"What happened?"

"We fought and I could not kill him. I had the chance, but I could not make the last blow. I stepped back and we commenced again. Then I slipped in the blood and went down on one knee. He came at me and just at the last minute instead of swinging and tearing my head off, he tapped me lightly on the shoulder with the flat of his sword."

"Dear God," Moira breathed.

"And then he stepped back and pointed to the gray horse and here I am."

She buried her face in his neck, as he gathered her wounded fingers gently in his hands and kissed each in turn. The ruby ring caught the light of the setting sun slipping almost horizontally through the trees. "See, my dearest love," he whispered, pressing his lips to the stone. "I told you the ruby was your heart held safe in my hand. I suppose it has always been the symbol of our love, but we knew it not until now."

"Until now, this very moment," she agreed, caressing the side of his cheek with her palm before turning her face against the side of his neck.

The light of day began to wane. Gently, he stroked her

hair until he thought she had gone to sleep. Her breathing was light and even. Suddenly, the baby kicked within her belly. He felt the force of the blow and tensed in wonder.

Moira raised her head and pressed Rhiannon's hand against her. "Take me home, my lord. Take us both home."

"Yes, my lady. Home it is."

EXCITING BESTSELLERS FROM ZEBRA

PLEASURE DOME   (1134, $3.75)
by Judith Liederman
Though she posed as the perfect society wife, Laina Eastman was harboring a clandestine love. And within an empire of boundless opulence, throughout the decades following World War II, Laina's love would meet the challenges of fate . . .

HERITAGE   (1100, $3.75)
by Lewis Orde
Beautiful innocent Leah and her two brothers were forced by the holocaust to flee their parents' home. A courageous immigrant family, each battled for love, power and their very lifeline—their HERITAGE.

FOUR SISTERS   (1048, $3.75)
by James Fritzhand
From the ghettos of Moscow to the glamor and glitter of the Winter Palace, four elegant beauties are torn between love and sorrow, danger and desire—but will forever be bound together as FOUR SISTERS.

BYGONES   (1030, $3.75)
by Frank Wilkinson
Once the extraordinary Gwyneth set eyes on the handsome aristocrat Benjamin Whisten, she was determined to foster the illicit love affair that would shape three generations—and win a remarkable woman an unforgettable dynasty!

THE LION'S WAY   (900, $3.75)
by Lewis Orde
An all-consuming saga that spans four generations in the life of troubled and talented David, who struggles to rise above his immigrant heritage and rise to a world of glamour, fame and success!

Available wherever paperbacks are sold, or order direct from the Publisher. Send cover price plus 50¢ per copy for mailing and handling to Zebra Books, 475 Park Avenue South, New York, N.Y. 10016. DO NOT SEND CASH.

BESTSELLING ROMANCES BY JANELLE TAYLOR

SAVAGE ECSTASY   (824, $3.50)

It was like lightning striking, the first time the Indian brave Gray Eagle looked into the eyes of the beautiful young settler Alisha. And from the moment he saw her, he knew that he must possess her—and make her his slave!

DEFIANT ECSTASY   (931, $3.50)

When Gray Eagle returned to Fort Pierre's gates with his hundred warriors behind him, Alisha's heart skipped a beat: would Gray Eagle destroy her—or make his destiny her own?

FORBIDDEN ECSTASY   (1014, $3.50)

Gray Eagle had promised Alisha his heart forever—nothing could keep him from her. But when Alisha woke to find her red-skinned lover gone, she felt abandoned and alone. Lost between two worlds, desperate and fearful of betrayal, Alisha hungered for the return of her FORBIDDEN ECSTASY.

BRAZEN ECSTASY   (1133, $3.50)

When Alisha is swept down a raging river and out of her savage brave's life, Gray Eagle must rescue his love again. But Alisha has no memory of him at all. And as she fights to recall a past love, another white slave woman in their camp is fighting for Gray Eagle!

TENDER ECSTASY   (1212, $3.75)

Bright Arrow is committed to kill every white he sees—until he sets his eyes on ravishing Rebecca. And fate demands that he capture her, torment her . . . and soar with her to the dizzying heights of TENDER ECSTASY!

Available wherever paperbacks are sold, or order direct from the Publisher. Send cover price plus 50¢ per copy for mailing and handling to Zebra Books, 475 Park Avenue South, New York, N.Y. 10016. DO NOT SEND CASH.